BROKEN HONOR

HORNET: BOOK 3

BROKEN HONOR

HORNET: BOOK 3

TONYA BURROWS

This book is a work of fiction. Names, characters, places, and incidents are the product of the author's imagination or are used fictitiously. Any resemblance to actual events, locales, or persons, living or dead, is coincidental.

Entangled Publishing, LLC
2614 South Timberline Road
Suite 109
Fort Collins, CO 80525
Visit our website at www.entangledpublishing.com.

Amara is an imprint of Entangled Publishing, LLC.

Edited by Heather Howland
Cover design by Kelly Martin
Cover art from iStock and Shutterstock

Manufactured in the United States of America

First Edition February 2015

To Bianca
(Although your mommy says you can't read this book for at least another sixteen years.)
Auntie Tonna loves you!

The spirit of a man can endure only so much, and when it is broken, only a miracle can mend it.
—John Burroughs

Chapter One

WASHINGTON, D.C.

New Year's Eve sounded like a war zone. With confetti.

As soon as the ball touched down, the room exploded with noise. Cheers. Those annoying tasseled horns. A champagne bottle popped open. Confetti shot into the air as if propelled from a cannon and rained down on the group.

Travis Quinn flinched at the assault to his pounding head and melted back, away from the chaos.

He should be happy and celebrating like the rest of HORNET. A month ago, they'd successfully rescued a man who had been left for dead. They'd stopped a maniac from getting his hands on a nuclear weapon and saved a women's shelter while they were at it. They all had a right to some happiness, but the only emotion Quinn could conjure up was…dread.

Another year.

They all seemed to blur together into one long battle, and he was tired. So tired, and he watched his team celebrate with a weird kind of detachment. None of the guys knew it yet, but Afghanistan had been his last mission with them.

Why did that knowledge settle like a ball of molten lead in his gut?

Gabe Bristow, the commander of the team, walked over and handed him a glass of the freshly poured champagne. "You okay?"

The guy was his best friend, the closest thing to family he had. More than anyone Gabe deserved the truth—which was fuck, no, he was not okay and might never be again—but when he opened his mouth to say it, nothing came out. So he shut his trap and gave a jerky nod instead, which sent pain singing through his skull.

Damn headaches had been worse since he'd taken that blow on the head in Kabul. How much more abuse could his already fucked-up head take? He was no medic, but if he had to guess, probably not a whole helluva lot more.

Which was exactly why he had to quit the team, and he should do it now. It was the perfect opportunity to tell Gabe everything about his traumatic brain injury and the blackouts he'd been suffering since their car accident last year. Just lay it all out and…

Then what would he do?

He was no longer a Navy SEAL. And he couldn't continue as XO of HORNET…

So who the hell was he?

Gabe eyed him. "Yeah, buddy, you sure look okay. That green complexion you've been sporting all night suits you."

"Too much to drink," Quinn muttered.

"I've seen you drunk, jackass, and you're not right now."

Quinn mustered up a smile and took a small sip of his champagne. He might not be, but Gabe was well on his way.

Across the room, Jean-Luc Cavalier, the team's linguist, who was currently wearing a ridiculous party hat and oversized sunglasses, grabbed Gabe's wife in a fast two-step and broke out into a horrible rendition of "Auld Lang Syne."

Gabe winced. "Jesus. Why does that man think he can sing?"

"Y'all love me, f'true," Jean-Luc called and dipped Audrey.

"Getting a little handsy there with my wife, Cajun. I suggest you remove them if you wanna keep them."

Jean-Luc grinned and straightened, setting a giggling Audrey back on her feet. "You can't blame me for trying. Look at her." He spun her, and her little red dress flared out from her hips. "She's gorgeous."

"Yeah," Gabe said with a big, dopey grin. "Why do you think I married her?"

Audrey laughed. "Oh, so it wasn't because I manipulated you into it?"

"Nah. I just let you think that."

"Liar," she called in singsong.

"Yeah," Gabe admitted into his glass before taking a drink, his eyes never leaving his wife. "Best thing that's ever happened to me, too." After a moment, he shook his head and looked at Quinn again. "Take some time off, Q. You look like hell, and that whack on the head you sustained in Kabul—"

"It's fine."

Gabe's jaw tightened, and as soon as there was a lull in the noise, he raised his hands to get everyone's attention. "Listen up, gentlemen! Mandatory one-month leave starting now. I don't want to see any of your ugly mugs until February, got it?"

"Hot damn," Jean-Luc said. "I know what I'm doing."

"Gettin' laid?" Jesse Warrick, the team medic, suggested dryly.

"Well, duh. That goes without saying. Why are there no

single ladies at this shindig?"

"We didn't want to subject them to you?" Seth Harlan, the newest member of the team, suggested.

Jean-Luc blew a raspberry. "That's ridiculous. Women love me. But that's beside the point. *After* I get laid, I'm going home to Louisiana and sweet-talking Grandmère into making me her famous gumbo."

"I don't believe your grandmother can be sweet-talked. I've tried," Marcus Deangelo said as he refilled his glass from the massive stash of alcohol laid out on a table. As the team's lead negotiator, he could talk his way into or out of almost any situation—except, apparently, if Jean-Luc's grandmother was involved. Marcus shuddered. "That woman scares me."

"Aw, *mon ami*. She ain't nothin' but a sweet old Cajun lady."

"Who wrestles gators in her free time," Marcus said.

"Really?" Harvard, resident hacker extraordinaire, perked up. Still recovering from a chest wound that had nearly killed him, he couldn't drink like the rest of them and had been unusually quiet all night.

"*Oui,*" Jean-Luc said. "Gator wrestlin' is a national pastime in the bayou. All the cool *grandmères* are doin' it."

"You're so full of shit," Harvard groaned.

As the chatter continued, Gabe sent Quinn a smug sideways glance, the meaning loud and clear. Executive order. Now he had to take time off.

Quinn sighed. "Yeah, I read you. I'll go home." He set his glass aside. "In fact, I'm gonna call it a night."

Gabe nodded. "Good plan. Go home, get some rest. Do you need a ride?"

"You're not driving anywhere right now, Gabe."

"No. Audrey is. She…" He winced and lowered his voice. "She wanted to start trying for a baby, and she refuses to drink a drop of alcohol until we know if it…took. Just in case."

Shock coursed through Quinn. Yup, Gabe was definitely drunk. He'd never share that bit of personal news while sober. "Whoa. Uh, congrats?"

"I'm fucking terrified about it."

"Understandably so."

"But," he added on an exhale, "she wants a family, and I want her to be happy. And…maybe a kid would be kinda cool." He polished off his glass in one long gulp, then shrugged. "Anyway, she's, uh, the designated driver tonight."

Quinn's gaze skimmed over the crowd until he found Audrey in her bright red dress. She was indeed drinking water, but she was also laughing with Seth and his girlfriend, Phoebe, and looked like she was having a good time. He shook his head. "Nah, don't worry about it. I'm good."

"All right. If you're sure." Gabe clapped him on the shoulder but hesitated a beat before adding, "I'll tell Audrey to expect you on Sundays this month for dinner. Raffi's already coming. I invited Michael, too. Audrey has been nagging me to be nicer to him because he's my brother, same as Raffi, and blah, blah, but I doubt he'll show."

Quinn winced internally. He liked Raffi, Gabe's youngest brother—except for the fact Raffi thought he was hot, which made him damn uncomfortable—but he'd rather not have to sit around and make nice with Michael, the middle Bristow boy. He got along with Michael about as well as he did The Admiral, Gabe's father. Those two were struck from the same puritanical mold.

"Yeah, I'm not—"

"C'mon," Gabe said. "It'll be like a family thing."

"Except I'm not family." The long stare Gabe sent his way made him feel like an ass. A subject change was in order. "You're not going back to Costa Rica?"

"Nope. We're hanging out here in D.C. for a while, which

is all the more reason you should join us. Who knows the next time we'll make it back to D.C. for an extended stay? And Audrey will be thrilled to have the company."

Quinn started to protest again, but Gabe had already limped away.

Christ. That was so like Gabe. Not an invitation, but a thinly veiled command with shades of a guilt trip, since Quinn hated the idea of disappointing Gabe's wife in any way.

Tricky bastard.

Yeah, well, it wasn't going to work this time. He'd give it a few days, then come up with some B.S. reason why he couldn't make it. All that happy-family-Sunday-dinner shit wasn't for him. Never had been. Never would be.

Gabe walked over to Audrey, picked her up in a tight hug, and kissed her thoroughly, shamelessly, right there in front of the entire team. The guys whooped and catcalled, and Gabe ignored them, all but bending his wife backward with the force of his kiss.

A hollow ache opened up in Quinn's chest, and he glanced away from the two of them, only to spot Seth and Phoebe being all lovey-dovey as they picked at the finger foods laid out on another table. And Seth—unstable, paranoid, jumps-at-his-own-shadow Seth Harlan—was laughing. Amazing. Somehow during the course of their mission in Afghanistan, Phoebe had gotten through his PTSD and drawn him out of his shell.

That hollow ache spread, got a little deeper, a little colder, and Quinn rubbed his chest. Yeah, definitely time to get gone. He grabbed his coat and headed toward the door.

"It's a fucking love plague," Ian Reinhardt said. The EOD tech was leaning against a nearby wall, swinging an empty leash as he watched all the happy couples. His lip curled into a sneer. "Don't stand too close. You'll catch it."

Quinn glanced at the couples again. First Gabe, then

Seth. Ian was right. Maybe it was contagious. And, Christ, he wanted it.

No. What?

Fuck, it was a good thing nobody could hear that kind of sappy shit going through his mind. He had a reputation to maintain. He was the hard-ass, the ice-cold unbreakable warrior, nicknamed Achilles by his BUD/S instructors because they had tried their damnedest to find his heel, his weakness. Too bad he didn't have one.

But men like him, the kind of guys who left the womb fighting? They didn't get fairy-tale endings. They burned bright until they burned out—and he was burning out. He knew it, accepted it, but it was not exactly conducive to a happily-ever-after kind of life.

And yet, he couldn't help but wonder what it would feel like to have that kind of intimate connection with someone.

No, not with just anyone.

With Mara.

Christ, that woman. Mara Escareno shouldn't still be haunting his thoughts. She'd been a one-night stand over the summer—one he couldn't seem to forget, sure, but still only a one nighter. But then he'd returned from Afghanistan last month and found himself on her doorstep, and suddenly that no-strings-attached fucking turned into a…he didn't know what. A fling? A booty call? It hadn't felt like either, and the memory of her in his arms was so vivid he could almost feel her there again. Would that memory ever leave him? He had a sinking suspicion the answer to that was a resounding no.

Ian snorted in disbelief. "Jesus. Don't tell me you're already infected?"

Quinn dragged himself out of his thoughts and pulled on his coat before flipping Ian the bird. "Hey, I'm not the one who fell so hard for a dog that I brought him home from Afghanistan."

Ian stopped swinging the leash and pushed away from the wall. "Fuck you, Quinn." He walked away, presumably to go find his new buddy, Tank, in the crowd.

He needed to make a quick, clean exit before anyone else noticed him, but as he opened the door, the little bell on the jamb rang, alerting everyone to his departure.

Audrey waved. "Bye, Q. See you Sunday for dinner."

Fuck. Gabe had already mentioned it to her?

Quinn raised a hand and called up a smile that hurt his face. And then he ducked outside, shutting the door on all the other farewells.

The party had been held at the private security firm owned by the Wilde brothers, who were all ex-military and had done some work here and there for HORNET throughout the last few months. Their office was in a disused strip mall, which had recently been damaged by fire at one end. Because of that incident, the parking lot was now well lit but quiet, muffled by new snowfall. Silence closed in, threatened to strangle him.

He should leave. Go home like he told Gabe he would. But all that waited for him there was more silence.

He didn't want to be alone.

Stupid. He gave his head a hard shake to dislodge the thoughts. He was a grown-ass man, and he'd been alone most of his life. How was now any different?

He zipped up his coat, and his footsteps crunched across a fresh layer of snow as he crossed to his car, parked in the far corner of the lot. He fished for his keys in his pocket and instead came up with his cell phone. He'd barely looked at the thing while in Afghanistan because the team had relied mostly on radios and sat phones to communicate, and in the weeks since he'd been home, he'd spent most of his time with Gabe and the team—the only people who ever called him—so he'd kept it shut off. But now he powered it up, and the screen showed he had several voicemails.

Who the hell would call him? He didn't recognize the number.

Maybe it had been Audrey checking up on Gabe. Or possibly Gabe's younger brother Raffi. Those two were the only people he could think of, because the rest of Gabe's family—the Admiral, his middle brother, Michael, and his mother, Catherine—were all assholes. And Quinn himself didn't have any family to speak of. At least nobody who would be calling and leaving messages.

He stopped walking and punched in the code to access his messages. The uncertain voice that came through the speaker was like a punch to the gut.

"Hi, Travis. Um, I know it's probably bad form to call like this, but...I need to talk to you. About something. So, um, could you please call me back?"

Mara.

The sound of her voice after so many weeks sent his heart galloping, and for a moment, he forgot how to suck air into his lungs. Mara wanted to talk to him. Even after the way he'd acted six weeks ago. He knew she was a good person, generous to a fault, but could she possibly be that forgiving? Could he possibly be that lucky?

More than anything else in his life, he wished he could turn the clock back to the night he'd walked away from her. If he could have a redo, he wouldn't let himself get all tangled up inside his head again, wouldn't let the intense, instantaneous attraction he'd felt toward her scare him away.

Was this the second chance he'd hoped for?

His stomach fluttered with nerves—a sensation he felt so rarely, he almost couldn't name it—and his fingers even trembled a little as he punched in the number she'd left. But then he hesitated over the send button.

Fuck calling her. He had an entire month free, and if he was going to get a second chance with her, he would do it the right way.

• • •

"He's leaving." Todd Urban smacked his palms on the steering wheel of the van parked next to Quinn's car, then reached for the door. "We need to grab him before—"

"No."

"Sir, if we don't—"

"Stand. Down. I'm sure the Wilde brothers have cameras everywhere around here. We can't risk being spotted."

Urban grumbled but released the handle and watched in the side mirror as Quinn climbed into his car. "If he's going on another op, who knows when we'll have this opportunity again? We have to neutralize him before he gets his memory back."

"He's not going on an op. Gabe and the rest of the team are still inside."

The car started, and Quinn pulled out of the lot. Good thing they'd had time to bug his vehicle.

Urban cursed under his breath and glanced over at Captain Cold in the passenger seat. He'd never call the captain that nickname to his face, but it was a fitting one, bestowed on him by the people that suffered under his command. "Your orders, sir?"

"I've never liked this idea. We're better than grabbing a man out of a parking lot like a bunch of thugs. We need a new plan of attack."

Urban grunted. "Like running him off the highway?"

"That was an act of desperation and never should have been given the green light. We're better than that."

Urban just barely managed to keep his eye roll to himself. That was Captain Cold's mantra. He was better than this, better than that, better than everyone and everything.

And Urban was starting to think he didn't like getting his officer hands dirty. Maybe he even resented that he'd been sent on this kind of wet work with a lowly grunt. "We should have sent some guys to take him out in Afghanistan. Nobody would have thought twice about it if he ended up with a bullet in his head there."

"Urban," Captain Cold said after a moment and looked at him with—well, maybe not respect, but with something close to it. "That's the best idea you've ever had."

"What idea?"

"We'll send him on another op, get him out of the country again. Preferably someplace hostile where we'll have a scapegoat for his death. Where there won't be an investigation when his body turns up."

"That…might work." At least, it solved the problem of trying to explain away a decorated ex-SEAL's body to the American police. "How do we get them out on another op?"

"They're mercenaries," Captain Cold said with disdain and picked up his cell phone. "We hire them. Pull up the GPS and follow Quinn, make sure he's going home. I have some calls to make."

Chapter Two

El Paso, Texas

Now that he was here, standing in front Mara's duplex, Quinn was starting to doubt himself. What if she'd only called to tell him he'd left a sock or something behind last time he was here? Or what if she'd only wanted to tell him off for sneaking away while she was sleeping? She had every right to rip him a new one for that act of cowardice, but that didn't jibe with the sweet, shy Mara he knew. And her voicemail hadn't sounded angry, but there had been a note of urgency in her tone.

Maybe she was in trouble? If so, he'd look like an ass showing up on her doorstep with flowers. But if the Juarez Syndicate was causing her family problems again like they had been over the summer, Jesse, as her cousin, would have known about it. He had been the one who hired HORNET to protect her and her mother in the first place, and he hadn't said a word about Mara recently, so it couldn't be more trouble. Maybe…

Maybe he should stop standing here debating it like a

pussy and ring the doorbell already.

Yeah. Good plan. Frustrated with himself, he jabbed the bell harder than he meant to and the resulting sound grated across his nerves.

A lifetime passed before the door finally opened.

And there she was, Mara Escareno, the woman he'd been thinking about far too often since he walked away from her six weeks ago. Her black hair was damp and she was barefoot, wrapped up in a fluffy robe that fell to just above her knees.

She looked good—no, amazing, all dewy from her recent shower with her hair curling around her shoulders and her cheeks rosy. She smiled at him, warm and bright, and in the second before she realized he was not the person she'd been expecting, he could almost pretend she was welcoming him home.

But then her smile faded. She sucked in a sharp breath of surprise and all the pretty color drained from her complexion. "Travis?"

"Uh, hi." Shit. This was a stupid idea. She was obviously expecting someone else. Someone she'd been happy to see. A boyfriend? His blood boiled at the thought, even as he told himself he had no right to jealousy when it came to this woman.

She blinked like she couldn't believe her eyes. "Wha-what are you doing here?"

"You, uh, called me."

"Yes, but that was almost three weeks ago." She touched her throat, drawing his attention to the gaping front of the robe and the lush swell of her breasts peeking out from between the lapels.

Christ, he wanted to touch her.

But, again, he had no right when it came to this woman.

He made himself lift his gaze to her face. "Yeah, I was... dealing with some things. I didn't get the messages until last night."

"So you flew to Texas? Just like that?" Now she was staring at him like he was one sandwich short of a picnic. Which, given his head injury, he probably was. And then some.

"Mara," he began, but couldn't pick out the right words from all the white noise inside his mind and instead shoved the flowers in her direction. "Things, uh, didn't end well between us back in November and—"

"Are you kidding?" She shook her head in disbelief. "You walked out in the middle of the night without a word. No note, no phone call…nothing. That's not ending things, Travis. That's disappearing. And then you show up weeks later and hand me flowers, expecting *that* to make everything okay?"

"I know it won't—" He broke off as a car turned the corner at the end of the block and spotlighted them in its headlights. The little hairs on the back of his neck prickled. "Can we do this inside?"

Mara sighed and backed up a step. "Yes. Come in. There are things we need to talk about."

Quinn followed her. The open-concept space looked exactly the same as he remembered it, except for the boxes and totes stacked along one wall where she used to have a bookshelf. He closed and locked the door behind him, then motioned to the boxes. "Are you moving?"

"Yes. I can't afford this place anymore."

"Did something happen with your job?" He remembered she worked at as a veterinary technician and adored her job.

"No, I'm still employed. I just…" She trailed off and turned away, grabbing her cell phone from the breakfast bar that separated the living room from the kitchen. "We'll talk. Right now, I need to call Lanie and cancel our dinner plans."

"Lanie?" The surge of relief was so profound, Quinn felt

light-headed with it. She'd had plans with her best friend, not another man.

"Yes, and I'm going to have to talk her down from coming over here and beating you senseless."

He tried for a smile that fell flat. "I like her already."

"You wouldn't if she came over, so give me a few minutes."

He set the flowers down on the coffee table and wandered around the living room, making an effort not to eavesdrop on her conversation with Lanie. He stopped in front of the window and parted the blinds. The car that had spotlighted them was now parked on the street in front of her neighbor's house. Something about the sight of it there sat like lead in his gut, but he didn't have time to analyze the sensation. The back door slid open and little claws clicked on the tile floor as Mara's dog came barreling in his direction, barking its fool head off.

"Jesus Christ." He dropped the blinds and backed away from the animal. It was only the size of a football, with wild blond fur, a curly tail, and three legs, but he'd rather face down a suicide bomber than the little mutt.

"BJ!" Mara scolded and hung up her cell phone. She returned to the living room and scooped the little dog up, and Quinn was able to draw in a breath again.

"BJ," he said on an exhale and then scoffed at himself. "Snippy as ever, I see."

"She doesn't remember you, that's all."

"I remember her." He reached out to pet the animal, ignoring BJ's grumble of annoyance. "And your ornery one-eyed cat, Hawkeye. You named them after the characters from your favorite TV show, *M*A*S*H*. You like it because it was your father's favorite, too."

"Your first day here we binge-watched it together," she said softly. "And you laughed. Like, really laughed. I'd never heard you do that before."

"Yeah, I did. It's a good show." He exhaled hard. "It was…a good week."

"Then why—"

"Wait. Please." He stepped toward her, but still didn't touch her. He didn't trust himself enough to touch her before he said what he needed to say. "Just let me… I need to say this. I didn't ever tell you why I came back in November. During my last mission, things got really fucked up and for a while, it didn't look like I was going to make it out alive. And even though the shit was hitting the fan and one of my teammates was bleeding out in front of me, the only thing I could think of was how much I wanted to see you again. How much I wanted more than only one night."

Tears gathered in her eyes and, dammit, that wasn't the reaction he'd been aiming for. He couldn't stay away for a second longer, not when she looked at him with those big brown eyes brimming with emotion. He stepped forward and risked losing a finger by taking the dog and setting it on the floor, then he pulled her against him.

Christ, she felt good in his arms again. She felt right. And it scared the ever-loving hell out of him.

Her fingers tightened in the fabric of his shirt. "I don't like that image," she said, her voice muffled against his chest. "You, nearly dying alone in some foreign country."

He didn't bother telling her that was very likely going to be his end. He didn't see himself living to be an old man in retirement, that was for sure.

He rested his cheek on top of her head and breathed her in. Her hair smelled faintly of berries, a scent he remembered from when she'd leaned over as she rode him and her hair had fallen in a curtain around them both. The scent memory triggered an erection he had no hope of hiding, and she drew away slightly, gazing up with lust-darkened eyes.

"Travis." She breathed his name, and the raspy sound of

it went through him like a lava flow.

Holding her gaze, making sure she read his intentions loud and clear, he lowered his head until their lips were centimeters apart, silently asking permission.

Her breaths came faster, and her eyes half closed. "We need to talk."

He weaved his hand into her drying hair. "I know."

"Oh, this is such a bad idea," she whispered, then pushed up on her toes to close the distance between their mouths.

The kiss was of the rock-your-world, knock-your-socks-off, never-gonna-stop caliber. In that moment, Quinn would have been perfectly content to stand there in Mara's living room kissing her until his heart quit beating. But then she moved, set a tentative hand on his hip and stood higher on her tiptoes, pushing her breasts against his chest, and that idea suddenly held a lot less appeal. Kissing was good. Burying himself inside her heat would be even better.

Quinn spun her around so that her back pressed against the wall, shocking a gasp out of her. He lifted his head and stared down into dark eyes gone wide with shock.

Cursing himself but unable to stop tasting her, he bent to nip her puffy lower lip. "If you want me to stop, I will."

She muttered something in Spanish. "No. God help me, no, I don't want you to stop."

"I don't do gentle, Mara," he felt compelled to warn even as he worked his way down from her lips, over her chin, to the tender spot where her neck met her shoulder. He scraped his teeth over the frantic beat of her pulse and reveled in the delicate shudder that shook her body. "So if that's how you think this is going to go, back out now."

"I know. I remember, and I don't want gentle. I want you to..." She sucked in a breath as he shoved aside her robe and found her nipple with his teeth and tongue.

"Oh, God." Throwing her head back against the wall, she

hooked one soft leg around his thigh. "I want you to fuck me, Travis. Hard. Right here."

Christ, how could a man say no to that? He scooped his hands under her ass, marveling that sweet, innocent Mara had answered her door while commando underneath her robe. He'd almost expected sensible cotton underpants like the pair she'd had on the first time he'd stripped her bare over the summer. But, no, not this Mara. There was something different about her now, something intoxicatingly female that called to his baser instincts. She was a dark, seductive flame, wrapping herself around him, all heat and spice. She might very well burn him alive, and he didn't care.

Using his body to pin her against the wall, he freed up one hand to explore lower and found her open for him, already wet. He growled and claimed her mouth in another hard kiss, swallowing her groan as he slid two fingers into her.

"Oh, Travis. Oh, God. I think…I'm going to come. I'm going to…" She screamed and bucked against his hand, riding his fingers so hard he almost dropped her. Seeing her like this, watching her take pleasure from him with her eyes squeezed shut, her lush breasts bouncing with every undulation of her hips, her hair a wild, living storm cloud around her head, he wondered how he could have ever thought her shy. She was the most sensual, uninhibited woman he'd ever had the pleasure of seeing come.

And he wanted to see it again, and again, and again. Maybe for the rest of his life.

When her climax ebbed, he half expected embarrassed color to fill her cheeks. Readied himself for the possibility of seeing regret in her eyes. But she didn't withdraw or demand he put her down. Her big brown eyes opened and met his as she reached a shaking hand between them and flipped open the button of his cargo pants. Then his zipper hissed down and his cock sprang free like the damn thing was spring-loaded.

He might have been embarrassed by his obvious eagerness, but her fingers wrapped around him and slid down his shaft until she was cupping him at his base. She guided him toward her opening.

"Travis, please. Fuck me."

Well, now. She was full of surprises tonight. He hadn't expected this when he'd flown to El Paso to see her. Hell, he'd expected her to say whatever it was she needed to say then throw him out of her house, and that would be the end of it. But, no, she was just as desperate for him as he'd been for her. And he knew in that instant he was in trouble. Big trouble. The kind that started with sex and ended in a trip down the aisle. Part of him had known it when he walked away from her six weeks ago, which was exactly why he'd walked, but he should have fully realized it as soon as he heard her on his voicemail. What kind of guy dropped everything and bought a six-hundred-dollar plane ticket just because he heard a woman's voice?

A love-struck guy, that's what.

Alarm bells that had saved his life on more than one occasion jangled inside his mind. If ever he were going to turn chicken, now would be the time—but for the first time in his life, he ignored that ingrained alarm system.

Later. He'd worry about the alarms and the consequences later. Right now, he needed this woman like he needed his next breath. Wanted the connection, craved the warmth she created inside that hollow area in his chest.

"Travis, please."

He lifted her ass in his hands and drove his hips forward, burying himself to the balls inside her. So tight. Christ, he'd forgotten how tight she was, like a fist squeezing him. He sucked in gasping breaths, almost afraid to move, afraid even the slightest friction would end this when he wanted it to last forever.

Except Mara moaned and wrapped her legs tightly around him, swiveling her hips against his, and his last gossamer thread of control snapped. He pinned her against the wall and pounded into her so hard a picture fell, and he wouldn't have been surprised to see a dent in the wall behind her when they were done. Someone started banging angrily on the wall next door.

Mara laughed. The sound soothed over him like a balm and he found himself grinning, too.

"Bedroom?" he asked.

She gripped the too-long strands of his hair and dragged his mouth to hers. "Not yet. Let's give Señora Ruiz something to talk about with her bingo friends."

"Roger that." He took her with everything he had in him, driving her to another orgasm with merciless focus. Only after she came again, screaming, and her body clenched around him, did he allow himself the pleasure of his own release.

Gasping, wrung out, he dropped his forehead to her shoulder. For the first time in months, his muscles unknotted, the constant noise inside his head calmed.

Christ, she was like his own personal drug, and he'd been jonesing for more of her since November. And now that he'd had her again, he didn't know if he'd ever be able to quit her.

Yeah. He was in trouble.

He let her feet touch the floor again but couldn't find it in him to let her go. They stood together on wobbly legs, both sweat slicked and breathing hard. A strand of hair stuck to the side of her face, and Quinn reached out to tuck it behind her ear.

She burst out laughing and clenched her robe together. "Look at the two of us. We're ridiculous. Can't keep our hands off each other for anything."

He winced and stepped back, tucking himself in and zipping up. "Sex wasn't my intention when I—"

"I know. Mine, either, but we can't seem to help ourselves, can we?" She sighed heavily, then started to say something else, but stopped short when he lost his battle against a massive yawn. She touched his stubbled cheek. "Oh, Travis. When was the last time you slept?"

He honestly didn't know the answer. As if his silence confirmed what she'd already expected, she nodded, entwined her fingers through his, and dragged him toward the bedroom. "You need some sleep."

He couldn't agree more. The sex had wrung every last bit of energy from him, and his limbs felt like they were encased in cement.

But…

He pulled her to a stop before she decided to tuck him into bed like a child. "You keep saying we need to talk."

"We do." She shooed her cat off the bed and drew back the comforter, then disappeared into the en suite. When she returned, she wore an oversized T-shirt that fell just short of her knees. She looked so damn adorable with her mussed hair and stubble-burned cheeks, and a deep shame turned his gut into an acid pit.

"Mara, what I did to you, walking out like I did—" He stopped, the words clogging his throat. There was no excusing his actions, he knew that. They were the actions of a coward, but at the time it had seemed like the right thing to do. If he had stayed, he would have subjected her to his unpredictable mood swings and migraines and blackouts and all the other unknowns that came with his medical issues. Not to mention all the other baggage he carried. He was a mess, not fit to enter into any kind of relationship with her beyond the physical, but after only a week together, they had been headed fast down that path. So he'd walked away before he got in any deeper. And he hated himself for hurting her like that.

"Christ," he finally managed. "I'm sorry. I know it's a little too late, but I am. That's why I came here tonight. Not for sex, not for—" He dropped to the edge of the bed and flopped his hands in a helpless I-don't-know-what-else-to-say gesture. "I wanted to apologize."

She opened her mouth, closed it again, and the hurt in her eyes as she stared across the bed at him tore him up inside. "Are you going to walk out tonight?"

"No." He infused the word with every ounce of conviction he could muster. "I'm staying this time." *As long as you'll have me*, he tacked on silently, but he had a bit too much pride to say it out loud. With a lump the size of an Abrams tank lodged in his throat, he was already dangerously close to a man card-revoking breakdown.

She glanced away, but not before he saw the flicker of doubt. And that hurt. Christ, did that hurt, but he couldn't blame her for keeping her expectations low. They both knew she was slumming it with him. And they both knew that, whatever this thing was between them, it had no hope of lasting very long. Still, he wanted to keep her. It was ridiculous and selfish and he knew it couldn't happen, but he wanted her as his woman. At least for a little while.

"Okay," she finally said and climbed into bed. "We're both exhausted, and to say the evening has been emotionally trying is an understatement. We can talk tomorrow."

He climbed into bed beside her and hesitated only a beat before wrapping her up in his arms. He nuzzled the back of her neck and felt a delicate shiver go down her spine. "I'm not going anywhere, Mara. I promise."

• • •

As the couple stepped inside the house, Urban continued past the duplex, then hung a right at the end of the road and cruised around the block. He parked down the street and shut off the Explorer he'd borrowed from a buddy stationed at Fort Bliss. As soon as he'd realized Quinn was headed to the airport, he'd checked flight records, then hopped the first direct flight he could find, landing in the city several hours before Quinn's plane arrived. He'd spent the extra time staking out the airport, wondering why Quinn would take a red-eye on New Year's Day to El Paso of all places, but none of his theories had hit anywhere close to the truth. And when he pulled his laptop out of his bag in the backseat and ran a search on the duplex's address, the result had him laughing.

Holy shit. This could not possibly get any easier.

He grabbed his cell phone from the cup holder and dialed Captain Cold. "Sir, you good to talk?"

"Yes. What's happening?"

"Quinn has a girlfriend."

A beat of silence passed. Then another. "You're sure?"

"Yeah, and get this. She's Marisol Escareno, the stepdaughter Senator Ramon Escareno just disowned because she got pregnant out of wedlock."

"And you think it's Quinn's child?"

"I'd bet my career on it."

"Yeah, you are. Yours, mine, and the careers of everyone else involved in this clusterfuck."

"It's his," Urban said without a doubt. "Why else would he fly out here to see her?"

More silence, and the lack of reaction was starting to piss Urban off. After all, he was practically handing Captain Cold a get-out-of-jail-free card wrapped up in a goddamn bow.

"Sir, this is better than anything we could have engineered. You want him out of the country so I can put a bullet in him without consequence? If we grab her, he'll go after her. Hell, maybe we'll even kill two annoying birds with one bullet—eliminate Quinn and HORNET, because they'll almost certainly follow him."

Finally, Captain Cold made a sound of agreement. "If they take on any more fucking missions like Colombia or Afghanistan, they're bound to stumble onto something we don't want them to find. They've already come too close."

Tell me about it, Urban thought. Captain Cold and the rest of them had gone batshit when they found out Quinn had been to Bagram Air Base back in November, trying to convince his former commander of an impending nuclear threat. Luckily, Commander Bennett had been able to brush him off as crazy, but Quinn had said just enough during that meeting to make Bennett sweat. For the past two years, they'd all banked on Quinn not remembering the events leading up to his car accident, since trying for him again so soon after the accident would have raised too many suspicious eyebrows. Last thing they needed was an investigation into his death when they didn't know what he had done with the damning information he possessed. But now all the signs pointed to his memory returning, and they had no choice but to do something about it. Hence, the start of what Urban liked to think of as the Kill Quinn Initiative, which so far had been the most pain-in-the-ass mission he'd ever taken on, full of missteps and false starts.

But not this time. This time, they had him. All they had to do was take Marisol Escareno.

After another long stretch of silence across the line, Urban lost the little bit of patience he had. He might be the low man on this totem pole, but he had just as much to lose as the rest of these fuckers. He had a family to feed, a wife with expensive tastes, and a ridiculous mortgage. If the navy had paid him better for risking his neck year after year, maybe he wouldn't have turned to the black market to make sure he could send his four kids through college debt-free. But now he'd grown to like the extra paycheck and the lifestyle it provided for him and his family, and he wasn't about to lose it because Captain No Balls here couldn't make a decision without debating it for hours first. "I'm grabbing the woman as soon as Quinn leaves."

"All right," the captain said, and he sounded relieved to have the decision taken out of his hands. "I'll make arrangements with one of our contacts to hold her somewhere OCONUS. Call me for your orders as soon as you have her."

Chapter Three

"I've never seen anyone sleep so hard," Mara whispered into the phone and cracked the bedroom door open to peek in on Travis again. Yup. Still sound asleep. "Lanie, he's been out for over twelve hours. I'm starting to worry. What if he's sick or—maybe I should call Jesse for advice?"

"And explain everything to him, including your condition?" Lanie said doubtfully. "And how do you think that overprotective cousin of yours will take the news?"

"Crap. You're right. Jesse's going to flip his lid." Just like her stepfather and mother had, and she'd prefer not to go through another ugly scene like that again. She winced and pressed a hand to her belly. Would Travis also reject her and the baby? In the weeks since she'd found out she was pregnant, she'd feared the answer to that question was a hard yes. But now…

"He says he's staying."

"Your cousin?" Lanie asked, confused.

"No. Travis."

"So you told him about the baby?"

"Um…"

"Mara! You didn't tell him? Don't you think you probably should? It's kind of a big deal. That's the whole reason I risked getting fired to track him down for you."

"I know! And I owe you for that more than I'll probably ever be able to repay. It's just…" She shut the bedroom door as softly as possible and moved into the kitchen, where her conversation was less likely to be overheard. She was fairly certain he was still asleep, but just in case he wasn't, she switched on her iPod dock for background noise. She sat down at the kitchen table and stared out through the sliding glass door into her backyard. "Lanie, I never expected to see him again. I called him several times, and he never responded to my messages. I mean, with the way he walked out, I assumed he wasn't interested in hearing from me. I had resigned myself to doing this alone, and then he shows up looking like death warmed over, and he's obviously upset about something, and 'hey, you're going to be a dad' is not exactly a great conversation opener and—"

"Whoa, whoa," Lanie said. "Take a breath."

Mara sucked in a lungful, as instructed, and let it go in a rush. "I slept with him again." Just the memory of the way he'd held her pinned against the wall had her cheeks heating up.

"Oh, Mara," Lanie sighed. "You didn't."

"Yes, I did." Groaning, she dropped her head to the kitchen table and banged it lightly against the wood a few times. "I don't even know how it happened. It was just like this summer all over again. One minute we were talking like somewhat reasonable adults, and then he was kissing me and I was kissing him back and…"

"And you ended up fucking like bunnies," Lanie finished.

Mara huffed out a laugh. It was such a Lanie comment. "To put it indelicately."

"Girl, I don't do delicate. And I gotta ask, was it as good as you remember?"

Mara felt her face go warm again against the cool wood of the tabletop and was glad her best friend wasn't there to see the blush. "Better."

"Wow. I'm…actually a bit jealous. How is the pregnant lady getting more action than me?"

BJ scratched at the back door and she got up to let the dog outside. The January morning air was crisp, the sky brilliantly blue, and she lounged in the doorway while BJ sniffed around the yard for a place to take care of business. "I don't know what to make of him showing up like this."

"Well, look on the bright side. At least he can't knock you up again."

"You're not helping."

"Do you believe he's going to stick this time?" Lanie asked seriously after an extended silence.

Oh, God, she wanted him to. She wanted to see if they had anything more between them beyond the explosive sex. When he came back and stayed for a week in November, she'd thought they might have something, the kind of something that could last. They had similar tastes in TV shows and movies, their views on religion and politics lined up, and he even shared her love of bowling, which had been a complete surprise.

But then he'd left without a word.

Mara sighed. "I…I don't know. Part of me hopes so. Really, *really* hopes so. And the rest of me's calling that part an idiot. Men like him don't stick." She noticed movement out of the corner of her eye and turned. Someone was walking through the kitchen of the empty house next door.

Strange.

She didn't think it had sold yet, but maybe they were having an open house today. And now that she thought about it, she remembered seeing an unfamiliar car parked out front when she took her trash to the curb this morning.

BJ came trotting over and dropped a half-dead lizard at her feet, distracting her. "Oh, gross. I have to go. BJ just brought me another lizard."

Lanie laughed. "Dumb mutt has about as many brain cells as a lizard. Call me if you need anything. I mean it. Anything, even if it's just to talk because that bastard walked out and broke your heart again."

"He didn't break my heart."

"Uh-huh," Lanie said before hanging up.

Mara set the phone aside and, fighting back a surge of nausea, dealt with the mess on her porch. She wasn't as naive as she'd been six weeks ago, and she had accepted Travis into her bed last night with no expectations of commitment. But, yes, they would have to talk when he woke up. She didn't expect commitment from him—wasn't even sure she wanted it at this point—but now that he was here, she couldn't very well let him leave without telling him about the baby.

He deserved to know. She just wasn't sure how he'd react when he found out. Would he be disgusted? Thrilled? Would he claim the tiny human growing in her womb wasn't his? She didn't know if she could take that rejection so close on the heels of her family's disownment.

Maybe she should wait a few more days, see how things went with him before she broke the news?

Mara shook her head. Such a coward. Putting it off longer would only make it harder. She knew that, and yet she hoped he was still sleeping as she ushered her dog inside and went to check on him again.

The bed was empty.

For a second, her heart stopped. Had he walked out again without a word?

But then her bathroom door opened and there he stood,

wearing the same clothes he'd arrived in, his hair damp from a shower. She took a step toward him, but the look on his face stopped her in her tracks. It wasn't anger but an emotionless void, almost as if he was wearing a stone mask, and it sent a chill racing over his skin.

"You said we need to talk?" He tossed her bottle of prenatal vitamins on the bed. "So talk."

• • •

The relief on Mara's too-expressive face when he stepped out of the bathroom was short-lived. Her smile faded, and she fiddled with the too-big watch on her wrist—a nervous habit he remembered from his previous stay. She stared at the floor as if she wanted it to open up and swallow her.

The little hairs on Quinn's arms stood at attention, and he got the distinct sense he was not going to like what was coming next. "What are those vitamins for, Mara?"

After an uncertain moment, she sucked in a deep breath and straightened her shoulders, lifted her gaze to his. "I called you because I'm pregnant. Six weeks."

Holy. Fucking. Hell.

Quinn opened his mouth, but his fucked-up brain was still scrambling to make sense of the words that had come out of her mouth, and no sound emerged.

Mara was pregnant.

And he...well, now there was only one explanation as to why she would have called him. He was the lucky genetic donor.

Mara clasped her hands together in front of her mouth and watched him with worried eyes. Silence stretched for several long minutes between them.

"Travis," she finally blurted, "aren't you going to say anything?"

Unable to remain standing since his knees had gone rubbery on him, he staggered a few steps and sank to the edge of the bed, feeling as if he'd just been dealt a second traumatic brain injury. He couldn't seem to make the thoughts in his head come out his mouth.

Or, no, scratch that. Speaking the chaos in his mind out loud was a bad idea. Very bad idea. If she knew about the firestorm of panic going on inside him—

"Travis?"

"You..." His voice came out rusty and he cleared his throat. "Don't look it."

She flapped her arms in a what-do-you-want-me-to-say gesture. "I won't start showing for another few weeks."

She'd always had curves—in fact, those curves were one of the things that had initially attracted him to her. He remembered kissing his way over the gentle swell of her belly, adoring the bit of fat that softened her figure. She'd been so self-conscious about it, claiming she'd recently switched to the night shift at the animal hospital where she worked and started eating too much junk food in an effort to keep awake during the wee hours of the morning. He'd told her he didn't like skinny women, then spent the next hour showing her just how much he enjoyed her body. He doubted he'd have noticed even if she were showing.

Mara crossed to her nightstand and took a string of grainy black-and-white pictures from the drawer. She handed it to him, and his mouth went dry. All he saw on the image was a tiny blob. But it was a blob that would eventually become a baby.

Mara's baby.

And...he was going to be someone's father.

Oh, shit.

He suddenly couldn't suck in an entire lungful of oxygen and bolted to his feet. He needed air. Needed to leave now before he did or said something stupid, and he almost made it to the front door before she caught his arm, looking so beautiful and...hurt.

Goddammit.

He should say something. He knew it, and yet he couldn't come up with a damn thing to say. He turned away from her searching gaze and opened the door.

"Travis, wait."

He hesitated only a second. "I don't want this."

She flinched as if he'd slapped her. "But..." Her voice was little more than a squeak.

"I gotta go." He didn't look back, but he could feel her eyes on him as he climbed into his rental.

Somehow, he managed to start the car and drive away, but Mara's scent lingered on his body and reminded him of the pain he'd put in her eyes. He stopped at a red light and only then realized he still had the sonogram clenched in his hand. He flattened the strip out on the steering wheel and studied the images. A chill raced over his skin, raising goose bumps on his arms, and a headache drilled into his brain behind his eyes. He rested his forehead on the steering wheel.

What was it about Mara that turned him into such a fucking coward? Why, when things started getting heavy, was his first response always to run away from her? Especially when he hadn't run from anything since he was ten and Big Ben had come home drunk and angry with the intention of killing his wife and son.

Was Big Ben the reason he kept running from her?

But, dammit, he wasn't his father. He'd spent his entire adult life trying to prove it, and now here he was, doing exactly what his father would have done.

Big Ben would be so proud.

A horn blared behind him, and he sat up to see the light had turned green. He gazed down at the sonogram again, then hit the turn signal and pulled a u-ey.

He had promised Mara he was sticking around this time, and as much as it fucking scared him, he wasn't the kind of man to break his promises.

He wasn't Big Ben.

Chapter Four

Mara stared in disbelief as his car all but burned rubber out of her driveway. She hadn't known what to expect from him when she broke the news of her pregnancy. Shock, for sure. Joy. Fear. Maybe even some anger. But she hadn't expected him to completely shut down and walk away.

Which, yes, had been stupid of her, since he'd done the exact same thing six weeks ago when it became obvious their fling had turned into something more intimate than either of them had intended. But it truly hadn't occurred to her that Travis wouldn't love the little heart she heard on the fetal monitor, working so hard to become a person.

How could he not love their baby?

Mara dashed away the tears streaming down her cheeks and straightened her shoulders. Fine. If he didn't want this, she'd have him sign away his rights as soon as the baby was born and then pretend her pregnancy was the result of artificial insemination. She hated that her baby wouldn't have a father, but she didn't need him. She didn't need her mom or stepdad. She could do this on her own, and she'd give her child the best life possible without help from any of them.

Mind made up, Mara shut the door, made it halfway across her living room, and froze in shock. The sliding glass door to her backyard was wide-open.

Crap. Had she not shut the door all the way earlier? BJ wasn't bright enough to get out of the fenced-in backyard, but Hawkeye might have tried to make a run for it. Wouldn't be the first time he'd made it over the fence. She ran to her bedroom and threw on leggings and an oversized sweatshirt, stepped into a pair of tennis shoes, grabbed Hawk's carrier from her closet, and was nearly to her bedroom door when a sick dread rose into her throat and stopped her in her tracks.

Something was wrong here.

She hadn't left the back door open. She was sure of it. Someone else had opened it…

And that someone was in her house.

Mara took a slow backward step, afraid to make any sudden moves even though her instincts screamed for her to throw open the door and run for it. The silence in her house was almost painful, scraping against her heightened senses.

No, not complete silence. There was a rattling sound like—like her phone vibrating across her nightstand, where she'd left it after taking off her robe.

Oh, God. It was ringing!

She spun to lunge for it, and the bedroom door burst open. A tall man in a gray hooded sweatshirt and black balaclava stepped through. He took one look at her, said, "Fuck," and launched across the room. She didn't have a chance at escape. Barely had time to think about running. In less than a heartbeat, he held her immobile with one big arm crushing her windpipe. He smelled like fresh paint, and as her vision swam from lack of oxygen, she thought, *the house next door.* He'd been the shadow she'd seen moving around inside. She should have said something to Lanie about it. And Travis.

Maybe this wouldn't be happening now if she had.

Tears trickled in hot streams down her cheeks. This was it. She was going to die, her baby was going to die, and nobody would ever know what happened to them.

Her knees buckled, and she wrapped her arms around her belly, afraid of landing on the baby when she fell. A pair of thick, strong arms caught her and picked her up with surprising gentleness. And in the seconds before she blacked out, she thought she heard him mutter, "I'm sorry. This will be over soon."

• • •

She wasn't picking up.

Quinn couldn't blame her. After the way he'd acted, he wouldn't pick up either if he were her.

Yeah, he'd fucked up. Big-time. But he'd make it up to her. Somehow. If he had to, he'd post up on her porch and stay there until she talked to him again.

Because they did need to talk about…hell, everything. He hadn't been lying when he'd said he didn't want the pregnancy. He wasn't father material. At. All. Just the thought of a baby sent a chill of pure fear down his spine.

What if he broke it?

Could babies be broken?

Yeah. Yeah, they could. He was living proof, which was yet another reason he should have sterilized himself years ago.

He finally wound his way through the gathering afternoon traffic and turned onto Mara's street—and the car he'd seen last night, the Ford Explorer that had been parked in front of her neighbor's house, was now in her driveway, engine running.

What the fuck?

All kinds of alarms started clanging inside his head, and he slowed his rental to a stop at the curb behind a minivan. Heart thudding, he reached into the backseat for his go bag and found the binoculars he kept in the side pocket.

A man in a hooded sweatshirt emerged from Mara's house moments later, carrying something big wrapped up in a blanket. And not just any blanket. The fucking one from her bed. He'd know that gray-and-yellow floral pattern anywhere, and his gut clenched with a sickening sense of dread. He couldn't think of one good reason why the man would be leaving the house with Mara's bedspread.

The man loaded his cargo into the back end of the Explorer and just before the trunk shut, the bundle moved. A small hand poked out, a woman's hand, and on her wrist was a too-big watch.

Mara's watch.

Mara was in that bundle.

And there went the ground, dropping out from under him. He grabbed the steering wheel for support, tightening his grip until he felt his knuckles pop.

The Explorer pulled out of Mara's driveway.

Shit. He had to get a grip. Focus. His only shot at getting Mara back was to stay latched onto the Explorer's tailpipe like a leech. He sucked in a breath, exhaled it slowly, and shoved everything but the mission out of his head. He waited until the Explorer was far enough down the street to avoid detection, then followed.

The problem with conducting one-car surveillance was that it was very easy to get burned by someone who knew what they were doing. And the fucker in the hooded sweatshirt definitely knew what he was doing. Whether he was just being careful or he suspected he had a tail was anyone's guess, but he weaved in and out of traffic, sped up through school zones, slowed down when the speed limit increased. At the first stoplight they came to, he signaled left and even moved over in the proper lane for the turn.

Was he actually turning or was he watching his rearview mirror to see who signaled over into the turning lane?

Damn. If Quinn didn't get over, and the Explorer did make the turn, he could lose them in the traffic. If he did move over, he could be spotted.

Quinn took a calculated risk and stayed where he was, in the non-turning lane several cars back. And sure enough, as soon as the light turned green, the Explorer shot forward, straight through the intersection, and cut off the lead car in the line to the sounds of tires squealing and angry horns.

Smart. Dangerous as hell with a vulnerable pregnant woman in the trunk—and Quinn would make sure he paid for that—but smart.

The Explorer took a one-way road in the wrong direction and Quinn turned down a parallel road to keep him in sight. He faked out two more turns, ran a red light, drove in patterns that didn't make any sense.

Yeah. The guy knew what he was doing. But so did Quinn, and he stuck close, sometimes close enough to see Mara struggling in the back. His chest ached with each breath he drew.

He. Was. Not. Leaving. Her. Again.

But if he stayed on this guy, they'd just keep going in circles and never get anywhere. He grabbed his phone from the seat beside him and speed-dialed Harvard's number.

"Uh, hey, Quinn." Harvard answered after two rings, sounding more than a little surprised. "What's up?"

"Do you have satellite access?"

"Do I have satellite access?" Harvard scoffed. "Duh. It insults me that you even have to ask. Why?"

"Mara's been kidnapped—"

"Hold up. Mara? Jesse's cousin Mara? Kidnapped?"

"Listen!" Quinn snapped. "I'm on her tail, but her abductor knows I'm here. We've been driving in circles for the last hour. I need to drop back, but I won't do it until I know you have eyes on her. I'm in El Paso, driving a gray Honda. Mara's in a green Ford Explorer with Texas plates."

"Holy fuck," Harvard breathed. "All right. All right. Hang on. Let me see if there's a satellite in the area." Computer keys clicked in the background and after far too many agonizing minutes, Harvard said, "I gotchu. Go ahead and drop back. I won't lose her." After another pause that seemed like an eternity, he said, "Yeah, he's moving. Getting on US-54, headed out of the city. Do you think it's the Juarez Syndicate wanting to cause problems for her stepdad again?"

"I don't know." Quinn pulled a u-ey and followed signs for the nearest highway on-ramp. "Whoever it is, they know what they're doing. They waited until I left and grabbed her fast. I was gone…twenty minutes, tops. And, Harvard, she's—" He choked on the word, had to clear his throat before finishing, "She's pregnant."

A beat of silence passed, and the little hairs on the back of his neck prickled. "What?"

"Yeah…" Harvard drew the word out. "I kinda already knew about the pregnancy."

"What?" he said again. If Harvard had reached through the phone and socked him in the eye, he would have been less stunned. "How the fuck do you know when I just found out this morning?"

"Look, Gabe asked me to keep tabs on the Escareno family after this summer, mainly because he suspects her stepdad isn't on the up-and-up."

"That's news? Senator Escareno's a prick and everyone knows it."

"Yeah, well. I noticed an OB-GYN charge on her credit card, followed by a flurry of activity from places like Babies-

R-Us. I put two and two together and it equaled pregnancy. I reported it to Gabe, but he decided it wasn't our place to tell you. We had no way of knowing for sure if the baby was yours."

"It's mine." And there was that chill of fear again, scraping its claws down his spine. What did it say about him that he was more afraid of a fetus than of the fuckhead who had kidnapped Mara?

"So," Harvard said slowly after another beat. "Congrats?"

He remembered saying the same to Gabe less than forty-eight hours ago and growled. It's a wonder Gabe hadn't punched him for that. "Harvard, do me a favor and don't talk about it. Just…tell me if they turn off this road, okay?"

"Okay. Sorry." And then there was nothing but radio silence from the former CIA intelligence analyst until an hour later, when Harvard spoke up again. "Quinn. They're about a mile and a half ahead of you, making a right off the highway."

"Yeah, I see a town up ahead." Really, it was more of a pit stop, its buildings clustered around the highway in crumbling clumps. There was only one intersection, and he could see the Explorer bumping along a desert road to his right.

Damn.

Quinn pulled into the gas station–slash–garage decaying on the corner of the intersection. "Hang on a second, H," he said into the phone, then popped open his door and called to a small Latino man who was poking around under the hood of a pickup. "Hey!"

"Hi, there. Need gas?" he asked with only a hint of a Spanish accent.

"No." Quinn studied the guy. He was about fifty and had a friendly, white smile that contrasted sharply with his leatherlike brown skin. The patch on his grease-stained overalls said his name was Antonio. "I need to know what's down that road."

Antonio's gaze followed the jerk of his chin to the road the Explorer had turned onto, then his eyes tracked away again. Big red flag.

"We don't want your kind around here," Antonio said.

Quinn sucked in a breath and fought for patience. "What kind is that?"

"The kinda people that go out to the airfield."

"An airfield? Who owns it?" All he got was a shake of the head in response. Whoever owned that field had the locals scared. "The Ford that just came by? You ever see it around here before?"

"Nope. And I don't want any part of this. I just go about my business and steer clear."

Yeah, that's what Quinn figured. He wasn't going to get any intel from this guy. He'd have to go in blind. "Is the road all open like this?" he asked instead, motioning to the desert around them. He could still see the Explorer bumping along, kicking up a cloud of dust in the distance.

"Oh, yeah. You can see for miles around here."

Which meant they'd see his car coming if he tried to get close to the airfield. Fuck.

Antonio let the hood of his truck fall shut. Considering, Quinn eyed the rust bucket on four wheels. "That thing run?"

"Good enough."

"I'll give you two hundred bucks if you drive me out there."

"Nope."

Christ, he was wasting too much time, felt each passing second as it slipped away and the Explorer got farther and farther from view. But continuing on in his rental was suicide. "Five hundred then."

"Uh-uh. I'm not going anywhere near there." Antonio headed for the garage. "No amount of money is worth getting killed for."

True, but this wasn't about money for him, and he was done fucking around. He grabbed his bag out of the backseat, left a couple hundred dollars and the rental's keys on the dash, and made a run for the truck.

And, look at that, good old Tony had even left the keys in the ignition. Quinn wouldn't have to revisit his days of misspent youth to hot-wire the thing after all. He fired up the engine and it sounded like a bear with a sore throat, but when he stepped on the gas, the truck shot forward with surprising speed. A quick glance in the rearview mirror showed Antonio cursing him out in the middle of the dust cloud his hasty exit had stirred up.

"Sorry, pal. Should've accepted the money." He raised his phone to his ear again. "Still there, H?"

"Did you just commit grand theft auto?" Harvard asked, voice dripping disbelief.

"Nah. This truck's not worth that much. Good power under the hood, though."

"Holy shit."

Quinn ignored him. "You still have her on satellite?"

"Uh...yeah. Yeah. I see the airfield, too, but if she gets on a plane, I'll lose her. I don't have a huge network at my disposal like the government does."

Of course it couldn't be that easy. "What about the way you tracked Gabe's phone in Colombia—can you do that with mine?"

"Yes, but—"

"Good. I hope that program of yours has a global reach, because if they put Mara on a plane, I'm going to be on it with her. I'll need you to lock on my signal and find us. Send the team."

"Oh, man. Quinn—"

"Does it have a global reach or not?"

"Yeah, of course. As long as your phone has battery power, I'll be able to track you."

"Then I'm getting on that plane one way or another." Quinn stared out the dusty windshield at the winding road in front of him. Adrenaline spilled into his blood, making him twitchy. "And, Harvard, you better make damn sure the team's right on my ass, got it?"

Chapter Five

The problem with deserts was that every move you made kicked up a cloud of dust as good as a neon sign screaming, "Incoming!" Quinn took the truck in as close as he dared, then dumped it and continued on foot at a dead run until he was within sight of the airfield. Only then did he force himself to slow down and flatten out on the ground. Except for a few rocks and some short desert plants, there was little in the way of cover here, but dust already caked most of his sweat-dampened skin and clothes, offering a bit of camouflage if he stayed low.

Quinn could be a patient man, but crawling toward that airfield one excruciating inch at a time was one of the most trying tests of self-restraint he'd ever endured. Every fiber in his being screamed that he had to get to Mara *now*. Make sure she was okay. Protect her. But he hadn't seen a plane take off or land, so she had to still be at the airfield, and running in like Rambo would only get them both killed.

Christ, he wished the team were here to back him up.

He halted in the shrubs alongside the runway and spotted

the Explorer parked in front of one of the two metal hangars about 150 meters away from his position. Was she still in the vehicle? He couldn't tell. And he didn't have a visual on the fuckhead, either.

Now what?

He had no team, minimal gear, and only a handgun. It was a damn fine weapon but still not enough firepower to take on…whoever he was about to take on. The Juarez Syndicate made the most sense, but it didn't sit right in his gut. The abduction had been too slick, and the Syndicate had too much of a gang mentality to pull off something like this. Their style was more like the sloppy drive-by assassination attempt on Ramon Escareno last July. They didn't do covert well.

But who else could it be?

Quinn rested his head on his forearms and gave himself a moment to breathe, which he hadn't done properly since he saw Mara snatched. His headache was nearing epic proportions, and he had to face the possibility it could explode into a full-blown migraine. Or, worse, a blackout episode. If he went lights-on-nobody-home right now, he'd lose Mara.

Possibly forever.

Yeah, sure, he'd already lost any chance he would have had with her, and he could live with that. Maybe. But losing her completely? Knowing he'd never find out if she'd give him another shot because she was just…gone? His stomach clenched at the thought. No. He wouldn't let it happen and fought against the headache with everything he had, separating himself from the pain, locking it away. He'd pay for it later, but right now all that mattered was getting to Mara. If he could free her now, before the plane they were undoubtedly waiting for arrived, he'd wouldn't have to worry so much about the unknowns—how to get on the plane, where they were going, how he'd keep track of her once they landed.

At least he didn't also have to deal with scorching heat. Even with the bright afternoon sun, the temperature was struggling to top fifty. A blessing now, but if he was still waiting out here when the sun went down, hypothermia would become a very real problem.

Which was exactly why he should make his move.

Quinn sucked in a deep breath and shoved himself upright. He sprinted across the open runway in a low crouch. Nobody tried to gun him down, which he took as a good sign that this was a small-time operation, possibly even a one-man job.

One man he could take. More than that… Well. He'd do whatever he had to.

He reached the first hangar, found a side door propped open a half inch, and peeked inside. Dark. The fuckhead wouldn't be sitting in complete darkness with Mara. They had to be in the other one. He backed away from the door and, staying close to the outside wall, moved around the back side of the building, then ghosted up the alley created by the two hangars. Even before he reached the second hangar's closed side door, he heard muffled female sobs inside, and his heart clenched.

I'm here, Mara. Hang on just a bit longer.

He tested the door. Locked. Because of course it was.

The distinct sound of a plane decelerating overhead caught his attention, and he squinted toward the sky. Whomever Fuckhead had been waiting for was only minutes away, and he'd prefer to be long gone with Mara by his side before that plane touched down.

Now or never.

Keeping to the shadows of the alley, he raced toward the front of the building, firearm up and ready. The main hangar door was open, the lights on, and he sensed movement inside. He sucked in a breath to calm the adrenaline-fueled jitters in his gut, then swung into the opening. The hangar was filled with three planes in various states of disrepair, the internal mechanics spread out on the concrete floor as if the planes had been gutted for parts. And there on the floor in the middle of it all was Mara, struggling against the zip ties holding her wrists, tears streaming over her flushed cheeks and a duct-tape gag.

Their eyes met, and the relief filtering through hers ignited a fragile spark of hope that maybe he hadn't fubar'd things with her yet—a spark he ruthlessly squashed. At this point she'd be relieved to see Elvis walk through that door—anyone but her attacker. She made a muffled sound behind her gag, and he pressed a finger to his lips. She nodded.

"Where he is?" he mouthed.

She shrugged, shook her head.

Quinn crouched in front of her. "All right. Let's get you out of here. We have to move fast. Can you walk?"

She lifted her feet to show they were also bound with a zip tie.

Rage sent fire roaring through his veins, and he clenched his teeth against it. He wanted to punch something. Or someone. Preferably the fuckhead who'd abducted her. He did another quick scan of the hangar, then set his gun down and reached into his boot for the knife he'd slid in there before leaving the stolen truck. He bent to saw through the tie—

Mara's shout from behind her gag was the only warning he had of an impending attack. He whirled, knife raised, and Fuckhead's fist glanced off his jaw. The blade flew from his hand, clattering to the floor somewhere nearby. He saw white. His knees buckled and he didn't catch himself soon enough to stop the fall. He was going down one way or another, but he couldn't stay down or he'd end up dead. That punch had been calculated to KO him. Truthfully, it was a wonder it hadn't.

Rattled from the blow, he clumsily rolled into the fall,

sprang back to his feet behind Fuckhead, and snaked an arm around his windpipe, squeezing tight. The guy grunted, and sweat soaked through his balaclava as he struggled for oxygen.

Quinn was sweating, too, breathing harder than he should have been. Choking someone out was nothing, a cakewalk, and yet his vision started to tunnel on him, and for one horrifying second, he thought he was going to pass out himself. His grip loosened enough on Fuckhead's windpipe that the guy was able to suck in a rejuvenating breath.

Shit. A quick, clean knockout wasn't going to be possible now.

Quinn blinked away the fuzzy gray dots clouding his vision and redoubled his grip, but the guy was huge, a good three inches taller and carrying an extra thirty pounds of muscle, and he'd tensed up his neck like a steel beam. He reared back, hitting Quinn's jaw with the top of his head.

Quinn released the chokehold and staggered. Barely had a chance to suck in a breath to regroup before Fuckhead made like a ram, plowing him in the stomach, and the fight was back on. Kicks and punches flew, Quinn battling for each blow he landed. Fuckhead fought like a machine and was quick for his large size. A punch glanced off Quinn's side, too close to his kidney for comfort.

Fuck this. The guy wanted dirty, Quinn would give him dirty.

Shutting off higher thought, he went into survival mode, all brutal action and reaction. He brought his knee up and connected with Fuckhead's balls hard enough that the guy's dark eyes bulged. When he bent double, groaning, Quinn grabbed him by the hair and slammed a knee up into his face. He made an *ump* sound and staggered sideways but still didn't go down. Blood splattered the floor from his nose, and he groped around under his jacket, no doubt going for some kind of weapon. Quinn wasn't about to give him the opportunity to pull it and drove his elbow into the base of the guy's skull. Finally, Fuckhead collapsed to the floor and didn't move again.

Christ.

Panting hard, Quinn swept his sweat-dampened hair from his face. All right. Who was this guy? He rolled his opponent over and pulled off the balaclava. The face underneath was a bloody mess and his nose was certainly broken, but…

No.

No way.

Recognition slammed through Quinn like a train. This wasn't right. It couldn't be. "Urban?"

Petty Officer First Class Todd Urban's eyelids were frozen half open, his eyes staring sightlessly at the ceiling.

No. Oh, fuck, no.

Quinn fumbled for a pulse and found nothing under his fingers but cooling skin. That final blow to the head had done more than render Urban unconscious.

Quinn sat back, head reeling, his stomach threatening a revolt that had nothing to do with the sudden, insistent pounding of a headache inside his skull. He scrambled away from the body and gulped in large drafts of air, silently talking his gut down before it went all *Exorcist* on him. Puking at the scene of the crime was not a good plan.

Really not a good plan.

Fuck! He'd just killed an active-fucking-duty U.S. Navy SEAL. A former teammate. A guy he'd once considered a friend…

And yet Urban had been fighting to kill. How had he not recognized Quinn? Sure, he'd lost some weight since leaving the SEALs, but he hadn't changed that much. And why was Urban here alone, without his team? They wouldn't have deployed on U.S. soil, no matter how important Mara's stepfather was.

What the hell was going on here?

Mara made a whimpering sound, and he gazed over at her. This time, there was no relief in her eyes. Instead, he saw fear. Of him. She was staring at him with sheer terror, her eyes too big in her pale face and showing too much white.

"Mara." Her name came out on a soft exhale. He reached for her, his knuckles bruised and bloodied, and she flinched back. The gesture was worlds away from last night, when she had arched into his touch, begged for it. He swallowed hard at the memory, his throat tight. After witnessing this, she'd never let him touch her like that again.

Which was for the better. A woman like her didn't deserve his brand of danger in her life.

He found his knife on the floor near a dismantled plane engine and crossed back to her, holding it up in a silent question. She nodded and shut her eyes, squeezing out tears to roll over her gag as he sliced through the ties on her feet and wrists.

He reached for the duct tape over her mouth last. "I'll do it fast, but this will hurt. I'm sorry." And he yanked it off.

She cried out in a string of Spanish curses and stomped her feet in a way that had him fighting back a smile.

Christ, he loved that feisty streak in her, the one she fought so hard to hide behind a demure outer shell.

Whoa, wait. Loved?

Ha. What did he know about love? He shouldn't even think that word in conjunction with Mara. He needed to stop that shit, because she was obviously terrified of him now. With good reason.

He backed away from her, careful to keep his face impassive. "We need to go."

Mara sucked in a shaky breath. Nodded. "Okay."

She climbed to her feet and looked so damn small and

fragile standing there, he wanted nothing more than to wrap her up in his arms and never let her go.

Bad idea.

He spun away, snatched his gun from the floor, and, after a moment of hesitation, he searched Urban and found another gun. He'd need all the firepower he could get his hands on to make sure Mara stayed safe.

He stared down into Urban's bloodied face. He hated leaving the guy here, but he didn't have much choice. Carrying Urban back to the truck would only slow them down, and Mara was his first priority. He'd take her back to El Paso, make sure she was secure, then turn himself in at Fort Bliss. The army would send someone out to investigate and collect Urban's body. There would be questions he wouldn't have answers for and possibly even a trial.

"Goddammit. This shouldn't have happened. I'm sorry, man." He ran a hand over Urban's face, closing his eyes for the last time. In his peripheral vision, he saw Mara cover her mouth with her hand.

"You know him?" she gasped.

"He was a SEAL. A friend." Quinn looked over at her, watched the color drain from her face.

"But—but why would he kidnap me?"

Wait. What? Sure, Urban had been wearing a hoodie and a balaclava like the abductor, but after Quinn uncovered his face, he'd assumed it had been a tragic case of mistaken identity on both of their parts. It hadn't once crossed his mind that Urban *was* the abductor, because that didn't line up with the Todd Urban he knew—a likable, hardworking family man who would sell his soul for his wife and kids. "*This* is the man that abducted you? You're sure?"

Mara nodded, her dark eyes wide and glassy with unshed tears. "He broke into my house and took me out of my bedroom." She started to tremble. Probably going into shock.

Again, Quinn wanted to hold her, to tuck her in against his chest until the shivering stopped and the bad memories faded. And again he restrained himself. She had flinched the last time he reached for her. She didn't want him or his comfort, and who could blame her for that?

He stared down at Urban. Why would his former teammate kidnap Mara? "This doesn't make any fucking sense."

Chapter Six

Mara gazed down at the man who had broken into her home, knocked her unconscious, tied her up, and driven her into the middle of nowhere. Travis's former teammate. "I thought SEALs were supposed to be the good guys. The nation's heroes."

"At one time he was. I don't know what happened to change that." Travis straightened away from the body and reached for her hand. She flinched, couldn't control the automatic reaction. He'd killed a man with those hands—the same hands that had wrung every drop of pleasure from her in bed, but the thought of him touching her now made her skin crawl. Or maybe that was just the shivers she couldn't seem to stop.

He'd killed his teammate to protect her. On a purely logical level, she understood that and was grateful for it. But, oh, God, there was such a huge difference between knowing Travis Quinn was a dangerous man and seeing him in action. And witnessing the sheer brutality he was capable of only drove home the realization that she didn't really know him at all.

Was this the kind of man she wanted in her child's life?

Travis's jaw tightened, and he dropped his hand. "We need to move."

She hugged herself against the chill in his tone. "Where are we?"

"Somewhere in New Mexico. I have a truck about a mile due west from here. If something happens and we're separated, run for it. The keys are in it. Take it and don't stop until you get back to El Paso." As he spoke, he strode to the hangar door and peeked out. "Aw, fuck me." He ran back to her, gripped her shoulders, and whirled her around. "Hide. Now."

Where? she thought, stalling out midstride, her heart threatening to beat a hole through her rib cage as her gaze boomeranged around the hangar, looking for a hiding place. Travis shoved her toward one of the disassembled planes, but she was too short to reach the doors. She wasn't getting inside without a ladder or Travis's help.

A large toolbox sat on the floor nearby. Better than nothing. She ducked behind it, crouching down in a tight ball, arms wrapped protectively around her belly. Voices sounded from the front of the hangar, but they weren't speaking English. Or even Spanish, for that matter. Was it… Russian? She strained her ears. Couldn't make out words, but yes, she was certain it was Russian. She'd spent a summer in St. Petersburg during a high school exchange program and used to know quite a bit of the language—at least enough to understand a conversation and to make herself understood—but it had been ten years since she'd last used it.

One of the Russians called out, followed by the sounds of struggle—fists landing against flesh, grunts of pain, something metal clattering to the floor.

Oh, God, had they found Travis? Had he even tried to

hide?

She peeked around the bottom edge of the toolbox. Two big guys held Travis captive on the floor, his face turned in her direction, his cheek smooshed against the concrete. Their eyes met, and his narrowed in an obvious warning.

Stay hidden. She could all but hear him issuing the order.

He resumed struggling, and she ducked back behind the toolbox and held her breath at the sounds of more punches, more things falling to the floor, some glass shattering.

A third Russian voice broke through the confusion. "*Stoy!*"

She knew that word. *Stop.* And just like that, the fight ended. Someone groaned in pain, and she couldn't stand not knowing what was happening to Travis. She again peeked around the toolbox. Two Russians dragged him to his feet, but he wasn't the one groaning. It was the bald one to Travis's left, who was favoring his leg and groaning with the strain of holding Travis still. She gazed past the three of them to the well-dressed man striding into the hangar. He had sharp features and dark hair pulled back into a ponytail at the base of his neck. He was in charge here. Of that, she had no doubt.

He eyed Travis up and down, then glanced over at the body of her abductor on the floor with a raised, perfectly manicured brow. He clicked his tongue against his teeth and said in English, "Well, this is interesting."

"Zaryanko." Travis all but spat the man's name. "What the fuck are you doing here?"

"I stopped to collect the merchandise Mr. Urban had for me," Zaryanko said placidly. "Where is she?"

Merchandise? Mara's stomach lurched. This man considered women merchandise? Oh, God.

"Gone," Travis said. "I let her go. She's safely in the hands of the authorities by now."

Mara shrank back, clearly hearing the implied warning

in his words. No matter what happened, she did not want these people to know she was still here.

Zaryanko sighed. "You and your friends have a bad habit of getting in my way, Mr. Quinn. First in Afghanistan and now here you are, disrupting another of my business transactions. You've cost me a lot of money these last few months."

"We stopped you from starting a nuclear war," Travis said, deadpan. "Cry me a fucking river."

"But in truth, you've also done me a bit of a favor here," Zaryanko continued. "I was supposed to hang on to the woman, tuck her away until you came for her, but you're already here and Mr. Urban's dead, so I see no reason to go through with their plan. Unless they pay me…"

"No honor among thieves," Travis said.

"Or dirty business associates." Zaryanko considered for a moment, nodded. "Yes, I think this works out much better. It's long past time I recoup my loses, and I believe they want the information you have badly enough to pay whatever sum I ask."

"Who are they?" Travis demanded. "What information? I don't have any information."

Zaryanko's gaze tracked over to Urban's body, but he said nothing more about it. He snapped his fingers, the sound sharp and echoing around the hangar's high walls. "Bring him," he said in Russian.

Mara eased back behind the toolbox and shut her eyes, listened to their footsteps fade away.

Travis had sacrificed himself for her.

Tears burned, and she fought them back. She didn't have time to break down. They had Travis, were taking him God knew where, and she was his only hope. She had to move. Run to the east, find the truck, and get to the nearest phone and call…

Who?

Obviously, the police were out of the question. The morning had been so Alice-down-the-rabbit-hole surreal, they'd never believe her. And if Urban had indeed been a SEAL, how did she know she could trust anyone in authority?

She'd call Jesse. Her cousin would know what to do—he *always* knew what to do, and he could bring in the rest of Travis's team. And Lanie. She was a Texas Ranger, one of their best investigators, and would figure this all out.

Except she couldn't go anywhere until she was sure the Russians were gone.

She waited, listened. Minutes ticked by, and shadows lengthened across the floor as the sun sank. She really didn't want to be wandering around in the desert after dark, but—what if Zaryanko and his two thugs were still out there? She hadn't heard any engines, car or otherwise. But neither did she hear any voices or footsteps outside the hangar.

The sun sank closer to the horizon, spilling orange-gold light in through the west-facing hangar door. The cold emanating from the concrete floor seeped through her leggings into her bones, and she shivered so hard her teeth clacked together. She couldn't stay here much longer. Desert nights were cold, especially in the winter, and she'd freeze to death. But was it safe to leave yet? She had no idea.

She peeked around the toolbox again. The hangar was empty, and she didn't see anyone on the tarmac beyond. Gulping down her fear, she stood. Her legs had cramped up, and she shook them out one at a time until she was positive they wouldn't collapse on her.

The hangar door beckoned with the promise of freedom, but she wasn't so sure about walking out that big door, exposing herself to whatever lay beyond, and scanned for—

There. A side door.

She scrambled toward it and fumbled with the lock, a wild panic overtaking her when she finally got it open and tumbled into the deepening shadows of evening. In front of her lay nothing but a vast expanse of desert. Gulp.

Suck it up, she warned herself. Travis had let them take him so she would be safe and able to send help. She wasn't about to let him down.

Judging by the sunset, she was facing south. Travis had said his truck was to the west, which meant—crap. She'd have to run straight across the airfield.

She stayed close to the wall of the hangar like she'd seen soldiers do on TV and edged around the corner. A plane sat on the tarmac. Zaryanko and his men were still here.

She shrank back. She should go hide again. Maybe find a blanket so she didn't freeze and just wait the night out in the hangar. They had to leave sometime, right? Except she didn't like the idea of staying overnight with a dead body only a few feet away. And what if they were waiting for more criminal types to arrive? Right now, there were only three of them, and she got the impression that Zaryanko didn't do much of his own dirty work. So, really, there were only the two thugs. Who probably had guns. And knew how to shoot.

She sagged against the metal wall of the hangar and lifted her face to the sky. After her mother had married Ramon Escareno, she had been raised in a strict Catholic home, and while she'd found the church's views too narrow-minded and confining, she'd taken comfort in the idea of heaven and that her dad could be up there, watching over her. She sent a quick prayer up to Jackson Warrick.

I love you, Daddy. Please, help me be strong and brave for my baby.

With that, she sucked in a fortifying breath, pushed away from the wall, and ran. She made it a quarter of the way across the pavement before she heard the shout behind her in Russian.

Oh, God, they were going to shoot.

She picked up the pace, her tennis shoes pounding as hard at her heart. Halfway there. Heavy footsteps thundered behind her, closing in fast. Three-quarters of the way. Up ahead, she saw the snake of an unpaved desert road, and a large black van kicked up dust as it sped toward her.

Help?

Unsure, she faltered a step, and that was all the Russians needed to catch up. One grabbed her around the waist and hauled her back against his rocklike body.

No, no, no! She kicked and screamed, but the thug seemed unfazed. He just banded his arm tighter around her, clamped a large hand over her mouth, and looked at his companion. "I win," he said in Russian. "Told you she was still here. Pay up."

"Later," the second man said, nodded toward the road, and added something more that she didn't understand. But it couldn't be good, because they weren't at all surprised to see the vehicle.

The Russians dragged her back to the plane, and Zaryanko smiled. "Well. Quinn was lying after all. Good work, Alexei."

"What do we do with her?" the bald thug holding her—Alexei—asked.

Zaryanko eyed her up and down, made an unimpressed sound, then turned his attention to the arriving vehicle. The van rolled to a stop near the plane, and several armed men wearing the gold-and-red colors of El Sindicato hopped out.

"What do you have for me?" Zaryanko asked them in English.

The lead gang member opened the back door. He pulled ten bound and gagged women out, one by one, and laid them facedown on the tarmac like fish at a market.

"Hmm." Zaryanko walked down the line, inspecting each of them, murmuring his approval until he reached the last woman. She was older than the others, with silver-streaked hair and a lined face. He grimaced and motioned to his thug with the flick of a wrist. "Pyotr. This one is too old and ugly. She's worthless to me. Do something about it."

Pyotr drew a gun and strode over to the sobbing woman. The shot was drowned out by the terrified screams of the others. Mara's stomach lurched into her throat and one word kept bouncing around inside her skull. *Merchandise.*

"I'll take the rest at half our usual rate," Zaryanko said.

"Fuck no!" the gang leader said. "You kill one of our women and think you can cheat us—"

"Pyotr," Zaryanko said softly, and his personal killer raised the gun and fired again. The gang leader dropped. The women's screams choked off into silence.

"Anyone else have objections?" Zaryanko asked. Nobody spoke. "Very well. Half our usual rate, and I will not be making the trip back to this wasteland until you have something better to offer me."

Money exchanged hands quickly after that, and the gang members didn't stick around. They were long gone before Pyotr ushered the nine remaining women onto the plane.

"So what about this one?" Alexei asked.

Zaryanko walked over and pinched Mara's face between his fingers, turning her head side to side. "She's fat and short," he said in Russian, "but her face is pretty enough." He added something else that she couldn't translate, but she swore she heard Travis's name mentioned. Then, "Bring her."

Alexei picked her up and all but tossed her into the cargo area of the plane with the other women. The door latching shut behind her was the most terrifying thing she'd ever heard in her life.

This couldn't be happening.

She sat up on her knees and blinked until her eyes adjusted to the near darkness. She was the only woman not bound or gagged, and she tried to calm the others in both

English and Spanish as she worked to free their hands.

Toward the front of the plane, she stumbled over a leg and groped around for the owner, finding a very large boot attached to the leg. That didn't belong to one of the women, and her heart fluttered with hope. "Travis?"

He jerked upright as if she'd electrocuted him. "Mara?"

"Yes, it's me." The darkness was too complete, and she couldn't see him, but there was no mistaking his voice. She ran her hands over him, searching for his ties, and discovered handcuffs securing him to a metal pipe welded to the wall. She wasn't going to be able to break through those like she had the women's duct tape, but she could remove the burlap bag from over his head.

"Fuck," he breathed and jerked on the cuffs. "What happened?"

"I tried to get away. I really tried, but I was afraid of being in the desert after dark and I ran for it. But they knew I was still here all along and they were ready for me."

"Fuck," he said again, and she couldn't quite muffle the sob that worked its way up out of her throat.

The cuffs rattled again. "Mara, I'm not angry with you. Okay? I'm not, but—" Another vicious yank made the whole wall rattle. "Goddamn these things! Come over here. Please. I need —" His voice caught. "I need to know you're okay."

She swallowed down another sob and crawled up beside him, wrapping her arms around his waist. "I'm okay."

"All right. All right," he repeated as if trying to assure himself. He rested his cheek on top of her head. "Who's in here with us?"

"Nine other women, most of them Mexican. I think they were kidnapped."

"Yeah, they were. Nikolai Zaryanko is a trafficker. Humans, drugs, guns, organs—if he can get his hands on it, you can bet he'll sell it. Rumor has it he sold his own sister."

He hesitated. "Mara, no matter what, he can't find out about your, uh…"

"My pregnancy?" she finished.

"Yeah. That."

Travis couldn't even say the word aloud. And here she'd thought she had done the right thing by contacting him about the baby. Now, hindsight being twenty-twenty and all that, she saw it for the mistake it was. She backed away from him and immediately missed the heat of his body. She was so cold, down to the very center of her being. "He'll try to sell the baby, too, won't he?"

"Yeah. He'll auction it off to the highest bidder."

"Oh, God." Sick dread surged into her throat. She swallowed it down, wrapped her arms around her middle, and huddled against the wall in the dark. Sobs and whimpers echoed around the plane from the other women. One was reciting the twenty-third psalm in Spanish over and over in a choked, hushed tone.

But she would not fall apart like them. She didn't have that luxury.

"Mara," Travis said softly. "We'll be okay."

"Please, don't do that. Don't coddle me." She lifted her head and looked toward his voice. "Tell me the truth."

He said nothing for several agonizing beats. "The truth is unless my team finds us, we're screwed. But I swear I will do *everything* in my power to make sure they find us."

Chapter Seven

El Paso, Texas

Jesse Warrick made it to the El Paso hotel that would be the team's temporary base just after ten p.m. and stepped into a wall of noise and activity when he opened the door. Seemed he was the last to arrive. Most of the team had still been in D.C. after celebrating the New Year, but he'd left for Wyoming right after the party, hoping to catch a few days of downtime with his son before another mission called him away again. He'd gotten only one day with Connor—one long day of trying to coax the kid out of his teenage shell of indifference—before the call had come in from Harvard about Mara's kidnapping.

Christ, he was tired.

Between the nauseating worry for Mara's safety eating away at his gut, his heartache at his son's complete apathy toward him, and the emotionally draining fight with his ex-wife when he'd told her he had to send Connor home early, he was running on fumes. Not to mention the calls to Mara's parents—who, he'd found out, had fucking disowned her, and that was a whole 'nother can of worms he didn't have the energy to open yet—and his own horrified family, the last twelve hours had been the longest of his life. He felt like a big steaming pile of manure, and the noise in the hotel room did nothing to help the headache pounding behind his eyes.

He stalled out in the doorway, unsure if he had the patience to deal with the team right now. Marcus and Jean-Luc had claimed the suite's couch and were arguing good-naturedly over the football game on TV. Harvard already had his tech stuff spread out on the large dining table and was tapping away at his keyboard while Ian stood at the sink in the kitchenette, filling a bowl with water for his dog, Tank. Seth sat in one of the two deep leather chairs that completed the living room arrangement and added his two cents to the animated football argument. The guy looked happy, more at peace with himself, worlds away from what he'd been only a few short months ago. Meeting Phoebe in Afghanistan had been good for him, had done what no doctors or psychologists had been able to accomplish: she'd given him a solid foundation of love and support on which to build his recovery. Yeah, he still struggled with his PTSD, but he was coping, and Phoebe was helping him do it.

At the thought of the happy new couple, a twist of longing snaked through Jesse's chest. He didn't begrudge them their happiness. He didn't. He simply...wanted a piece of it for himself.

And wasn't that goddamn foolish? You'd think he would have learned by now. He'd already tried the whole falling-in-love thing—not once, not twice, but three times, and they had all ended in divorce.

He glanced away from Seth and noticed a stranger looming in the corner.

Who the hell...?

Eyes narrowed, he studied the man. Big guy, close-cropped dark hair, olive skin—most likely of Hispanic decent. Recognition clicked. This was Jace Garcia, HORNET's new pilot, hired on shortly after they had returned from Afghanistan. Jesse had met him only once, very briefly, when he was first introduced to the team, but he remembered the pilot wasn't much of a talker, liked to keep to himself.

Garcia seemed competent and came highly recommended by Camden Wilde, who had served in the air force with him. Still, Jesse was surprised to see him here. This op wasn't exactly situation normal for the team.

Marcus spotted him loitering in the doorway. "Hey, Jess. You have any idea why Gabe called us all back to El Paso?"

Yeah, he wasn't in the mood for chitchat. Ignoring the question, he crossed to the window and stared out over the parking lot, but it wasn't well lit and there wasn't much to see but the blackness of a desert night.

"Hello to you, too. What bug crawled up your ass, Warrick?"

The door opened again, and Gabe Bristow's quiet, commanding voice overrode the chatter of the TV. "All right, gentlemen. Everyone here?" He scanned the room, nodded in Jesse's direction. "Good. Time to get down to business, then."

Yeah. Business. Jesse snorted in disgust. Like they should've been doing hours ago instead of sitting here on their asses, watching football and twiddling their thumbs while they waited for him to arrive. Mara could be on the other side of the world by now, and he shuddered to think of the horrors his sweet, softhearted cousin might be facing at this very moment. She didn't belong in this world—his world, so full of death and destruction. None of his family did, and he'd done his damnedest to make sure they never got involved in this portion of his life—which had cost him all of his marriages and, now, his son's love. And yet despite his efforts to keep his two very different worlds from colliding, he couldn't shake the feeling that he'd invited this danger to Mara's doorstep by asking his teammates to help him protect her this summer.

Gabe shut off the TV and positioned himself at the front of the room. "We have a situation, gentlemen."

Seth straightened in his seat and glanced around. His shoulders tightened. "Hey. Wait a minute. Where's Quinn?"

For the first time since convening on the hotel, the rest of the guys took notice of their missing teammate. Both Marcus and Jean-Luc turned and scanned the room with nearly identical *WTF?* expressions. Ian stood propped against the wall with his arms crossed, his dog faithfully by his side. He merely lifted one brow in question, but his reaction was downright animated next to Jace Garcia's impassive poker face. Harvard still didn't glance up from his laptop, which was par for the course for the ex-CIA intelligence analyst.

"That's who we're here to talk about," Gabe said.

"Goddammit," Jesse said. "I warned ya, boss. Back in Colombia, I warned you."

Gabe sighed. "I know."

"Warned him about what?" Marcus asked.

Jesse started to answer—that Quinn was a walking medical case study for traumatic brain injury and shouldn't have been allowed to go on missions—but Gabe spoke over him, bringing the guys up to speed on the situation. Mara had been abducted midmorning yesterday. Quinn had witnessed it and had been on the HT's—hostage taker's—tail with Harvard tracking him until the satellite moved out of range. There had been no word from Quinn since his last contact with Harvard.

Surprise rippled through the room.

Gabe held up his hands and spoke over the growing noise.

"We're assuming whoever took Mara now also has Quinn, and we'll need all hands on deck to find them. This won't be a paid op, and I know it's asking a lot when we just came back from that clusterfuck in Afghanistan. I understand if any of you prefer to stay behind this time." His gaze went to the new guy. "Especially you, Garcia. You have no stake in this. You don't know Quinn from Adam, so if you want to bow out, nobody's going to hold it against you."

Garcia shrugged. "I have nowhere better to be."

Gabe nodded and focused on Seth. "You've been through a lot in the last month and a half—"

"Fuck that," Seth said. "Quinn saved my hide once. I'm not staying home while he's in trouble."

"Fair enough. Harvard, you—"

"Not happening, boss," Harvard answered without looking up from his screen. "Quinn's the only reason I'm sitting here right now instead of inside a box six feet under."

A rumble of agreement came from everyone in the room.

Marcus got to his feet. "I'll call Giancarelli and have the FBI—"

"What?" Jesse snapped, impatient with all of them. "What's Giancarelli goin' to do? He's not even that high up on the FBI's bureaucratic totem pole."

"Do you have a better idea, Jess?" Marcus asked. "Because we gotta do something. I don't plan to sit around while a friend's in trouble."

"Friend?" Jesse gave a bitter laugh, the word leaving a bad taste in his mouth. "Yeah, Quinn's some friend. Last I checked, a friend doesn't go behind your back and knock up your cousin. I told him Mara was off-fuckin'-limits."

And…cue the crickets.

"Yes," Gabe said with a *nice going* scowl in Jesse's direction. "Mara's pregnant, and Quinn confirmed to Harvard that it's his kid. Which, in regards to this situation, only means we have to locate them a-sap. Harvard, what have you got for us?"

"Not much, I'm afraid," Harvard said and fumbled to find his glasses in the mass of papers strewn across the table. "Quinn wanted me to trace his phone like we did yours in Colombia," he said to Gabe. "And as long as he has it on him and the battery holds out…no biggie. The phone doesn't even have to be turned on for my program to work. Thing is, the phone is still at the airfield in New Mexico, and that's not sitting right with me because I've been monitoring the area via satellite and I saw a plane land shortly after I last spoke to Quinn. It took off again about an hour later."

"What about Mara?" Jesse asked.

"Quinn said he'd stay with her, no matter what." He met Jesse's gaze with deep regret in his own. "I'm sorry. At this point, all we can do is hope that's true. But I don't believe either of them is in New Mexico anymore."

"Do we suspect the Juarez Syndicate is behind this?" Marcus asked the room. "The FBI only got a couple low-level Syndicate punks this summer. Maybe they came back, figured instead of trying for another hit on Senator Escareno, they'd kidnap his stepdaughter and get some money out of him."

"No." Harvard finally found his glasses and rubbed his eyes before putting them on. He looked paler than usual, had lost some of the muscle weight he'd packed on during training this summer. The medic in Jesse sat up and took notice. The man had been severely wounded just over a month ago, after all, and he was still healing. He shouldn't be involved in any of this. At the same time, if they had any hope of finding Quinn and Mara, he had to be.

"I wondered if it was El Sindicato at first, too," Harvard admitted. "But this doesn't fit their modus operandi."

Jace Garcia spoke up. "He's right. I know El Sindicato.

If they kidnapped the woman for ransom, they would have disappeared over the border into Mexico. It's not them."

Unease slipped through Jesse's gut as he studied the pilot. "How do you know El Sindicato?"

Garcia raised a brow. "How do you think? I grew up in Laredo, Texas, and everyone in the border states knows them."

Jesse made a noncommittal sound. Sure, everyone in Texas was aware of the threat El Sindicato posed, but the way Garcia talked…

Something more there.

Garcia pushed away from the wall. "Are you implying something, Warrick? 'Cause that, *esé*, is textbook racial profiling. I'm a Mexican immigrant so I must be corrupt, is that it?"

Jesse winced. Shit, he really must be tired. "That's not what I meant. I'm not—I don't think like that."

"I'd hope not, since your pretty little missing cousin looks to have some Mexican blood in her, too." He nodded toward the photo of Mara among Harvard's papers, then scowled at the rest of the group. "Way I see it, you *cabrones* need me far more than I need you, so I'd appreciate some respect. I can easily walk out that door and you can find yourselves a new pilot. No skin off my ass."

Gabe waved a hand toward the door. "I told you you're under no obligation here, Garcia. If you want to leave, leave. But if you're going to stay, I need you 100 percent committed to this mission."

"Hey, man," Jesse added. "I apologize. I'm…freaked out. Mara's like a sister to me."

Garcia scratched his jaw but otherwise didn't move. "Like I said, I have nowhere better to be." He glanced toward the photo again, and his lips tightened. "And I don't like seeing women hurt."

"All right," Gabe said after a moment of silence. "Marcus, I want you and Ian to check out the airfield in New Mexico. We need to know who we're dealing with. Harvard will give you the directions. Take Tank, see if he can pick up Mara's scent. I want confirmation that they are together and we aren't dooming her by chasing after Quinn."

Jesse's gut tightened. As angry as he was at Quinn for fucking around with his baby cousin, he needed the guy to be with Mara right now.

God, please let him be with Mara.

"We're on it." Marcus nodded and got up from the couch to gather his gear from the pile near the door.

Ian followed, whistling to Tank. "If her scent's there, we'll find it."

Gabe continued, "I'm going over to Mara's place to take a look inside—"

"I'm goin' with you," Jesse said, leaving no room in his tone for argument. He had to do something. Couldn't stand the thought of pacing around this suite with nothing to occupy his time except worry.

Gabe studied him for a long second, then gave an abrupt nod. "Good idea. Harvard, keep working the computers. And, Marcus, I do want you to call Giancarelli and see what he can do, if anything, to help. Everyone else, rest up and be ready to go. As soon as we know where Quinn and Mara are, we're going after them."

• • •

ISTANBUL, TURKEY

The whore was a useless waste of air. Her mouth was so dry he'd get more pleasure out of rubbing his cock with sandpaper, so when his cell phone rang, Liam Miller was more than happy to kick her skinny ass out of his bed. She landed on the floor with an unseemly shriek.

He rolled over and grabbed his phone from the nightstand. "Get out."

"What about my money?"

"I don't pay for whores who can't do their jobs right. Get out."

"But—"

He grabbed his gun from its spot next to his phone and pointed it at her. She gasped and backed up a slow step, hands raised. But she showed no real fear in her dark eyes. In fact, her nipples puckered and that…was interesting. Was she turned on by the threat? His cock stirred from the slumber her untalented mouth had put it in. Yes, he liked that thought. Maybe she wasn't so useless after all.

"Don't move." Without taking his gun off her, he reached for his phone. He'd prefer not to answer it now, but only a select few had his number, or even knew he was alive. "Miller."

"I need your help."

Liam smiled and sat up. Well, now. Hell must be frozen over if his American associates were reaching out to him. Especially since it was the big man in charge himself, the brains behind the whole black market operation, and not one of his underlings or his nitwit son. "What can I do for you, mate?"

"Your pal Zaryanko just fucked us over."

And that surprised them? Nikolai Zaryanko was a right dodgy bastard even on his best days. "And what do you expect me to do about it?"

Silence. Then, "He has Quinn."

Bloody hell. Liam dropped his weapon and waved the whore away. This conversation was far more interesting than anything she could do for him. "Does he now? In Transnistria?"

"We assume so. Zaryanko was only supposed to lure

Quinn out of the country so we could dispose of him without raising too many eyebrows. Instead, I have a dead operative in New Mexico and Zaryanko is trying to ransom Quinn back to us."

Liam swung his legs over the edge of the mattress and watched the whore gather her clothes, his stomach fluttering with a sensation he couldn't name. Not nerves. Anticipation, maybe? He'd been stewing in boredom for the last seven months as he healed from the fucking chest wound that had very nearly killed him in Colombia—courtesy of Quinn's fucking team—and it'd been too long since he'd anticipated anything. He grabbed his jeans from the floor. "Quinn is *mine*."

"Fine," his caller said with a superciliousness Liam would love to beat out of the man. "I'm sending you a team. If you can convince Zaryanko to turn Quinn over, you can do whatever you want with him. As long as he ends up in a body bag by the time you're done."

Quinn in a body bag.

It was the stuff of wet dreams. To have this opportunity fall into his lap now was almost too good to be true. "What's the catch?"

"No catch. I'm letting you off your leash. Quinn can't walk away from this alive."

Liam sneered at the phone as the line went dead. A leash? That arsehole couldn't be serious. He had never been *leashed*. He didn't answer to them. Never had, never would. If anything, *he* owned *them*. He'd lost everything to keep their operation running—his wife, his career, every-bloody-thing—and he'd only gone to ground after the fiasco in Colombia to give himself time to heal, not because they had insisted he should.

Fuck keeping a low profile now. It was time to show HORNET he was still alive and kicking.

And well past time to get his revenge.

Chapter Eight

The jolt of the landing gear thunking into place snapped Quinn out of the kind of dead-to-the-world sleep only exhaustion brought on. And for a moment, despite all of his training, he didn't know where he was. Or even who he was. He scrambled through his memory for a sliver of identity—a name, a place, something to latch onto and kick-start his stalled brain—but all he found was darkness, a void of nothingness, and he was falling deeper into it.

His heart hitched, and pain speared through his head. He squeezed his eyes shut and breathed in ragged pants, suddenly needing more oxygen than he could draw in.

Why couldn't he remember anything?

Someone moved beside him, and a terrified murmur near his ear sliced through the worst of his panic. "Travis?"

Yes, that was his name. Travis Benjamin Quinn. He lived in Baltimore, used to be a SEAL until a car accident ended his career two years ago, and he was now the executive officer of HumInt Consulting, Inc.'s Hostage Rescue and Negotiation Team, better known as HORNET.

Okay. That was a start. At least he wasn't amnesic.

"Travis, are you okay?"

And that voice was Mara, the woman he'd dreamed about far too often. The woman who was now pregnant with his child. The woman he had to protect no matter what. The sound of her saying his name settled him like nothing else could have. He had to get his shit together and keep it there, because she needed him.

Mara. Needed. Him.

He opened his eyes again and took stock of his condition. His fingers were numb, his arms tingling, and his back ached from the odd angle he'd had to maintain to keep the handcuffs from completely cutting off his circulation.

"Travis!" Her voice picked up a panic-induced shrillness.

"It's okay," he rasped. His throat felt like sandpaper and clearing it did nothing to help the problem. "I'm good. Fell asleep for a moment, that's all."

A beat of silence. "No," Mara said slowly, "you were just singing to me and then you stopped."

Panic lanced through him. Oh, hell. Had he blacked out on her? "I don't sing."

"But…you were." She started humming a melody he hadn't heard in years, then sang softly, "Too-ra-loo-ra-loo-ral, too-ra-loo-ra-li, that's an Irish lullaby."

"I—" His voice caught. He hadn't thought about that song since he'd lost his adopted mother. She used to sing it to him when he was ten years old, fighting for his life in an unfamiliar hospital, surrounded by the kindness of strangers.

He cleared his throat. "I don't sing."

"How can you not remember—"

"We're landing." The words came out like a whip, and she flinched back. Fuck. He hadn't meant to lash out at her like that, but he'd be damned before he talked about that song or admitted to her that he did not remember singing it.

He took a second to gentle his voice before speaking again. “How are you doing? Okay?”

“I’m…” She swallowed audibly. “Yes. A-are you?”

“Yeah, I’m good.” *Not even close.* He lifted his head and glanced around, the nerve in his neck pinching at the movement. In the cloying darkness, he picked out the shapes of the other abducted women huddled together in clumps along the plane’s walls. The acrid stench of sweat-soaked fear and urine saturated the air.

He had no way of knowing the time, but his internal clock told him they’d been in the plane for damn near twenty-four hours. They could be anywhere in the world and his phone—with its lifesaving GPS tracker—was lying on the floor of the hangar in New Mexico. He’d managed to type out one word before Zaryanko’s men attacked him, and although he’d never sent the text, he had no doubt Gabe and the team would find it. And, hopefully, find them.

The plane touched down with a jolt, shocking gasps out of several of the women, and after a few minutes of taxiing, it finally came to a stop.

“Where do you think we are?” Mara whispered.

He winced. “If I had to guess, Zaryanko’s base of operations.”

“Are we in Russia?”

“No. Transnistria. It’s—”

The cargo door dropped open, flooding the interior with blinding white light. Mara winced and huddled closer, hiding her face against his side. After so many hours of darkness, the light was disorientating, even for him, and he’d had training to fortify himself against these kinds of torture techniques. But the women didn’t have his training, and many of them panicked, scattering like mice to the darker corners of the plane.

At his side, Mara trembled. He held her as best as he could

with his hands cuffed and blinked until his eyes adjusted.

Zaryanko's two thugs, Alexei and Pyotr, started plucking the women out one by one and separating them into two groups. One group was hustled through the swirling snow onto another waiting plane. The other into the back of a van.

Then they came for Mara.

Alexei grabbed her arm and yanked her to her feet.

"No!" She hauled off and punched him. It didn't do much, damage-wise, but after the docile compliance from the other women, it surprised the asshole enough that he let go of her. She tried to get back to Quinn's side, but Pyotr rushed up the ramp to help his buddy and grabbed her around the waist. She screamed and kicked, and it got her nowhere. Pyotr clamped a hand over her mouth, and her frightened eyes locked on Quinn.

Oh, no. She couldn't give up now. He yanked on the handcuffs, but nothing happened. Fuck.

"Mara!" He held his hand next to his mouth and pretended to chomp down. Her eyes widened with realization and a second later, Pyotr shouted with pain as her teeth sank into his hand. He dropped her hard to the floor. She crawled over and tucked herself into Quinn's side. He felt her shudder with sobs and wanted to hold her more than anything, but there was no give at all in the fucking handcuffs. All he could do was scoot his body in front of hers and shield her against the wall. If they really wanted her, they would have to go through him first, and since he was Zaryanko's golden goose, he was about 80 percent certain they wouldn't kill him.

Pyotr shook out his hand—he was bleeding from her teeth marks in the fleshy part between his thumb and forefinger—and unsheathed a wicked-looking blade from his belt.

Okay, so maybe the percentage was more like sixty-five, because that fucker had murder in his eyes.

"Stay behind me," he said for Mara's ears only. "No

matter what."

Her fingers curled into his shirt, and she nodded against his back.

Pyotr lunged, and Quinn swept out a leg, taking his knees out from under him. The thug went down hard, but not before a gash opened up on Quinn's thigh from the knife. He didn't feel the pain. Yet. He would once the adrenaline in his system ebbed, and he needed to be in a more defensible position when it happened. He kicked out again, knocking the knife from Pyotr's hand.

Alexei snapped it up from the floor and took a step forward but was halted by a sharp command from the bottom of the plane's ramp.

"That's quite enough. We're wasting time." Zaryanko shook his head in disgust and turned away. He added something else over his shoulder in Russian, and Quinn's gut bottomed out. He didn't speak a word of the language, but Zaryanko's tone made it clear that had been kill order.

Behind him, Mara whimpered. "They're going to kill me."

Holy shit. She understood Russian?

He didn't have time to process that fact, though, because the two thugs moved forward as one hulking entity, the knife glinting with blood in Alexei's hand. They were going to use that on Mara, and he couldn't do a fucking thing to—

Wait. Yes, he could.

"Zaryanko!" he shouted. "Killing her is a mistake!"

Zaryanko stopped moving, the wind whipping his coat around his legs, but he didn't turn back. "How so?"

Quinn schooled his face into a mask so as not to let the fragile spark of hope show. "She's the stepdaughter of a U.S. senator. She's worth twice what you'll get for me in ransom."

"Ah, yes." Zaryanko waved a dismissive hand. "That would be true if Senator Escareno hadn't already flatly refused to pay for her return. He told me in no uncertain terms that she was to never come home. So she's no use to me now."

Mara gasped. "Oh, God."

Quinn could practically hear her heart shattering at the news, and his broke right along with hers. Fucking Ramon Escareno. All she'd ever wanted from the man was acceptance, maybe a bit of affection, and instead he abandoned her to the whims of a human trafficker?

Yeah, when they got out of this, he was going to pay the crooked senator a visit, and Escareno would be lucky if he limped away from the encounter.

But that had to wait until later. Right now, he needed leverage or she wasn't going to live through the next few minutes. And Mara was going to hate him for what he said next, but it was the only thing he could think of that would catch Zaryanko's attention. "She's pregnant."

Mara jerked like he'd hit her with a Taser. "Travis…"

"I'm sorry. It's the only way."

This time, Zaryanko turned. His eyes narrowed and he studied her for several endless moments. Finally, he snapped out a command to his minions.

Quinn twisted enough that he could see Mara's face. She'd gone white and her chapped lips stood out in bright red contrast against her complexion. "What did he say?"

"Um, I—I think…" She swallowed hard, shook her head.

"Mara, what did he say?"

"H-he told them not to hurt me."

"Okay." He released the breath caught in his lungs and willed his heart to slow. She was safe. For now. At least until Zaryanko confirmed that yes, she was pregnant.

Then both she and the baby would be in grave danger.

• • •

EL PASO, TEXAS

"So," Gabe said, drawing the word out.

Jesse clenched his jaw but didn't look away from the rental car's passenger side window. "I'm not in the mood to chat, boss."

"Yeah, I got that." Gabe sent him a questioning sideways glance. "But I never pegged you as a brooder."

"I'm not brooding."

"Uh-huh." Silence. One beat. Two. "How about you tell me what's up with you?"

Jesse finally looked over at his boss. The occasional streetlight illuminated Gabe's hard, square-jawed profile as he navigated the car through the empty streets. Funny how you could have so much respect for a man and yet still want to punch that knowing expression off his face. "What? You want to share a warm fuzzy Oprah moment? 'Cuz I gotta warn you, it's goin' to look more like Jerry Springer."

Gabe blew out a long breath. "C'mon, man. You can't blame Quinn when she—"

"I'll blame whoever the hell I want."

"She was just as involved," Gabe finished, his tone full of reason. "It takes two to make a baby, and you know damn well Quinn never would have laid a hand on her if she didn't want him to."

"Still, he shouldn't have touched her. Shouldn't have even *thought* about her like that. She's family."

"Yeah, *your* family. Not his. He's not gonna see your baby cousin when he looks at her. He's just going to see a gorgeous woman, because she's exactly the type he goes for. Curvy, smart, sweet, a little bit shy—I hate to tell you, but if you had asked me to describe the perfect woman for Quinn, Mara would be pretty damn close."

"Doesn't matter. I told him she was off-limits."

Gabe smacked his forehead with an open palm as if he'd just had an epiphany. "That's right. You're Saint Jesse, who's never once had an impure thought about an off-limits woman."

Jesse growled. There was one woman who popped instantly to mind—Lanie, Mara's best friend from high school—and it pissed him off. "I'd never act on it."

"Bet you'd never have a one-night stand, either."

"Fuck you."

"Sorry, I'm married." He held up his left hand, wiggled his ring finger, then flipped the bird before replacing his hand on the steering wheel. "So, tell me, Saint Jesse. You call up every woman you've ever slept with to make sure you didn't have an oops? Can you say with 100 percent certainty there are no other little Jesses wreaking havoc somewhere out there? No? Huh, imagine that. And, wait. If I remember your dossier correctly, your son came along a few months before you married your ex. Some saint you are."

"That's different."

"Because we're talking about Mara," Gabe concluded.

"Yes." And, yes, he realized how ridiculous that double standard was, but he'd always felt more like her big brother than her cousin and had done his best to keep her safe. "Mara's always been…fragile, especially after her father died and her mother married Ramon. She was cut off from our family, made to change her last name, and she just went along with it all. She doesn't have the courage to stand up for herself, and before my uncle died, her brother and I promised to look out for her. I kept that promise as best I could right up until I invited Quinn—" He stopped, shook his head. "Goddammit. I can't even say his name now without wantin' to punch somethin'. I invited him and all of his fucked-up issues into her life."

Gabe stayed silent for three long minutes until Jesse

instructed him to turn down Mara's street. He pulled to the curb several houses down from Mara's, shut off the car, and turned in his seat.

"Okay, listen up, Warrick. I get you. I get why you're pissed off at Quinn. But you need to pull your shit together, because even as angry as you are you know Quinn is not the kind of guy to shirk his responsibilities. Am I right?"

Jesse wanted to say no. He wanted to remain silent and stubborn on principle alone, but he knew better. Gabe could read people like the Sunday funnies.

"Yeah," he admitted, but not without a huge load of grudging reluctance in his tone. "You're right. Quinn wouldn't do that."

"And we all want to find him and Mara and the baby and make sure they're safe, right?"

"Yes." No reluctance in that answer. Jesse hadn't yet told Mara's brother, Matt, who was stationed overseas in Japan, about her disappearance. It was a call he really did not want to make without the news that she was now safe and okay.

"So we need to focus on finding them." Gabe climbed out of the car and retrieved his cane from the backseat. "And then we'll worry about working out the rest of it. But right here, right now in this moment, I need you with me on this. You know Mara better than any of us."

Jesse followed him to the sidewalk. "Why do you have to make so much goddamn sense?"

"Because, as you so often point out, I'm the big, bad, all-knowing boss."

Jesse snorted a laugh. "All right. I'm here. I'm focused. Later, though, when we find them…I can't make any promises I won't punch Quinn."

"Good enough for now." Leaning more heavily on his cane than usual, Gabe studied the street. "Which house is hers?"

“This one.” Jesse led the way up the walk to Mara’s duplex, a tan stucco house that she shared with Mrs. Ruiz, a seventy-year-old widow. “And it’s 98 percent.”

“What?” Gabe said as he followed.

“I’m 98 percent sure there are no other little Jesses out there besides my son.”

“That high?”

“Never had much time for baby makin’. I was married to the army for eleven years, and she’s one jealous, demanding bitch.”

“So’s the navy,” Gabe said. “What’s the other 2 percent?”

“Well, there was this weekend leave in Hawaii right after my first divorce was finalized.” He rubbed his jaw. Winced. “I started drinkin’ soon as our plane touched down, and I don’t remember much after leaving the base. Pretty sure I was so hammered that even if I’d wanted to try some baby makin’, I wouldn’t have been able to get it up, so—”

Mara’s front door swung open and a tall, lean figure stood silhouetted there, weapon aimed. “Who are you and what are you doing here?” Her voice was soft, but there was an edge in her tone that said she meant business.

Jesse reached for his own firearm and saw Gabe doing the same out of the corner of his eye. “Good question.” He aimed at the woman, although he had no intention of firing unless she did. “How about you go first? You know, since you’re outgunned right now.”

“Oh, a lady never gives it up that easily, cowboy. At least buy me dinner before you go asking me to spill all my secrets.” But she relaxed, dropping the muzzle of her gun toward the ground and clicking on the safety. When she stepped into the light, he about swallowed his tongue.

Dayam.

He should have known, but she looked so completely different from the last time he’d seen her at her and Mara’s high school graduation. She'd…grown up. A lot.

"Hello, Jesse," she said. "Thought you might show up here."

"Lanie." He lowered his weapon. "Mara's best friend since high school," he explained to Gabe, who also relaxed. "She's a Texas Ranger. And a mighty pain in the ass."

"Aw, I'm hurt you think so. Look at me cry." Lanie smirked at him as she holstered her weapon and approached. In the muted light of the street lamps, her skin glowed a gorgeous mocha and she wore her tightly curled black hair pulled back in a ponytail. She used to be all awkward, gangly limbs—which he'd found appealing as an awkward, gangly-limbed teenager himself—and her clumsiness had always reminded him of a baby giraffe learning to walk. But not anymore. She had to be close to six feet tall now, with jeans-clad legs that stretched for miles, and she moved with the lithe confidence and purpose of a predator.

She held out a graceful, long-fingered hand to Gabe. "You must be Gabe Bristow. We never had the chance to formally meet when you and your team were here last summer, but you briefly met my partner, Dennis Aranda, and he had nothing but good things to say about you."

Gabe nodded and holstered his gun to accept the handshake. "I remember him. Good guy. Solid cop."

"Yes, he—"

"Jesus, we don't have time for this chitchat." Jesse scowled at the two of them before turning his full attention to Lanie. "What are you doing here?"

Her dark eyes flashed annoyance. "I already said I was waiting for you. The local authorities were notified about Mara's disappearance when her neighbor noticed her door was hanging open and found her dog pacing around the yard. They launched their own investigation, but I knew that Travis Quinn guy had been here and—"

"And you thought he might have had something to do it," Gabe finished.

"It crossed my mind," she admitted. "She hadn't told him about the baby yet when I last spoke to her. I thought—"

"Hold up. You knew she was pregnant?" Jesse demanded. Betrayal soured his blood. Why would Mara confide in Lanie before him or even her brother?

"Of course I knew," she said like he was an idiot for asking. "I was with her when she bought and took the pregnancy test. What kind of friend would I be if I abandoned her when she most needed one?" She looked at Gabe. "And when I heard about the abduction, I worried maybe her baby daddy flipped his lid when she broke the news."

Gabe shook his head. "I can assure you, Quinn has nothing to do with this. But he did witness the abduction and went after Mara to rescue her. We've been tracking his phone."

"So do you know where they are?"

There was no mistaking the fragile hope in her voice, and Jesse hated to crush it. "No, we don't."

"But we will," Gabe added.

Lanie nodded, closed her eyes for a moment, and drew in a soothing breath. Then she opened her eyes again and nailed them with the gaze of a woman determined to do something stupid. "All right, here's the thing. Mara's my best friend. Honestly, one of my only friends, and I know y'all have a better chance at finding her than anyone else—but if you think for one hot second I'll let you leave me behind on this, you need to think again."

Gabe arched a brow, but he appeared more amused by her demands than angry. "Oh, yeah?"

"Yeah. And if you try, I'll turn your asses in to the local police faster than small-town gossip, and you'll be tied up in so much red tape you won't be able to move. Please don't make me do that."

"You wouldn't," Jesse said.

"No," Gabe said slowly. "I believe she would."

She nodded. "If you get in my way, absolutely. I don't think it needs to come to that, though. Gabe here seems like a reasonable guy."

Meaning Jesse wasn't. Heat crawled up his neck, and he realized he was grinding his teeth. "No, you're staying here."

She ignored him and met Gabe stare for stare. "Well?"

Gabe considered her for a long moment. Then he lifted a shoulder. "Okay."

Jesse whirled on him. "Boss—"

"She's had some training, knows how to shoot, and from what I can tell, has balls of fucking steel. Nothing against my wife or Phoebe, but she's better than any of the assets we've had to work with in the past, and we need all the help we can get." He held up a hand, cutting off all further protest, and reached into his pocket for his buzzing phone. "Bristow," he answered and walked away.

Jesse scowled over at Lanie. "You're not going anywhere, Elena."

She scowled right back. "It's Lanie. And oh, yes, I am. Didn't you hear your boss? I have balls of fucking steel, and you're stuck with me, cowboy."

Gabe returned a moment later, his face set in grim lines. "Marcus and Ian found three bodies at the airfield, two men and a woman."

Lanie sucked in a sharp breath. "Are they…?"

Jesse had the strangest urge to pull her into his arms and comfort her. Jesus. Instead, he faced Gabe. "It's not Mara and Quinn?"

"No."

He'd guessed as much because of how calm Gabe was after ending the call, but it still felt like a weight off his chest to hear it confirmed. "Any sign of them?"

"Tank picked up on Quinn's scent in the hangar and led them to a cell phone."

Jesse's body went cold. "Quinn's?"

"Yeah."

"How do we trace him now?"

"Ian said he left us a clue," Gabe said. "They're headed back to the hotel. Lanie, I'm assuming you already searched Mara's house?"

She nodded. "After the police cleared it, I had to go in and round up Mara's animals. Mrs. Ruiz next door has them for now. But if there was anything in there to help us, it's now in the possession of the El Paso Police Department."

"Then we're wasting our time here." Gabe walked to the car, opened the driver's side door, and arched a brow in question. "You two coming or what?"

Chapter Nine

Somewhere in Transnistria

"Clothes," Alexei said in heavily accented English. "Off. Now."

Quinn glanced around the tiled room, which was like a crappier version of his high school gym locker room. Besides him and Mara, three of the other women had been transported to this place via a van with blacked-out windows. All of the women were exhausted, beaten down, but not one of them moved. They all looked toward him, as if he had all the answers.

He lifted his still-cuffed hands. "Handcuffs," he said, mocking Alexei's accent. "Off. Now."

Alexei just grunted in response and walked over to a hose coiled up on the wall.

Well, it had been worth a shot. Now that his body wasn't contorted, he could theoretically break out of the cuffs, but he wanted to save that little party trick until he really needed it. Until then, he'd have to live with them on.

He gazed over at the women and nodded. "Do what they say."

Mara translated his words for the women, then touched his shoulder. "What are they doing?"

"They're going to hose us down, probably cavity search us."

She shuddered, and he turned to her, cupping her face in his bound hands. "Any way you cut it, the next few hours are going to suck. I can't do anything about that."

Nodding, she covered one of his hands with her own. "I know." Then she let go of him and glared daggers at the thugs before yanking her sweatshirt off over her head and throwing it to the floor.

Even before they finished undressing, Alexei hit them with a powerful spray of icy water, nearly knocking them both off their feet. It was like needles piercing Quinn's flesh, stealing away his body heat almost before he could produce it, and it transported him back to his days in Coronado when his need to become a SEAL had been the only thing keeping him going during Hell Week. His BUD/S instructors had loved pushing him to the brink of hypothermia and even one step over, and he'd never forget how cold the Pacific was at oh-dark-thirty when your body was beyond exhausted and you'd taken only the briefest of naps in the last twenty-four hours.

This water was colder.

He gritted his teeth to keep them from chattering and caged Mara between his body and the wall, shielding her from the worst of it. He couldn't do anything to help the other women and winced with each new scream as the water sprayed back and forth over the line of them.

Mara huddled against his chest. Her skin was warmer compared to the ice of his, but not by much. She was amazing, never making a sound, enduring the torture silently each time the water rained over them. Trembles raced just under the surface of her skin, and he rubbed her back, trying to generate more heat.

Finally, the damn hose was shut off, leaving the room silent except for dripping water and chattering teeth. Alexei and Pyotr laughed as they led the other women away, one by one, until only he and Mara were left.

"Oh, God," Mara whispered against his chest. "They're going to separate us. Travis, please don't let them take me away. I'm scared."

He looped his cuffed hands over her shoulders and squeezed her tight. "Shh. I've got you. You're not going anywhere."

"They're going to—" Her voice caught on a sob. "They're going to sell the baby."

Yeah, that would be their plan. He hugged her closer and eyed the two thugs standing guard by the door. They hadn't come back into the room since removing the last of the women. Seemed to be waiting for something. Or, possibly, someone.

The door opened moments later to admit a man in a white coat. A doctor. They wanted confirmation she was pregnant.

"I need to examine the woman," the doctor said with a deadness in his voice that chilled Quinn more than the cold water had.

Christ, he hated doctors.

"I don't think so." He removed his arms from her shoulders and stepped in front of her, again using his own body as a barricade. She pressed her face into the middle of his back. Hot tears trickled down his spine to mingle with the water still clinging to his skin.

He had to get her out of here.

He lunged for Pyotr first because out of the three of them, that guy was the most dangerous. He had soulless eyes that spoke of the depths of his brutality and depravity. But for all of that, Pyotr wasn't trained, and the surprise attack threw him off guard. Quinn had him disabled and on the ground, gasping for breath, in half a heartbeat. He sneaked his hands into Pyotr's coat pocket, found his cell phone, and drew it out as he spun on Alexei, knocking a knife out of the guy's hand with a roundhouse kick.

"Travis!"

Pain stabbed into his shoulder, but with his hands cuffed, he couldn't reach around to dislodge what he thought was a knife. Fuck. He'd miscalculated, had focused too much on the thugs and hadn't thought of the doctor as a real threat.

The room fuzzed and wobbled around him. Not a knife, then. Drugs of some kind. He dropped to one knee, gagging as bile threatened to come up. A boot connected with his gut, bending him double.

"Stop it!" Mara shouted. "Leave him alone!"

There was a strangled cry of pain, and Quinn glanced up in time to see Mara break free from the doctor's grasp. The guy was doubled over, too, one hand cupping his crotch, the other braced against the wall for support.

Despite another surge of nausea, a smile pulled at his mouth. Christ, she was amazing. "That was fucking stupid, Mara."

"Yes, it was. I don't know why I did that." She knelt beside him and set a hand on his back. "Are you okay?"

"C'mere." He gripped her face in his hands and dragged her closer until their lips touched. Just a quick, hard kiss, but it did all kinds of hot, unwanted things to his body. Which wasn't part of the plan. If he could even call this sloppy kiss-and-grope a plan. With the drugs numbing his system, he was mostly just winging it at this point.

Mara's body stiffened up in shock.

Shit. He probably should have given her some kind of

warning first. He pressed his lips harder against hers, silently urging her to play along as he fumbled with the cell phone, pushing it into her bra, down between her breasts, where it would be hidden.

"Get them out of here," the doctor ordered in a strangled voice. He straightened away from the wall, tugging his jacket back into place with as much dignity as a guy could muster after getting kicked in the nads by a woman half his size.

Yeah. Mara was freaking amazing, and Quinn kissed her again because—well, he had to. She'd stunned the hell out of their captors just now, and he couldn't be more proud of the way she'd handled herself.

Alexei pulled them apart, and panic flashed in her eyes as she was dragged toward the door.

"Mara, it's okay," he called after her, not bothering to fight when Pyotr yanked on his cuffed hands, pulling him to his feet. His world was spinning, and his feet were numb. If he tried to fight anyone right now, he'd just get himself dead. "Hey, you hear me? We'll be okay. Just go with them. I promise you, we'll be okay."

• • •

EL PASO, TEXAS

The clue left on Quinn's phone was an unsent one-word text message: *Zaryanko.*

Jesse's heart nose-dived into his gut when he saw it. "Are you fucking kidding me? Nikolai Zaryanko has them?"

"Uh, I'm sorry," Lanie said and lifted her hands. "Newbie here. Who is Zaryanko and why do you all look like you just bit into a lemon?"

The hotel room went pin-drop silent, and all eyes turned in her direction.

Jesse couldn't pinpoint why, exactly—if he were in the

men's shoes, he'd be suspicious of her, too—but all that mistrust directed toward her pissed him off in a big way. "This is Lanie," he said. "She's Mara's best friend, and I've known her since she was knee-high to a grasshopper. We can trust her."

The tension eased, then evaporated altogether when Gabe added, "She'll be helping us on this. Harvard, can you bring up our file on Zaryanko?"

Harvard nodded and hit a few keys on his computer. A photo popped up on screen. It wasn't the best picture, having been taken during a recon mission in Afghanistan that went to shit shortly thereafter, but it was the only one they had of the man.

"That's Nikolai Zaryanko," Gabe said, motioning to the photo. "He's known for trafficking arms, drugs, organs, and humans. He first popped onto the radar five years ago after the discovery of his association with Liam Miller, a disgraced British SAS operative. Since Liam had a nasty habit of cultivating friendships with the scum of the earth, the spec ops community learned pretty damn fast it behooved us to keep tabs on his associates. And Zaryanko was one of Liam's closest friends. Shit." He pinched the bridge of his nose as if a tension headache hammered behind his eyes. Made sense, since his wife had been the one to finally take Liam Miller out, and he'd worried about the repercussions ever since. "What are the chances that we cross paths with Zaryanko twice in the eight months after Audrey killed Liam?"

"I don't like coincidences, either, boss," Jesse agreed and dropped his head into his hands as a headache thundered between his own temples. "Goddammit."

Gabe grasped his shoulder. "I know it doesn't seem it, but this is good."

"Good? My cousin's in the hands of a man who supposedly sold his own sister into sexual slavery. How the fuck is this good?"

"You're not thinking like an operative, Jesse. We know where Zaryanko lives, where he runs his businesses. Now we can find her and maybe shut him down for good before he tries for anyone else."

Like Audrey.

Gabe wouldn't be cruel enough to speak those words aloud, but they hung in the air between them anyway. Jesse couldn't blame the stark fear he saw in his boss's eyes and tried to calm himself.

Think like an operative. Think like an operative.

Of course Gabe was right again, but that still didn't make the whole goatfuck of a situation any easier to stomach. "All right. So what's our game plan?"

Gabe rubbed a hand over his face. "They're most likely headed to Transnistria."

Similar reactions came from everyone in the room, except Lanie, who frowned. "Trans what? Never heard of it."

Harvard hit a few more keys and pulled up a map. "Transnistria," he said, turning the laptop around so everyone could see the screen. "It's an unrecognized breakaway republic sandwiched between Moldova and Ukraine. They have tight ties with Russia, and many in the intelligence community fear it'll be the next Crimea."

"So, basically, it's only a matter of time until Russia invades?" Lanie asked.

Harvard winced. "Wouldn't be so much as an invasion as a 'welcome back.' Transnistria is very much stuck in the Soviet era. Their economy completely collapsed when the Soviet Union fell, and they've never recovered. That and the fact they are unrecognized and have largely unprotected borders has turned it into a hotbed for smuggling and sex trafficking." He slid an apologetic glance in Jesse's direction. "My research indicates our best option is to infil by parachute here." Harvard brought the map up on his computer again, indicating a spot just outside the Transnistrian border in Ukraine. "Once on the ground, it's about sixteen klicks southeast to the capital city of Tiraspol."

"Let me get something straight," Jace Garcia said, speaking up for the first time. He walked forward, placed his hands on the table and leaned toward Harvard. "You want me to fly into Ukrainian airspace? You do know they recently shot down a passenger jet that had nada to do with their war."

Gabe nodded. "We're aware."

"HumInt has a small airfield just outside of Odessa, Ukraine," Harvard said, pulling up another map. "It's about an hour's drive from Tiraspol on the main roads. Obviously, HumInt pulled their people out of there when the crisis started, but the field's still functional for our needs. After we parachute out, you can land the plane and stay hidden there, keeping our exfil route open."

Gabe met the pilot's gaze across the table. "Can you manage that?"

Garcia grunted. "Yeah. Yeah, I can. But y'all are more loco than I am. And that's saying something."

"What about border guards?" Jesse asked.

Harvard tapped a spot on the map. "There aren't any border checkpoints or patrols. Not here, at least. Satellite imaging shows this location's a field in the middle of nowhere. There's not even a sign to indicate which country you're in."

"So we can walk in without anyone the wiser?" Jesse asked with more than a little surprise. He hadn't expected anything about this op to be easy.

"Yes. The problem won't be getting in, as far as I can tell. Or even getting out, as long as we stick to the back roads on our way to Odessa. It will be staying undetected while there. Tiraspol is crawling with Transnistrian KGB officers—"

"Whoa, what?" Lanie straightened away from the table.

"Didn't the KGB go the way of the Berlin Wall?"

"They did," Harvard agreed. "For the most part. But like I said, Transnistria is stuck in time, desperately hanging on to their Soviet roots, and the KGB is still very much alive there. They will stop anybody who looks like they don't belong."

"So we best not be spotted," Gabe said and also straightened. "Pack your bags, gentlemen—"

Lanie cleared her throat loudly.

Gabe sighed. "Gentlemen *and* Lanie. We just got an open invitation to the black hole of Europe."

Chapter Ten

As far as prisons went, Quinn had been in worse.

He seemed to be in some kind of hotel. Although there were no other guests, there was a dance club off the lobby, thrumming with music heavy on the bass. Through the open doors, Quinn spotted a handful of skimpily dressed girls and an otherwise empty dance floor. Which made sense. Transnistria wasn't usually found on Average Joe Tourist's destination list.

Was Mara in that club?

He craned his neck, but Pyotr stepped into his line of sight and shoved him forward. He stumbled sideways and unfortunately, it was only partially an act. He still wasn't steady on his feet, but pretending to be more off-kilter than he was gave him a better view into the club.

He didn't see her.

Pyotr dragged him upright. "Walk."

"If you'd wanted me to walk, you shouldn't have drugged me, asshole."

He got another shove for his sarcasm and shuffled across

the tiled floor on bare feet. Judging by the desk clerk's non-reaction when Pyotr marched a handcuffed, naked man across the lobby, the place had to be owned by Zaryanko or one of his associates—which was pretty much everyone running the corrupt government here. He wouldn't be able to count on getting help from any civilians he came across.

Unless the team found them—and soon—they were well and truly fucked.

Pyotr dragged him upstairs to a room at the far end of the hall, unlocked his cuffs, and pushed him inside.

"Travis?"

He spun at Mara's voice, and relief like nothing he'd ever known crashed through him. She was still in her bra and underwear, and fresh bruises marred the skin on her arms. Before he even realized he was moving, he'd crossed the distance between them and pulled her into his arms.

"Christ, Mara. Are you okay? Did they hurt you?"

She released a shuddering breath and shook her head. Her hair tickled his bare chest.

"No," she whispered. "Not really. They held me down to draw some blood." She showed him the bruised flesh of her inner arm. The fresh needle mark was still dripping a thin line of blood.

"To confirm you are pregnant."

She nodded. "Then once they had it, they brought me up here."

"They didn't search you?"

"No."

Quinn shut his eyes and hugged her to him again, burying his face in her hair. Just for this one moment, he'd let himself hold her, let himself give in to the overwhelming relief that they hadn't subjected her to the same kind of invasive search they had done to him.

The door opened again and a tray of food landed on the

floor along with the rest of their clothes. And like that, the moment ended.

Mara pulled out of his arms and picked up her sweatshirt. "Oh, thank God. I'm freezing." She hesitated over the food. "Can I...?"

"I wouldn't," Quinn said. "We already know they're willing to use drugs to subdue us. Don't risk it."

She sighed and nodded, but still gazed longingly at the tray before pulling the sweatshirt on over her head.

Quinn grabbed his pants and stepped into them, then did a lap around the room to check for cameras. The only furniture was the bed, which had been bolted to the floor. The bathroom—if it could be called that—consisted of a hole in the corner.

No surveillance equipment monitoring them as far as he could tell, but if the room was used for what he suspected, Zaryanko wouldn't care what happened inside. Outside, though, the hallway was probably monitored, if not guarded.

He crossed to the room's one dingy window, ignoring the wave of dizziness that crashed over him. Outside, thick gray slush covered a city full of boxy concrete buildings, and low-slung clouds promised more snow on the way. In the empty park across the street from the hotel rose a statue right out of the Cold War.

"What the...?" Mara came up to the window beside him and rubbed her eyes as if to make sure she wasn't hallucinating. Nope, she wasn't. That was a statue of Lenin standing there in all of its communist glory.

"Where are we?" she whispered.

"Fucking Transnistria." He shook off another wave of dizziness. It had been over an hour since he was hit with the syringe of drugs, and although it never completely knocked him out, he'd been groggy and disoriented ever since. Not to mention, his head was splitting like a cord of firewood and he was starting to see zigzagging patterns flashing in front of his eyes, which meant he had about twenty minutes before a migraine knocked him on his ass.

"Do you still have the phone?"

"Oh," she gasped and reached into her bra. "I made sure they didn't find it. Does it work?" She handed the old flip phone to him and he checked the screen.

"Would if we had a signal." He picked up his coat from the floor, dropped the phone into the pocket, and glanced out the window again. Didn't appear to be any balconies nearby and no fire escapes, but the roof of the dance club was only about eight feet straight down.

Finally, a lucky break.

He tried the window, but it was nailed shut. Okay. A half-lucky break. But if he could get the window open, they had a chance at escape. The drop to the club's roof was completely doable.

Annnnd then what?

That was where his plan came to a screeching halt. Even if they were able to get out of this place, they had nowhere safe to go in the country. There were no embassies here, and rumor had it the streets were crawling with Transnistria's version of the KGB, who had very close ties to Russia. And nowadays Russia was about as cuddly as a sewer rat.

The only choice they had was to make a break for the border, but with no money and no winter gear, the going would be rough—possibly too rough for a woman in Mara's condition.

Then there was the question of which border? Ukraine was the most logical choice, but they were on the verge of war with Russia, and it wasn't the safest option. And crossing into Moldova would be nearly impossible to pull off with Russian peacekeepers manning the frozen conflict zone between that country and its breakaway state.

Fuck.

Quinn pressed his throbbing head to the cold glass and shut his eyes. He heard Mara moving around behind him but didn't turn to see what she was doing.

"What is this room?" Her voice shook.

"If I had to guess, it's for training."

"What kind of training?"

He glanced over his shoulder. She stood by the squat toilet, staring into the hole like she was trying to decide whether she should use it or not. "Zaryanko's a sex trafficker, Mara. Take a wild guess."

She moved away from the toilet and hugged herself. "He brings girls here to traffic them?"

"No, to break them. He'll have recruiters lure girls from their homes by promising them work abroad, but instead he'll lock them in a room like this one, have them repeatedly raped, and addict them to drugs until they have no will left of their own. Then he ships them off to his clubs in Dubai or Istanbul, where they'll work off their debt, which is just some arbitrary number he decides. If they ever manage to work off that debt, he'll let them come home if they agree to send two more women to take their place. It becomes a vicious cycle."

She shuddered. "Oh, God. How do you know all that?"

"The spec ops community has been watching Zaryanko for a long time."

"Then why hasn't he been stopped?"

"We know what he does, how he operates, but he's never been caught in the act."

Mara stayed silent for a moment. "He said he's going to sell me and the baby." She twisted her too-big watch around on her wrist—a nervous gesture he remembered from the summer. Then she lifted her eyes, tears streaming down her face. "Why is this happening?"

"I don't know. Why would Urban kidnap you and ship

you off to Zaryanko? It doesn't make sense." A memory flitted along the outside edges of his consciousness, but when he tried to grasp it and bring it into focus, his headache grew claws. He winced, pinching the bridge of his nose in an effort to relieve the pressure. "What am I missing?"

He shook his head. The whys didn't matter right now. All that mattered was escape, but he had no weapon, and the phone wasn't going to do squat for them until it had a signal. He scanned the room for anything else that could help them. The place was pretty much barren, save for the tray of food on the floor.

He crossed the room in three strides and grabbed the tray. Transnistria wasn't a rich country and didn't have access to a lot of disposable goods like plastic utensils, so if they were at all lucky…

Yeah, there it was. He picked up the scarred metal spoon and tried to bend it.

"What's that for?" Mara asked. "I thought you said we shouldn't eat the food."

"And we're not going to." He studied the window again. "This spoon's fairly sturdy. I might be able to get us out of here with it."

She followed his gaze. "How?"

He shrugged. "Haven't you ever seen *The Shawshank Redemption*?"

"You're going to dig a tunnel?" she said, incredulousness in every word. "Um, you do realize it took Andy Dufresne twenty years in the movie, right?"

He tried for a smile, but it felt forced on his lips. He sucked at jokes, he really did. "I'll get you home before that. I promise."

• • •

Mara didn't doubt that.

At first.

But time passed one excruciatingly slow minute after another, and the longer she watched him unsuccessfully try to dig the nails out of the window frame, the less and less she started to believe him. Besides, he'd promised her he wasn't going to walk away again, and that was exactly what he'd done when she told him about the baby, so why should she believe his promises now?

God. This was never going to work.

She'd lived the past day in a state of numbed shock, but now, in the quiet of this awful room, the hopelessness of their situation crashed into her full force. Travis was just as lost as she was. Her SEAL. Her protector. He didn't have a clue how to save them.

And he was in a massive amount of pain.

She straightened at the realization, ashamed at herself for not noticing his clenched jaw and the strain around his eyes sooner. Yes, he had broken his promises to her, but he'd also gone through hell trying to keep her safe. He'd been beaten up, slashed with a knife, had endured a pounding of icy-cold water, and had been drugged. And, still, he was trying to do something about their situation. Maybe it was hopeless. Maybe it wouldn't work. But at least he was being proactive and not sitting there wallowing in self-pity.

She walked over to him and laid a hand on his shoulder. His complexion was pasty, tinged with a green-gray hue, and he was sweating despite the chill in the air. "Travis?"

The spoon slipped out from under a nail. "Fuck!"

"Are you okay? Do you need me to—"

"I'm fine," he snapped, which told her all she needed to know. Travis was not the kind of man who lost his patience like this.

"No, you're not. Anyone looking at you can see you're in

pain. Why don't you take a break from that? Let me try for a while."

"I'm fine," he repeated. "What time is it in El Paso right now?"

"Uh." Thrown by the sudden topic change, she shook her head. "I don't know."

He glanced over his shoulder. "You're wearing a watch. Unless you've changed it to local time—which would save me from having to do math with a splitting headache…?"

She shook her head again in answer to his half question.

"Then you should still have El Paso's time on it," he finished.

"But it doesn't work."

"Of course it doesn't," he muttered and returned his attention to the window. "Why the hell would anyone wear a watch that worked? It's ludicrous."

Self-conscious, she twisted the band around her wrist. "It was my dad's."

Travis exhaled hard. "Look, I'm sorry, okay? But I don't need a break. Even if I did, we don't have time to—" The spoon slipped from his hand. He bent double, cradling his head, then dropped to the floor on his hands and knees and dry heaved. The sound he made could only be described as a whimper of pain.

Alarm shot through her. Travis Quinn, or at least the stoic man she'd met this summer, didn't whimper. He didn't show pain, period. Yet here he was, nearly curled into a fetal position on the floor.

And she had no clue how to help him. "What can I do? What do you need?"

"Lights," he gritted out. "Off."

She looked around, but there were no switches in the room. She had no control over the lights and instead found his coat where he'd left it on the end of the bed. She draped the material over his head. “Better?”

He groaned.

Her heart was racing, but she refused to break down when Travis needed her to be strong for the both of them. She rubbed his back. “What’s wrong?”

“Just…migraine.”

A migraine dropped him to his knees like that? She’d never gotten one before and had no way of judging how normal this was. “Do you get them a lot?”

He made a sound in the affirmative. “On meds to control…them.”

And that medicine was probably well out of his system by now. “What can I do?”

“It’ll go away. Need…dark. And quiet.”

Okay, she could take a hint. She straightened away from him and noticed the spoon on the floor near his hand.

Something clicked inside her mind, like a missing puzzle piece snapping into place. If she really wanted to help him, she should continue his work.

She carefully stepped over Travis and picked up the spoon.

Chapter Eleven

Nikolai Zaryanko hung up the phone and pushed away from his desk, pleased with the outcome of his phone call. The ransom for Quinn was inching toward the million-dollar mark, and with the involved party having such deep pockets, he could easily see it reaching seven, maybe even eight digits before it was over.

And that deserved a bit of celebration.

He poured himself a glass from the bottle of Kvint on his desk and breathed in the scent of the top-notch cognac found only in his country. If you asked him, it was the best in the world, and he savored the burn of the first sip sliding down his throat.

As he lowered the glass, a slow round of applause from the doorway caught his attention. There wasn't much left in the world that could shock him, but when he spun and saw a dead man propped in his doorway, it startled him so much he spilled his drink.

"Liam." He set the glass down. "My old friend. I—I was told you were dead."

"I have risen," Liam Miller said, spreading his hands in a godlike gesture. "And you've been plenty busy since I've been dead."

Zaryanko swallowed hard. "You know, business as usual."

"Ah," Liam said on a laugh. "Not what I've heard, Nicky. And I've been racking my brain, trying to decide if you are extremely clever or if you have a secret death wish."

Zaryanko got up and found a towel in a nearby cabinet to blot the front of his shirt. A fissure of panic tried to claw up his spine, but he suppressed it and forced a smile. "I'm sure I don't know what you mean."

"Yes, you do." Liam strolled in and made himself comfortable in one of the leather chairs. "It is brilliant, I'll give you that. Brilliant, but you've already gone and cocked it all up."

Realizing he wouldn't get away with playing dumb, Zaryanko filled a second tumbler with Kvint and offered it to Liam. "How so?"

Liam set his drink aside without touching it. "You've given both sides time enough to rally the troops."

"HORNET doesn't know they are dealing with me. And the other? They won't risk coming here when Mother Russia is in such a bad temper. They'd start a war."

"Ah, my shortsighted friend. They know exactly with whom they are dealing. I heard rumblings about the con you have going all the way in Istanbul, and I found you within an hour of arriving in Tiraspol. What makes you think that HORNET won't? As a matter of fact, I have little doubt they are here now, as we speak. And as for the Americans, you'd be wise not to underestimate their willingness to start wars. Or their ability to justify them. If there's one thing Yanks are good at, it's that." He didn't wait for a response but instead picked up his drink again and leaned casually back in his chair, slinging a leg over the arm. Only a slight tightening around his brown eyes spoke of the pain he still felt from the bullet that had supposedly ended his life back in May. "You've painted a bull's-eye on yourself, mate. Give Quinn to me."

"*Nyet.* I cannot. He's worth too much money."

Liam made a tsking sound. "Nicky, Nicky. Do you truly believe they'll pay up? They'll kill you first and take Quinn by force. Do yourself a favor and hand him over to me."

"No, but you're welcome to bid on him. If you can pay more than our American comrades, he's yours."

Liam said nothing for a long moment. "I think you're forgetting. Who gave you your start? Who scraped you off the street and made you rich in this shithole fake country?"

Zaryanko clenched his jaw, pride warring with a deep sense of self-preservation. In the end, self-preservation won. Always did. "You," he ground out between his teeth.

"And yet you cannot grant me a favor when I ask it?"

"I have to recoup my losses," Zaryanko tried to explain. "HORNET cheated me out of my money in Afghanistan. I want it back."

"Heard about that. So you've seen them in action." Liam sat up slowly, the strain around his eyes tightening even more at the movement. "You know better than to underestimate them. Give Quinn to me, and they'll have no reason to come after you."

Zaryanko's hand shook, jingling the ice in his glass. He set his drink down, unwilling to give Liam the satisfaction of seeing his nerves. While he had witnessed firsthand what HORNET was capable of and he wanted no part of that, he couldn't very well hand over his own personal gold mine. "My answer is still no. As I said, you're welcome to join in the bidding. It's at one million."

Liam didn't move for a moment, then finished his drink

and produced a wallet from his back pocket. He peeled off a one-ruble note and stuffed it into his empty glass. "There's my bid, and I have no doubt you'll accept it sooner rather than later."

Relief made Nikolai light-headed as Liam left. He downed his cognac and sat forward, reaching for his phone. He needed to move his merchandise to a more secure location. He'd just made an enemy, and Liam Miller was not someone you wanted as an enemy.

• • •

Noise from the hallway startled Mara awake, and she groaned at herself when she realized she'd fallen asleep. She hadn't meant to. Last thing she remembered was taking a break from working on the window after she managed to get the first nail free sometime in the early morning hours. She'd wanted to share her triumph with Travis, but he was out cold and with how much pain he'd been in before he fell asleep, she didn't dare wake him. Instead, she'd settled down on the floor beside him, planning only to rest her eyes for a few minutes.

Should have known better. She was beyond exhausted and now, judging by the angle of the light filtering through the window, it had to be late afternoon. They'd slept all day.

Travis's arm rested across her ribs, and when she tried to move away, he unconsciously pulled her closer. She exhaled hard as emotions threatened to swamp her. She couldn't let herself fall for this man who made promises and walked away. And yet, he still made her belly jitter and her heart pound, and the less rational part of her never wanted to leave his arms again. She curled toward his body and buried her face in the crook of his shoulder, enjoying the moment of intimacy for the fleeting thing it was.

He'd broken her heart six weeks ago. It was a stupid thing to fall for a one-night-stand-turned-fling, but they had connected on more than just a physical level, and she hadn't been able to help her foolish heart's involvement. Having him walk out on her in the middle of the night should have killed all of the tender feelings she harbored for him. But, no, it really hadn't. She was just as attracted now as the first time she'd laid eyes on him on that insanely hot July day.

She remembered she'd been worried about the guard Jesse had told her would be sitting in a car outside her duplex, so for the first time ever, she'd broken the rules. Jesse had laid down a strict no-contact law, but she'd still decided to take her bodyguard some of the fresh lemonade she'd made that morning. Except her visit had startled him, and he'd pulled his gun, which in turn had startled her. She'd tripped over her own feet, and Travis had jumped out of the car to catch her.

The spark had been instantaneous and electric. She'd never before experienced lust at first sight—but Travis Quinn, with his stormy gray eyes, hard, unsmiling lips, and lean, muscular body had made her formerly dormant libido jump up and do a samba. As they stood there on the sidewalk with his hands on her hips for a beat too long, she'd realized she'd break any and all rules to be with this man, even if it was only one time.

And she had. They had. Broken every rule in the book together. Repeatedly.

Next to her, Travis stirred and opened his eyes. They were clear again, and although he was terribly pale, his complexion didn't have the greenish hue of nausea that it had last night. He smiled—just a sleepy upward quirk of his lips—and memories of their first time together flooded her.

Before Travis, she had never understood the appeal of sex. It had always been more obligation than pleasure, something she had to do to make her boyfriends happy—the same two boyfriends that her stepfather had handpicked for her. But sex with Travis was different. Fun. Thrilling. A little dirty. A lot hot. And the man had stamina for days…

"You're ready again so soon?" She opened her eyes in time to catch the look of awe that crossed his face.

"Apparently," he muttered, schooling his features back into a mask of concentration.

She laughed, caught his jaw in her hands and placed a soft, lingering kiss on his mouth. "I can't tell if you sound happy about that or annoyed."

"Happy." When she lifted her hips into his downward thrust and he sank in even deeper, he groaned. "Oh, fuck, yeah. Definitely happy."

"Then smile, Travis. I promise it won't hurt." She stuck her pointer fingers in the corners of his lips and pushed them upward, then mimicked his scowl. "Actually, that stern face of yours might just break. You should start small. A smirk. C'mon, let me see it…"

Travis cupped her cheeks in his hands, much the same way she had his that day in her bedroom, and Mara snapped back to the present. Her body hummed from the all too vivid memories.

"Travis?" Her voice came out a shaky whisper.

He drew her in closer and claimed her mouth with commanding lips and an exploring tongue. A little alarm chimed in the back of her mind. He must not be fully awake yet and didn't realize what he was doing, because since finding out about the baby, he'd barely been able to look at her, and the only time he'd touched her was to protect her from something. For that reason alone, she should pull away, but he took the kiss deeper, his hard mouth demanding a response, and she melted. She couldn't help it. Like it or not, she'd always melt for this man.

Her breasts ached and her peaked nipples scraped

uncomfortably against the material of her bra. She arched her back, pressing against his chest, seeking some kind of relief. His hand left her cheek, skimmed her neck, her shoulder, and finally settled over her breast, cupping her through her shirt. She wanted skin to skin. Oh, how she wanted it, and she moaned her encouragement.

In a burst of movement, he rolled, tucked her under his body, leaned down to kiss her again—

And froze when his hard stomach brushed hers.

"Fuck." He shoved back onto his knees and dragged his hands through his too-long hair.

She propped herself up on her elbows. "What's wrong?"

"What isn't wrong is the better question. Wrong place, wrong time. Everything I just did was fucking wrong. Christ." He got up and paced across the room like he couldn't get away from her fast enough.

Chilled to the bone by his abrupt rejection, she snapped up his coat from the floor and pulled it on. It smelled like him, and that rankled. "Pregnancy is not a communicable disease, Travis."

With his back to her, she clearly saw his spine stiffen. "I know that."

Oh, if he wanted a fight, she was ready to give it to him. It was about time they discussed the proverbial pink elephant in the room. "Do you? Because you've done everything but put on a hazmat suit to avoid touching me."

"Mara," he said and massaged his temples. "Just—be quiet for a minute."

Be *quiet*? She stared at his back in disbelief. "No! I will not. Everyone always wants me to be fucking quiet. To be unseen. To be a lady. To not make trouble. Well, you know what? I'm done with being *quiet*." She climbed to her feet. "And, you, Travis—"

"Quinn," he said in an icy tone. "My name's Quinn.

Nobody calls me by my first name."

"Excuse me?" She planted her hands on her hips. "We've slept together, and I'm carrying your child. I think if anyone gets to break that rule, it's me."

He finally faced her again, and his expression was a frighteningly blank mask.

Smile, Travis. I promise it won't hurt...

Oh, God. This complete shutdown wasn't what she wanted from him. Why couldn't he let himself get mad? Break down? Maybe even tell her how terrified he was of his impeding fatherhood? Because, dammit, he was terrified, and they both knew it. Why couldn't he give her some kind of reaction to work with? At this point, she'd take anything other than this emotional vacuum.

"Well, say something! If you—"

The door banged open behind him, and Mara jumped, but he didn't even blink. Alexei and Pyotr tromped into the room. Pyotr grabbed Travis in a chokehold and wrestled him to the floor while Alexei secured his hands behind his back with a zip tie. He didn't fight back. If anything, he appeared startled. Frightened, even. Not like himself at all.

"Travis?"

He didn't respond. Alexei hauled him upright and marched him out the door.

No! Where were they taking him? Why wasn't he fighting back?

She lunged forward, but Pyotr blocked the doorway and said something nasty in Russian. She didn't need to be 100 percent fluent in the language to know he'd made a sexual suggestion, since he grabbed his crotch and thrust his hips.

Classy.

She dug around in her rusty memories of Russian for an insult and only came up with, "*Yeban'ko maloletnee.*"

Adolescent jerk.

But it was enough. He stopped with the lewd gestures and, scowling, slammed the door as he left.

At a loss, Mara glanced around the room. Until this moment, she hadn't been aware of how much she had depended on Travis to get her through this. Even with him recovering from the drug injection and suffering from migraines, she'd believed he'd get them out of here.

But he hadn't even fought to stay with her. He'd let them just…drag him off, and she had a sinking sensation in her heart that, one way or another, he was always going to leave her.

Exhaustion dragged her to the floor. It would be so easy to just lie down and give up hope. She was alone in this, and the weight of that realization crushed her, very nearly broke her. In fact, if it wasn't for her baby, she was pretty sure it would have.

But, no, that was the old Mara. The one her stepfather dominated, the one who let everyone walk all over her without a peep of protest. That Mara was gone, because her baby needed her to be strong. Needed her to keep going, keep hoping, keep trying, even without Travis.

So she would.

Mara grabbed the spoon from the floor and hauled herself to her feet as she contemplated the window. It was a daunting task, considering how long it had taken her to work the first nail free, but she wouldn't think about that. Nor would she think about the eight feet down if she did manage to pry the window open.

One nail. That's all she needed. And then one more. She'd keep at it until her fingers bled if she had to. Because she was so over being the meek little mouse everyone—including Travis—pushed around. Nobody else was going to look out for her. Nobody else was going to rescue her.

If she wanted to be rescued, she'd damn well do it herself.

Chapter Twelve

When Quinn's brain clicked online again, his first thought was, *did Mara notice the blackout?* They'd been talking—no, fighting. Or on the verge of it. Shit. If they had been fighting, then she'd definitely noticed.

He should have expected the blackout. Prepared for it. Stress triggered the migraines and more often than not, the migraines triggered a blackout event. At very least, he should have warned Mara about—

Wait.

He wasn't with her anymore.

Backseat of a car. Hands bound. And he was still shirtless.

Fuck, how had he gotten here?

He scooted around in the seat to look out the back window. Zaryanko stood on the street, talking to Pyotr and Alexei, and he did not look happy.

No Mara.

Quinn's hands were zip-tied behind his back, but even in his blackout state, his training had still kicked in, thank Christ. He'd clutched his fists when the ties were applied, making his wrists bigger, and now with his hands relaxed, he had some wiggle room. Enough to slip free.

He began working his top hand loose while keeping an eye on Zaryanko in the rearview mirror. Bastard seemed worried, antsy, talking fast with a lot of hand motions and scanning the street as if he expected an attack at any moment. With good reason. If he had hurt Mara in any way, Quinn would end him. Right here, right now, and in the bloodiest way imaginable.

Quinn's thumb popped loose of the tie, and it was quick work to free the rest of his hand after that. Still, he didn't move from the seat. He used his thumbnail to release the catch on the zip tie. Now he had a weapon.

Had to time this right if it was going to work.

In the rearview, he spotted an old cable car trundling down the center of the street. A half block back, a cargo van pulled away from the curb and followed. Alexei left the conversation and circled to the passenger seat.

Quinn still didn't move.

Alexei cranked down the window and lit a cigarette. Muttering to himself, distracted by his own thoughts, he didn't view Quinn as any kind of a threat.

Good.

The cable car let out an unholy screech as it slowed for a stop at the next corner, and Quinn took full advantage of the noise. He looped the zip tie around Alexei's neck and yanked it tight. The guy gagged and flailed, his feet making a dull metallic thumping sound in the foot well. But he didn't have a lot of fight in him, and when he slipped into unconsciousness, Quinn lunged across the seat, grabbed his gun, and pressed the barrel to his temple. The blast was deafening in the close confines of the car and left Quinn's ears ringing.

One down, two to go.

He shoved open the door and rolled out onto the street, keeping low to avoid putting himself in Pyotr's line of fire. Still, a lucky shot blasted through the car's window, raining bits of broken glass on him and coming way too fucking close to his head for comfort. Zaryanko screamed at Pyotr, most likely telling him to stop shooting at the golden goose, but Pyotr was in a rage now and there was no stopping him.

Good. Angry people made mistakes.

One bullet tore through the flimsy door Quinn was hiding behind, and he felt the heat as it skimmed by his neck.

Fuck.

Just as he was about to say a Hail Mary and leave cover to return fire, the cargo van he'd spotted earlier pulled up alongside him and the back doors flung open.

"Quinn!"

Jean-Luc? No. He had to be hallucinating, because he couldn't possibly be that lucky...

Could he?

But he definitely knew that voice, and as Pyotr peppered the pavement around him with bullets, he crouched, readying to surge to his feet at the first lull—and froze. Across the street, under the statue of Lenin, was a ghost. Liam Miller made a gun with his forefinger and thumb and aimed it at Quinn. Smiling, he pretended to shoot.

Holy Christ. How could he be alive?

"Q, c'mon, move your ass!"

A bullet ripped through the car inches from his neck and, yeah, he couldn't stick around any longer. He took a running leap for the van. Jean-Luc and Jesse caught him by the arms and hauled him inside, then Jesse returned fire.

For a moment, with the bullets continuing to fly and his guys shouting orders at each other, Quinn could do nothing but lie on the floor, shocked into immobility. Had he actually seen Liam, or was his fucked-up brain playing tricks?

Jean-Luc tried to pull the swinging door shut and almost got a bullet through his hand for the effort. He cursed in a livid string that ended with the word "mama."

"Did you just insult Zaryanko's mother in Russian?" Seth's voice called from the driver's seat.

One of Jesse's bullets blew through Pyotr's left cheek and the gunfire came to an abrupt end.

Jean-Luc finally caught the door and yanked it shut. "The Russians know how to do two things well, grasshopper: make vodka and swear. I told him his mother sucks cow dicks."

Christ, Quinn thought and finally let himself relax. He loved these guys. He really did.

Jesse lowered his weapon and glanced over his shoulder. "Where's Mara?"

Mara.

He bolted upright. "We gotta go back. She's still in the hotel." As far as he knew. Unless they had moved her, too. Fuck, he wished he could remember. "Seth, turn around!"

Jesse cursed a blue streak that rivaled Jean-Luc's. "We can't. Zaryanko's on alert now."

Of course he was right. Going back without a solid plan was akin to suicide and wouldn't help Mara.

But still. "Guys, we can't leave her. She's pregnant."

"We know," Jesse muttered.

The van slowed, then rolled to a stop on an empty side street. Seth shifted it into park and glanced through the metal door that separated the front from the cargo area. "Someone take over up here." He grabbed the bag that contained his sniper rifle. "I'll find Ian and Marcus and we'll keep the hotel under surveillance until we can come up with a plan of attack. If they move her, we'll know."

Jesse stepped over Quinn without as much as a glance in his direction. "Go," he said to Seth. "Keep in touch."

"Copy that."

The van lurched forward again with Jesse at the wheel. Quinn leaned his head back against the wall and shut his eyes. Guilt churned in his stomach. If he hadn't blacked out on Mara, leaving her to fend for herself, maybe they'd both be safe now.

Jean-Luc squeezed his shoulder. "Cajuns have a saying, *lâche pas la patate*. Translated literally, it means 'don't drop the potato.' But it's commonly understood to mean 'don't give up.' So *lâche pas la patate*. We'll find her and bring her back to you."

Quinn met the linguist's intense blue eyes, and emotion surged, blocking up his throat. This team, as dysfunctional as it sometimes seemed, was one of the best he'd ever had the privilege to work with.

He reached up and clasped Jean-Luc's shoulder in return. "I know we will."

• • •

The door burst open a second time, banging hard into the wall, and Mara fumbled the spoon. It landed on the floor with a soft *clink*, and she kicked it up against the baseboard, doing her best to hide it with her sneaker as she turned to face Zaryanko.

If he noticed the spoon, he didn't acknowledge it. He was livid, and maybe even a bit shaken. Blood spattered one side of his face.

Mara's heart lodged in her throat. "What did you do to Travis?"

He crossed the room in several long strides and grabbed her by the arm.

"No!" She ducked out of his reach. "Where. Is. Travis?"

"You wish to know what kind of coward he is?" Zaryanko

sneered and withdrew a handkerchief from his pocket to wipe away the blood. "He escaped. Saved his own ass and left you here without a second thought. Some savior he turned out to be, yes? So now you will go to Dubai and work off all the money he cost me on your back. And when your child is born, it will work, too. You will never again know the taste of freedom."

A strange sense of peace settled over Mara, calming her racing heart. If Zaryanko was telling the truth, if Travis had escaped, he'd come back for her. He'd probably walk away later when she was safe, but as long as she was in danger, he'd always come back. She knew it with every fiber in her being. Travis was a lot of things, and not all of them were good, but he wasn't a coward.

And neither was she. Not anymore.

She planted her feet. "I'm not going anywhere with you."

Zaryanko's eyes all but spit fire at her. She had never seen such hatred before and recoiled despite her intentions to remain steady.

"You don't have a choice." He snapped out a command in Russian and a thug—not Alexei or Pyotr, but a new one—strode into the room. This guy was built like a pit bull and looked about as mean as a half-starved one trained to fight. The last thing she saw was his meaty fist on a collision course with her face…

Until a blast of cold air shocked her awake.

How long had she been unconscious? Seconds? Minutes? She wasn't sure, but she was outside the hotel now, draped over the pit bull's shoulder, and her jaw ached. She squirmed, and he dropped her to the pavement like she was nothing more than a sack of potatoes.

Maybe to him, that was all she was worth.

Her hands and knees took the brunt of the fall, and she bit her tongue at the jarring impact. Tasted the copper tang of her own blood. And her fear.

She wasn't a coward, but oh, God, was she frightened.

"Are you willing to behave now?" Zaryanko asked.

She gazed up and found herself face-to-face with the license plate of a car. T219AX. She stared hard at it, committed the number to memory.

"Well?" Zaryanko demanded.

She spit out the blood pooling in her mouth. Told herself she would not cry the tears blurring her vision in front of this animal of a man. "Yes."

"Yes what, *cyka*?"

"Yes, I'll behave."

"Then get the fuck in the car and keep your mouth shut."

Swallowing back a surge of bile, she wobbled to her feet and used the car to steady her progress toward the door Zaryanko pulled open. She slid into the backseat and something jabbed her side.

The seat belt?

No, someone had shoved all of the buckles down into the seat. So what—?

Cell phone. The one Travis had stolen off Pyotr. He'd put it in his coat pocket, and she was still wearing his coat.

Zaryanko had gone back into the hotel, and his thug was walking around the hood of the car toward the driver's seat. She only had a tiny window of opportunity to get out a call for help. Had to make it count. She slid the phone out and positioned it between her thigh and the door. Hopefully they'd just think she was cowering. She opened a new text message and plugged in the only number she knew off the top of her head besides her mother's: Travis's cell phone. She'd dialed the number over and over again after Lanie gave it to her, and all those failed attempts to call him had left his number burned into her memory.

She stuffed the phone back into her pocket before the

pit bull was fully settled in the driver's seat, but he didn't so much as glance back at her. He started the car, cranked on the music, and began humming along as if he wasn't driving a woman somewhere against her will.

Mara slipped her hands into both pockets as if she was cold. Which, she was, but the move was more about disguising the fact that she was hiding something in one pocket than it was about keeping warm. She dragged a finger over the old flip phone's number pad, trying to remember which letter corresponded with each number.

Oh, she hoped she was right.

Slowly, precisely, she began to type out a text.

Chapter Thirteen

"You'll never guess what we found wandering in the streets," Jean-Luc called out as he led the way inside the small house they had commandeered as their operating base. He'd explained to Quinn on the ride over that the house had been abandoned when the family that called it home up and moved abroad, leaving most of their possessions behind. And judging by the state of the living room, they hadn't been a rich family. An old, lumpy couch sat against the tapestry-covered wall, and Gabe rested there with his bad foot elevated and an arm thrown over his eyes. There was also a TV in the corner that was such a technological dinosaur it actually had rabbit ears. Other than that, the place was empty.

Gabe groaned at the sound of Jean-Luc's voice and didn't lift his arm. "Please don't tell me Ian found another dog. No more dogs. And no cats. No furry animals, period."

"Well, he is a little furry." Jean-Luc ruffled Quinn's overgrown hair.

Quinn ducked out of his reach and pointed a warning finger at him. "If you want to keep that hand, I suggest you never do that again."

Gabe dropped his arm and slowly sat up, his eyes as wide as Quinn had ever seen them. "Q?"

Jean-Luc grinned. "You still so sure you don't want to keep him?"

"Jesus," Gabe said. His mouth worked silently for a second, completely at a loss for words. "Quinn, shit. You okay? Where's Mara?"

Quinn rubbed the back of his neck. "Honestly, man, I don't know. I was with her and then…I don't know." And it made him sick to his stomach, but he wasn't ready to get into the conversation as to why he didn't know, so he nodded toward Gabe's leg. "Foot okay?"

Gabe grunted a reply that could've been anything from "just peachy" to "fuck you," but the answer was obvious. If his foot wasn't bothering him, he would have been at the club with the rest of the team. He pushed himself to his feet, limping as his weight settled. He held out a hand, and Jesse slapped his cane into his palm.

The medic's mood was dark as a storm cloud. Not that Quinn blamed him. "Hey, Jess, I—"

Jesse ignored him and said to Gabe in a carefully flat voice, "Where are Harvard and Lanie? We need to brief everyone on the recent developments."

Gabe hitched a thumb over his shoulder. "Half of our radios don't work, which is driving Harvard to drink. Last I saw, he was in the kitchen trying to jury-rig them, and Lanie's helping." At that moment, a vicious curse came from the kitchen. Female voice.

Jean-Luc winced. "Annnd from the sounds of it, they are not having much luck. Looks like we'll be racking up international charges on our cell phones again."

"Which reminds me," Gabe said to Quinn and reached into his bag on the floor, "I have your phone."

"You got my message."

"Yeah, it was in your drafts folder. Tank found the phone at the hangar in New Mexico."

Quinn's lip twitched in a small smile. That dog was worth his weight in gold and completely worth the hassle of bringing him back from Afghanistan. "Man, I take back everything bad I've ever said about Tank. I'm buying him the biggest rawhide he's ever seen when we get home. Where is he?"

"We had to leave him behind on the plane," Gabe said. "We parachuted in, and he hasn't had the training for that yet."

Quinn nodded and turned his phone on. The screen lit up and showed he was doing good in the battery department. "No signal."

"Harvard warned it would be spotty at best, which is why he's trying so hard to get those radios up and running."

"Well, wouldn't be right if we didn't have one snafu."

"I hear you. No easy day, right?"

"Hooyah." He pocketed the phone. "You mentioned the name Lanie. You're not talking about Mara's friend?"

"He sure is," Jean-Luc said. "Lanie Delcambre. She's..." He gave a wolf whistle.

"I heard that, Cajun," the woman said from the kitchen.

He shrugged and called back, "Well, ya are!" Then added in a lowered voice, "But she plays for the other team—which, you ask me, is hot as hell."

Jesse stopped short halfway across the living area and spun back. If anything, his scowl only got darker. "What, she's a lesbian 'cause she didn't drop her panties at your feet?"

"Or yours."

"I can hear you, assholes," Lanie said and appeared in the doorway between the two rooms. A mixed-race woman with sharp, exotic features, she was all long, lean muscle, but it was her eyes more than her build that commanded respect.

She had the eyes of a soldier ready and willing to do what was necessary to get her friend back. And right now, those eyes were spitting fire at Jesse and Jean-Luc.

"And, no," she said, "I'm not a lesbian. I like men. A lot. Just not any of you, so how about y'all get your minds out of my panties and—" She broke off when she finally spotted Quinn, and the radio in her hand clattered to the floor. Her gaze darted around the room. "Mara…?"

"We were separated," Quinn answered, because he felt like it was his responsibility. "Zaryanko still has her. I'm sorry."

For a moment, her shoulders slumped in defeat. Then she sucked in a breath and straightened to her full height. "Well. We need to find her then."

Quinn nodded. He could see why Gabe had chosen to bring her along on this mission.

"Let's take this to the kitchen," Gabe said. "More room in there."

Harvard glanced up when they all filed into the room but returned to tinkering with a radio without much concern. Quinn waited, counting the beats in his head before—

Harvard did a double take.

And there it was.

"Quinn?" He leaped to his feet and opened his arms like he was about to give one of those backslapping hugs.

Quinn held up his hands to ward him off. "Mara's not safe yet. We still have work to do."

"Yeah, uh…" A flush worked up Harvard's neck. Dropping back into his chair, he adjusted his glasses. "I assume Gabe's already filled you in—"

"Not yet," Gabe said and proceeded to do just that. Once they figured out where Zaryanko was holding Quinn and Mara, they had planned to have Ian set a charge as a distraction for the rescue, and then they'd hump it over the border to Ukraine, where Jace Garcia was waiting with the plane.

Then it was Quinn's turn to talk. He took the guys through the events of the last forty-eight hours, but when he got to the shoot-out, he hesitated. He still couldn't be entirely sure he'd seen Liam Miller, but…he decided to mention it anyway.

As he spoke, Gabe's usual unreadable expression hardened. He had sat down in one of the kitchen chairs to take pressure off his foot during the lengthy discussion, but now he stood. "What the fuck do you mean Liam Miller is alive? I saw him after Audrey shot him. It was a fatal wound."

Quinn shook his head. "I know what I saw, man. It was Liam."

Gabe dragged a hand over his face. "Goddammit. Where's the sat phone? I—I need to call Audrey."

Harvard dug around in a box and found the only satellite phone they had. Gabe grabbed it and walked from the room.

"Shit," Harvard breathed, staring after him. "I've never seen him that shaken."

"If I'm right and Liam's alive," Quinn said quietly, "and he knows we're here, there's a good chance he'll try for Audrey. She did almost kill him. He'll want to get even."

"And Audrey's on the other side of the world," Jesse snapped. "Ask me, we should be more concerned 'bout Mara."

Quinn stared at the medic in disbelief and a roiling heat filled his stomach. He stood. "If you think I'm not tied up with worry for her and the baby, you're a fucking idiot, Warrick."

Jesse stood as well, and his chair banged against the wall hard enough to leave a divot in the floral wallpaper. "Family is off-fucking-limits, Quinn. Off. Limits. You know what that means?"

"Yeah, I do." His jaw ached and he realized he was

grinding his back teeth. "I also know that Mara is her own goddamn person, free to make her own choices. You have no right to control her life."

"I was trying to protect her from the likes of you!"

Quinn flinched internally, the words hitting like a physical blow. *The likes of you.* Meaning the bastard son of a crack whore and an alcoholic murderer, the kid from the way wrong side of the tracks. Yeah, who could blame Jesse for not wanting him in Mara's life?

But he didn't let his thoughts show and leaned across the table, got in Jesse's face. "You weren't protecting her. You were smothering her. You're no better than her jackass stepfather."

"You know what, fuck you, Quinn. If it wasn't for your inability to keep your dick in your pants—"

"Enough!" Gabe's voice boomed from the doorway, shocking the room into silence. "We have work to do, and this bickering is a waste of time." He limped over to the head of the table and stared down the length of it, very much like a king presiding over his knights.

Which, as much as Quinn loved the guy, really grated on his last paper-thin nerve. "Our leader has spoken. Tell us, oh great one, what are your commands?"

Gabe's brows climbed toward his hairline. "For you? Something anatomically impossible that none of us want to see. Here." He tossed his cane across the six feet of space separating them, and Quinn caught it. "Use that so I have a good goddamn reason not to drag it around with me."

And now he felt like a complete asshole. What the hell had happened to his infamous control? Where was the man that his BUD/S instructors had started calling Achilles because they had been so determined to discover a weakness? The warrior who'd never let them find one? He'd taken everything they had thrown at him and asked for more.

Christ, he'd give anything to be that man again.

"Gabe, I don't know where that—" Quinn shook his head, blew out a long breath, and tossed the cane back. "I'm an asshole."

Gabe's eyes narrowed, but he said nothing. Didn't accept the semi-apology, but didn't reject it, either. Typical. Very little hurt his best friend, but Quinn knew that snide remark had cut deep and wished he could recall it.

Gabe left the table and crossed to the other side of the room, where Jesse was pacing furious holes in the floor. They exchanged a handful of words too soft for Quinn to hear, then both looked up as he approached.

"Warrick, man, if you want to have it out with me, fine. I get it. But Gabe's right. Let's find Mara first."

Jesse shrugged off Gabe's restraining hand. "Don't talk to me right now, Quinn. Seriously, just—don't."

"I didn't mean for any of this to happen. You gotta know that."

Jesse whirled around, broadcasting his intentions so loudly the next block probably heard them. Quinn had plenty of time to maneuver out of the way of the punch, had plenty of time to launch a counterstrike that would have taken the medic to his knees in less than a heartbeat.

But he didn't.

Jesse had to get this out of his system, so Quinn took the full force of the blow without even twitching in defense. Blood bloomed on his tongue as his lip split. His vision flared white, rivaling a flashbang for brightness. He even staggered a little from the shift in his equilibrium when his brain rattled around in his skull, but he stayed on his feet—

Or not.

He blinked and realized he was staring up at the ceiling. Not the kitchen ceiling, either. He was in a bed with a thin, uncovered mattress, and something was poking him in the ass.

What the…?

Another blackout. Christ, they were happening more and more frequently now.

"You're a fucking medic, Jess," Gabe was saying from somewhere nearby. "You of all people should know you don't punch a guy with brain trauma in the head."

Quinn blocked out their voices, squeezed his eyes shut, and breathed a soft sigh of aggravation. Now both Gabe and Jesse knew how bad of shape he was in.

He sat up on the edge of the bed and cradled his head in his hands. He didn't look over when he heard a door close, nor at the distinctive tap of Gabe's cane as it crossed the room.

"So," Gabe said. He pulled up a rickety chair and sat down, his boots directly in Quinn's line of sight.

All right. Quinn mentally steeled himself, then straightened to meet his best friend's gaze. Apparently, it was time for that talk he'd been putting off for far too long.

"You know about the blackouts," he said, point-blank.

Gabe nodded. "Since Colombia. Jesse told me about them after he did your physical in Bogotá."

"Goddamn Jesse." Quinn rubbed both hands over his face and then sighed in resignation. "And that's why you've been sticking me with B.S. bodyguard assignments. First Mara, then the shelter girls in Afghanistan…"

"Yeah, that's why. I know it hurt you to leave the teams. Believe me, I know exactly how much it hurt. I didn't want to take HORNET away from you, too."

"But," Quinn added since the word hung in the air between them like an anvil waiting to drop. "I'm a danger to have out in the field."

"Yes, you are. And you know it, which is why you've been accepting those B.S. assignments without protest." Gabe was silent for a moment. "Have you been checked out?"

"I've gone to specialists," he hedged. "They don't know

what's causing it." Which was why he'd stopped going months ago. After a while, all the inconclusive testing seemed pointless.

Gabe scowled down at his bad foot like he wanted to rip it off. "That fucking car accident."

"Yeah," Quinn agreed softly. "That fucking accident. Do you remember that day?"

Gabe winced. "In vivid detail, unfortunately."

"I wish I could."

"No, Q, you don't. I was awake the entire time. The whole four hours I was pinned in that car, I didn't pass out for more than a few seconds at a time. Wouldn't let myself until they got me free. I remember every painful second of it. Keeps me awake sometimes, remembering it."

That was a surprise. Gabe's nickname in the teams had been Stonewall because he was usually just about as reactive as one. Nothing much rattled him beyond fear for his wife's safety, so those memories must be a special type of hell to keep him awake at night.

Still, Quinn would prefer the nightmares. "There's this blank spot in my mind. I can remember dinner the Friday before the accident, right down to how much it cost, what my waiter's name was, and what I left for a tip. Then…nothing until I woke up in the hospital. Almost a whole month—just gone. Like it never fucking happened."

"Pretty sure with brain trauma that's normal," Gabe said.

"Yeah, that's what the docs all say. Thing is, I've had this nagging feeling since I woke up in the hospital. Like there's something I have to do or… Fuck, I don't know." Full of restless energy, he stood. Paced across the small bedroom, then returned. "Before the accident, did I tell you anything?"

Gabe snorted. "You never tell me shit."

"Gabe, I'm serious. I need to know what I said, what I did."

Gabe hesitated. "You acted pissed off about something when you picked me up that morning, but I brushed it off as a bad night or a lack of caffeine or both. Whatever had your dick in a twist, you never said anything about it to me."

Quinn stopped moving, a sudden thought pinning him in place as surely as glue on the bottom of his boots. "Do you blame me?"

"What?" Gabe said with an expression of genuine surprise.

"Do you blame me for the accident?"

"What?" he repeated with a shake of his head. "Shit, no. Why would I?"

"Because I was driving."

"Q, c'mon. It was that asshole in the pickup truck's fault. It's damn lucky he didn't hurt anybody else weaving in and out of traffic like he was. When he shoved us into that semi, there was no stopping it, no avoiding it. The same thing would've happened had I been behind the wheel. Hey, hey." Gabe stood and caught his shoulders, forcing him to stop pacing. "Listen to me, bro. I don't blame you."

Quinn let out the breath he hadn't realized he'd been holding for nearly two years. Gabe didn't blame him for ruining their SEAL careers. Good to know.

Now if only he could stop blaming himself.

Outside the bedroom door, he heard the team moving around. Jean-Luc cracked a joke, as usual. Harvard laughed. Jesse told them both to fuck off.

Good men. They all were.

Quinn was going to miss them.

Mind made up, he drew a breath and met Gabe's eyes. "I'm resigning as HORNET's XO."

"Whoa. Wait a second, Q. You—"

"No, you're right. I'm a liability. I shouldn't even be going on this op now, but—well, this one's non-negotiable. I have to find Mara. But once she's safe…" He glanced toward the door and something cracked in the vicinity of his heart. "Yeah, I'm done."

Chapter Fourteen

Gabe said nothing for several endless minutes. Finally, he walked toward the door but paused next to Quinn and handed over two slips of what Quinn first thought were white paper.

No, wait. It was a photo, ripped in half.

"I went by your place before I left Washington," Gabe said. "Your house was ransacked. Looked more like someone was searching for something than a run-of-the-mill burglary."

What the hell was going on? He shook his head. "This doesn't make sense. I don't have anything anyone would want."

Gabe shrugged, then motioned to the photo. "On my way out, I found that on the floor. The rest were destroyed beyond saving. Thought you'd want it."

He left.

Quinn stayed rooted to the spot, staring at the closed door until he worked up the nerve to look at the photo. He knew what he'd see, and chills raced through his body as he turned the two pieces over.

Samuel and Bianca Quinn. Their faces smiled up at him from the ruined photo. The doctor and the ICU nurse who'd felt bad enough for a poor, abused ten-year-old that they'd agreed to open their home and hearts to him as he recovered from the gunshot inflicted on him by his own father. They were the one bright spot in the darkness that was Quinn's life. For six all too short years, they were his family. Not Big Ben and Cherice Jewett, the man and woman who'd given him life. No, it was Sam and Bianca, who had shown him life could be good.

Quinn bowed double over the photo, his heart riding high in his throat, choking off the dry sobs that racked his body. Gabe had said the few other photos he had of them were destroyed. They were gone. Now he had nothing left of them but unreliable memories that got fuzzier and fuzzier each day.

Whoever did this would pay.

No, fuck that. Whoever did this would die.

On a shaky breath, Quinn straightened and dragged his hands through his overgrown hair. Sorrow and rage iced over into a solid layer of determination. He spotted the bag Gabe had packed for him in the corner of the room and snapped it up before going in search of the house's bathroom. The guys and Lanie looked up as he passed through the kitchen, but nobody said anything—not even Jesse.

The bathroom was a closet off the living room, but it had all the amenities of a Western bathroom, including a shower with hot and cold running water. He set his bag down on the toilet and took stock of his appearance in the scratched mirror over the sink. It showed him a man he barely recognized. Sunken eyes, cheekbones that stood out in stark relief on a face that hadn't seen a razor blade in a very long time. His dark blond hair had grown so long that it brushed the tops of his shoulders and hung in limp tangles.

Look at him. Sam and Bianca would be so disappointed in what he'd become these past few months. Drunk and self-medicating when he wasn't on a mission with HORNET. Perpetually pissed off at the world, at himself…

He'd become Big Ben after all.

Christ.

Bile burned on the back of his tongue at the realization, and he unzipped his bag. His battery-powered razor lay right there on top, and he said a mental thank-you to Gabe for packing it and his shave kit. After hunting up the crappy pair of scissors he kept in the kit, he hacked off chunks of hair, cutting it as short as he could with the dull blades. The razor got the rest and tamed his beard. He jumped in the shower, dipped his head under the cold water, and scrubbed his hands over the remaining stubble, then cleaned up with the small bar of soap from his shave kit. He found a T-shirt and fresh pair of urban-print cammies at the bottom of his bag and pulled them on without bothering to dry off. Gazing up, he met his own bloodshot eyes in the mirror.

That was more like it. The man staring back at him looked more like the Quinn he remembered from before the damned car accident that destroyed his career.

All conversation came to a halt when he returned to the kitchen. Their stares brought on an uncomfortable flush along the back of his neck. Damn. He must have looked in bad shape before if this was their reaction to seeing him looking somewhat like himself again.

He cleared his throat. "What's going on?"

Silence.

"Guys?"

"Oh." Harvard dropped his gaze to the radio in his hand. "Uh, I was just saying I haven't been able to raise Seth, Ian, or Marcus by radio. The radios suck, so the one they have could have just crapped out, but still. And Garcia missed his last check-in, which could mean trouble. If our exfil route is compromised…"

"Let's work on finding Mara first," Gabe said. "Worry about Garcia later."

Quinn nodded his agreement. "I'll try Seth's phone." He fished his cell out of his leg pocket and turned it on, pleased to see that Ian and Marcus's efforts installing satellite dishes and signal boosters on nearby buildings had come to fruition. For the first time since he got his phone back, he had a signal. Weak, but maybe enough to—

A text message popped up from a number he didn't recognize.

in car license t219ax going NE

"What the hell?" He read it again. And again. And then scrolled down when he realized he had several other messages from the same number.

nz sent me 2 olesea says i go 2 dubai 2morrow

hide phone now leaving on please find me travis

Every last molecule of air hissed out of his lungs. He swayed a little as the room started a spin that couldn't be healthy.

"Q?" Gabe said, concern in his voice.

"It's Mara."

All motion in the room stopped and suddenly Jesse was by his side, snatching the phone from his hand.

"Thatta girl," Jesse murmured.

Lanie grabbed the phone next and grinned. "Way to go, Mara."

Quinn smiled a little, pride shining a brief beacon of light inside his dark soul. Mara was smart. Stronger than anyone gave her credit for. Resourceful.

And his.

Even if she never forgave him for…well, everything, his heart had her name carved into it for eternity. He'd known it from the very first time she'd kissed him in her living room all those months ago—exactly why he'd tried to run as fast and as far away from her as he could.

What a fucking fool he was.

Quinn took the phone from Lanie and passed it to Harvard. "Can you track a Transnistrian license plate?"

Harvard winced. "You know I hate to doubt my own abilities, but I'm not entirely sure it's possible. Because Transnistria is unrecognized, there might not be any records to trace. Or, if there are, they might not be digital. I can take a peek, but it will take time we can't afford."

"Do it," Quinn said. "Fast as you can."

Harvard gave a solemn nod and sat behind his computer, his fingers already tickling the keyboard like an expert pianist. "I'm on it, boss. Wait." He straightened away from his computer and smacked his palm against his head. "I'm an idiot. We don't need to trace the license. All we need is the phone. There are so few cell towers in the country that finding out which the messages pinged off should give us a search area."

Pride morphed into something even more dangerous. Hope. "How long will it take?" Quinn asked.

"Give me…a half hour. I'll also run a reverse lookup on the phone number, but I doubt we'll get anything. It's probably a burner."

"It belonged to one of Zaryanko's people," Quinn said. Until now, he'd completely forgotten about the phone.

"Well, we have another clue." Harvard tapped the phone. "She mentioned Olesea. Is that a place?"

Jean-Luc shook his head. "*Non*, it's a woman's name.

Somewhat common in Moldova."

"Well, it's something. While my programs are running, I'll pull that research string, too. Something's gotta fall loose."

"Go ahead and do your thing," Gabe said and faced the remaining members of the team. "While Harvard's on that, we need to pack up. As soon as we find Mara, we're gone, and we're not coming back. Make sure we leave nothing behind that will trace to us. We were never here."

"What about Garcia?" Jesse asked. "We need the plane to be ready."

Quinn's gut told him something was wrong there. He glanced a question at Gabe, who shook his head.

"This is your show, Q. What do you want to do?"

Mara was their priority objective right now. She had to be. At the same time, if Garcia was in trouble, that compromised their exfil route, which compromised Mara.

Damn. He hated making these judgment calls, and Gabe knew it, too. "Keep trying to raise him by phone and radio," he decided. "If we still can't get him by the time we have Mara in hand, we may have to come up with another plan. And someone try Seth, Marcus, and Ian again. If we're lucky, they'll have been watching when she was moved and will already have her location."

• • •

Mara curled herself around her belly, hoping to conserve as much body heat as possible even as the icy air whisked it away almost before her body produced it. When the pit bull dropped her off, she'd been stripped of Travis's coat—and the lifesaving phone. Then she was shoved into this shed by a nasty woman named Olesea and left without any protection against the cold. She couldn't stop shivering. Was the baby suffering, too? What kind of mother was she, already subjecting her child to this kind of danger?

God, she was an idiot. Such a naive, foolish idiot. This had started as a fantasy, a simple, harmless one-night stand—they were harmless, right? Women had them all the time. Lanie had them all the time and always came out the other side no worse for wear. So how had her one night of abandon gone so horribly wrong and ended like this? Trapped in a sordid room in some godforsaken foreign country she'd never heard of. Cold, hungry, and terrified beyond anything she'd ever felt in her life. Of course, her one-night stand hadn't stayed one, and part of her wished Travis had never showed up at her house in November, wished she'd never had the opportunity to know him beyond a one-night stand, wished she'd never had the opportunity to fall in love with him.

Was she being punished for her recklessness?

But, no, she really hadn't been reckless. She'd been on birth control when Travis showed up at her house six weeks ago and she'd welcomed him back into her bed.

Meant to be.

That's what her mother had said before her stepfather decided the family should disown her for her promiscuity. And of course Mama had gone along with him, because that's what she always did, but at first she'd been thrilled to be getting a grandbaby.

Maybe Mama was right. Maybe this was all just meant to be.

The door to her prison opened, and she lifted her head from the bare mattress. Zaryanko stood in the doorway, outlined by the snowy-white light of the winter day outside. She again wanted to ask what he'd done with Travis but couldn't form the words around the lump of terror in her throat. He scanned the tiny room, then studied her for a long moment with flat eyes. His breath clouded against the air as he made a *tsk-tsk-tsk* sound and shut the door.

"Olesea!" he roared.

Mara sat up. Curiosity and a fragile spark of hope made her heart hammer, and she nervously twisted the band of her watch around her wrist. He obviously wasn't happy with the way she'd been treated since arriving here.

"Olesea!" he yelled again, and Mara heard the crunch of boots running over snow, followed by Olesea's scratchy, too-many-cigarettes-a-day voice.

The two carried on a rapid-fire conversation that Mara had no hope of deciphering. She listened anyway, straining to pick up anything familiar.

Nothing. They were speaking too fast, and from this distance, it all sounded like gibberish to her.

Desperate to hear more, Mara climbed to her feet and crept toward the one window in the room. She'd peeked out it once before, knew it overlooked a short stretch of snow-covered yard and a ramshackle barn that housed a handful of goats and chickens. Through the ice-frosted glass, she saw Zaryanko and Olesea standing by the shed, deep in an argument that was fast escalating to violence.

"*Nyet!*" Zaryanko shouted and hit Olesea so hard her head snapped to the side and blood spouted from her red, pockmarked nose.

Olesea took off the kerchief covering her salt-and-pepper hair, pressed it to her nose, and said something muffled. Zaryanko raised his hand again, and she flinched back like an abused dog. She nodded and disappeared around the edge of the barn. Zaryanko lit a cigarette and stood there smoking until he caught sight of Mara in the window. He threw his cigarette down and crushed it out in the snow, then strode toward the door of her prison.

Mara scrambled backward but had no place to go, no place to hide, and her legs bumped the mattress. She sat down, arms automatically wrapping around her belly as she waited and worried.

Zaryanko threw open the door. "Come with me."

She hesitated.

He muttered something in Russian, then held out a hand and wiggled his gloved fingers. "Do you wish to stay in the cold? Come."

An image of lambs being led to slaughter popped into her head. They all probably thought they were going someplace better, too. But she had to go with him. What other choice did she have? To stay here in this freezing room was nothing but a prolonged death sentence.

Ignoring his outstretched hand, she stood and followed him across the yard, her feet numbing inside her tennis shoes with every step. The house that came into view as they circled around the barn was bigger than she would've guessed, two stories tall and painted with absurdly cheerful colors.

Zaryanko led her up the porch steps and opened the front door. It was warm inside, and the front foyer looked the same as any country cottage found in the United States. The clash of her expectations versus reality gave her an instant headache.

Nikolai motioned her inside. "In."

Despite the warmth spilling from the house, beckoning her inside, she hesitated. "Are you really going to sell me?" The question popped out before her brain weighed the pros and cons of asking it, and she expected him to hit her like he had Olesea, but he merely shrugged.

"Would you rather I kill you?" He asked the question casually, like it was one he posed every day.

She recoiled. "No."

"Nothing to do with you," he repeated. "Just business. All of this? Just business. I have a family to care for."

"What about my family?"

He said nothing more and gestured to the house.

Trembling from the cold, she walked inside and then climbed the stairs when he motioned for her to go up. On the second floor, he unlocked a door and pushed it open. It was dark inside and the stale air stank of unwashed humans. She swallowed hard, prayed to her dad for strength, and stepped over the threshold, but turned around to meet his gaze before he shut the door.

In that instant, she thought of her mother. Would Rosa Escareno miss her if she disappeared forever? Would Rosa even know? Ramon had such a firm grip on her, she might not even find out Mara was gone. Her brother, Matt, would notice. Jesse and his parents definitely would, and they'd all miss her. Her throat closed up at the thought of never seeing any of them again. "My family needs me, too, Nikolai."

He cocked his head slightly as if giving real consideration to her words. "Hmm, yes. But in this world, some people are…sheep. You are sheep. Others are like wolf."

"And you're the wolf?"

"No." He gave a toothy smile. "I am a businessman, nothing more. I simply sell the sheep to any wolf willing to pay."

Her body froze down to the bone as the door shut in her face. The soft *thunk* of the lock sliding into place sounded very final.

She released a breath in a shudder. She wouldn't cry. It would only exhaust her, and if Travis found her—no, *when* he found her—she'd need her strength. Because he would come for her. She had to hang on to that hope or go insane.

A scrape of a footstep sounded behind her. She whirled and groped for a light switch, but her hand slid along nothing but bare wall.

"You will not find a light," a soft female voice said in Russian.

Mara froze. It took her a moment to translate and then another to find the words she needed to communicate. "Who are you?"

"Dasia." Movement in the darkness, and then a curtain opened to let in a pale square of yellow light from outside. A woman stood near the window, a hand resting on her hugely pregnant belly. She was so big she must have been having twins.

Two more women stepped into the light, both little more than girls and both pregnant. Mara touched her own belly as a swell of nausea rolled through her. These women—girls—were here to be sold. Did they know that? She scanned their faces and saw exhaustion and resignation in each.

Yes, they knew.

She swallowed back the lump of sorrow blocking her throat. "How long…uh, have you been here?"

Dasia winced. "You are not from here. Your Russian is bad."

Mara shook her head. "American," she said in English. "Do any of you know English? *Español?*"

She received nothing but blank looks in return. Okay. They'd just have to suffer with her mangled Russian. "How long have you been here?" she repeated, trying to enunciate clearly and make sure her tone and inflections were correct. She must have still bungled it, though, because it took several moments of soft discussion among the women before they figured out what she meant.

"A week for me," Dasia said. She motioned to the youngest looking of the group, a small blonde who was maybe halfway through her pregnancy. "Lizabeta arrived three days ago. Oxana"—she indicated the short brunette who was also very pregnant—"yesterday."

"Do you know why you're here?"

Again, the three murmured among themselves, then Dasia nodded. "We're going abroad to sell our babies."

"You want to?"

All three nodded enthusiastically. "It will pay off our

debt to Nikolai," Dasia explained, "and we'll be free to go home. It's a good thing."

Oh, God. They truly thought Zaryanko would let them go if they sold their children.

Mara remembered in vivid detail how Zaryanko had so coldly ordered the execution of a woman on that runway in New Mexico because she was too ugly and how he'd originally planned to kill Mara herself for being too fat. She pressed a hand over her mouth to hold back a sob. These women would have baby weight after they delivered. Would Zaryanko consider them too fat to be of use then?

How could she make them understand they'd never be free unless they escaped? She didn't have a good enough command of the language to tell them the information she knew from Travis or about the brutality she'd seen. But she had to try. "Dasia—"

The doorknob rattled, and the three women scattered like frightened woodland creatures as the door swung open.

Mara turned to face Zaryanko again, but it was that nasty woman Olesea this time. She snapped out a command Mara didn't catch and the other women darted from the room. Mara didn't move. She didn't know what Zaryanko had said to Olesea by the shed outside, but she had little doubt it was something along the lines of "don't damage the merchandise."

"You won't harm me," Mara said in English. "You're as afraid of Zaryanko as the rest of us."

Olesea's sunken eyes widened. She stalked forward and grabbed a handful of Mara's hair, twisting hard. Pain exploded across Mara's scalp, and she dropped to her knees.

"I will harm you," Olesea said in heavily accent English. "I leave no marks. Nikolai never knows." She shoved Mara out of the room. "In my house, you work for the roof over your head. Now go."

Chapter Fifteen

"Here's what we have." As the van bumped over an unpaved road an hour later, Quinn briefed the team. "The last message Mara sent me pinged off this cell phone tower here." He marked an X on a topography map, then braced himself against the wall when the van hit a pothole that nearly sent it airborne.

"Sorry," Harvard said.

"Fuck, where'd you learn to drive?" Ian asked.

"Do you think you can do better?" Harvard demanded. "This road doesn't have ruts. It has canyons."

"Don't listen to them," Lanie said from the passenger seat. "Just get us there in one piece."

Once the van evened out, Quinn returned to the briefing. "Based on the topography, the cell tower's range, and the low population density of the area, the call originated from this village of about fifty people." He called up satellite images of the area on Harvard's laptop and turned the screen toward the guys. He zoomed in on a blue two-story house seated just outside the village. "This place is our target. The property is gated, and we have no intel on security. It's on a hill, and the land around it is flat, with only these trees here"—he drew a circle with his finger around the tree line at the back of the property—"for cover."

"It's a logistical nightmare," Seth muttered.

"Pretty much," Gabe said.

"The house is owned by a fifty-one-year-old woman named Olesea Alistratova," Quinn continued. "Which matches the name Mara gave us, so it's a safe bet this is the right place."

Lanie glanced back. "Why would this woman help Zaryanko?"

"She was probably once trafficked herself," Marcus explained. "That's how these rings work. They'll trick a woman into going with them by offering her employment abroad, then addict her to drugs and make her work off some arbitrarily assigned debt that she'll never be able to pay back. If the women survive that, many of them are so broken they can't return to their lives before they were taken and end up as recruiters for the traffickers. It allows them to continue paying off their debt and even make a living without being forced to prostitute themselves."

"Jesus," Lanie breathed.

Stomach knotted, Quinn met each of the guys' gazes in turn, finally settling on Jesse. "This might be our best chance to rescue her before Zaryanko ships her to Dubai. We can't fail. We—" His voice cracked, but he didn't bother clearing the emotion from his throat. He needed Jesse to know how sorry he was for all of this. Needed the medic to know that if it came to it, he'd give his life to make sure Mara made it home safe. "We can't fail," he repeated softly.

Jesse glanced away and sucked in a choppy breath.

Gabe grasped each of their shoulders. "We won't fail. We'll get her back."

A beat of heavy silence passed. Quinn knew if anyone could do it, it was this group of men bouncing around with him in a van going way too fast on the rutted road. But fear still ate at him with jagged teeth. He had to lock that shit down and concentrate.

Finally, he straightened and pointed to the map again. "There's about a foot of snow on the ground around Olesea's house, which is going to make a covert attack hard to pull off. I'm open to ideas here, guys."

They pored over the maps and satellite images for several bumpy miles.

"Looks like the biggest area of weakness is the back of the house," Jean-Luc finally said. "More cover for us."

Quinn shook his head. "We don't want to be fighting uphill. Nothing drains you faster."

"So we sniper crawl in," Seth said. "We have our snow camo. If we take it easy enough, we can be on their back porch before they realize it."

"They're not expectin' us," Jesse said with a nod of agreement. "We have that to our advantage, and the slow crawl in will give us time to scope out the opposition force."

"If there is one," Ian said.

"Yeah. If." Quinn rubbed his hands over his face. There were too many fucking ifs for his liking and only two certainties: Mara was in that house, and he wanted her back.

• • •

As darkness fell, Mara stopped scrubbing the living room floor to peek out the windows whenever Olesea wasn't looking. Ever since she'd sent that text to Travis's phone, she'd hoped…

But maybe he hadn't gotten the messages. Or maybe he had received them, but her blind typing made no sense.

There were so many ways her plan, as feeble as it was, could have gone wrong, and with each passing hour, she grew more and more desperate.

She couldn't stay here and wait for Zaryanko to whisk her off to Dubai. But without help, she didn't see how she could possibly—

"Psst."

She glanced over at Dasia, who made a scrubbing motion with her hands and whispered in Russian, "Work."

Mara shook her head and searched for the words she needed. "Four of us. One of her."

Dasia's blue eyes rounded, huge in her too-thin face. "No. Keep working! We'll all be punished."

Didn't Dasia realize that breathing was a punishable offense in this place? Olesea enjoyed hurting them. And if she was going to be punished anyway, simply for existing, she might as well attempt an escape. She shook her head again and stood.

"What are you doing?" Olesea stalked across the room and backhanded Mara so hard she drew blood. "Get back to work, *cyka*!"

Mara straightened from the blow and tasted copper on her lips. Realizing she clenched the sponge so hard her nails dug half moons into her palm, she loosened her fingers until it fell out of her hand and hit the floor with a wet slap. "*Nyet*."

Olesea's mouth dropped open. Apparently, she was so used to blind compliance from the women she housed, she hadn't expected a rebellion. "Excuse me?"

"*Nyet. Ya ne tvoy rab*," Mara said, struggling to make sure the Russian came out clearly.

Olesea laughed. Actually laughed, and the skeletal fingers of fear scraped down Mara's spine, but she held her ground. The other three women recoiled in terror.

"*Ya ne tvoy rab*," she repeated, and even though her voice

trembled, she lifted her chin in defiance. "I am not your slave, you bitch."

"Not my slave?" Olesea's hand whipped out again, striking Mara across her cheek so hard she stumbled sideways. "We shall see."

• • •

"Cajun to Achilles." Jean-Luc's voice crackled through Quinn's earpiece, loud in the muffled winter evening as he lay, belly to the snow, still fifty yards from the house. He stopped crawling and flattened himself out on the snow as much as he could, scanning the area around him for any immediate threats before he answered the radio call. "Cajun, Achilles. Go ahead."

"Be advised, there is movement in the house. Looks and sounds like a fight in there. How do you copy?"

"Good copy. Do you have eyes on any tangos?"

"Negative."

Damn. "Anyone have eyes on?"

"Ace to Achilles," Seth said. "I count one female tango in the house and one female hotel. Three female unknowns. I have visual confirmation of hotel's identity. Over."

Visual confirmation of the hotel—hostage. Of Mara. Quinn rested his forehead on his arm for a moment and gave himself a chance to recover from the explosion of pure joy that sang through him at the words. He had to stay focused. Think like an operative. Just because he now knew Mara was inside didn't mean he could let down his guard until she was safe in friendly territory. This was always the most dangerous part of any snatch-and-grab mission.

The radio crackled again. "Harvard to Achilles. Be advised, I have a car headed toward your position. ETA three mikes."

Quinn lifted his head and squinted toward the house. Harvard waited in the van a mile down the road, but Quinn could already hear the incoming car. Hard not to when the struts squeaked with every bump on the road. "Copy that. How many passengers?"

"Four," Harvard said. "Driver looks like Nikolai Zaryanko. Over."

"Copy that." All ideas of doing this covertly just went to hell. They had made a tactical mistake, wasting too much time trying to sneak up on a house that was barely guarded, and now they had four likely armed men bearing down on them. Quinn would kick himself for it later. Right now, he needed to get Mara out of that fucking house.

"Achilles to team," he said into his mic. "You have permission to engage. Go in hot."

Chapter Sixteen

The door blasted inward with a small explosion. Mara slammed her eyes shut against the blinding flash, and the other three women let out deafening screams. She wrenched her hair from a stunned Olesea's grasp as two men in white filed into the house, rifles aimed. One shouted commands at Olesea in Russian. The other moved toward Mara with single-minded intent in his shadowed eyes.

No. No, dammit. She was not going to Dubai. This was not how it was going to end for her. She knocked the bucket of dirty water into his path, then bolted toward the kitchen at the back of the house, intent on getting her hands on the butcher knife she'd been planning to steal since she first saw it, the one that Olesea hung right out in the open by the kitchen sink like a taunt. The knife wouldn't do her a lick of good if one of the white-clad men decided to shoot her, but it didn't matter. She needed a weapon. She would fight for her baby until the very last breath left her lungs—and then she'd come back and haunt her murderer's ass.

A third man caught her around the waist just on the other

side of the kitchen door. She kicked and screamed and clawed at his white-and-gray-paint-smeared face, but his hard arms only tightened around her.

The man chasing her skidded to a stop. "Got her?"

"Yeah. Go help the others, Ian. We have incoming," the man holding her responded, and every muscle in her body went to water at the sound of his voice. She sagged, her legs no longer able to hold her upright. As he easily took her weight and scooped her up in his arms, his hood fell off his head.

Travis. Under all of that war paint and white winter gear, it really was him. He'd found her.

"You cut your hair." Such a stupid thing to say, but it was the first thing that popped into her dazed mind. She lifted a hand and rubbed her palm over the prickly dark blond stubble. His eyes closed and the room, the noise from the rest of the house—it all vanished with his soft exhale. It was just the two of them in that moment. The outside cold clung to his coat, but she huddled closer until her nose touched the bare skin of his neck. Oh, his scent. Sandalwood and a dark, warm spice. She breathed it in and wanted to hold it—hold him—inside her forever.

Tears blurred her vision. "Travis..."

He said nothing, but his arms tightened around her in a fierce hug, and for the first time since Zaryanko took them captive, she felt truly safe.

All too soon, reality crashed through their tender moment. Gunshots thudded into the kitchen door, splintering the wood. Someone screamed in agony and other voices from men she didn't know shouted in Russian. No English, though. Where were all of Travis's men?

He lowered her to her feet the exact moment the kitchen door banged open, and Zaryanko stumbled to a halt in front of them.

Mara felt the muscles in Travis's arm tighten to steel

cables under her hands. He reached into an inside pocket under his white coat.

Zaryanko's gun, which had lowered a little in surprise at the sight of them, came up again. "Don't move!"

Travis produced a ripped photo and held the two pieces between his gloved fingers like playing cards. "Did you send someone to ransack my house?" His voice took on a dark edge she'd never heard from anyone before, as sharp and lethal as any blade.

Zaryanko's gaze flicked to the photo, but he dismissed it with a sneer. "So you came back for your little whore after all?"

Travis waved the photo, his hand trembling a little. "Did. You. Do. This?"

Zaryanko lowered the pistol a fraction and stared at him like he'd lost his mind. Maybe he had. Mara was starting to fear it herself and rubbed a hand soothingly up and down his arm.

"Travis, it hardly matters right now."

"It matters," he said through his teeth.

"Why?"

"If he's responsible, I'm going to kill him."

She flinched at the implacable way he said those words, as if killing were a matter of fact, not of choice. And, again, she saw him standing over Urban's body in New Mexico. He'd seemed genuinely remorseful for what he'd done—but that Travis and this one were two totally different people. This Travis looked intent on murder. And, yes, Zaryanko deserved to be punished for his crimes, but she did *not* want to see Travis be his judge, jury, and executioner.

"Please, don't," she whispered, and that seemed to finally break through whatever rage had enthralled him. He dropped the photo like it had caught fire and Mara caught the two pieces of it, partly out of curiosity, partly because it seemed to mean so much to him.

"You've become more trouble than you're worth," Zaryanko muttered and raised his gun again.

Travis pushed her behind his body. She stumbled at the force of his shove and grabbed his coat to catch herself just as Zaryanko's gun exploded. She held her breath and waited to feel the impact slam through Travis's body into hers, but nothing happened. Stunned, she lifted her face from his shoulder and looked around. Her tug on Travis's coat had thrown him off balance enough that the bullet had streaked harmlessly by him and burrowed into the wall, sending plaster dust into the air.

Time stilled, caught in a tableau of violence. It was like slo-mo in the movies, except everyone moved at once and it probably all happened within five heartbeats. Travis pushed her aside and raised his own weapon. Zaryanko's eyes rounded and he tried to level his gun again, but he was too slow. Far too slow. The quick one-two blast of Travis's rifle left her ears ringing. Two holes opened up close together on Zaryanko's shirt, and, with plaster dust falling like a fine snow, he dropped to the floor. Just like that, her kidnapper was dead.

Her nightmare was over.

It almost seemed impossible.

Rifle still aimed, Travis walked toward the obviously dead body and grabbed Zaryanko's pistol, which had slid across the floor when he dropped it. Travis holstered it on his leg, then crossed to the door. Took a breath, held it, and swung out into the hall, leading with his rifle.

A moment later, she heard him say, "Clear," and he came back to the door. He held out a hand to her but didn't stop scanning the hallway. "You okay to walk?"

She nodded and tried not to look at Zaryanko's body as she accepted his hand and followed him out of the kitchen.

"I'm okay."

"You're lucky." He stepped over another body sprawled across the hallway—Olesea, her gray hair matted with blood—then held up a fist in a halt gesture and checked around the next corner into another room.

"It's clear, but stay behind me." He took hold of her wrist in a firm grip. "I'm not risking you or your baby again."

Your baby.

Not *my baby.* Not even *our baby.*

Your baby.

Mara's heart sank. "Well, I guess that answers that question."

His head never stopped moving, scanning for threats. "What question?"

"How you feel about our baby."

He said nothing and stopped at the front door, which sat propped open. Cold outside air wafted into the foyer, and a shiver raised goose bumps on her bare arms.

"Coming out?" he called.

"Coming out," someone answered.

Shouldering his rifle, he scooped her into his arms again and whisked her through the door into the swirling snow. Over his shoulder, she caught glimpses of two other men dressed in the same white-and-gray camouflage as him, their faces covered with paint. Both men also carried rifles and brought up the rear, always scanning, scanning, scanning for threats. Three more bodies stained the snow in the yard red.

Travis bundled her into the back of a cargo van with one of the two men from his team, then left without so much as a word of good-bye. A second later, two doors slammed shut up front, and the van rumbled to life. She craned her neck to see who sat in the driver's seat, but a hand reached out and shut the mini door in the steel partition that separated the front from the van's cargo area.

Travis's hand. Shutting her out. Again.

She tried to convince herself that it didn't hurt. Failed miserably. Why was he shutting her out?

"Mara," the man beside her said in a comforting, twangy drawl that reminded her of home. He removed his ski mask, and his dark hair stuck up in sweaty spikes. His eyes were a warm, caring brown filled with relief—so unlike the snowy gray of Travis's.

"Jesse!" She let the tears come and flung herself at him. His arms felt good around her, strong and safe, like a little bit of home.

"Hey, buttercup." He held her tighter for a moment, then set her back at arm's length and rubbed his thumb gently over her bruised cheek. "We'll be stopping to pick up the rest of the team in a minute. They took the three women from the house to safety down in the village. But before they get back I wanna look you over, okay? Make sure you're not injured."

"I'm not," she said but lay down on the pallet he indicated anyway, because she knew he wouldn't relax until he'd seen for himself. "Have you spoken to my parents?"

Jesse's brows slammed together and he opened his mouth as if about to say something, but then he shook his head and started his exam with her vital signs. "Does anything hurt?"

"My heart." Her eyes filled with tears again. She couldn't help it, but she'd be damned if she let any more fall. "Is Travis always…" *Cold. Calculating. Unfeeling. Grim.* She couldn't settle on the right adjective and trailed off.

"Quinn?" Jesse scowled. "Yeah, he's always everything you're thinking."

Mara turned her head away on the makeshift pillow as he performed the physical exam on her. "I'm such a fool."

"Love does that to people." When she blinked up at him, his lips quirked in a self-deprecating smile. "Don't deny it. You know me—I've fallen enough times myself to know love when I see it."

"I'm not denying it, but it doesn't matter how I feel."

"You're probably right. Quinn's goin' to do what he's goin' to do. I suppose it won't matter if I tell ya he's absolutely the wrong man for you."

"No. It won't matter."

"Figures." He smiled down at her. "Little Mara's goin' to do what little Mara's goin' to do. Isn't that what Uncle Jackson always said about you?"

"Yeah." She huffed out a laugh and rested her hands on her stomach. "But I think Daddy would be surprised to see I'm not so little anymore."

"Yeah, I bet so. Surprised the hell outta me when I found out."

"I'm sorry I didn't tell you."

He waved a hand. "Nah, don't be. I know why you were afraid to. And you were right to be worried. I've been actin' like a jackass about it—as Lanie has delighted in tellin' me throughout this whole mission."

"Lanie's here?" She started to get up, but he gently held her still.

"Yes, she's with the rest of the team. You'll see her when we stop. May I?" He indicated her stomach, and she nodded. He lifted her shirt and did a quick exam, then set his hand reverently on her belly. "Tell me the truth now. Do you feel okay?"

She nodded. "I'm fine. Banged up, tired. Hungry," she added with a little laugh when her stomach gave a mighty growl.

Jesse smiled. "I can do somethin' 'bout that. How do you feel about MREs?" He reached into one of the packs lining the wall and grabbed a small pouch. "Let's see what we got here. Apple-cinnamon oatmeal. Sound good?"

"Sounds amazing, and I'm sure the baby will appreciate

it, too. I…am a little worried," she admitted because, well, this was Jesse. She could tell him anything without facing judgment—something she'd forgotten about him until just now. "I haven't eaten in days, and I've been really nauseous since yesterday morning."

He started heating the oatmeal for her, then opened the other packages included in the kit. "Sounds like normal morning sickness, but we'll get you checked out as soon as we're back in friendly territory."

"Thank you." She pulled her shirt down over her belly and accepted the toaster pastry he handed her. She was fairly certain it was the most wonderful thing she'd ever tasted, especially when she washed it down with a swig of the fruit punch drink he handed her next. Then came the oatmeal, and crackers with peanut butter, and applesauce. By the time the van rolled to a stop, she'd demolished it all and was sipping from a foam cup of cocoa.

Someone pounded on the back of the van and Jesse called, "One minute." He turned to her and enclosed his hands around hers on the cup. "Mara, listen. I'm only goin' to say this once, because it'll hurt like hell to admit."

She set down the cocoa and held his gaze. "Okay. I'm listening."

He drew in a breath and let it out in a sigh. "I wasn't happy about what happened between you and Quinn. I'm still not. Quinn is not the kind of guy I want for my baby cousin."

"What if he's the kind of guy I want?"

"Thought you might say that. And when I saw the way you looked at him back there… Well, I realized it's not my decision to make, is it?"

"No," she said as gently as she could, because she knew her bluntness would sting. "I know you mean well, Jesse. You and my brother both, but you've always been too protective. Between you two always worrying and Ramon always dictating, I haven't been able to breathe. That's part of the reason this happened. I just wanted…freedom, and Travis offered me that, even if it was for a short time."

"Yeah." He glanced away, obviously uncomfortable. "Thing is, I like Quinn, but I saw a lot of guys like him when I was with the army. Burned out, but they keep doin' the job until they completely flame out or get themselves killed because they have nothin' else. Quinn's right on the edge of that. He needs somethin' to care about."

Her heart gave a hard thump. "Like?"

Jesse smiled a little and flattened one hand on her belly again. "You have that somethin' right here. If you really do love him, you won't let him push you and the little one away. He needs you both if he has any hope of making it."

Relief surged through Mara, leaving her light-headed and nearly giddy. Her arms and legs even felt light, as if her shackles were truly broken and she was finally free to make her own decisions for the very first time in her adult life. No matter what she did, whatever mistakes she made, Jesse and her father's side of the family would always love her. So would her brother. And her stepdad had never loved her to begin with, so why waste energy trying to please him? Or her mother, who was too weak to stand up to Ramon's tyranny?

Mara wrapped her arms around her cousin and buried her face in the front of his coat. There were so many things she wanted to say to him. Instead, all that came out of her mouth was a teasing, "You love Travis, too, don't you?"

Jesse scoffed and pushed her back at arm's length. "Horrified" was the only word to describe his expression. "Straight guys don't love each other."

"Yeah, sure you don't." She smiled and stole his cowboy hat off his head, setting it on her own. "How about we let the rest of the team in now? I'm sure they're freezing, and I want to see Lanie."

Chapter Seventeen

Near the Transnistria-Ukraine border

Without the winter sun's meager rays and no cloud cover to speak of, the night's temp plummeted from cold to freeze your balls off. When Quinn slid from driver's side of the van, the cold ripped the air from his lungs like a punch to the gut and seared the insides of his nostrils. Christ. He'd considered abandoning the van here and humping it the rest of the way to the plane, but no way would he make Mara stay out in this weather for any extended period of time. She didn't have the right gear, they were still a good ten klicks from the plane, and it'd take far too long to make that walk on foot.

Not to mention, the closer they got to the Transnistria-Ukraine border, the more warning alarms clanged inside his mind. He rubbed his temple, only now realizing how much his fucking head hurt. The strain of the last few days was taking its toll. He'd be lucky if he didn't crash and burn before the end of this mission. "Something's wrong."

Gabe, in the passenger seat, glanced over the center

console at him. "You okay?"

"Headache. But that's not what I mean. Garcia should have answered our radio calls by now."

Gabe nodded. "Yeah. I was thinking the same thing." He jerked his chin toward the back of the van. "Go check on Mara—I know you want to, so don't deny it—and see if any of the guys are injured. I'll try Garcia again."

Quinn shut the door and walked the length of the vehicle, boots crunching over the ground, too loud in the winter night. Damn snow. It made staying covert difficult. Might as well wave a giant red flag and scream, "Here we are!" Of course, that worked both ways, and the woods surrounding the rarely used road were silent.

They were safe. For now.

He joined the guys, who spilled out of the van's back end like clowns from a subcompact. "Anyone injured?"

"Had worse," Seth said.

Quinn studied each of them as they exited the van. Seth had a wide streak of blood smeared on his coat under his left arm, but whether it belonged to him or one of Zaryanko's dead thugs was anyone's guess. Everyone else seemed no worse for wear, except for Jean-Luc, who scowled as if someone had pissed in his cornflakes.

"You hurt?" Quinn asked.

"No. But I'm freezing to death. This cold is ungodly." He crossed his arms over his chest and stomped his feet a couple times, but if anything, the crunching of his boots on the snow only made him look more unhappy.

"Get over it." Ian blew on the ends of his fingers. He always cut off the tips of his gloves, leaving his fingers free so that he could handle sensitive items—like bombs. Everything the EOD tech did, in some way, shape, or form, related back to making things go boom. "We're all cold."

Gabe joined them. "Not everywhere can be like the

bayou, Cajun."

"And that's a damn shame," Jean-Luc said and his breath clouded in the air. "See? Look at that! I'm making freaking clouds. That's not natural. I'm telling ya. Ungodly."

Jesse was the last to leave the van. He hopped out, took off his Stetson, ran a hand through his hair, then resettled the hat on his head. He'd taken off his snowsuit and wore nothing but black cargo pants and a denim jacket over a thermal undershirt.

"Aw, c'mon. This ain't nothin' but T-shirt weather, Cajun."

If looks could kill, Jesse would have died in a hundred brutal ways from the glare Jean-Luc sent him.

Quinn had to admit Jean-Luc had a point. The temperature hovered somewhere in the single digits if he had to guess. Add in the wind chill and it made for a wicked shock to the system, even for someone as hardened against the cold as him.

Was Mara warm enough?

He stole a glance inside the van. She lay on a pallet underneath a survival blanket, curled around her belly like she was trying to protect it. So deep asleep she didn't even twitch at the cold seeping in from the open door.

A hand landed on his shoulder, and he glanced over in surprise at Jesse.

"She's goin' to be fine," the medic assured. "She's healthy. Best I can tell, the baby's healthy."

Right. Okay. Quinn shrugged out of Jesse's grip and shut the van's door to keep the heat inside. He turned to the group. "Has anyone had luck raising Garcia on the radio?"

They all shook their heads.

"Damn." Quinn glanced at Gabe. "What do you think?"

"This is your game, Q. Your play. Your call."

He shut his eyes and, frustrated, scrubbed at his face

with both hands. He really hated being in command. Taking orders was so much easier. When you're given orders, you follow them to the best of your ability. Black-and-white. Simple. Issuing those orders? Not so simple. There were so many varying shades and levels of gray murkiness involved. He had to consider the team's safety. Mara's safety. Even freaking ethics came into play—right versus wrong and all that. But how did a guy know when he was right? It was enough to make his head pound if he allowed it.

Quinn shoved aside all thoughts of a headache even as one wrenched at the nerves behind his eyes. He held out a hand to the group. "Someone give me a radio."

He tried Garcia one last time. Got a whole lot of nothing but radio silence.

Quinn clicked off the radio and tapped the handheld against his palm a couple times in thought. Maybe he was paranoid. Probably he was paranoid—another lasting gift from the head trauma.

But…

He looked at the van, pictured Mara in there, curled up under the Mylar blanket, hugging her belly. Well, dammit, he had a right to a bit of paranoia. He wasn't about to put Mara or the baby in any kind of danger.

Then again, keeping them out in this cold longer than necessary wasn't exactly safe, either.

"Ruble for your thoughts?" Jean-Luc said.

"Nah." Quinn jammed the radio into one of his inside jacket pockets. "They're not worth even that. How do you guys feel about this?"

"It fucking stinks," Ian said.

Seth nodded. "Something's not right."

"I'm getting me all kinds of bad feelings about this," Jean-Luc said.

Well, at least he wasn't alone in his paranoia. And the

longer they stood here discussing it, the more the idea of taking Mara to the rally point sat like a lump of slimy coal in his gut. "So, what are our options?"

"Play it safe," Harvard said. "Zaryanko's dead, yeah, but Liam is out there. Let's take Mara to friendly territory, then come back for Garcia. If he's in trouble, then he has been since we left and can handle himself for another day."

"And where precisely do we find friendly territory?" Seth asked. "We're in the black hole of Europe."

"There's a temporary air force base in Constanta, Romania, set up to help with the transition of American forces out of Afghanistan," Harvard said and searched in his bag for a map. He spread it on the side of the van and found his glasses in the front pocket of his coat. After a moment's study, he indicated a city on the coast of the Black Sea. "Here. About five hundred klicks southwest of our position. We'd be looking at a sixteen-hour drive round-trip and it'd mean crossing two borders: into Moldova, which is going to be a problem, and then into Romania."

"Shit." Quinn stared up at the sky, at the vast expanse of night dotted with tiny shimmers of starlight and the bright, nearly full moon. The blows just kept coming. Had to wonder if they'd ever stop. "I'm not comfortable with that plan. There's something I haven't told you guys yet. In New Mexico, I killed the guy who abducted Mara." He lowered his gaze until he found Gabe. "It was Todd Urban."

"What?" Gabe said and for maybe the first time ever, his expression showed pure shock. "Urban abducted Mara? Are you sure?"

"Yeah."

Harvard looked back and forth between them. "Who's Todd Urban?"

"A SEAL," Quinn said and looked at the rest of the team. "I killed an active-duty SEAL, a former teammate."

Silence.

Finally, Jesse muttered, "Dayam. That's going to be a problem."

"We can't trust anyone, guys. A week ago, I would have told you Todd Urban was one of the best men I knew, but he was in league with Zaryanko." He remembered the way his gut had churned at the revelation. *He* was the reason Mara had been kidnapped, not her stepfather's crooked dealings with the wrong people like he'd first assumed. Somehow, this all centered on him, and he'd been the one to put her in danger by showing up at her house.

Quinn glanced toward the van and tamped down the urge to check on her again. He had a job to do if he wanted to keep her safe, and part of that job would be to make her hate him so she'd walk away and never look back. The thought sent shards of ice spearing through his chest, but he'd do it if it meant keeping her safe.

Marcus finally broke the silence. "There's always a chance Garcia's radio just crapped out on him. Mine did and so did Ian's. For all we know, Garcia could still be waiting for us and we're just a bunch of assholes who don't like trusting the newcomer."

"I can vouch for that," Seth said. "I mean, you guys full-on hazed me, for fuck's sake."

"Okay," Quinn said slowly. "What do you suggest, then? I'm not taking Mara anywhere near the plane unless we know for sure it hasn't been compromised."

"Recon," Seth said. "Send out an advance team to make sure all is clear. And if it's not safe…" He opened the back door of the van and grabbed his rifle from the floor. "Then let's make it safe."

"Charge recklessly into the fray with nothing but a hope and a prayer?" Jean-Luc asked.

Seth held up his rifle. "And an AK-47."

"You're crazy." Jean-Luc grinned and clapped him on the shoulder. "I love that about you, *mon ami*."

"I'm with Seth on this one," Jesse said.

"Me, too," Ian said. "My fucking dog was on that plane. I want him back."

Everyone else agreed, and Harvard threw up his arms. "Guess I'm vetoed."

"So you in or out?" Quinn asked.

Harvard heaved a weary sigh. "You know I'd follow you and Gabe into the lowest pits of hell. I'm in."

"All right, let's do it." Quinn opened the van's door wider and leaned in, taking the opportunity to check on Mara. Still out cold. His heart lurched at the sight of her pale face so still with sleep.

"We'll get you home, sweetheart," he promised under his breath, then grabbed the straps of several more AKs and hauled them out. "Who's going with me?"

"I will," Jesse and Ian said at the same time and looked at each other with almost identical sneers of disgust.

Quinn bit back a groan. Those two. When would they realize that they got along like fire and nitro precisely because they were, like fire and nitro, the same explosion waiting to happen, packaged in two different forms?

"Jesse, you're the best tracker out of all of us, so you should come with Gabe and me." When Ian scowled, he added, "And if we have a chance to get Tank back, we'll take it. He's a member of this team, too, and we won't leave him behind, but right now, I want you here to protect Mara. Nobody can beat you at hand-to-hand."

After a long moment, Ian gave a curt nod. "Nobody will touch her on my watch."

"Thank you."

"I'm coming, too," Lanie said.

Jesse opened his mouth to protest, but Quinn didn't give

him a chance. He'd seen the Texas Ranger in action, and she would be nothing but an asset in the field. "Good. Jean-Luc, Seth, Marcus, Harvard—you guys stay behind with Ian. If you don't hear from us by morning, or feel this position is compromised, get out of here. Follow Harvard's plan and take Mara to Romania."

Chapter Eighteen

The airfield was empty.

No wonder Garcia wasn't answering their radio calls. He wasn't fucking there.

Quinn stepped out onto the tarmac from the cover of the forest and did a quick safety check of the area. Found nothing. Cursing under his breath, he leaned against the ruins of an old storage shed as he heard Gabe, then Jesse, and finally Lanie confirm what he'd known as soon as they approached the field.

Clear.

Abandoned.

Jesse came up beside him. "Goddammit. I had a bad feelin' about Garcia from the start. He was too quiet."

"Then why didn't you say anything when we hired him?"

"After the way Gabe went all papa bear when you brought Seth onto the team and I didn't think that was a good idea? Nah. I was keepin' my mouth shut."

Gabe appeared around the side of the building and scoffed. "Papa bear?"

Jesse puffed up his chest and deepened his voice. "'There'll be no hazing of every new guy I bring onto this team. Is that understood, gentlemen?'"

"I don't sound like that," Gabe said.

"Actually..." Lanie said as she joined them. "You kinda do."

He pointed a finger at her. "Watch it. They're going to haze your ass when we get home, and for that, I'm not stopping them."

"You're assuming a lot there, Bristow. Who says I even want to stay in your dysfunctional little boys' club when we get home?"

Quinn got that they were just blowing off steam. They were all as frustrated and exhausted and cold as he was. Hell, any other time, in any other situation, he might've been joking with them—but this wasn't any other situation, and he couldn't find it in himself to be amused by the banter. In fact, the only thing he felt was a rising surge of anger that all but choked him.

"Fuck!" He ripped off his snow mask and threw it on the ground, then felt stupid for the uncharacteristic outburst when everyone went silent. He dragged his hands over his head and slid down the wall, his exhaustion weighing him down as much as the gear on his back. "Fuck Garcia. And fuck Cam Wilde for recommending him."

"Cam couldn't have known the guy would leave us hanging like this," Gabe said, ever the voice of reason. "We'll come up with a new plan."

"No." Quinn sucked in a breath and stood. "Let's go with Harvard's plan. We'll take Mara to the air force base in Romania."

"Quinn, we don't know how far this thing reaches. Urban—"

"Is dead. I killed him, took away a husband and a father

from a family I've had dinner with. I have to face up to that."

Gabe pulled off his mask and ran a hand through his hair. "Yeah, you killed him. And, yeah, I know it's eating you up. But Urban was corrupt—"

"Do we know that?" Quinn demanded. "Really? All we have to go on is Zaryanko's word, and that bastard was a liar."

"You said Urban tried to kill you," Gabe pointed out.

"But I'm not convinced it wasn't a case of mistaken identity."

Lanie spoke up. "We also have Mara's statement that Urban was the man who abducted her."

"For all we know, he had a damn good reason for it. But you're missing the point. Even if he was corrupt, I can't condemn the entire military for one man's actions. Our priority is Mara's safety. That's it. And the safest place for her right now is an American military base." When he got nothing but stubborn silence from Gabe, he turned to Jesse. "C'mon, you want Mara safe just as much as I do, and you could give a fuck what happens to me. So why aren't you backing me up here?"

Jesse sighed heavily. "Way I see it, the air force base is our only option."

"Thank you. Finally someone with some sense," Quinn muttered.

Jesse grabbed his shoulder hard enough that he had no choice but to face the medic. "But don't you dare say I don't give a fuck about what happens to you. Bein' angry with you is not the same thing as wantin' you dead. Mara's my family by blood, but everyone on this team—including you—is my family by choice."

Quinn blinked. Jesse considered him family? That was... He tried to think of something to say in reply and came up empty.

But suddenly Jesse's anger made a hell of a lot of sense. It hadn't been about Quinn sleeping with Mara or even about the pregnancy. It had been about betrayal. Jesse had felt betrayed and…

Man. He had a shit ton of amends to make when this was over.

Jesse let go and stepped back. "So," he said after an awkward beat. "You go with us as far as Romania, then disappear. Maybe call Tucker Quentin for help or whatever, but you're not settin' foot on the base. Even if I have to hog-tie you, you're not goin'. Got me?"

"Good idea," Gabe said. "That's—"

The crunch of a boot on the snow behind the shed caught Quinn and Gabe's attention simultaneously. They both spun, weapons raised, and the shock of recognition almost made Quinn lower his. Four men stepped out behind the shed, and there was no doubt in his mind—at least three of these guys were SEALs. The fourth man moved like he had some military training but was no longer comfortable in the field.

The leader of the team was shouting, "Weapons down! Hands up! Put your fucking weapons down!"

Another shock of recognition. Christ. They weren't just any SEALs. They were from Team Ten. They were friends. Quinn glanced at Gabe, who nodded.

Right. What other choice did they have at this point?

Together, they laid their weapons on the tarmac and raised their hands. Jesse and Lanie hesitated, then followed suit. The leader motioned for his men to secure the weapons.

"Hey, Bauer," Quinn said. "Long time."

Edward Bauer didn't so much as flinch at the sound of his name, nor did he lower his own weapon. "Quinn. You know you have to come with us, so let's make this easy."

The little hairs on the back of Quinn's neck prickled. This wasn't right. No way was this a sanctioned mission. "Nah. Easy's not in my vocabulary. Wanna tell me why they'd send you after me?"

"Urban was one of ours."

"Urban was corrupt," Gabe said, then froze as the fourth guy stepped forward. His eyes narrowed. "What the hell are you doing here?"

The guy pointed his weapon at Gabe and fired.

Twice. In the chest.

At the same time, Bauer spun and shot at Jesse and Lanie, grazing them both.

Quinn didn't have time to process the shock and horror as Gabe collapsed face-first into the snow. He could only act on his instincts, and his instincts were screaming for him to get the hell back to Mara at all costs, because Urban hadn't been the only corrupt SEAL on Team Ten and who knew how many others were involved?

Jesse must have been thinking along the same lines because, despite the bleeding wound in his shoulder, he lunged at Bauer. "Quinn, go!"

Lanie followed his lead and went for her weapon. She got off a lucky shot as one of the other SEALs charged her, and he went down. Still, the odds were not in their favor.

Quinn ducked, just missing a bullet from the same man who had shot Gabe. He scooped up his weapon and returned fire, but the coward ran.

Fucking *ran*. No way that guy was a SEAL, but Gabe had recognized him, so who the hell was he? Quinn wanted to give chase. The asshole deserved a bullet for every one he'd put in Gabe—

Gabe.

Christ. He couldn't leave him just lying here, bleeding out in the snow. Wouldn't do it. He watched the shooter disappear, then swung his weapon toward Bauer, squeezing off several rounds. Bauer retreated into the tree line and returned fire, the bullets hitting the ground way too close to

Gabe's head. Cursing, Quinn grabbed Gabe's legs and pulled him toward the cover of the shed.

"No," Gabe said through clenched teeth. "No, no, no. Stop. Stop. Stop."

He rolled his best friend over. Oh, Christ. Blood. There was too much of it spreading across the front of Gabe's chest, the bright red a gory contrast against his winter camouflage jacket. If he didn't get medical help fast, he was not going to make it.

"Okay. Okay. We're covered now. Where you hit?" As the firefight abruptly ceased, plunging the airfield into a hair-raising silence, Quinn dropped to his knees and pulled apart the front of Gabe's coat. He didn't have the level of medical training Jesse had, but he had enough to know he didn't have the skill to treat this wound. The first bullet had impacted Gabe's vest and spun him just enough that the second bullet tore into the unprotected area under his arm. Quinn could stop the external bleeding, but there was no way of fixing the internal damage without surgery.

And without surgery, the wound was fatal.

Still, he had to do something.

He found the case of tampons he'd started carrying since Jesse told him they worked better than combat gauze to stop bleeding. Ripped open one of the packages and pressed the bullet-shaped cotton into the wound.

Gabe groaned. "Quinn. Get—outta here. Mara—the team—" He fumbled in his leg pocket and brought out two envelopes, thrust them at Quinn's chest. "Go. That's—order."

He knew what they were without looking—good-bye letters to Gabe's wife and brother. No. That wasn't happening. Not today. Not ever. He clasped Gabe's hand, gave it a hard squeeze. "I'll be giving these back to you later."

Gabe's smile was weak and bloodstained. And in that moment, they both realized he was lying. Gabe was already fading, his breathing labored. If he didn't get to a hospital fast, he wasn't going to make it.

"Keep—Au-Audrey—safe for me."

"I will. Until you heal." Quinn tucked the notes into a pocket. He glanced around, searching for Lanie and Jesse, and spotted movement in the woods. Someone had called in reinforcements. Man, they could do with some of that themselves.

Holding his hand over Gabe's wound, he found his phone in his pocket. No signal. Fucking figured.

The crunch of a boot on the snow had him swinging his weapon up in an automatic reaction. Jesse and Lanie all but dragged each other behind the meager cover of the shed.

"Friendly," Jesse croaked.

Quinn lowered his rifle. "Sitrep?"

"We took one out, wounded another. They retreated into the woods. No doubt waitin' for reinforcements. They'll have us pinned down before long. We need to move now." Jesse straightened away from Lanie and made sure she was steady on her feet before kneeling to examine Gabe's wound. His jaw tightened. Quinn saw exactly what he'd feared in the medic's eyes. They couldn't move Gabe anywhere but to a hospital. If he'd even make it that far.

"Take over here. Do what you can." When Jesse's hand replaced the pressure of his own on the wound, he stood. "They want me. If I turn myself over—"

Lanie shook her head. "We've *seen* them. They're not going to let us go."

"She's right," Jesse said. "Our best chance is you. Go warn the others, call Tuc Quentin for backup, and make sure Mara's safe. We'll take care of Gabe."

Mara.

He had to go back to her.

Quinn squeezed Gabe's hand again to draw his attention,

only to realize the big guy had gone unresponsive. His chest constricted and leaving them was the hardest thing he'd ever done, but Jesse was right. Someone had to go now or none of them would survive this, and Gabe needed Jesse to stay.

"Go," Lanie said and readied her rifle. "I'll cover you."

Quinn took one last look at the man who was more like a brother to him than a friend, motionless in the snow with a red stain spreading beneath him. That wasn't going to be the final image he had of Gabe. Audrey was not going to lose her husband, and Raffi Bristow was not going to lose his hero big brother.

Hang on, buddy. I'm bringing back help. You just hang on a little longer.

"Go!" Lanie said again and sprayed bullets into the woods.

Chapter Nineteen

Mara woke to an urgent need to relieve her bladder and realized she was alone. When she fell asleep, she'd been in the midst of strong, capable men, all of them fussing over her like she was someone important. Even Ian had scrambled to make her comfortable by giving her a leather motorcycle jacket from his pack. Going by the way Jean-Luc and Marcus started mercilessly teasing him about it afterward, the act of kindness must have been very uncharacteristic. She had to remember to give him a thank-you hug when she returned the jacket. He looked like a man who had received too few hugs in his life.

Crammed into the van with them, she had felt as secure as she could without being tucked into Travis's arms and soon found that she could no longer keep her eyes open. She had drifted off to the sounds of their voices joking and laughing, congratulating each other on a mission well done.

But now the van was silent, empty, and for those foggy moments between sleep and full wakefulness, she panicked that it had all been a dream. Lanie and Jesse both hovering like mother hens. Jean-Luc making her laugh with that delicious Cajun accent. Sad-eyed Ian, so willing to give up his jacket. Affable Marcus, sweet Harvard, quiet Seth…

Had her imagination conjured them all?

And Travis…?

No. His arms had felt real and solid around her for those too-brief moments he'd held her in Olesea's kitchen. And his cruel words as he led her to safety still hurt too much.

Your baby.

Well, she thought as she sat up and pushed her tangled hair out of her eyes with both hands. If that was the way he wanted it to be, fine. Her baby. Nobody else's.

Mara glanced around the van, hoping to find that one of the men had had the foresight to grab her tennis shoes from the foyer in Olesea's house. Seeing as she was barefoot, she couldn't very well walk out into the snow. She saw nothing except a discarded snow camouflage outfit. Between Ian's jacket and the silver Mylar blanket someone had draped over her, she was warm enough, but one look at the van's windows told her how cold it was outside. Fog from the heater and her breath had iced the windows and crystalline spiderwebs glittered across the glass in the moonlight. It would have been pretty if it wasn't so potentially deadly. She pulled on the white camouflage coat over Ian's jacket and wiggled into the pants. A born and bred Texan, she wasn't used to this kind of cold. The more layers, the better. Now if only she could find something for her feet—

She pushed aside someone's pack and found what she'd been hoping for. Her tennis shoes. Yes! She stuffed her feet in and tied the laces.

Voices outside the van caught her attention, and she crawled over to the door with the intention of telling Travis or whoever was on the other side that she urgently needed a bathroom.

But the voices…

She stopped before opening the door, her hand on the lever, and a chill clawed over her skin that had nothing to do with the cold. The voices were wrong. American, yes, but where was Jean-Luc's singsong Cajun lilt? Even Travis had a slight blue-collar Baltimore accent that delighted her southern ears when he said "youse" instead of "y'all."

Careful not to make any noise to alert the men outside to her presence, she scraped ice off the window with one nail and peeked out. Jean-Luc, Seth, Harvard, Marcus, and Ian sat on their knees in the snow, their hands raised and locked behind their heads. A group of men stood several feet away with rifles pointed in their direction.

Oh, no. Had Zaryanko's thugs come to take her back? Somehow, that didn't seem right. She'd seen most of his thugs, and none of them had been American. Still, the possibility of it terrified her. She ducked below the window and pressed a hand to her chest, trying to convince her heart that it didn't need to jump out of her throat.

Where was Travis? The rest of his team? Were they hurt—or worse?

No, she wouldn't even think it.

She sucked in a fortifying breath. Okay, she'd come this far. She could handle this, too. She just had to breathe and think…and observe. As much as she didn't want to, she had to look out the window again. Not knowing where they were or what they were doing to the guys was so much worse than watching. She sat up on her knees, lifting her head just enough that she could see through the frosted glass.

One of the men had shouldered his gun, tied Jean-Luc's and Harvard's hands behind their back with zip ties, and was now working on securing Seth's hands. Seth seemed to be hyperventilating and struggled like a wild animal. One of the men whacked him over the head with the butt of his rifle, and he collapsed into the snow.

All of their captors wore snowshoes, the same camouflage as Travis and his team, and the same gray-and-white face paint. For all she could see of their features, they might as well have been abominable snowmen with guns.

Once everyone was secure, the man who had tied them up started walking toward the van. Mara inched away from the door until her back pressed to the steel partition that separated the cargo area from the seats up front. She tried the small lever that would open it.

Locked.

Trapped.

The partition opened suddenly, and a hand clamped over her mouth before she even had the chance to draw in a breath and scream. None too gently, the hand's owner yanked her backward through the partition and threw her into the passenger seat before slamming the door shut and flipping the lock.

"Buckle," Travis ordered and cranked the van's engine. "And stay low."

"W-w-what about the guys?"

He grabbed her by the back of the neck and shoved her head toward her knees. "Ow! Travis—"

"Get down!"

She heard it then. The blast of gunfire. The ping of bullets bouncing off the van's exoskeleton as the wheels spun, searching for traction in the snow. Finally, the van lurched forward, and Travis hit the gas.

God, this couldn't be real. This wasn't the kind of life she lived. She was a veterinary technician who worked not because she had to but because she loved it. She was a daughter who put up with her mother's tyrannical husband out of sheer loyalty. A sister who looked up to her big brother with something close to hero worship. She ran errands and took care of her pets and kept a clean house and stayed in close contact with all of her friends. She'd enjoyed a glass of wine here or there before she'd become pregnant, but she didn't drink to excess. Didn't smoke, had never tried drugs, didn't indulge in any other risky or self-destructive behaviors. She'd led a safe, normal life…

Until Travis Quinn. He had destroyed so much more than her heart when he walked out her door and, suddenly, she didn't think she'd ever be able to forgive him for it.

Squeezing her eyes shut, she hugged her knees and focused on breathing. Just like they taught in birthing classes, which she'd have to register for. And she didn't have a partner. She turned her head enough to look at Travis. Such a strong profile, an angular jaw with a sexy dimple in the center of his chin. He also had dimples on the rare occasions he smiled.

Would the baby have his straight nose? His dimples?

Travis must have sensed her gaze, because he glanced down just as the tears she'd tried so hard to keep at bay overflowed her defenses.

His lips compressed into a thin line, but she saw no softening in his expression. He'd closed down on her at Olesea's, and she doubted he'd ever open up again. And right now, she didn't know if she even wanted him to.

"It's okay," he said stiffly. "We're out of range now."

Slowly, she sat up and stared out the window. Trees and darkness. Up ahead, in the splash of the van's rattling headlights, there was nothing but more darkness, more of the bumpy road. She sniffled and scrubbed away her tears.

"Are you crying because we left the guys?" Travis asked after a long moment of silence.

Disbelief that he even had to ask roared through her. "Yes! And because I want my old life back! And because I'm trapped in the middle of frozen nowhere and I have to pee and I don't have a partner for my birthing class and the baby will have your nose and your dimples and I won't be able to stand it when I see a smile and I'm reminded of you!" She paused for a breath but couldn't seem to stop the tirade now that she'd unleashed it. She glared at him, putting everything she felt into it. Fear. Anger. Pain. So much pain. "And because if I could do one thing in my life over, I'd go back to July and leave you to die of heatstroke in that car in front of my apartment. I really, really hate you, Travis Quinn."

His mouth opened but no sound came out, and he closed it again. He exhaled a breath that, if she didn't know any better, she'd think was a suppressed sob. When he spoke, his voice was a little hoarse. "I know you do, Mara, and I'm sorry for that. As for the rest, I don't know how I can help. Once we're a little farther away, I'll stop to let you pee and—yeah. The…birthing…partner thing, you don't want me for anyway. But don't worry about the guys. They can take care of themselves."

"How can you say that? You just left them there! In the cold, with a bunch of armed men!"

His hands tightened on the steering wheel. "I didn't have a choice. They killed—" His voice broke and she looked over at him again. Dread wrapped icy fingers around her spine at the tortured expression on his normally stoic face.

"Killed who?" Oh, why did she ask that? She didn't want to know. Was terrified to know. What if…?

Travis swallowed hard, his Adam's apple bobbing with the effort of it. "Gabe."

Relief crashed over her with such force she slumped back in the seat. Not Jesse. Or Lanie. Thank God. Then the relief twisted into a dull blade composed of equal parts sorrow and shame that cut deep in the vicinity of her heart. Her cousin and best friend were both alive—as far as she knew—but Gabe…

He had been Travis's best friend, hadn't he?

She reached for his hand, surprised at how cold and stiff his fingers felt on the steering wheel. "What happened?"

He pulled his hand away on the pretense of wiping his eyes. "We were ambushed. We let down our guard and Gabe was shot. He was bleeding out in the snow and instead of taking him to a hospital, I left—" In a burst of emotion fiercer than any she'd ever seen from him, Travis swore and banged his fists against the steering wheel. "What am I supposed to tell his wife? She's going to hate me for not taking care of him like I promised. She's going to…" He trailed off, his outburst hanging in the air like a thick, wet blanket, making it hard to draw a decent breath.

"What about Lanie?" Mara whispered. "Jesse? Are they…?"

"I don't know." He keep his eyes on the road, but she had a feeling his reluctance to look at her had little to do with the driving conditions. "I had to get back to you. I couldn't risk Bauer and his guys sending you back to Zaryanko's people. Or worse."

"And yet you left your men with them."

"My men can take care of themselves," he said with a lot less conviction in his tone than before. "And they all know and accept the possibility of sacrifice. Your safety is our first priority."

Our priority. Not *my priority.*

She reached over and set a hand on his muscled forearm. "We need to go back, Travis. We need to go help your team. Help *Gabe*. If there's still a chance he could be okay—"

"No." His profile was set in stone, not letting even the faintest hint of his thoughts through. He glanced over, and in a passing sliver of moonlight, she thought she saw wetness glimmering on his cheeks. "We can't go back. I'm not willing to risk you."

Claws of pain dug into her heart, and she rubbed at her

chest. “At the expense of your best friend’s life?”

“Yeah,” he said and returned his attention to the road. His voice was raw. “Even at the expense of Gabe’s life.”

Oh God. If he were willing to sacrifice his best friend for her, what else would he sacrifice?

Chapter Twenty

"We'll crash here for the night."

As Travis shifted the van into park, Mara blinked open her gritty eyes and looked around. More darkness, more trees, but the landscape had flattened out while she was trying and failing to sleep. "Where's here?"

"We're still in Transnistria, if that's what you're asking. We can't leave until I figure out how to get us through the border checkpoints into Moldova and then to the air force base in Romania."

"Why not take me to the closest consulate?"

He gave her a dry look before he crawled out of his seat and ducked into the cargo area of the van. "My former teammates are after me. They want me badly enough that they killed my best friend. Do you really think they wouldn't warn any government officials of my presence in their country? If I show my face at a consulate, the marines stationed there will arrest me"—he snapped his fingers—"like that. Someone high up has to be involved in this, too, and then it will only take some paper shuffling to get me where they want me.

Besides, the only embassy I'd be comfortable taking you to is in Bucharest, and the air force base is closer."

She stretched out a crick in her neck before following him. "Won't the air force arrest you?"

"Yeah." Grim lines hardened his mouth as he shook out a sleeping bag from his pack and laid it on top of the pallet she'd slept on earlier. "But the air force is a completely separate entity from the navy. They're less likely to be corrupted by… whoever the hell is behind this."

"The lesser of two evils?"

"Pretty much. At least if I turn myself in to the air force, I might live long enough to set foot on U.S. soil again. Hell, maybe I'll even get a shot at a decent trial."

"Trial for what?"

"For killing Todd Urban."

Outrage seared the lining of her throat. "But you did it to protect me. He kidnapped me!"

Travis pointed a finger at her. "Exactly the reason I need to keep you alive. You're my get-out-of-jail-free card."

"Oh, of course." She snorted in disgust. "Silly me for thinking you'd want me alive because I'm carrying your child. Or, say, because you care about me."

"Dammit, don't make me sound like a heartless asshole."

"I don't need to. You do a good job of sounding heartless all by yourself." She sat down with her back to the wall of the van and ignored his creative cursing. Folding her hands across her belly, she watched him put together a makeshift bed until the silence between them started to weigh on her, pressing down on her lungs, making breathing difficult. "Are you physically incapable of carrying on a genuine, personal conversation?"

Without a word, he grabbed another pack from along the wall and unbuckled a second bedroll. He tossed the second sleeping bag over the first with a lot more force than necessary.

Then he sighed, and his shoulders slumped forward.

"What I said before…it came out wrong." He turned toward her with an expression of complete exasperation. "I do care about you, Mara."

The words sounded like he had to drag them from his throat. Not exactly the romantic declaration she'd fantasized about when he showed up on her doorstep again. God, that felt like a lifetime ago, but it had only been a few days.

"If you truly care, then you have a strange way of showing it."

"It's the only way I know how," he snapped. "If you want to be cuddled, I'm not your guy. I told you, I'm not gentle."

I don't do gentle, Mara.

As much as she hated herself for it, heat crackled over her nerve endings and her nipples tightened against the fabric of her bra at the reminder of the way he'd held her pinned up against her living room wall. "I remember."

In the bright moonlight filtering through the windows, she thought she saw those same heated memories flare in his eyes.

"I do, too." He sucked in a breath, and his gaze dropped to her mouth. "It's one of the few things I haven't forgotten."

But then his gaze dropped lower and settled on her belly and the heat fizzled, replaced with the snowy indifference he had down to an art. He stared at her as if the baby was a potential threat and he had to calculate a strategy to combat it.

"Travis." She reached for his hand and placed his palm over her belly. "This is our baby."

He jolted like she'd electrocuted him and yanked his hand back so fast he whacked his elbow on the wall. He gritted his teeth against a curse and hurried to finish laying out the sleeping bags.

Mara sighed. "You're never going to be okay with this,

are you?"

"Honestly?" He glanced over his shoulder. "I don't know, but it's not on the top of my list of concerns at the moment."

"It should be."

"Yeah, you're probably right about that, but my head's all kinds of fucked up. I really can't imagine what a nice, respectable woman like you ever saw in me." As if he realized he'd said too much, he pulled back the edge of one sleeping bag and motioned for her to lie down. "Now let's get some rest. We're hidden well enough here. We should be safe until morning."

Beyond exhausted, both physically and emotionally, she was past the point of arguing with him and nestled into the makeshift bed. Travis had zipped the two sleeping bags together on three sides, making them into one big sack. He slid in beside her before zipping up the final side and, despite his earlier comment about cuddling, he wrapped his arms around her and drew her against his too-lean body.

"You've lost so much weight."

He grunted. "This changes nothing, Mara. It's only a survival tactic to keep us warm. Body heat."

Mara couldn't put her finger on it, but something in his tone told her he was lying. Maybe he was even trying to convince himself of it. But everything had changed. She had Travis in her life again, and she was safe with him. He was a warrior, born to right wrongs and built to protect. For all of his faults, she knew that to be one undeniable truth about him.

The van's floor was hard under her back, and the blankets were cold, but she didn't care. He threw off a furnace of heat beside her, and it all felt like a small slice of heaven after living in Zaryanko and Olesea's cold world for…

How long?

"What day is it?" she asked. "I've lost track."

"The fourth of January. Well, probably fifth now," Travis said after a second of thought.

Five days. She'd lost nearly a week of her life. "With everything...needing to move and, well, everything else...I completely missed out on the holidays this year. Christmas, New Year's. It's like they never happened."

"They'll come back around," he replied with a complete lack of enthusiasm that she couldn't understand. She'd always adored the holiday season.

"Don't you like Christmas?"

Under her cheek, his shoulder lifted in a half shrug. "I'm not religious."

"Even so, you can still enjoy it as a celebration of life and love and family."

"Family?" He gave a humorless laugh. "Yeah, right, except when you don't have one. Then Christmas is just a day like any other."

She lifted her head to look at him, but he had his head tilted back and his eyes closed and all she could see was his throat and stubbled chin. "Don't you have a family?"

"I did. The SEALs." His throat worked as he tried to swallow. "But they're dead to me now."

"Your parents?"

"The only parents I want to remember are dead."

She thought about the picture he'd had in Olesea's kitchen. The one that had sent him into a rage. "But what about—"

"I'm going to sleep now. You should, too, Mara."

She settled against his shoulder and bit her lip. His reluctance to touch her belly was starting to make sense. He wasn't doing it to be a jerk. It was the self-defense mechanism of a child who never knew what it meant to be part of a family.

But they're dead to me now.

Those words, spoken in that carefully emotionless tone

of his, said so much more about his life than he probably intended. He'd suffered loss the likes of which she couldn't begin to understand. Her father's death when she was eight had left a gaping wound in her heart that refused to close, so how must it feel to have lost everyone you ever cared about?

Jesse had been right. Travis Quinn was a very lonely man.

On impulse, Mara lifted her head again and pressed a kiss to the underside of his chin. He didn't move, didn't acknowledge the affection in any way, but she knew he wasn't asleep yet. His breath caught.

"You're not alone anymore, Travis," she whispered.

Chapter Twenty-One

Airfield near Tiraspol, Transnistria

When Tucker Quentin had financed the redesign of HORNET's jet over the summer, he'd not only included dorm-like rooms for the team, but also a prison barracks down below for any captives they might take on a mission. Although the billionaire head of HORNET's parent company probably hadn't reckoned said prison could be used against them if there was, say, a traitor in their midst.

Fucking Jace Garcia. Jesse had known he was trouble from the second he'd laid eyes on the man. Should have listened to his gut.

The door to the prison slammed open, flooding the room with light, and Jesse raised an arm to shield his eyes. Five big somethings landed in a chaotic heap on the floor between the bunks. Ever since he, Lanie, and Gabe had been dragged aboard the jet, they'd been kept in complete darkness, and his pupils didn't adjust to the change fast enough. He only caught the impression of five men before the room plunged into blackness again.

Lanie stirred. She'd been asleep beside him on the narrow bunk—more out of necessity than any kind of attraction, since Gabe occupied the only other bed.

"Who is it?" she whispered close to his ear.

He set a hand on her shoulder, once again thankful that their captors had removed the zip ties before locking them in. "Not sure."

"Jesse?" Jean-Luc's groggy voice said from the floor. "That you?"

Shit. Jesse stood and blindly groped his way toward Jean-Luc's voice. "Cajun, who's with you?"

Jean-Luc hissed out a breath. "Ian. Seth. Harvard. Marcus. We fucked up. Didn't notice…ambush. Until too late."

"What about Quinn and Mara?"

"Far as I know, he got her—" His voice caught and he inhaled sharply. "Got her away in time."

Jesse's searching hand landed on someone's face and came away wet. Ian? He ran his hands over the rest of the EOD tech and found Ian's left arm twisted at an unnatural angle. "Lanie, I need help. Ian's unconscious and bleedin' bad. Pretty sure his arm's broken."

A few feet in front of him, he felt the air stir. As his eyes adjusted to the darkness again, he could see Jean-Luc limping up the aisle toward him.

"I'll help," Jean-Luc said.

"No. You're injured, too."

"I'm fine."

"Unless 'fine' has been redefined as 'stubborn asshat,' you're not fine. Sit down, Cajun, before you fall down."

Lanie's slim figure appeared next to Jean-Luc and guided him over to the wall. "Let Jesse do the doctoring. It's the only thing he's good at."

"*Merci.*" Jean-Luc groaned as she helped him sit down. "I like ya, Lanie. F'true."

"You like all women, Cajun." She laughed and leaned over him. Jesse heard the unmistakable sound of a smooch and had to ruthlessly beat back an irrational surge of jealousy. But…damn. Why'd she have to kiss freakin' Jean-Luc, of all people? And where had she kissed him?

"Lanie, help me." As soon as the words left his tongue, he knew he'd put too much command in his tone, but fuck it. He couldn't have her standing around kissing one of his teammates while another was possibly bleeding to death on the floor. For once, she didn't argue with him and together they hefted Ian onto the bunk she had abandoned moments ago.

Once they got Ian settled, Lanie went to the door and pounded on it hard enough that she'd probably have a bruise on her hand. The noise must have echoed through the whole plane, because footsteps sounded on the other side, coming down the stairs in a hurry.

"Hey!" she shouted. "We have wounded in here. How about some lights?"

Jesse shook his head. He had to admire her bravado, but it wasn't going to—

The overhead light flashed on, momentarily blinding him.

"Thank you," Lanie said. Whoever was on the other side of the door hesitated for a moment, then the sound of his footsteps faded as he climbed the stairs again.

"Nice job."

She smirked. "It's 'cause I have tits. Guys just can't resist a damsel in distress."

Jesse snorted. "Nobody's goin' to mistake you for a damsel in distress, Delcambre." Now that he had sufficient light, he studied his teammates. Seth's right eye was swollen shut, his lip was split open, and he was sitting against the wall, staring off into space like he was shell-shocked. Which, given his past, he probably was. Ian's complexion rivaled plaster for colorlessness. Jean-Luc, Marcus, and Harvard looked like *Carrie* on prom night, they were all so drenched with blood. Whatever else happened out there, they'd put up a hell of a fight.

Ian's eyes popped open, and he tried to sit up, but Jesse placed a hand on his shoulder to keep him still. "Relax, Reinhardt."

"What happened?" Ian blinked a couple times and lifted a hand to scrub blood out of his eyes.

"We were ambushed," Seth answered, his voice far away.

Ian craned his neck until he could see Seth and scanned the sniper as if looking for serious injuries. "Hey, Hero. Stay with us."

Seth blinked and straightened his shoulders. "Don't call me Hero, asshole."

Ian nodded, apparently satisfied that Seth was okay, and settled against his pillow again. He heaved out a breath before visibly gathering his strength and pushing himself upright. "Has anyone seen Tank?"

"He's here." Jesse motioned to the bed where Gabe lay, still as death. Tank was stretched out beside him, keeping watch.

Ian climbed to his feet and shuffled over, cradling his broken arm to his chest. Tank's tail thumped twice, but it was a halfhearted greeting, and he still didn't move from Gabe's side. Ian rested his good hand on the dog's head and stared down at their boss's pale face for a long time. "How did this happen?"

Jesse scowled over at the door. "Jace Garcia sold us out."

• • •

"*¡Oye!* I'm on your side. Or did you *cabrones* forget that already?"

At the sound of Jace Garcia's annoyed voice, Liam glanced up from the maps spread across the table in front of him. Two of the SEALs muscled Garcia up the plane's steps with their weapons pointed at his back.

"What's going on?" the captain asked, straightening away from the table. Captain Cold, his men called him. It was a fitting nickname, considering whom he'd been willing to kill to get this job done. Even Liam had higher moral standards than that guy.

"We found him sneaking around down by the prisoners," Bauer said and shoved Garcia forward.

Garcia straightened his jacket and snarled something in Spanish, then added in English, "I wasn't sneaking anywhere."

"Yeah?" Liam studied the pilot, but damn, he was starting to feel sluggish, his mind fogged, and he didn't see anything in Garcia's face to arouse suspicion. Was he losing his edge? Probably. It had been a long time since his last hit, and the bag of coke in his coat called to him. He slipped a hand into his pocket, drew it out, and dumped some on the table. Over to his left, Captain Cold made a disdainful sound, and because of that, he took his time with the whole process. Picking a card from his wallet, smoothing the coke out, lining it up. "So what were you doing down there with the prisoners, Garcia?"

The pilot ignored the two weapons pointed at him and stepped forward. "The woman asked for light. I didn't see the harm in turning it on. They have wounded down there."

Liam bent over the table and snorted three lines in succession. The rush was instant, leaving him giddy. He laughed. "Having a change of heart about betraying them?"

"No," Garcia said. "My heart goes where the money is,

and they weren't paying me for this op."

"Mmm." Head buzzing, Liam wiped at his nose and scanned the notes and maps left on the table by the jet's previous occupants. Looked like this area had served as HORNET's makeshift war room. And now he was in command of their nest.

Perfect.

He picked up a notebook with Gabe's handwriting in it and grinned as he flipped through the notes.

Ah, Gabe and Quinn. Those two had always been too meticulous, too honorable, too goddamn good. If the shine on their saintly halos got any brighter, they'd start blinding people.

But halos didn't stop bullets, now did they?

Liam's gut jittered with excitement that the legendary Gabe Bristow was dying down in the belly of the plane at that very moment, trapped with all of his honeybee minions, and there was nothing any of them could do to save him. That was the only reason Liam hadn't ended Gabe's life on the spot. A slow death was much more satisfying.

When this was all over, he'd take Gabe's corpse to Costa Rica and pay the spunky Mrs. Bristow a visit. What grieving widow didn't want to see her husband one last time, after all?

"So what's the plan?" Garcia demanded, and his impatient tone severed the pleasant line of Liam's thoughts, dragging his wandering mind back to the here and now.

"We find Quinn," Captain Cold said.

Liam held up a hand for silence. *He* was in charge here, not the captain. He met the pilot's stony gaze. "Tell me. Why turn on your team?"

Garcia's face remained carefully impassive. "As I said, they weren't paying me. I have no loyalty to them."

"Right." Liam tapped his fingers in quick secession on the table, then pushed out of his chair, because his skin was threatening to jump off his bones if he didn't move. "Nor to me. Should I be worried about that, mate?"

"The only loyalty I have is to myself and my family. But I'll tell you what you can count on, amigo. My well-established sense of self-preservation. I'll do what I have to do to keep breathing, so don't put me in a position where I might stop, because then I'll have to turn on you, too."

Liam clapped. "Now that, I believe. Don't you?" He directed the question to Captain Cold, who said nothing in response, just pulled up a file on his laptop and passed it across the table.

Liam stared down at the screen, waited for his eyes to focus on the jittering words there. "Ah, Garcia, we seem to have your dossier. Ex–air force, huh? And your record has more than a few dings. Ex-cartel, as well? Now that's interesting. Wonder if we share any mutual friends in Mexico?"

Garcia ground his teeth so hard a muscle jumped in his jaw. "I'm not a part of that world anymore."

"Maybe not." He glanced up and pinned the pilot with a glare. "Still, why the fuck would Gabe trust you?"

Garcia shrugged. "I lied. Didn't tell him everything, and he didn't have access to the redacted portions of my file."

"Of course he didn't," Cold said, then added in an undertone, "Should've taken the Pentagon job, Gabe. It would have kept you out of all of this."

If Liam wasn't mistaken, there was a touch of regret in the captain's voice. Maybe Captain Cold wasn't as cold as he wanted to appear? Pity, that. Emotions made people unpredictable. Liam would have to keep an eye on him.

"So," Garcia said after a beat of silence. "What's the plan?"

"It's need to know," Cold said.

The pilot bristled. "And I need to know if you expect me to fly this jet anywhere. I can't just pick it up and throw it like a paper airplane. There are checks to be done…unless you want us to end up in the Atlantic when the engines quit."

Liam smiled. Now Jace Garcia, on the other hand, was all emotion. It made him unpredictable, sure, but not as much as the captain, because a hothead could always be relied upon to be a hothead. "For now, we wait."

Garcia let another beat of silence pass. "That's it?"

"That's it. I know Quinn's been dealing with some… mental issues." He sent an amused sideways glance toward the SEALs. "Isn't that right?"

Bauer's lip lifted in a sneer. "The captain told us to make it look like an accident, so Urban and I made it an accident. Nobody could have known Quinn and Gabe would survive that crash."

Cold made a frustrated sound in the back of his throat, and Liam laughed. "You're all lucky Quinn cracked his skull and his memory loss has worked to your advantage this long. But sooner or later, Quinn *is* going to fuck up. And when he does…" He returned to his seat and reclined back, sighing as satisfaction buzzed through his veins. "I'll finally have the pleasure of killing him."

Chapter Twenty-Two

"You've gotta be fucking kidding me." Quinn slapped the van's dashboard and experienced a sense of déjà vu. The day he met Mara, he'd been beating on his rental car for its faulty air conditioning. "A/C CPR," he'd called it. Except this time, it was more like whole-car CPR. And it wasn't one hundred degrees out. And he was in fucking Transnistria instead of fucking Texas.

Quinn drew a breath and forced a leash of restraint on his frustration. Okay, so the van wouldn't start. Judging by the *tick tick tick* sound when he cranked the key, the battery was dead. He stared out the windshield at the pitted dirt road that had never seen a plow and had little more than faint ruts left by a vehicle long since gone. No way was he getting a jump out here.

On the off chance he had a signal, he searched his many pockets for his phone. He didn't know whom he'd call—maybe Tucker Quentin?—but realized it was a moot point when he turned it on and checked the screen. The phone's battery was still holding up, but there wasn't even half a bar of signal. In the military they'd had an acronym for middle-of-nowhere places like this: BFE. Bumfuck, Egypt.

He rested his head against the steering wheel. Dammit, he should've kept on driving last night, should've gotten Mara as far away from his former teammates as he could. Which had been his general plan until his world started graying around the edges and he feared he'd have another blackout. It tended to happen in times of stress or when he hadn't gotten enough sleep, so pulling over on this secluded road for some shut-eye had seemed like his best option. If he went zombie, where would that leave Mara? Unprotected, that's where, and he would die before he let that happen again.

He turned in his seat and gazed through the open door into the cargo hold. She always slept curled up on her side, tucked around her stomach into the smallest ball she could manage, as if she wanted to retreat from the world even in sleep. That innate vulnerability of hers had been a turn-on at one time. Something in him needed to protect and care for those that couldn't do it for themselves. He was sure a shrink would have a field day dissecting that character trait, but there it was.

The air inside the van was warmer than outside but still cold enough to cause frostbite or worse if they stayed too long. He hated the thought of her traveling anywhere in this weather, but what choice did they have?

He ducked into the cargo hold, knelt beside Mara, and reached for her shoulder, intending to shake her awake. Almost without his permission, his palm skimmed down her arm to her waist instead. He hesitated over her stomach, his hand trembling.

"C'mon," he muttered to himself and wiped his damp palm on his pant leg. He had to get over this ridiculous fear of touching her stomach. It was distracting and…well, ridiculous. Still, he kept picturing scenes from *Alien* and found himself holding his breath as he slowly, oh, so slowly laid his palm across her belly, touching her as if the baby was a bomb that would explode at the slightest jostle.

Mara gave a soft sigh in her sleep, but nothing else happened. He let out his breath in a whoosh that left him a little dizzy.

Her belly was softer than he'd expected and worry chased away the dizziness. Wasn't it supposed to be…Christ, he didn't know. Like a rock? And protruding more? He had no idea what was normal. What if something was wrong? The only thing he knew about this pregnancy shit was the part he'd had a hand in. He'd never even been this close to a pregnant woman before. It was embarrassing to admit, even to himself, but he'd always shied away whenever he'd seen a baby bump in public.

Gabe had ragged on him mercilessly about his almost-phobia for years. Not that the guy was completely phobia-free himself. He'd avoided babies with near-religious zealousness, always saying, "Nothing that small should be that loud."

What a pair they had made.

Gabe.

An arrow of pain sliced Quinn in half at the memories, and he bent over, laying his cheek on Mara's belly. He'd lost another person he loved. His best friend. His brother.

First his adoptive parents. Now Gabe.

He couldn't risk falling in love with this baby. Wouldn't risk it. Bad things happened to the people he loved.

"Travis?" Mara's voice, all soft and sleepy, nearly broke the dam he'd constructed to hold back his emotions. Her hand lifted to stroke his hair, and it felt so good. Too good. And horrible, because it was a reminder of something he could never allow himself to have. Something like her waking in his bed every morning after running her fingers through his hair all night as they made love.

Christ.

He locked down everything soft and tender he felt toward her. It was wrong to fantasize about her like that when he was somehow the reason she was in danger.

Keeping his back to her, he sat up and pressed his fingers to his eyelids. Told himself to man the fuck up and do the right thing. Keep her at arm's distance to keep her safe.

She touched his back. "Trav—"

"We need to go." Damn, was that his voice, all rough and thick? He cleared his throat. "Dress warm. The van's battery ran down during the night, so we're continuing on foot."

"On foot?" she echoed. "To Romania?"

If it were only him, he could do it. Or die trying. But it wasn't just him anymore. He glanced over his shoulder to see her mouth parted in a small, sexy O of disbelief, and he remembered all too clearly that night in her bed when her mouth had…

Yeah, whoa, okay. Better to avoid looking at her from now on.

"No," he said and winced at his harsh tone. But he wasn't going to dial it down. If she hated him, she'd stay away from him once they were home. He'd make sure all of his enemies knew she meant nothing to him, and she'd be safe. "We're going with plan B."

"What's plan B?"

"Still working on it."

"Great." Sarcasm weighted heavily in the word as she scooted out of the sleeping bag. "Plan B."

"I'll think of something." Quinn grabbed the nearest pack and riffled through it for supplies. Luckily for them, Jean-Luc, Seth, Harvard, Marcus, and Ian had left all of their stuff in the van. Not so lucky for the guys, but like he'd told her before, they could take care of themselves.

After a pause, he heard Mara moving around behind him

and resisted the urge to check on her.

"I have to pee again," she said finally.

"Hold it."

"God, you're such a—a—jerk!" She planted her hands on his back and shoved him. Not hard, but enough that he wobbled in his precarious half-crouching position.

"What the—" He started to turn toward her, but she pushed him again. This time, he did lose his balance and smacked into the wall.

"Pregnant women pee. That's what we do." Fury etched lines between her brows, and she kicked out a bare foot, catching him in the shin.

"Okay. Okay." He held up his hands in helpless surrender. "I'll take you outside, find you a place—Mara, no. Shit, don't cry."

"You should know this stuff! You *would* know all this if you hadn't disappeared without leaving me any way to contact you." As tears streamed from her eyes, she fisted her hands and hit him again, pounding on his chest to punctuate each word. "Why couldn't you have just left it a one-night stand? Why did you have to come back and break my heart? You asshole!"

At a complete loss, Quinn caught her wrists and drew her into his arms. He soothed a hand down her back, tucked her head underneath his chin, and started a gentle side-to-side rocking motion. He had no clue what to say, but obviously this was about way more than needing a bathroom break, so he made soft shushing noises and let her cry it out.

Long, long minutes passed before she lifted her head. Her eyes were bloodshot and puffy, her nose red, cheeks splotchy. She wasn't a woman who cried prettily, and yet…

Christ, she was still so beautiful to him.

He tucked a limp strand of hair behind her ear. "Okay now?"

She nodded. "I'm sorry."

"No, don't be. I deserve it and more."

"Yes, you do."

Despite everything, he smiled. He liked this bold, mouthy version of her even more than the shy mouse she'd been when they first met. And maybe he'd gone straight-up masochist, but her new attitude was kind of hot.

He caught a tear on his finger and flicked it away. "Don't look now, your backbone is showing."

She arched a brow, then her gaze dropped pointedly to his lap. "Don't look now…"

Laughing softly, he cupped her cheeks in his hands and swept away more tears with his thumbs. "I can't help my reaction to you."

Her eyes widened in disbelief. "You're still attracted to me?"

Christ, he shouldn't tell her the truth. This was the perfect opportunity to push her away, but when he opened his mouth, he couldn't lie, couldn't hurt her like that.

"Ah, Mara." He dropped his forehead to hers. "Always. That's never going to change."

Her lips curved into a trembling smile, and he was transported back to her house, when she'd opened the door in her robe and he'd wanted nothing more in that moment than to feel her mouth against his.

He couldn't help it. He had to taste her again. Just one more time…

• • •

Travis caught her lips with his and swallowed her gasp of surprise. Then his tongue caressed her lower lip and begged entrance, and all other thoughts vanished, consumed by flames of pure lust. Somehow, he always did that to her. Had the power to sweep away her rational mind and replace it with a wild seductress she hardly recognized. His tongue invaded her, claimed, thrusting in a pantomime of sex as his hands curled into her hair and held her head still for the kiss.

Commanding. Rough. Her Travis, kissing her like there was nothing broken between them. God, how she'd missed him.

All the memories of long, sleepless nights filled with yearning coalesced into a desperate need. She wrapped her arms around his neck and poured her soul into the kiss, trying to explain every emotion that was too complicated for words. She didn't know if she loved him, didn't know if she wanted him long-term, couldn't take him walking away from her again somewhere down the road.

But right now, in this moment, she wanted him.

She rubbed her aching breasts against his hard chest, wanting nothing more than to peel away the layers of clothing separating them, to feel him flesh to flesh again. His hands slid to her shoulders, slipped down her back, pressed her closer…and he froze. His lips stopped moving against hers. His muscles locked up until he might as well have been a marble statue.

"You won't hurt me," she assured, still breathing hard from his kisses. "Or the baby."

No reply.

The baby. Right. Her pregnancy freaked him out, so the reminder of it probably sent up big, flashing off-limits signs in his mind. The frustrating, impossible man. Mara pulled out of his arms, her hands bunching into fists at her sides.

Do not smack him. Do not smack him.

Why couldn't he see past the pregnancy? She was still the same woman she'd been before the baby. A little fatter, yes, but her weight gain hadn't bothered him one bit when he'd held her up against her apartment's wall and pounded into her with savage intensity. Her sex dampened at the memory, and she clenched her thighs together to relieve the throb of need.

She wanted him, but he had to understand that if he wanted her, he had to want all of her, including the baby.

Do *not* smack him.

Mara sucked in a fortifying breath before lifting her gaze to his. "Okay. I'm trying really, really hard to understand this…issue…you have about the baby, but I thought we'd at least gotten past the—"

She realized he wasn't looking at her. His eyes were open, but he stared over her shoulder. She whipped around, half expecting to see something terrifying behind her, but there was only the van's wall.

"Travis, what's wrong?"

He didn't acknowledge her in any way. Just continued to stare at the wall with a vague, out-of-focus look in his eyes.

"Travis!"

He turned his eyes toward her, followed by his head in a slow, almost robotic sweep. "Who?"

Oh, God. Something was wrong with him. First the migraine, and now he had the same blank look in his eyes that he'd had when Zaryanko dragged him from the hotel.

"Quinn!" Her voice cracked. "Travis Quinn. You."

"No," he said and his features scrunched in confusion. "Paulie."

"You're not making sense, Travis, and you're really starting to scare me."

"My name's Paulie. Benjamin Paul Jewett Jr. Granddad's name is Travis. I gotta go home," he added and crawled toward the doors. "Big Ben will be mad."

"Travis—Paulie, wait." She reached for him, but he shrugged out of her grasp and opened the door. Snow swirled inside with a burst of frigid wind. "Please, don't leave me."

"Big Ben will be mad," he said again and jumped out of the van.

Mara scrambled to the door, but she was too late. His figure disappeared into the snow at a full-tilt run. She stared after him for a long time, until her nose started to run and her eyes stung from the cold. With her breath hitching on a sob, she closed the door and leaned against the van's wall. He'd come back. As soon as he snapped out of it, he'd come back for her. Maybe even before that. He had to come back.

Tears burned on her cold cheeks. She stared at the pack he'd left on the floor.

Yes, he had to come back. He wasn't wearing his boots.

Chapter Twenty-Three

He had to go back.

Quinn blinked and looked around, his heart stuttering at his unfamiliar surroundings. A house. He sat at a kitchen table, a spoon poised midway to his mouth. He stared at the plate in front of him. Some kind of meat stew and a corn porridge. He'd eaten half of it and could still taste the spices and onion on his tongue. How did he not remember eating that? Or even sitting down at a table to eat?

Had to go back.

He dropped the spoon and shoved away from the table so hard his chair banged on the floor. The constant hum he'd heard since coming around stopped, and only then did he realize it was not a hum. It was conversation. Three people he didn't recognize sat around the table, staring at him in open-mouthed surprise: an older woman with a round, pleasant face and white hair tucked underneath a bright red-and-green head scarf; a man who looked close to the same age as the woman and had a wide nose and skin hardened to leather by too much time in unforgiving environments; and an androgynous child of about five with a fringe of blond hair held out of pale blue eyes by a red headband. The small room consisted of the creaky four-person dining table and nausea-inducing candy-striped wallpaper.

"Where am I?" The question came out as little more than a croak. "Where's Mara?"

The man and woman shared a glance, then the man stood up. He motioned to himself and spoke in broken, heavily accented English. "I am Rustam Belyakov." He indicated the woman. "My wife, Valentina." And the child. "My granddaughter. Nadejda." Then he said something long and complicated in Russian.

Quinn shook his head. "I don't speak—"

Nadejda said something to Rustam and received a nod of approval. She jumped up from her chair and took hold of Quinn's hand, tugging him toward a splintered wood door as she chattered happily in Russian. He glanced back at the older couple, who both watched him go with frowns of concern.

Obviously, these people meant him no harm.

The next room wasn't so much a room but an open alcove that contained a rusted sink and a hand-crank well. It let out onto a courtyard where several small, bright blue buildings squatted around a wide patio. Nadejda pulled him across the concrete and through a narrow alleyway created by two of the buildings. Up ahead, a fence held back a flock of chickens and geese and one gigantic turkey that cocked its wrinkled head and peered at them with large black eyes. A dog chained to a coop whimpered and pawed at the fence as they passed.

"Where are we going?"

The girl tugged on his hand and continued to talk enthusiastically, pausing for a moment to point through the fence at a goat, then at a small pig, then at the rabbit coops lining the shed that made the goat's home.

Finally they came to another small building painted the same turquoise blue as the others. Nadejda marched up the steps and peeked through the door, then turned to smile at him. She didn't seem inclined to go any farther, so he ducked inside and found a large room set up to look like a living room with two wood chairs, a futon-like couch, and a TV older than he was. Burnished gold-and-brown tapestries decorated each white-painted wall and clashed with the bright teal-and-pink-flowered rug covering the floor, and yet the place felt homey, lived-in, and well loved. His pack leaned against one of the chair legs.

He glanced back to ask Nadejda what he was supposed to do in here, but she was gone.

"Okay," he muttered and scratched at the stubble coming in on his jaw. So he'd just have to determine what happened himself and find a way to get back to Mara.

Christ. He'd left Mara out there somewhere. Alone.

If he had to take a wild guess, he figured another lights-on-nobody-home episode had landed him here with the Belyakov family. Sometimes when he woke up, he was in the exact spot he'd been in when he blacked out. Other times, he found himself on a bus or in a mall or on a street halfway across the city. Rustam and his family must have found him wandering and brought him home with them.

He didn't know how he'd ever thank them for their kindness, but right now, his number-one objective was Mara. He strode forward and reached for his pack, but a whisper of sound from the other side of the room caught his attention. In truth, it was barely a sound, more like the shift of air with the softest rustle of fabric, but he sensed he was no longer alone and glanced up.

The moment his eyes met Mara's, his emotions ran the gamut from a brilliant joy to fear that he was dreaming to an extreme need to take her into his arms and never let her go.

The only thing that stopped him from running forward and scooping her up was the fear that his knees would give out from the intense relief that she was safe and he'd land on his face like an idiot. She stood in another curtained doorway, her hair hanging loose and damp around her shoulders, and looked so very tired, her complexion shades paler than it had been, the tender flesh around her eyes bruised.

She yawned but covered it with the back of her hand. "Paulie, you need to go eat. I told you I'd be there in a minute."

Quinn's heart stuttered to a halt, and every drop of saliva in his mouth evaporated. "What—" The word came out high-pitched and strangled, and he had to clear his throat twice before he found a semblance of his real voice. "What did you just call me?"

"Pau—" She stopped short, and her eyes narrowed a fraction as she studied his face like she was seeing him for the very first time. "Travis?" She launched across the five feet separating them and hugged him so tight he felt his vertebrae shift. "Oh, God. You're back? Please tell me you're back. Are you back?"

He awkwardly patted her back, his mind still reeling from the name she had…

No, but she couldn't have. Nobody had called him that in over twenty years. He hadn't even thought of himself by that name since he was eleven.

He grasped Mara's shoulders and set her away from him.

"You're pushing me away?" She gave a short, sniffling laugh and wiped at her eyes. "You are back!"

"Where did I go?"

"Physically, nowhere. Well, you ran off into the snow, but Rustam was out fixing a broken fence and found you right away. You led him to the van. We were on his property, and so here we are. Rustam and Valentina have been wonderful."

Quinn shook his head. "I'm sorry. I'm not following. Did

you call me…Paulie?"

Mara bit down on her lower lip, then entwined her fingers around his and urged him over to the couch. When he refused to move, she dropped his hand and sat herself, clasping her hands together in her lap.

"What happened?" he asked again.

"You went into a fugue state and I think…I think you regressed back to your childhood. You called yourself Paulie and kept telling me you had to go home or Big Ben would be angry with you."

Quinn shut his eyes against the words that registered like a blow. He sank to the couch beside her. "Paulie died a long time ago."

"I don't think so, Travis. He was here not even fifteen minutes ago. He's been here for the last twelve hours."

"Twelve—?" Groaning, Quinn leaned against the couch cushions. "That's a new record."

"How long has this been happening to you?"

He lifted his head and looked at her. Surprise rippled through him. He actually wanted to answer her question, and honestly at that. He glanced away again. "It started after the car accident that ended my SEAL career. I suffered a traumatic brain injury and…I started losing time. A few minute here, a few there, but it's been getting worse. I knew I was functional during the blackouts because I've interacted with people and then didn't remember it later." And ever since one such encounter during the team's last mission in Afghanistan, he'd had an uneasy suspicion he was reverting back to the worst years of his life during the blackouts. Now he had confirmation.

Mara touched his arm, drawing his attention. "Have you told your doctor about it?"

He opened his mouth to give his usual line—yes, he'd already been checked out by doctors and they didn't know what was causing it—but stopped short without uttering a sound. He drew a breath, exhaled softly. "I stopped going several months ago."

There was no condemnation in her eyes, no pity. She didn't lecture him about the importance of seeing his doctor, and that was a relief. Of course he knew he had to see his doctor, but honestly, he dreaded what he'd find out when he went. Healthy, normal people didn't black out or regress to being a kid. He was obviously not healthy…but what if he was sicker than even he thought?

Mara remained silent for several seconds, then curled one leg up underneath her, settling in for a long story, and he knew she wasn't going to leave until he spilled everything.

"Okay," she said, "who is Benjamin Paul Jewett Jr.?"

Chapter Twenty-Four

Quinn glanced away from her. Up at the paint-chipped ceiling. Across at the faded tapestry on the wall. Down at the frayed rug covering the floor. Searched for anything to look at but her.

"So?" she prompted after a moment.

"He's nobody important."

"You're lying."

Annoyance spiked through him. Annoyance and something else that had the acrid, hated metallic taste of fear. "He's dead."

"No," Mara said without a shred of doubt. "I have a feeling I'm looking at him right now, or at least part of him. Why won't you tell me?"

"What, you think you can heal poor Paulie like one of your blind, three-legged pets?" He clenched his jaw against a swell of bitterness that he couldn't quite rein in. "You can't."

Her chin lifted to a stubborn angle, and the fires of determination sparked in her eyes. "Maybe not. But we won't know that for sure if you don't tell me, now will we?"

"You really want the whole ugly story?"

She nodded, and something twisted inside him. He didn't want to go back. Christ, he really didn't want to go back there, and the telling of it would suck him right down into the black abyss. Was he capable of clawing out a second time? He didn't know, but the concern and understanding in her expression worked as a fortifier. She was carrying a child that contained his DNA. At very least, she deserved to know the kind of people that child had come from.

He sucked in a sharp breath through his nose, readying for the cold plunge into the dark. Then he jumped. "Benjamin Paul Jewett Jr. is the name I was born with. It was a miserable childhood, full of drugs and alcohol and violence. My first clear memory is of my father punching a hole in the kitchen wall after kicking the shit out of my mother in an alcohol-fueled rage. I went hungry more often than not. Half the time we had no running water, and I went weeks without a bath."

"And nobody helped?"

"Child services came in at my elementary school's request one time. They removed me and put me in foster care, which wasn't so bad, but it didn't last long. You have to understand, I was all but feral. I'd never lived with rules, and suddenly I had a bedtime and homework, family dinnertime and baths. Within three months, I drove my foster family away. But by then, Big Ben had landed himself a couple years in jail for dealing, and my mother went to rehab, so I was returned to her when she completed the program. She didn't stay clean long. The very night I came home, I found her passed out on the couch with a needle still in her arm. I realized I hated Cherice then for what she did to herself, to us. I don't think I've ever really stopped hating her. I don't think I can."

"Tell me what happened to Paulie." Mara reached out and laced her fingers through his as if she realized he felt like he was drowning and needed the contact of another human being. "When did he become Travis Quinn?"

The contrast of her dainty hand next to his big one settled him a little, and he focused all of his attention on their joined fingers. "When I was ten, Big Ben came home drunk and murdered Cherice, then walked into my room and shot me." He lifted their joined hands to show her the scar on his pointer finger.

Mara traced the ridge that extended from his knuckle to the web of his thumb, and even that light contact from her stirred his body. Christ, he was in so much trouble with this woman. Then again, he'd known that from day one, hadn't he?

"That's where you got the scar," she whispered. "A bullet?"

"I was playing with a Game Boy I'd stolen out of a classmate's backpack. We didn't have money for shit like that. I was jealous of the kid and his picture-perfect family, so I took it and one of his games. *The Amazing Spider-Man.* It was the coolest thing I'd ever seen. Then Big Ben got home, and I thought he was going to slap me around for taking it. I was trying to hide it when he came in with the gun. The bullet went through the game, sliced open my hand, and hit me in the chest. I stayed in ICU for two weeks and in the hospital for another eight because I was malnourished, my immune system was shit, and I kept getting infections. Sam Quinn was my doctor and his wife, Bianca, my nurse. They saved me. In more ways than one."

"Sam and Bianca Quinn," Mara said, realization in her voice. "They adopted you."

He nodded. "I wanted nothing to do with Big Ben, so I legally took the Quinns' last name and my maternal grandfather's first name, because he was the closest thing I'd had to a father before Sam."

"Were they good to you, Sam and Bianca?"

"The best. They were my parents in every sense of the word except biology. I wasn't a somewhat inconvenient visitor in their home like I'd been in my first foster family's. I was their son, and for once, I had a real family. That's all I ever wanted. A family." His gaze dropped to her belly, but he couldn't bear the sight of it and shut his eyes. "At the time."

She stayed silent for another moment that felt like ages. "So what happened to them? Where are they now?"

"Dead." Like so many others, and a chunk of his heart had died with each and every one of them. Including Gabe, but he wasn't about to tell her all that. Couldn't quite face it yet himself, because when he did, when he finally let himself grieve for his best friend, he was going to lose himself. Maybe forever. Just like Sam had. "Let's leave it at that."

"No," Mara said and squeezed his hand reassuringly, even though her tone allowed no room for argument. "You need to talk about it. How did they die?"

Christ, her and her questions. He wanted to say it was none of her business. Wanted to lash out so that she'd drop the subject. But he didn't.

"Mom got cancer." He had to force each word out of his constricted throat. Why did it still hurt so much? After all these years, the wound was as fresh as ever and, if possible, even more jagged around the edges. "We watched her waste away for eight long months. When it was over, Dad couldn't stand the grief of losing her and I—I wasn't enough to keep him alive. He killed himself."

"Oh, no," she breathed. "Oh, Travis. You're not responsible for any of that. You know that, don't you?"

He couldn't look at her, couldn't bear to see the pity he knew must be in her eyes. "Yeah, of course. I didn't put the gun in Big Ben's hand. I didn't give Sam the rope for the noose."

Mara touched his cheek, drawing his gaze to hers. No

pity. He searched her face. No, she didn't pity him. She understood. How could that be when nobody else ever had?

"How old were you?" she asked.

"Sixteen. I'd just passed my driver's test. I was saving up to buy this old Impala that sat in my neighbor's yard. With some work, it would have been a beautiful car. I was going to buy it and fix it up before prom so I could ask this girl I wanted to..." A whisper of laughter escaped him at the memory. "Well, I was a teenage boy. You can guess what I wanted to do. I was just a normal kid with a normal life, normal teenage concerns...and then one day, there was nothing left of that life. Mom died, and Dad shriveled up until he couldn't take living without her any longer. I was all alone again, and I didn't know how to cope."

Mara scowled. "I'm sorry, but Sam should have protected you."

Everything in him revolted at the suggestion. "He didn't owe me anything."

"You're so wrong. He owed you everything. He took on the responsibility of caring for you when he adopted you. He should've been stronger for you, should've realized you were hurting just as much as he was."

What could he say to that? If he was honest with himself—and he didn't want to be—her words were the same thoughts that had tortured him for years. Why hadn't he been enough for Sam?

"What happened after they were gone?" Mara asked after his silence stretched a moment too long. "Were there no relatives?"

"No. Neither had siblings, and their parents were all long dead. I ended up in foster care again, ran away, got into as much trouble as I could find, and generally had a 'fuck you, world' attitude for the remainder of my teenage years."

"But you straightened up."

"I wouldn't have. I was so angry at everyone, but then…" He trailed off as memories he hadn't thought of in years emerged from the chaos that was his fucked-up head. The things he'd seen and done…to survive. He hadn't stooped as low as he could have, and he had only one person to thank for that. "It was the winter of '98. I stayed in this slum boarding house in East Baltimore. Horrible place. Rats in the walls, and half the time the furnace didn't work. My neighbors were all heroin addicts, and there was always blood in the kitchen sink, needles scattered across the bathroom. But one of my neighbors was a drunk, homeless World War II vet everyone called Froggy, short for Frogman."

"Frogman?" Mara smiled. "He was a SEAL."

"Close. He was in the Underwater Demolition Teams, the predecessor of the SEALs. He always told stories and nobody ever listened, but for some reason, that morning I sat down and talked to him over a bottle of Jack Daniel's. He was amazing. The stuff he'd done… He was a hero. It wasn't right that he was wasting away on booze and PTSD in a slum house." He lifted a shoulder. "Seth, our sniper, has PTSD. Nobody wanted him on the team, but I fought so hard to keep him because I saw Froggy every time I looked at him. Saw that future for him if someone didn't step in and help. I didn't want that for him."

Mara smiled. "Seth's lucky to have such a good friend."

He didn't know what to say to that, so he said nothing. But he didn't see anything good when he looked in the mirror, that was for fucking sure.

After several minutes, Mara softly said his name and he cleared his throat. "Yeah, so that day, I listened to Froggy's stories and the world seemed to click into place. I realized I was heading down the exact same road I'd been on before the Quinns took me in, and I wasn't going to sully their memories by destroying myself. I left everything I owned except a photo album at that boarding house, found the nearest navy recruiter, and signed up."

"And you never looked back."

"And I never—" He stopped short. Shook his head. "No, that's not true. I did once. When I graduated BUD/S, I went back to show Froggy my trident, but he'd died the winter before of pneumonia. I still visit his grave occasionally." He lifted his sleeve and showed her his one and only tattoo on his left bicep, a cartoon frog with a stick of dynamite in its hand. "That was for him."

Mara ran her fingers over the design, a reminiscent quirk to her lips, and he remembered her doing the same all those months ago while they lay tangled together in her bed. She'd traced the tattoo over and over again, as if fascinated by it.

"I've wondered about that frog for months," she said now. "It seemed so...unlike you. But I was wrong. I didn't know you well enough then. It suits you perfectly." She smiled up at him. "Can I visit Froggy's grave with you sometime?"

He sucked in a breath and told himself to say no, because they had no future together. Instead, when he opened his mouth, "I'd like that," came out instead. "My place back in Baltimore was ransacked, all my pictures of the Quinns gone. Froggy's all I have left—"

Mara jumped up, smacking him in the chin with the top of her head. His teeth cracked together, and his head spun for a second.

"Oh. Oh, God. Sorry." She bent over and kissed his forehead. "Just...hang on to that thought for a second." She disappeared through a curtain into the other room.

"I don't have any thoughts left in my head after that blow," he muttered, rubbing his chin. He heard her talking to herself as things rustled around.

Curious, Quinn stood and followed her. The room on the other side of the curtain was a tiny bedroom with barely enough space for a guy his size to hold out his arms. A narrow bed sat on a platform that jutted from a wide concrete column built into the center of the wall. Fire crackled behind an iron grate at the base of the column.

He walked over and placed his hand on the concrete. Warm. Huh. He looked at the bed and tried not to think of how easy it would be to share that warm, narrow space with Mara. "Interesting way to keep a bed warm."

"Valentina said it's called a *soba*," Mara said as she continued searching for something in another one of the packs she must have brought from the van. "It's their version of a furnace. There's one in each section of the house."

He lifted a brow. "You speak Russian?"

"I was an exchange student in Russia during high school. Spent a summer in St. Petersburg, studying history." A shadow crossed her features. "I used to love history until Ramon told me it wasn't a practical field of study. Oh, here it is." She pulled something out of the pack but wouldn't let him see it and held it behind her back. She nodded toward the bed. "Sit down."

He did as she asked. "Now what?"

"Now…" With a flourish, she produced a photo. And not just any old photo, but the one he'd dropped at Olesea's house. He slowly took it from her with hands that trembled. She had taped the two ragged halves together, and Sam and Bianca once again smiled up at him over their anniversary cake.

"I knew it was important to you," she said, "so I picked it up before we left Olesea's. I tried to tape it back together."

"Mara." His voice came out raw. "This is…" Nobody had ever done something so thoughtful for him, and he couldn't find the words to express the emotions warring inside his chest. But he'd never been very good at saying the right thing anyway, so he set the photo aside and stood, wrapping her up in his arms. He poured everything he felt into the hug and hoped it was enough.

"You're welcome, Travis." The warmth in her brown eyes as she smiled undid him. Everything that had gone wrong and soured between them suddenly didn't matter. It was all drama and senseless baggage that needed unpacking, but for now…

For now, she was here with him, and he had to hold her. He cared about this woman deeply, and in this perfect moment, none of the rest of it mattered.

"Now what?" She trembled ever so lightly in his arms.

Quinn cupped her cheek in his palm, tilting her head back until he had unrestrained access to her mouth. "Now, I'm going to kiss you." He tugged at her lower lip with his teeth. "And more if you want." He soothed the nip with his tongue, then claimed her mouth in a searing, soul-melding kiss. "Please say you want."

"Oh, I want." Her head fell back as he cupped her heavy breast through the fabric of her shirt, and he delighted in the expanse of smooth neck she exposed. He dipped his lips to trace the sleek column of her throat.

Too many layers between him and her skin. She was wearing far too much clothing, and he pulled his lips away long enough to rip her out of the button-up shirt. Metal buttons clinked to the floor and scattered underfoot, and he experienced a half second of sanity to worry that he'd just destroyed a shirt that impoverished Rustam probably all but gave her off his back. But then it didn't matter because the fabric of her bra was so thin that she might as well have been wearing nothing at all. He took a moment to feast on her lovely round breasts with his eyes before returning to her with his hands and lips. Lush now, her body was the same and yet…very different. He wondered at how he'd missed it before. But this time, he would take his time and explore every inch of her, rediscover all the curves he'd found so enchanting over the summer.

"Oh, yes, I want," she gasped and clutched at his head, her nails biting half moons into his skull. "I want so much. Always. I can't seem to stop wanting around you."

Nor could he around her. And he had to tell her that, to let her know about all the hot, foreign emotions she brought bubbling to the surface of the ice shell he'd locked around his heart long ago. But his voice deserted him. He had no words to describe what she made him feel.

She touched his cheek. Just a light caress of the tips of her fingers, but it sizzled across his nerves like a torrent of electricity, and his cock pulsed with need in response.

Straightening to his full height, Quinn gazed down into dark, expressive eyes that held nothing back, and for the length of a heartbeat, he saw himself the way she must see him. Too proud to let the world know how much he hurt inside, and too damn stubborn to know what was good for him. To her, he wasn't a mercenary. He wasn't a SEAL. He wasn't an abused kid. He wasn't a lost soul fighting hopeless wars with himself.

Not when he was with her. No, with her, he was a man. Her man.

"I'm here, Travis," she said.

It was all he needed. He wrapped her up in his arms and stole her breath with a hard kiss. Far less gently than he'd planned, he spun around and tossed her on the bed. She bounced a little on the squeaky mattress and laughed, then sat up and wiggled out of her pants. She flung them at him, and he found himself smiling as he snatched them off his face. Mara laughed again and crooked a finger in a come-here gesture before reaching around behind her and unclasping her bra. Her breasts fell free, and his mouth watered for a taste of her.

Quinn all but ripped the fabric from his body then stretched out on the bed beside her, kissing her, feeling the weight of those lovely breasts in his hands, the rasp of her peaked nipples against his palms. He let his hands slide lower until he found her hot and ready for him.

He would taste her.

He licked his way down her body, pausing only to lave each nipple until she squirmed. He released her nipple with a popping sound and continued over her belly to the curly thatch of dark hair at the vee of her legs. Closing his eyes, he buried his face in her and drew her scent deep into his lungs. A pleasant buzz started in his head, and he realized he was getting high off her, off their lovemaking. He chuckled and dragged his tongue up her slit.

"Travis," she moaned and bucked against him.

"Not yet, honey." He smiled and licked her again, slowly, ending with light suction on her clit as he slid a finger inside her. Mara arched off the bed and let loose with a melodious string of Spanish, her body spasming around his hand.

"Mmm," he breathed against the soft flesh of her thigh. "You know I love it when you talk dirty."

Cheeks ablaze with color, she looked down the length of her body and met his gaze. Her breasts heaved with each gasping breath she took. "I think I cursed you to hell and called you a god in one breath."

"A god?" He nuzzled her. "I really like that."

"No, you don't. You'd hate being a god. You'd rather be a god's bodyguard."

She knew him too well. She was already closer to him than he'd ever let anyone get before, and a hazy part of his brain told him to slam on the brakes now before she burrowed past his every last defense, but his brain wasn't the organ in charge at the moment.

"I'd rather be your bodyguard, sweetheart."

"You were already." When his lips closed over her clitoris again, she moaned and dug her nails into his scalp. "You're torturing me, Travis. I want you inside me."

"Is that an order, ma'am? I'm good at taking orders." He swirled his tongue around that sensitive nub and sucked it into his mouth.

Convulsing again, she cried out. "Yes!"

"Roger that." Quinn sat up and parted her legs, taking a moment to enjoy the sight of her wide-open and glistening with her desire for him.

"Travis, please."

"Yes, ma'am." He positioned his tip at her entrance and plunged into her, catching his breath at the exquisite pleasure. Her body was silk heat as it clenched around him. He had to grit his teeth against the urge to come.

No, he wasn't letting this end. Not yet. Maybe not ever. Good thing he had phenomenal control, because this was going to last all night if he had anything to do with it.

Needing to go deeper, he propped himself on his arms and thrust into her, suddenly very aware of her gently rounded belly between them. Knowing what lay beneath should have turned him off. It should have scared him so much that his cock shriveled into a useless lump of flesh. But it didn't. Impossibly, the idea that his seed had taken root inside her only hardened him to the point of pain, especially with her body clutching at him with every withdrawal, unwilling to let him go.

Her breasts were slightly larger than he remembered them, her nipples rosy brown. He had to taste them, had to feel those peaks puckering under his tongue as he moved inside her.

"Travis…" She shuddered. "I can't. Oh, I can't. It's too much. I can't."

Quinn froze, tightening his muscles to keep from losing

all control even as his cock bucked inside her, demanding he continue.

"Do you want to stop?" He would. Didn't know how and it'd probably kill him, but if she called a halt to this, he would stop. "Are you uncomfortable?"

Big brown eyes opened and gazed up at him, brimming with emotions he didn't dare put a name to. She bit her lip. "No. No, I want this. You. I need you, but I'm so sensitive. My breasts and…everything. It's overwhelming. Just…go slow."

"Okay." He hung his head between his shoulders and breathed in and out a couple times, reining in his instincts to take her hard and fast, to claim her, brand her as his. There would be time for that later. Maybe. Right now, his priority was her comfort. Her enjoyment. She was always going to be his priority.

Slow.

Her breath hitched as he pushed into her, inch by excruciating inch. Slow, slow, so very slow that his muscles ached from the tight leash of restraint and sweat dripped into his eyes. After what seemed like a blissful and yet devastating eternity, he was seated inside her again. And she felt so good, so right. So his. His mind splintered, all intelligent thought fleeing except for one.

Home.

Finally, *finally*, he had a home. With her.

But that was ridiculous.

Quinn shoved the thought away and forced all of his attention to focus on her again. She was his priority, nothing else. Propping himself up on one elbow for leverage, he started an easy rocking rhythm and traced his lips along her jaw. He brushed her hair back from her ear and whispered, "Better?"

Mara arched her back on a moan, pushing against his thrusts. "You told me you don't do gentle."

"I don't." With his lips still on her jaw, he felt her smile and added, "At least I never have before. But for you—" His voice caught, but he didn't bother trying to clear away the rustiness brought on by emotion. "Christ, Mara, you gotta know I'd do anything for you."

Chapter Twenty-Five

He'd do anything for her. Yes, she knew that. He'd risked his life and his team's lives to rescue her. But—and this thought nagged at her even as she basked in the immense pleasure of making love to him again—what about the baby? He hadn't mentioned their baby once, and the oversight sat in the back of her mind until his intimate coaxing drove her up and up and brought them both to an orgasm that shattered all other thoughts.

Spooned against him, with his arms wrapped tightly around her and his body still buried deep inside hers, she let herself drift. Oh, she had needed this. She hated that about herself, wished she could be strong and self-reliant like Lanie, but she wasn't cut from the same sturdy fabric as her best friend.

"You're shaking." His voice rumbled in his ear. "Are you cold?" He didn't wait for an answer and reached down for the quilt folded at the bottom of the bed. He pulled it over them both.

That did it. The tears she'd refused to cry before flooded

her eyes and seeped into the pillow.

Travis soothed a hand over her hair, down her shoulder and arm, and rested it on the curve of her hip. "What can I do for you, Mara?" He sounded at a complete loss and maybe a little bit terrified. "Please, don't cry. Tell me what I can do to help."

She shook her head and turned her face into the pillow. "It's hormones. They've turned me into an emotional mess."

He was silent for a long time, and in that moment, she wished desperately for the ability to read minds. She could only imagine what was going through his head. Part of her still feared he would deny the baby was his and demand a paternity test. But then his hand drifted from her hip to her belly and, dang it all, that made her start crying again.

Mara shut her eyes and let herself savor the embrace for one short second. She couldn't allow herself more than that before shifting away, because the gesture absolutely did not mean the same to him as it did to her. He touched her belly like that out of curiosity, not any sense of possessiveness or love.

Was he even capable of love? She wanted more than anything to believe so but feared his life had broken him beyond repair. Maybe he didn't have the ability to connect beyond sex. He'd already walked away from her twice, once after promising he wouldn't. And, yes, maybe he had come back the second time, but who was to say he'd come back a third, or fourth, or fifth? She'd live every day with him in fear that he'd walk out the door and never come back.

She couldn't do that. As much as she wanted to love him, she couldn't put her baby through that kind of uncertain life.

She inched a couple centimeters away from him on the narrow bed, but it might as well have been a chasm for all the figurative space between them.

"Mara—"

"Don't."

"We need to talk about—"

"No, we don't," she insisted. "I expect nothing from you."

He hooked a finger under her chin, forcing her to meet his gaze. "Listen, you gotta know I wouldn't have…if I'd known…"

"Oh, real nice, Travis." She welcomed the rush of anger and wiped away her tears with the backs of her hands. "You wouldn't have touched me had you known you'd knock me up?"

Color rushed into his cheeks. "Uh, yeah. No. I mean—"

"Well, it's too late. You did touch me, and I did get pregnant." She struggled to a sitting position and threw her pillow at him. "So either grow up and deal with it or leave us alone. We don't need you."

Wincing, he caught her hand. "Wait. Mara, that came out wrong, too. Goddammit, I never say the right things."

"You think?" She shook off his grip and pushed herself to stand on her aching feet. She found her clothes on the floor. The memory of tossing her pants at him heated the back of her neck, but she shoved the shame ruthlessly aside and stepped into the leg holes. Her shirt was ruined, the buttons gone, so she grabbed his T-shirt instead. Let him find his own clothes.

"Okay, so maybe I meant that exactly like it sounded," he admitted and sat up, apparently unconcerned with his nudity. His penis was still half hard. "But you can't tell me you didn't think the exact same thing when that test first turned pink or blue or whatever it does when you're pregnant. You've had six weeks to come to terms with this. I've only had a couple days, so you'll have to forgive me for not running out and buying myself a World's Greatest Dad T-shirt."

"You are such a jerk." She turned toward the door but whirled back. "And for your information, I was happy. After you walked out like you did—leaving me in the middle of the night without a fucking word—you broke me, Travis. I fell in love with you that week, though God knows why, and I thought I'd be alone for the rest of my life because I couldn't forget you."

His mouth dropped open. "You…what?"

Her cheeks heated, but she refused to take it back. "When I realized I missed a period, I bought a pregnancy test hoping it came up positive, despite the fact I knew my asshole of a stepdad would throw a fit. I was excited. I thought if I couldn't have you, I'd at least have a piece of you."

Emotions battled over his face for an instant before he slammed that blank, expressionless mask of his back into place. "Mara," he said very evenly. "You didn't purposely get pregnant, did you?"

Oh. My. God. She stared at him in stunned horror. Had he really just asked that?

"Mara," he said again, a soft note of warning in his voice. A tone she imagined he'd use when their baby misbehaved. That was, if she ever let the jerk see their baby. Right now, she was having serious doubts about that.

"No, I didn't." She flung back the curtain covering the door. "And screw you for even thinking I'd do something like that."

• • •

That had been the wrong thing to say. Wrong, wrong thing to say. Especially since he knew better. Mara didn't have a conniving bone in her body. The thought of getting pregnant on purpose to trap him wouldn't have even entered her mind.

Why could he never find the right words when she was around? Seemed like every time he opened his mouth, a bunch of bullshit came spilling out and he couldn't stop it.

Groaning at his own stupidity, he leaped to his feet. "Mara, wait."

Her shoulders straightened. She whirled around, stalked back into the bedroom, and the hurt in her eyes as she glared at him cut him to the bone. "The least you can do is tell me why. Why did you leave?"

The thought crossed his mind to play dumb, but that was the coward's way out. He knew exactly what she was asking him about. That night. She wanted to know about that beautiful and goddamn awful night he'd walked out six weeks ago.

Quinn sat down on the edge of the bed and pulled the quilt over his lap. "I turned chicken. I could see it—us—" He motioned toward her midsection. "This. I could see it so clearly, and I wanted it. Christ help me, I wanted it, but I don't deserve it or you. And that baby doesn't deserve to be stuck with a pathetic excuse of a man like me for a father."

"Travis, you're not giving yourself enough credit." She shook her head, her denial plain on her face. "Our baby's privileged to have such an honorable man as a father."

Honorable. Right. Because honorable men always ran away from the women they cared about. Honorable men were always terrified of their children.

Who was she trying to fool? He knew where he stood, and it hadn't been on the honorable side of the line since he'd left her back in November. Maybe he'd crossed the line even before that. Why else would his former teammates want his head on a platter? Had he betrayed their trust long before he'd betrayed Mara's?

A half memory bobbed to the surface of his conscious, but when he reached for it, it sank under again. There was something about this whole mess he was missing. Something hidden by all the scar tissue in his brain.

He glanced at her, but the tears streaking her cheeks broke

his heart. Instead, he grabbed his pants and concentrated on stuffing his legs into the holes.

He wished he could be what she needed. If he knew how to change to be her perfect man, he'd do it without a second thought. But he was just…him. Travis Quinn, a mess of a man barely holding the strings of his manufactured life together, a warrior at constant war with the world and with himself. He didn't know how to be anyone else. He could certainly never be what Mara needed, and he was a fucking idiot if he let himself believe otherwise for even one breath of a moment.

"I shouldn't have called you," she whispered. "I should have kept the baby a secret."

He knew he should say that he was glad she'd told him. It was what she wanted to hear. Probably what she needed to hear. But with his former teammates riding his ass, with Gabe most likely dead and his current team scattered in the wind, he couldn't muster the words to comfort her.

He found he couldn't even look at her. Couldn't see the hurt he'd put in her eyes, but she refused to move when he tried to leave the room, so he manned up and met her glare.

Pain. Yes, it was there just as he thought it would be, but what surprised him was the unflinching strength, the iron will of someone who had made a decision there was no coming back from.

"This is never going to work between us," she said, and he inwardly flinched at the uncharacteristic shards of ice in her tone. "And I can't keep doing this dance with you. When we get home, I want you to give up your parental rights. I want you out of our lives."

Wasn't that the story of his entire existence?

Quinn shut his eyes as pain unlike anything he'd ever felt before lanced his heart. He was barely able to squeeze words through his constricted throat. "Consider it done."

Chapter Twenty-Six

Consider it done.

God, how could he just give up their baby without a fight?

Mara skidded to a stop halfway across the Belyakovs' courtyard. Her heart felt as if he had cracked it open and scrambled it like an egg. He truly didn't want the baby. Or, by default, her.

She tilted her head toward the sky, filling her lungs with the biting-cold air. Clouds had rolled in during the day and snow swirled all around her, dusting her nose and frosting her eyelashes. Despite the cold, there was something magical about it all. Too bad she wanted nothing more than to forget this entire day.

Nadejda called out from the door to the kitchen. Fortifying herself with another slow breath, Mara plastered a smile on her face and joined the child.

"He's back," Nadejda said in Russian. Or at least Mara was fairly certain that's what she said. "The real him is back."

"*Da,*" Mara agreed. "He's back."

"That's good. We saved you some *tocana* and *mamaliga*."

"*Spasibo,*" Mara said and she truly did appreciate the family's kindness.

Nadejda's brow wrinkled. "How do you say *spasibo* in English?"

"Thank you."

"Spanish?"

"Gracias."

"*Gracias,*" Nadejda parroted. She was a curious child, always asking questions. Mara got the feeling the little girl didn't have the opportunity to talk to many other people besides her grandparents. Especially not any nonwhite people. Nadejda had come right out and told her she was the first brown-skinned person their family had ever seen, which made their kindness that much more poignant. Humans of any race, creed, or culture tended to shun that which they were not familiar with, but the Belyakovs had welcomed her with open arms despite the differences in their appearances. She didn't know how she and Travis would have survived without them.

Travis. Even when she tried to block him from her thoughts, he always managed to ninja his way in somehow.

Nadejda took her hand and dragged her into the kitchen. Rustam and Valentina were both gone, probably retired to their section of the house for the night, but they had left several platters covered on the table. Guilt stabbed through Mara's conscience. It had been rude of her and Travis to disappear and not join the family for dinner.

"Sit," Nadejda urged and started uncovering the food. "Where is Paulie?"

"Sleeping. Very tired." Mara made her hands into a pillow by her cheek and mimed sleep. She decided not to try correcting his name. That whole situation would require a big explanation and she didn't have a firm enough grasp on the language to provide one.

"Oh." Nadejda stopped spooning the traditional corn porridge called *mamaliga* onto a plate and set the dish down. "*Sotovyj telefon!*"

Now that, Mara didn't understand. She watched the girl cross the room to a cupboard and climb onto a stool to reach for a small square device on the shelf.

Travis's cell phone.

She had looked for it in the van and thought it lost. He must have had it on him this whole time.

Mara jumped out of her seat and took the phone from the girl's hand, powered it up and checked the battery. Half dead. Only half. And there was a signal! Not much of one, but enough that she should have little problem making or receiving calls.

Except…

She didn't know any of his teammates' phone numbers, and there was nothing in his contacts or recent call history, which meant she had to swallow her pride and face him again tonight. Damn. She had wanted to throw a tantrum and give him the silent treatment for a while.

Nadejda bent down to put herself in Mara's line of sight. "Good?"

Mara nodded. "Thank you."

"You're welcome!" Nadejda said in exuberant English. "Are you going to call your mama?" she then asked in Russian. "I miss mine. She's in Turkey. Had to go to Turkey because there is no work here…"

The girl's Russian blurred together, and Mara lost the thread of the conversation, but one word transcended the language barrier and stood out to her like a beacon.

Mama.

Oh, her mother must be worried sick. Why hadn't that occurred to her until now?

"Yes," she said to the girl and flipped open the phone.

"I'm going to call my mom."

• • •

AIRFIELD NEAR TIRASPOL, TRANSNISTRIA

"Lots of movement up there," Seth said.

From his seat on the floor, Jesse opened his eyes and craned his head around. Seth sat against the wall at the foot of Gabe's bed, nursing what the sniper claimed was "nothing but a cracked rib." Still, Seth's complexion had taken on a greenish-gray hue in the last couple hours, and sweat plastered his hair to his forehead. He was in far more pain than he wanted them to know.

Then again, everyone was worse for wear. Lanie had a minor concussion—not that it had slowed her down much. Ian a broken arm. Jean-Luc, Marcus, and Harvard all sported a variety of cuts and bruises. He himself had a black eye, a swollen jaw, and his body was one massive throb.

And Gabe…

Jesse checked on him. Found him still alive, but in a coma. And fading. That he'd hung on this long was a miracle in and of itself.

Jesse gritted his teeth against a flood of anger born of impotence. The SEALs hadn't even left them with the first aid kit that usually sat bolted on the wall by the door, and he'd done all he could do for his boss.

Footsteps sounded overhead, fast, moving with some kind of purpose. Rustling. Banging. Muffled voices.

Jesse looked at the ceiling. "What the hell are they doin'?"

"Sounds like they're mobilizing." Ian sat up on his bunk across the aisle, wincing as he jostled his arm. Unfortunately, the two bunks had been stripped of linen and the only thing available to fashion a sling had been their clothes. Most of their clothing was filthy, wet, and torn. Lanie had offered her shirt, but Jesse wasn't about to let her parade around in her bra in front of the guys, so he'd given up his instead.

"Think they found Quinn and Mara?" Jesse walked toward the door. Listened, trying to make out words from the murmur of voices upstairs. The sounds faded away. "They're gone."

"Would they leave us unguarded?" Lanie asked and also stood.

"Why not? Not like we're goin' anywhere. They—" On impulse, he tried the door's handle…and it moved.

It. Moved.

He let loose a surprised string of curses and shoved the door open.

Yup. Should've known it was too good to be true.

Jace Garcia stood on the other side, decked out in winter gear, face painted white and gray under his floppy hat, an M4 held loosely in his hands. Except he didn't seem inclined to shoot anyone. Yet.

"What are you doing, Garcia?"

"Oh, you know." Garcia shrugged. "Betraying my team, throwing away my career. The usual shit."

"You already did that, asshole."

"Did I? Or maybe I was just playing a part. Keeping myself breathing and our exit open like I was supposed to. Why do you think I didn't answer any of your radio calls? I was trying to tell you to stay the hell away from the airfield without ending up dead." He glanced over his shoulder toward the stairs. "We don't have a lot of time, but you need to know Quinn and Mara are alive."

A heavy weight lifted off Jesse's heart, and from the collective sigh behind him, he imagined the others felt the same thing at the news.

"The SEALs received intel from a tap on the family's

phone that Mara contacted her mother," Garcia continued, "and they were able to lock on her general location about thirty klicks southwest of here, but it's going to take them some time to pinpoint exactly where she is. No doubt Quinn's with her, and when they go in, they're going to be shooting to kill. Can you find him first?"

"I can," Harvard said and got to his feet. "I just need a computer and two minutes, tops."

Garcia nodded and stepped aside, tilting his head. "Get to it."

Harvard slid past both of them and jogged up the stairs. Jean-Luc and Marcus followed, grabbing weapons from the bag sitting at Garcia's feet.

As the room cleared, Garcia stepped inside and stared down at Gabe. His lips tightened. "Is he alive?"

"Barely," Jesse said. "He needs surgery."

Garcia nodded and handed over his weapon. "There's a vehicle waiting for you outside. Go help Quinn. I'll make sure Gabe gets to a hospital."

Jesse took the weapon and shoved the barrel into Garcia's chest. He couldn't shake the feeling they were being played—again. "You sold us out. Why should we trust you?"

The pilot said nothing for a long time and, damn, he could even teach the great Gabe "Stonewall" Bristow lessons on impassivity. It was impossible to read his intent from his eyes or expression.

Finally, Garcia shrugged. "Because you have no other choice. How's that for a reason?"

• • •

The curtain over the door rustled, and Quinn moved his arm away from his eyes, hoping like hell his visitor wasn't Nadejda, since he hadn't bothered to finish dressing. Yeah, his cock was covered, but he still didn't like the idea of the girl seeing him in a sex-rumpled bed wearing nothing but his jeans and his bad mood.

Mara appeared in the opening, and for one glittering second, he thought everything would be okay now. She'd come back to him.

But instead, she handed him something. His brain, numbed by all the emotional turmoil, didn't immediately recognize the device.

Cell phone. And it was turned on.

Everything else faded away as his training kicked in. "Mara, did you call anyone?"

She crossed her arms over her chest. "My mother. I had to let her know I'm okay."

Fuck. "How long ago?"

"I don't know. Fifteen, twenty minutes."

Quinn ripped the battery out of the phone and strode over to the *soba*. Heat singed his eyeballs when he opened the metal grate, but he paid no attention to the discomfort and tossed everything except the battery into the flames. The plastic hissed and cracked as it melted.

Mara made a distressed squeaking sound. "What are you doing? We could have called for help."

"There's no help. Gather your things. We need to leave." He slammed the grate shut with a metal *clang*. "Now!"

"Why?" Mara dogged his heels as he finished dressing and started gathering anything they might need. Blankets, clothes. He probably should have kept his cell phone, because the components would have been useful in a survival situation, but he couldn't risk the chance that someone had a lock on its signal.

"Shouldn't we wait until morning?" Mara asked.

"No time."

She caught his arm and pulled, forcing him to stop

packing and face her. “Travis, tell me why.”

“You called your mother. Did she ask any specifics about where you were? Did she try to get you to admit you’re with me?”

Mara’s lips pressed into a thin line. “No. She didn’t. In fact, she had no idea I was even missing.”

Quinn froze. No doubt her mother’s obliviousness was the work of that goddamn stepfather of hers. What a prick. “I’m sorry,” he said and meant it. “But calling her was a mistake. At very least, the SEALs have a lock on the signal and now they know to come here looking for us—” A thought, the memory that had eluded him for months tickled the back of his skull. Something…important…dangerous… A sliver of hazy recollection… He squeezed his eyes shut, straining to bring it into focus, but as soon as he closed his mental hands around the half memory, it slipped from his grasp like a fish diving back into the ocean. He rolled his fingers into a fist and punched his thigh for a lack of anything else to punch. “Goddammit. Why can’t I remember?”

“Remember what?”

“I don’t know, but something’s going on here, Mara. I just can’t…remember.”

“So that’s it? You’re just going to run away?” She shook her head, sorrow and disgust warring on her beautiful face with an expression he couldn’t name. “Figures. That’s what you’re best at, aren’t you, Quinn?”

He flinched at her use of his last name instead of his first. “It’s more than—Mara, you gotta understand, this is something big. And now that Liam Miller is back—”

“Who’s Liam Miller?” she demanded. “You talk about him like he’s the devil or something.”

“That’s not too far off.” When she planted her hands on her hips and scowled at him, he added, “Liam’s a former British Special Forces operative—basically a sociopath with delusions of grandeur and advanced training. Our history goes way back. The short of it is Gabe and I caught him snorting coke during a mission, and we got his ass canned. We found out later that he had been selling us out to the highest bidder for years. He was so far into the black market at that point he couldn't see the light of day, and he was pissed when we refused his bribes and reported him. He's had it out for us ever since, but he has a special place in his black heart for me."

"Why?"

He shoved one more blanket into the pack then yanked the elastic cord to close it. "I killed the woman he loved."

Mara blinked. "You—what?"

"It was during an op, and she was on the wrong side. I was doing my job, protecting my team—but Liam doesn't see it that way. Which is why he can never know about you and the baby. If he does..."

He didn't have to finish the thought, let her draw her own conclusions. She swallowed audibly.

"They plan to kill me, Mara." And, Christ, that hurt. Men he'd once considered friends, brothers, were now hunting him down like public enemy number one. And the kicker was, he had no clue why. He could only guess that they were working with Liam and this was all that crazy motherfucker's doing. "You won't get the chance to tell anyone I killed Urban to protect you. The only way they'll allow me to go back to the States now is in a body bag, and as much as I sometimes hate my life, I'm not ready for it to end."

And wasn't that a surprising realization? Two weeks ago, his desire to keep on keeping on had been next to nil. "I need to get you to safety and then disappear."

Mara's lips trembled as she fought to hold back the tears shining in her dark eyes. "Where will you go?"

"Dunno. Maybe someplace warm and tropical. I've

always hated the snow." He smiled a little and reached out to cup her cheek. She pressed her hand over his and lost the battle with her tears.

"I didn't mean what I said before about not wanting you to see the baby. I was pissed off at…everything. This whole situation. It isn't fair."

"No, it's not, but my life has rarely been fair." He whisked away her tears with his thumb. "I'm glad you told me about the baby. You gave me a reason to live."

Sniffling, she lifted drenched eyes to meet his. "I don't really want you to give up your parental rights."

"Nah, it's for the best that way." Quinn hesitated for a beat before mentally scolding himself and dropping his hand from her cheek to her belly. Emotions, dark and bittersweet, swamped him until he was afraid he'd break down and sob like a pussy. And beg her to run away with him, which logic dictated just wasn't feasible. He couldn't put her and the baby through a life filled with danger. He wouldn't. "Probably better you don't put my name on the birth certificate at all."

"No way."

"Mara, think about it. Once you're home, I can't guarantee Liam or any of my enemies won't come after you both to get to me."

Mara's chin jutted stubbornly. "Let me rephrase that in a way you'll understand. No fucking way. And I should slap you for even mentioning it."

He grinned. Couldn't help it. He snaked an arm around her waist and pulled her in for a quick, hard kiss. She melted into him, clinging to his shoulders with both hands as her tongue met his. His body stirred, and he wished he had time for a longer good-bye.

Breathing hard, she drew away a fraction of an inch. "Promise me something. If it's ever safe, you'll come back to us. Even—" She stopped short, cleared her throat. "Even if you can't stay."

A promise he couldn't possibly keep. He rested his forehead against hers and sighed. "I'd like to."

"But?"

"But I don't know if it will ever be safe."

Chapter Twenty-Seven

A panicked shout from outside startled Mara, and she looked toward the door that led to the courtyard. Travis's muscles tensed underneath her hands.

"It's Rustam," she said. "Are we too late?"

"Christ, I hope not." Travis let go of her and slung his pack over one shoulder. "Can you make out what he's saying?"

Mara focused on the words Rustam kept shouting. She wasn't sure, but it sounded like…

Oh, no. She knew that word. "Help. He's shouting for help."

Travis leaned down and kissed her hard. "Stay here. Hide in the corner behind the *soba*. The concrete should stop any bullets."

"What are you going to do? You're not armed."

"I'll do what I've been trained to do. I'll improvise." He bared his teeth in what might have passed for a smile—if he was a shark. She watched him go, and the hair stood at attention along her arms. He enjoyed the prospect of facing down impossible odds.

How on earth could he enjoy it?

For all of her newfound strength, her heart pounded a conga beat against her ribs, and she wanted nothing more than to do exactly what he said: hide. While he faced down a well-equipped, well-trained enemy by himself, she wanted to hide. Disgust rolled through her, sweeping away the most ragged edges of her fear. Oh, yes, she was still afraid, but she wasn't going to let the crazy man get himself killed for her. She also wasn't stupid enough to think she stood a chance against his enemies. Still, she could help by getting the Belyakovs out of the house and to safety. Without the added weight of worrying about all of them, Travis would be able to focus on…doing whatever he had to do.

Mara tiptoed across the room and peeked out the crack where the two halves of the wooden double doors didn't sit together quite right. In the courtyard, a group of soldiers stood around Travis in a loose circle. Surrounded.

Her heart turned a somersault in her chest. They had the father of her child surrounded, and all of them appeared to be armed with huge guns. The Belyakovs huddled together in the alcove by the kitchen, Rustam with one arm around his wife and the other protectively holding his granddaughter against his barrel chest.

This wasn't fair to them. The Belyakovs had been nothing but friendly, welcoming two strangers into their home with open arms and warm hearts, and now they were in terrible danger. She and Travis never should have stayed here.

Weighing her options, she glanced back at the group of soldiers. They stood far enough up the narrow courtyard, near the main gate by the road, that she might just be able to stay out of their line of sight if she clung to the deeper shadows alongside the building. If she could sneak across to the Belyakovs without being spotted, she might be able to lead them through the chicken coops into the garden behind the house. Jumping over the fence around the property would be difficult for her, but she wasn't planning this escape for herself—she was staying with Travis. No matter what. But if the Belyakovs could get over the fence, they could run to a neighbor and be safe. At the very least, they deserved that much from her.

Mara drew a steadying breath and pushed one half of the door open several centimeters. The creak of the wood sounded like nails on a chalkboard to her ears, but nobody else seemed to notice. Except Rustam. He met her stare across the courtyard and shook his head once. She pretended not to see and pushed the door open another couple centimeters, wincing at every squeak of metal hinges and groan of old wood. It seemed to take forever to open it wide enough that she could slip out. Then she was out in the cold, pressed against the side of the building, silently gulping in air to make up for the oxygen deprivation from holding her breath too long.

She made it halfway to the Belyakovs before Travis's head lifted and turned in her direction like a predator scenting its prey. He cursed viciously and shoved between two of the soldiers.

No! Was he trying to get them all killed? Why was he drawing attention to her? Now the soldiers knew—

Except they didn't shoot him or try to stop him in any way.

He caught her by the arms and yanked her against him in a tight hug. "I told you to stay inside, you insane woman."

Mara stared over Travis's shoulder at the soldiers. They didn't attack when his back was turned. Gasping, she pushed on his chest until he let her go. As she walked toward the group, she didn't dare to hope. Not yet. She studied each of the faces in turn. Harvard. Jean-Luc…

Poor Jean-Luc. She lightly touched his cheek underneath

one hideous-looking black eye. "Are you okay?"

"Of course, *cher*," he said, lifting her knuckles to his lips. "Nothing I haven't had before."

"Laying it on thick there, Cajun," someone muttered from across the circle. She looked over at the owner of the voice.

"Ian! Oh, and Seth. You have no idea how happy I am to see you guys! I was afraid—"

"What 'bout me?" a familiar voice demanded. She spun and threw her arms around Jesse. He all but lifted her off her feet.

"Jesus Christ," he whispered in her ear and hugged her tighter. "I'm so happy you're safe."

"Okay, enough." Travis pulled her out of Jesse's arms, and she experienced the pure thrill of feminine power. Travis was jealous. Of Jesse. Her cousin, of all people. It was laughable, but she couldn't help herself for enjoying the moment. Travis wouldn't be jealous if he didn't care.

She smiled at Jesse, expecting to see him smile back like they were sharing an inside joke. Instead, he glared at Travis with an equal amount of anger, and that feminine thrill morphed into alarm. No. Uh-uh. It wasn't happening. She was not going to let two of the most important men in her life ruin their friendship because of some testosterone pissing match.

She shoved between them. "Oh, my God. Really? You two are idiots. Jesse, stop being an overprotective jackass. This"—she motioned to her belly—"is just as much my doing as it is his. And Travis..." She couldn't think of an appropriate scolding for him, so she decided to show him exactly how she felt instead. She pinched his earlobe and pulled his lips down to hers, ending the hard kiss with a punishing nip to his lower lip. "Okay?"

He smiled and tucked her hair behind her ear. "Roger

that."

Jesse's eyes narrowed, and he acted like he wanted to protest, but after a tense moment he nodded and backed away. "Is he treating you right?" he asked in his rusty version of Spanish, knowing full well Travis couldn't speak the language.

"He's still learning," she replied, also in Spanish. "But he's a smart man. Give me time and I'll have him trained."

Jean-Luc burst out laughing. Of course. Given all the languages he was fluent in, he probably spoke Spanish. Her cheeks heated up, but then she surprised herself by shrugging off the embarrassment. There was no point to it. It wasn't like they all didn't already know she and Travis had been intimate.

"She's a spitfire," Jean-Luc said when he caught his breath. "I like her."

"You like all women, Cajun," the group chorused, but one female voice stood out from the drone of baritones. Lanie.

Mara took a step in her direction, but hesitated. Lanie had never been the hugging type, and at the moment, she looked as if she'd gone a round with a heavyweight boxer.

Lanie gave a soft laugh and held out her arms. "Aw, come here."

Mara buried her face in her best friend's coat and told herself she wasn't going to cry. Again. Dammit, she'd spilled enough tears already. "Thank you for coming to get me."

"Girl, you think I wouldn't? Hey." She pushed Mara back at arm's length and smiled. "I'm a ornery, overbearing bitch on my best days, and there aren't many people who put up with me, not their mention call me their friend. I won't risk losing one of them."

Mara looked around the group of men and smiled when she realized Jesse was hovering close to Lanie—like, possessively close, and she didn't think his proximity had anything to do with his familial need to protect her. "Looks like you have a few more friends than you think."

Lanie followed her gaze, but noticeably skipped over the area where Jesse was standing. "Eh, they're not a bad bunch. I might keep them."

Uh-huh, Mara thought and had to fight to control her grin. Lanie had always had a thing for Jesse, and he obviously had a thing for her and…oh, yes. Mara would be doing some serious matchmaking when they got home. Why hadn't this dawned on her before now? Her cousin and her best friend. The two of them were cast from the same mold. Perfect for each other.

Completely unlike her and Travis.

She met his gaze, and her amusement faded to concern. He'd slammed the shutters down over his expression again, letting nothing of his thoughts show through. But somehow, she knew. Part of him had hoped Gabe would be here with the rest of the team, alive and okay.

He cleared his throat and asked the team, "How did you find us?"

"Same way we found Gabe in Colombia," Jesse said. "Harvard's encrypted GPS system on your phone. Lucky for you Harvard's a genius or else the SEALs would have found you long before Mara made that phone call to her mother."

"I'm sorry about that," Mara said, shame heating up her face. "I had no idea they could track us like that."

Travis soothed a hand down her back, then returned his attention to Jesse. "Sitrep?"

Jesse gave him a quick rundown of everything that had happened to the team in the past twenty-four hours. Being held captive inside their own plane. Their traitor of a pilot suddenly growing a heart and letting them go before taking off for Romania with Gabe—still alive, but just barely—on board the jet.

"Can we trust him?" Travis asked.

"Hell, no," Jesse said. "He's a loose cannon. But under the circumstances, we didn't have much other choice. Gabe needed hospital care, and Garcia was the only person who could get him to one."

"And I had to leave my dog with him again," Ian grumbled. "Tank wouldn't leave Gabe's side. I swear if my boy comes back with so much as a fucking flea bite, Garcia's a dead man."

Jesse nodded. "For once, Reinhardt, we are in full agreement." He returned his attention to Travis. "The bad guys aren't here yet—"

"Because they don't have the boy genius at their disposal," Jean-Luc said and scrubbed his knuckles over Harvard's head.

"Right," Jesse said. "But they are zeroed in on this area. They will be coming in hot, and we're black on ammo."

"So basically, we're fucked," Travis said.

"Yup," Jesse agreed. "About sums it up. What is it you SEALs say? No easy day, right?"

"Hooyah." Travis reached out, bumped his fist to Jesse's, and just like that, whatever had been broken between them was fixed. They both seemed to relax, as if accepting that they each played an important role in her life.

Mara opened her mouth to ask how on earth a fist bump suddenly made everything all better, but Lanie set a hand on her shoulder and whispered next to her ear, "Don't even try understanding the dumber sex. Just be happy they're getting along now and not punching each other's lights out."

Mara groaned. "Please tell me they didn't get into a fistfight."

"They sure did. Jesse KO'd Quinn a few days ago. Like I said, just be glad they're getting along."

"All right, guys," Travis said and faced the team. "We need to get gone. Jean-Luc, explain the situation to the

Belyakovs and tell them to pack their bags. It won't be safe for them to stay here…" He glanced toward the front gate and trailed off.

"Travis?" Mara whispered, following his gaze. She didn't see anything beyond the gate but the pitted street.

"Are we out of time?" Jesse asked.

"Yeah. Fuck!" He whirled and grabbed Mara's hand, dragging her toward the house. "Inside! Now!"

Chapter Twenty-Eight

The Belyakovs' house was big by Transnistrian standards, but pack seven built warriors all but steaming with testosterone into the kitchen and the house became claustrophobic.

Mara sat with Nadejda, trying to keep her entertained and out of the way while also keeping one eye on the guys. Travis stood at the head of the table, discussing defense strategies, and looked every bit the warrior in snow-camouflage fatigues with a pistol strapped to one thigh and a large knife secured to the other. He was convinced they were under attack, even though there had been no rain of bullets, no grenades, no sounds from their attackers—nothing for nearly a half hour.

The silence was almost more terrifying than an overt attack would have been, and Mara's nerves frayed with each passing minute. What were they waiting for?

"So our weakest point is here." Travis pointed to the hastily drawn map that Rustam had provided for them, indicating the east side of the property, which bordered a forest. The house and farm areas were enclosed by a six-foot-tall concrete wall, and beyond, Rustam's vineyard surrounded the house on two sides. Travis said the SEALs wouldn't attack from the vineyard because it'd leave them wide-open as they navigated through the tidy rows of dormant vines. So their only options were either a frontal assault from the road or a covert attack from the forest.

"How solid is the wall on that side of the property?" Travis asked.

Jean-Luc repeated the question in Russian, and Rustam shook his head as he replied.

"He says the wall isn't sturdy," Jean-Luc translated. "The winter has been hard here, and that whole area has multiple holes. Concrete doesn't set well in this weather, so he can't fix it until it warms up."

"That wall isn't going to do a fucking thing to keep anyone out," Ian said. He'd just returned from scooping out the perimeter with Seth. "It's about as defensible as Swiss cheese."

Lanie straightened away from the map. "I really hope this last-stand shit goes better for us than it did for the guys at the Alamo." She held up her hands in defense when several sets of eyes narrowed in her direction. "Just sayin'."

A beat passed in silence.

"Ideas?" Travis finally said.

"I know one thing we can do." Ian hoisted a burlap bag from the floor with his one good arm. He dropped it on the table, and a handful of pellets rolled out. "Fertilizer. And plenty more in the barn. We can cook us up some ANFO."

"Nice," Travis said. "Grab someone with two hands to help you."

Ian tapped Lanie on the shoulder and jerked his chin in a let's-go motion.

Scowling, Jesse watched them leave. "So we rig up a couple bombs. Then what?"

Travis dragged a hand back and forth over his head in

thought. "It'd help if we knew how many men we were up against."

"When I was out with Ian, I spotted a nice hide on the roof," Seth said. "I'll climb up with my scope and see if I can't get a head count."

"Good idea. How are you on ammo?"

"In the black. Could really use the pack I left in the van."

"Yeah, we all could, but I don't think we'll be getting anywhere near that van now. Jean-Luc, ask Rustam where—"

He didn't have to finish the question. Jean-Luc was already translating, and as he spoke Rustam grinned. He said something in an exuberant tone, and Jean-Luc's jaw dropped open. They carried on a fast conversation, then Jean-Luc laughed.

"Guys, we have the van. Rustam towed it here with his tractor. It's in the shed."

Travis slapped the table. "Rustam, man. You are a saint. Jesse—"

"On it." He followed Rustam and Jean-Luc to gather their weapons from the van. Seth trailed them out.

Once the room was empty, Travis sank into a chair and sighed, massaging his temples.

Poor guy looked exhausted.

Mara crossed to stand behind him and dug her fingers into the knots in his shoulders. "Headache?"

"It's not bad."

"Liar."

He dropped his hands and leaned back to smile up at her. "Yeah, I'm lying. Hurts like a bitch."

"You should try to rest. At least until something happens. We can't afford for you to have another migraine. Or another Paulie episode."

He winced. "You're right. I know you are, but I can't—"

The screech of electronic feedback split the air, making

them both jump.

"Quinn!" A voice called through a megaphone. "Oh, *Quinn*! Come out, come out. I know you're in there."

He straightened in his seat. "Liam. Christ, the SEALs *are* working with him." Hurt shone in his eyes before he blanked his features, and until that second, she hadn't realized just how much he'd been hoping it wasn't true.

"Come on, Quinn," Liam said. "Don't make me be the big bad wolf here, mate. All that huffing and puffing is tiring, so how about you come out and talk to me, man to man?" A pause. "No? Ah, I see you have some backup with you. Is that your sniper climbing up on the roof?"

A shot rang out.

Liam laughed. "Not anymore."

Mara's heart dropped. She covered her mouth with her hands. "Oh, God. Seth?"

Travis leaped to his feet and was out the door before she could stop him. She hesitated a second, then chased after him, but he stopped her in the kitchen alcove just short of the patio and pushed her down beside the hand-crank well. "Stay here. Stay hidden."

"So our mate Garcia flipped sides again, did he?" Liam continued, amusement threading through his voice. "He's slippery, that one. Good thing I never trusted him. Let me guess, he told you he's on his way to take Gabe to a hospital? You really believe that, Quinn? He's not exactly the all-for-one, one-for-all type. My bet, he dumped Gabe off in the snow somewhere and is on his way to Fiji as we speak."

No, that couldn't be true—their pilot couldn't be that heartless. But one look at Travis's darkening expression told her he believed it was very possible. He didn't trust Jace Garcia any more than he trusted Liam.

"Speaking of Gabe," Liam continued. "How is that spunky wife of his? Audrey?"

Travis squeezed his eyes shut as if the words were a knife flaying open his heart.

"Last I heard, she was on the beach with her easel painting a gorgeous sunset. No, wait. She's going inside that gorgeous house of theirs now. Should I tell my man to pop in and say hello for you? No, I don't think so. He won't leave anything left of her for me, and I plan to hop the first flight to Costa Rica as soon as we're done here and spend some quality time with that little bitch—oh! Look, there's your medic running across the courtyard. I should say hello."

Another shot.

"Jesse!" Heart hammering, Mara lurched toward the patio. Later she'd realize how stupid the move was, but in that moment, she was only reacting, panicking for her cousin, and not thinking rationally.

Liam laughed again. "Now who's that pretty woman there with you, Quinn?"

"Fuck!" Travis grabbed her around the waist and hauled her back inside. He slammed the double doors shut and ushered her behind the concrete column of the kitchen's *soba*. "Stay here."

Liam's voice chased after them. "Mean something to you, does she? That's brilliant. I'll be sure to cut out her heart and lay it on Rachael's grave. You remember my wife, Rachael, don't you?"

Travis's hands curled into fists at his sides, and she caught his arm. "Don't! He's trying to make you angry."

"It's working."

"Exactly why you shouldn't respond!"

His lips thinned into a hard line.

She tightened her grasp. "Please, Travis. Don't let him bait you."

"No snappy comeback?" Liam tsked. "Stubborn as a mule, you are. Here's how it'll be, then. You have until midnight tonight to turn yourself over to me. If you don't, I'll raze the house and kill everything with a heartbeat. Oh, and you might not want to leave that building. Anyone else sets foot in the courtyard, they're dead."

• • •

"This is a waste of time."

"I don't think so." Liam Miller turned and handed the loudspeaker to Captain Cold. He walked back toward the warmth of his vehicle, parked on the pitted road outside the Belyakov farm. "Why the hurry? They won't be going anywhere."

Captain Cold followed at his heels. "I want this over with. I want the threat Quinn poses to us neutralized."

"If you hadn't been so sloppy in the first place, this wouldn't be an issue."

Cold grabbed him by the front of his jacket and shoved him against the car door. "Listen, you prick. You're only here because my father doesn't know how to say no to you."

Liam leaned in until he could smell the stink of the captain's breath and lowered his voice. "The only reason you and your father haven't been tried for treason is because I took the fall for all of you. I lost everything to keep this operation functioning, including my wife. You fucking owe me this."

After a tense second, the captain backed off. "I'm telling you, waiting is a mistake. We should go in now."

Liam tugged on his coat to straighten it. "Ah, but that's not as much fun, is it?"

"This isn't about fun."

"Of course it is. That's why men like us, we never retire. We keep at it until someone eventually gets the better of us."

Like Quinn had gotten the better of Rachael.

His wife had been his match in every way, with her killer body and touch-me-and-I'll-kill-you attitude. Just as heartless and bloodthirsty, always hungry for more. More action, more money, more sex.

Jesus, the sex.

It had always been a war. She'd play it like she didn't want him, then flaunt around in her skimpy outfits, flashing a tit or her pussy at him until he was wound so tight he couldn't concentrate on anything but her. Then she'd fight him, drawing blood with her nails and teeth. But, in the end, she always submitted.

He missed it. Missed her more than he thought he could miss anything.

Sometimes when he closed his eyes, he could still see the expression of shock on her face in the moment before Quinn's bullet burrowed into her skull.

Fucking Quinn.

He wanted nothing more than to wipe that tosser and his team from the planet, but until that moment came, Liam wanted them all to sweat.

He again pictured the pretty Hispanic woman he'd gotten a glimpse of through his binoculars. Quinn had pulled her out of range fast, but the way he handled her…

Something there.

"Who was that woman with him?" he asked.

Cold's lips tightened under his snow mask. "Her name's Marisol Escareno. She's the stepdaughter of Senator Ramon Escareno, Republican, Texas. Big oil family, lots of money, very conservative. Recent intel suggests she may have been quietly disowned in all but name for fucking around with a man her stepfather didn't approve of."

And now she was here. With Quinn.

Interesting.

Liam climbed into his vehicle, then rolled down the

window. "Shoot into the courtyard every once in a while. Keep them on their toes, huh? I'll be back in a few hours."

He needed more information about this Marisol Escareno. Because as per the big man in charge, he was *off his leash* and had permission to do whatever he wanted to Quinn. Overrunning the house and flat-out killing everyone they found inside wasn't enough. He wanted Quinn to suffer the gut-wrenching heartbreak he had suffered, and he had a good feeling that Marisol was the just the key he needed to make that happen.

As Liam drove away, he glanced in the rearview mirror and saw Captain Cold give him the finger. He laughed. He'd have to do something about that cocksucker and his band of not-so-merry SEALs.

If they didn't appreciate his sacrifice, he'd just have to sacrifice them.

Chapter Twenty-Nine

"What are we going to do?"

Travis stopped pacing and dragged his hands over his head. "I don't know."

"We can't stay here."

"You want to try walking across that courtyard?" he snapped.

"No." Her voice wobbled, and she hated herself for it. Wasn't she stronger than that now? She straightened her shoulders and matched his snappishness with her own. "Don't yell at me. This isn't my fault."

To her surprise, he actually flinched as if she'd struck him. "Yeah. It isn't your fault." He sighed. "I'm sorry."

Dang it. Now she felt bad. "Travis…"

He held up a hand. "No, don't. I get it. We're both stressed out. It's fine. Just…let me think, okay?"

She nodded, and he began pacing back and forth across the room again. For a long time, the only sound was his boots on the floor, the *thunk thunk thunk* of his steps muffled by the throw rug.

But wait. He wasn't moving anymore.

Thunk. Thunk. Thunk.

So where was the sound coming from?

The floor moved under Mara's feet, and she let out a startled cry before she could stop herself. Was someone down there? She hadn't even realized there was a down there under the house, but she definitely wasn't imagining the sound she'd heard.

Another *thunk*. It vibrated through the floor and up her legs, and she clamped a hand to her mouth to keep from making any more noise in case it was the SEALs. Travis whirled around to face her, a question in his eyes. She pointed to the floor.

"Someone's down there," she mouthed.

His brow wrinkled in confusion, but he still drew his weapon and waved her back. Moving like a cat, he crept forward and pulled back the throw rug she'd been standing on.

A door. Under the rug.

It was latched shut, and someone was definitely trying to get through from the other side.

Mara wanted to tell him not to open it. Going to the basement never ended well for people in horror movies. But she kept her hand clamped over her mouth and watched as he slid the latch free from the metal loop keeping it secured. He flung the door open…

And Jean-Luc popped through like a Whac-a-Mole. The instant rush of relief was so overwhelming a bubble of hysterical laughter worked up from Mara's chest and burst free.

"Whoa. Friendly," Jean-Luc said.

Travis lowered his gun. "Christ. Who are you, Tunnel Rat?"

Jean-Luc grinned and called behind him, "Harvard!

Quinn just cracked a G.I. Joe joke."

"G.I. Joe was before my time," Harvard's voice called. "Are you all set? I'm going back down to help Ian."

"Yeah, we good up here." Jean-Luc made a face. "Fuck me, I'm getting old. Marcus would have thought that was funny."

"What's down there?" Travis asked.

Jean-Luc hoisted himself up and dusted off his clothes. "Rustam makes wine for a living. Ya think he wouldn't also have a wine cellar?"

"Honestly?" Travis said with a note of surprise in his tone. "I didn't know he was a winemaker."

"I tell ya, or what? Russians know how to swear and how to drink. Hey, Mara, what's so funny?"

She gave up trying to smother her giggles behind her hand. "Whac-a-Mole."

"What?" Jean-Luc and Travis said at the same time.

"Nothing." Reining in the rising sense of hysteria took more effort than she thought she possessed but, eventually, she managed tamp down the giggle fit and smooth her features to appear at least somewhat sane again. She didn't feel sane—her nerves were paper-thin and headed for a shredder—but that was a problem to deal with later.

She slid a cautious step forward and peeked into the cellar. The ladder didn't look at all sturdy, and it was dark beyond. "Is everyone else down there?"

"Yup. When Liam's men started firing, Rustam told me about the cellar, how it was connected to most of the buildings on the property. He led the way and we started collecting people."

"What about Jesse?"

Jean-Luc's features softened. "No worries, *cher*. They shot at him but missed."

"And Seth?" Travis asked.

"Same deal. Shot and missed. *Mais*, they wouldn't have missed, but he lost his footing on a patch of ice and slid off the roof just as they took the shot. They probably think they did hit him, and he is a bit banged up from the fall, but he's alive." He motioned to the cellar door with a flourish. "See for yourselves."

Travis went first but paused at the bottom to help her down the last few rungs of the ladder. It was pitch-dark until Jean-Luc joined them with a flashlight, and the bright white beam illuminated a tunnel wide enough for two people to walk shoulder to shoulder and tall enough for Jean-Luc to stand up straight, and he was a big man. It was only a dozen or so feet long and let out into a larger tunnel lined with barrels stacked three high.

"Is this all wine?" Mara asked.

Jean-Luc nodded. "Russia has been trying to destabilize this region by putting bans on Moldovan wine, which is one of their biggest exports. So all these people are making wine and there's nowhere for it to go."

She ran a finger over one dust-covered barrel. "But they keep making it?"

"What else are they going to do? It's all they know."

"That's sad."

Travis walked ahead of them. "And nothing we need to be concerned with. Where's the rest of the team?"

Mara scowled at his back. He might not need a distraction, but she did, and wine was a much better topic than death and destruction. "Too bad I can't drink right now. I could sure use a glass."

"F'true." Jean-Luc gave her a conspiratorial wink. "There's another room just up ahead," he told Travis. "You'll see a door. Team's inside."

Travis found the door and ducked through. "Move it, you two. We need a new plan."

"God." She threw her hands up in disgust. "Can't he just give me a moment to catch my breath?"

Jean-Luc held open the door for her. "He has only one setting, *cher*, and it's warrior. But that's what we love about him."

On the other side was a large, square room with several floor-to-ceiling racks of bottled wine. Travis and the rest of the team had gathered around a scarred workbench and Ian was showing them all how to mix fertilizer into bombs. Lanie glanced up when Mara entered, gave a quick nod of hello, then went back to helping Ian. Jesse also checked on her, his gaze warm and assessing and like a balm to her frayed nerves. But all too soon, he returned his attention to the work at hand.

They all seemed to have a warrior mode, even the affable Jean-Luc.

Everyone except her.

The hysteria was creeping back, and she needed an escape before she completely lost it. She looked around, hoping to spot Valentina and Nadejda, but they weren't in the room. For that matter, neither was Rustam. "Where are the Belyakovs?"

Jean-Luc pointed upward. "In their section of the house."

"Is it safe for them to stay up there?"

"Just as safe as down here. We're not hidden, Mara. If Liam's men stormed the house right now, they'd find the wine cellar without problem. So Rustam thought keeping Nadejda in her room, among the familiar, was best."

"Oh." She glanced around again. She had thought the cellar offered them a safe haven, and to have that pretty illusion shattered completely deflated her. It was just one blow after another and she couldn't take it anymore. She just wasn't as strong as the rest of them.

She swayed on her feet, and Jean-Luc caught her arm.

"Hey. Whoa. Medic!"

In the space of a heartbeat, she had Jesse on one side and Travis on the other, and they led her over to a chair Lanie pulled out by the workbench.

Jesse squatted in front of her. "Mara? Hey, Marisol, look at me. Are you havin' any pain? Any blood?"

Oh, God. This was embarrassing. "No, I'm fine. No pain. No blood. I was just…overwhelmed."

"She needs a place to sit," Jesse said. "And someone needs to go up to the well, get her some water."

"I'll go," Travis said.

"Put on a vest," Jesse said, but his focus was still 100 percent on her.

"Stop it." She waved them all away and stood to prove she was fine, but Travis had already gone. She called after him and got no response. "Jesse, I'm okay now. Call him back. Nobody has to risk their life to go out to the well."

"He'll be fine. I'm more worried about you. Are you sure you're not havin' any pain?"

"I swear I'm fine. Nauseous and tired, but those are my defaults anymore. If I had even an inkling that something was wrong, I'd tell you."

"Okay," Jesse said after a moment and stroked a hand over her hair. "I believe you, but I still insist you take it easy until things start rollin'. Put your feet up. Eat somethin', drink some water. Try to relax. I know under the circumstances that's damn near impossible—"

"Understatement."

"But you've been through a lot of trauma lately, and we don't want to risk your or the baby's health."

He was right. Mara knew it, even though it bothered her that she was more of a burden than a help. But she didn't have any usable skills in this situation, so it'd be better for everyone if she just stayed away for a while.

Seth threw blankets down in the far corner of the cellar to make a comfortable spot, and she allowed Jesse to lead her over. On the way, they ran into Valentina coming downstairs. The older woman made a big fuss over her and insisted she'd make something warm for everyone to drink.

At Jesse's urging, Mara sat down and put her feet up on the pillow Harvard had retrieved from one of the bedrooms. Valentina reappeared, and Jesse rushed to help her with the tray she carried. Valentina fussed around Mara some more, covering her with a blanket, finding more pillows to prop behind her back, urging her to drink a fragrant tea. Eventually, and despite the language barrier, Jesse convinced the woman that everything was okay and she should go back to her own family.

Mara watched her go. The Belyakovs were such gracious hosts, even when under siege. And she feared the only thing they would receive in return for their endless hospitality was, at best, a destroyed home. At worst…

No. She couldn't consider the worst-case scenario. It was too terrifying.

"I hate this. I'm doing nothing but distracting everyone. I feel so useless."

"I know, buttercup." Jesse sat down beside her and lightly bumped his shoulder to hers. "How you holdin' up?"

"I'm…" She couldn't find the right word and stalled by lifting the mug of tea to her mouth, but her stomach was too tied up in nervous knots to drink. She set it aside. "Tired. Just so tired of all this. What if—"

"No, don't. There are no what ifs, okay?" He tugged on a strand of her hair. "We will get you home, Mara."

She scoffed. "All I have at home is a dwindling bank account and a duplex I can't possibly afford now that Ramon's cut me off."

"C'mon, now. You have a job you love. You have Lanie.

And Aunt Rosa—"

"Yeah. Mom." She recalled the phone conversation she'd had with her mother, and her heart broke all over again. "You know that call I made to her? Mom had no clue I'd been abducted. She was just worried Ramon would find out she was talking to me."

"That fucker's a waste of air." Jesse looped an arm around her shoulders and squeezed her gently against his side.

A lump clogged up Mara's throat, and she had to swallow it back before speaking. "I wish she'd stand up for once and choose me over Ramon."

She gazed across the room as Travis emerged from one of the tunnels carrying a bucket of water. It was like he had a sixth sense, always appearing when she most wanted to see him. Their eyes met, and his narrowed a faction.

"Oh. Dammit." She wiped at her tears. Last thing any of them needed was for her wild hormone fluctuations to distract Travis, but sure enough, he left the water on the floor and strode toward her like a man on a mission.

Jesse leaned in and gave her a hard hug. Before pulling away, he whispered, "You're not your mother, Mara. You're stronger than she's ever been."

With that, he got up and walked across the cellar, clapping Travis on the shoulder as he passed.

• • •

Christ, he hated seeing Mara's tears.

Everything in Quinn revolted whenever he saw her cry. She kept assuring him it was only a result of pregnancy hormones wreaking havoc on her emotions, but it still fucking slayed him.

Jesse hugged her and then got up—which was a damn good thing because, cousin or no, Quinn still didn't want to see another man's hands on her.

As they crossed paths, Jesse clapped him on the shoulder. "We have hours until Liam's deadline. Take some time. You both need it."

"I don't—"

Jesse's fingers dug into his shoulder. "Let me rephrase. She needs it. She's making herself sick with worry."

His stomach tightened with dread. "Is she all right? And the baby?"

Jesse nodded. "Make sure she stays hydrated and off her feet."

"Got it. Call me when you're ready to place the bombs."

Jesse gave a thumbs-up before striding over to help the rest of the team manufacture as many of the fertilizer bombs as possible.

"You should go with him now," Mara said from her little nest on the floor. "I wish everyone would stop fussing over me. I'm fine."

No doubt she had a point, but as worried as he was about her and the baby, he'd be useless to the team. When Jean-Luc had called for a medic and he'd glanced over to see Mara pale as bone and on the verge of passing out, his heart had all but slammed to a stop. He still wasn't sure if it had started beating again.

He should tell her all that. Should let her know in that moment, when he'd thought she was injured or ill, he'd never been more frightened in his life. But the words sounded ridiculous in his head and felt hollow on his tongue, so he kept his mouth shut. She'd needed water, so he had to go boil some and—

"Travis."

He closed his eyes. Christ, he loved the way his name sounded when she said it—even when she was clearly exasperated with him. He opened his eyes again and faced her.

"Go help your team," she said.

He shook his head. "I need some downtime."

"You're a horrible liar."

He scratched at his jaw. Winced. "Uh, I'm usually pretty good at it."

"Not with me, you're not."

And that should terrify him. It didn't. In fact, he liked that she could see through his bullshit and wasn't afraid to call him out on it. And again, he should probably tell her that, but the words wouldn't come.

After too many minutes of silence stretched between them, Mara sighed. "So are you just going to stand there, or are you going to come over here and hold me like we both want?"

Thank Christ. He'd been aching to wrap her up in his arms but hadn't known how she'd react, or even how to approach the subject with her.

He sat down and pulled her onto his lap, securing her against him with his arms around her and her head tucked under his chin. He wrapped a blanket around them both to keep away the chill of the concrete floor.

Tension seeped out of his muscles, and like that, he could breathe easily again. He kissed the top of her head. "I wish I could send you away from here."

"If you could send me safely away, you'd be going with me."

"Yeah, I would. In a heartbeat."

He felt her lips curve into a smile against his neck. "Where would we go?"

"Oh, man. Someplace warm. I don't want to see snow again for a while."

"Same here. I've always wanted to go to Costa Rica. I've heard it's beautiful. We could visit Gabe when he gets better.

I'd like to meet his wife."

A cold pit opened up in his chest. Was Gabe alive? Or had Jace Garcia simply dumped him off somewhere to die before running away like the two-faced coward he was? Fuck, he hated having to trust the pilot with something as important as Gabe's life.

Did Audrey know yet that her husband had been shot, or was she still whiling away the hours at their beach house, waiting for his return?

Mara's hand cradled the back of his neck and she lifted her head to look up at him. "Travis?"

"Uh, yeah. It is beautiful." His voice came out rough, and he cleared his throat, kissed the tip of her nose. "Costa Rica, I mean. The beaches are amazing. We could sit there in the sun with those fancy umbrella drinks—"

"Except I can't drink," she reminded.

"Okay, I'll drink yours, too. I'll need that and a few more to get use to this whole daddy thing."

She gave the short hairs at the base of his skull a playful tug. "You'll be better at it than you think. And, dammit, I want that umbrella drink, so let's fast-forward things a bit. We'll both enjoy drinks and help the baby build a sand castle."

Christ, he could picture it so clearly. Mara and a mini version of her—because the baby had to look like her, right?—playing in the sand on a sunny, tropical day. And he wanted it. Wanted umbrella drinks and sand castles and both her and the baby in his life forever.

Yeah. Nice fantasy, but they couldn't run away together. They might not even live through the next twelve hours, so there was no point in dwelling on the what ifs of the future when now might be all they had.

And right now, he wanted nothing more than to kiss her.

Lowering his head, he claimed her lips, keeping the kiss soft, drugging, needing some way to show her the feelings he couldn't put into words. She returned the kiss with so much passion and raw emotion his body began to stir. He wished he could make love to her again, once more, in case it was their last chance to be together. But the team was right across the room, and this was no time for sex. The kiss was the best he could do, and he infused it with his heart and soul.

When he finally broke the contact of their lips, he met her gaze. Tears cascaded from her eyes. This was the woman he'd fallen in lust with the moment they met, the woman he'd fallen wildly in love with he didn't know when, and the soon-to-be mother of his child. Holding her gaze, he leaned over and kissed her belly. He wasn't good with words, couldn't vocalize how much she and the baby meant to him.

All he could do was show her and hope it was enough.

Chapter Thirty

At eleven o'clock, one hour before Liam's deadline, every light at the Belyakov farm flickered and died.

Mara tightened her hand on Travis's as the room plunged into darkness. Everyone had abandoned the cellar, which would essentially be a concrete death trap once the siege started, and again gathered in the kitchen. Since it was the heart of the house, it was the best spot from which to make their stand.

"It's okay," he whispered next to her ear. "They only cut the electricity. We were expecting this."

A flame sparked to life in the center of the room, and Jean-Luc set a candle down in the middle of the table.

Outside, an electronic screech split the night.

"Quinn!" Liam's voice echoed through the house and sent chills racing over Mara's skin. She again tightened her hand, afraid to let him go. "Have you made your decision? You only have an hour left before everyone in that house dies—including your girlfriend, Marisol."

"Fuck," Travis said under his breath.

Mara felt him tense beside her and let go of his hand in favor of wrapping her arms around him. She didn't trust that he wouldn't offer himself up as a sacrifice.

"Yes, I know her name," Liam said. "Marisol Escareno, but she prefers to go by Mara. I've spent the last few hours reading up on her. Seems you knocked her up, and her stepdad didn't like that very much. You still have…fifty-four minutes. If you're not standing in front of me by midnight, I promise you I will put a bullet in her head like you did Rachael's."

"Quinn," Jesse said and leaned over the table. "You better not be thinkin' 'bout goin' out there. He will kill her either way if he gets the chance. We stick to our plan."

Travis's teeth ground together, but he nodded.

"What exactly is the plan?" Mara asked the room.

Lanie picked up one of the AK-47s on the table and checked it. "Basically, we're going to shoot them so they can't shoot us."

Mara glanced from one grim face to the next, waiting for someone to elaborate further. Nobody did. "Wait. Do you mean that's it? I thought y'all had a real plan."

"This is a real plan," Jesse said.

"A real shitty one," Ian muttered.

"Yeah, but all we got."

Oh, God. They were all crazy. They had to be to go up against these men with little more than a handful of bullets, a few bombs, and a prayer. "What happens if we run out of ammunition?"

Travis extracted himself from her arms and also picked up one of the guns. "Hopefully we'll run out of targets first."

"And if not?"

He met her gaze. "You don't want to know the answer, Mara."

She exhaled hard. He was right about that. She really didn't want to know. "Okay. What can I do?"

Travis set down the weapon again and accepted the bulletproof vest Jesse handed him. But instead of putting it on himself like the rest of the team was, he slid it over her head.

"No!" she protested.

"Yes."

"You need this more than me."

"What I need—he leaned in and pressed a quick kiss to her mouth—"is for you to be safe. I want you to stay in here, in the corner behind the *soba* with Valentina and Nadejda."

"What about Rustam?" She spotted the Russian man with one of the AK-47s and gasped. "Oh, no. He's not fighting, is he? He's too old!"

"It's his home, remember? Good luck trying to stop him from defending it." Travis gave a small smile and rubbed her chilled arms. "He'll be okay. We all will."

He didn't believe that. She could see the truth of it in his eyes but didn't call him out on the lie. Maybe he'd needed to say it as much as she had wanted to hear it, even if it wasn't true.

He finished securing her vest, then gave her shoulders another quick squeeze before returning to the table, where the rest of the team was talking strategy. From the sounds of things, the conversation grew heated when Travis joined in, but they might as well have not been speaking English for all she understood of it.

What a mess.

She tried to distract herself and Nadejda by teaching the girl some more English and Spanish words. And it worked for a few minutes...

Until she realized the men had gone quiet.

She glanced in their direction. Jean-Luc passed Travis a small makeup compact and he dipped his fingers into the gray paint. Using the handheld mirror in the compact, he smeared the paint over his face.

Wait. Face paint?

Mara cut through the crowd and positioned herself in front of Travis with her hands on her hips. "Where are you going?"

Several of the men shared a look that said *uh-oh* and promptly backed away with their hands raised in supplication when she glared daggers at them. Ha, afraid of a pregnant woman. Some warriors they were.

Travis kept working with the paint, dabbing streaks of white over the gray base coat.

"Where are you going?" she demanded again. Didn't take a warfare genius to know that he wouldn't need the face paint if he were planning to defend the house from inside like the other guys.

"Most of our team is wounded," he said matter-of-factly. "And we're up against at least two SEALs that we know of. I don't think there are as many men out there as Liam would like us to believe, but it only takes one determined SEAL to dispose of seven injured men and a seventy-three-year-old winemaker."

Mara shivered at the ice in his tone and had to wonder how many men he'd *disposed* of in his career. Probably more than she cared to know about. "So, you're going to…what exactly?"

"Even the odds."

"You're *not* going after Liam by yourself."

"Liam's not the real threat here. He's dangerous, yeah, and plenty crazy, especially if he's still into the coke. But it's the SEALs I'm worried about, so I'm going after them."

Was that supposed to make her feel better? Because it didn't. At. All. She turned to her cousin. "Jesse, you told him not even ten minutes ago that he had to stick to the plan."

"Yeah, but I also knew it would come to this. You were

right to be worryin' about our ammo situation, Mara. It's not good. Even with the help of Ian's bombs, we'll run out of bullets long before we run out of targets unless something is done."

"I know the two SEALs," Travis added. "I've trained with them, know their strengths and weaknesses. So what's the best way to make a gun safe?"

Mara frowned at the non sequitur. "Uh, you…take the bullets out, I guess."

He nodded. "And I'm going to take the bullets out of Liam's gun."

She caught her breath. "Are you going to kill them?"

"If I have to."

"But…" She bit back the protest she'd been about to speak and glanced over her shoulder at the rest of the team. All of them tried very hard to pretend they weren't listening, but their ears were tuned in to every word. Travis probably wouldn't appreciate her announcing to his team that he was unwell. At the same time, she couldn't bear the thought of him going out into the snowy darkness and lapsing into another fugue. If Paulie came back, he could get lost and freeze to death. Or, worse, be captured by Liam. That wouldn't do any of them any good. "Why can't someone else do it?"

"I've had arctic warfare training."

"And they haven't?"

He shook his head. "Not enough. Gabe was the only other guy with the skills to take on a mission like this, and he's not here." He lowered his voice. "Besides, look at them, Mara. They're all injured."

Her gaze traveled over each of the men. Even in the flickering candlelight Ian's complexion was ashen, and a makeshift sling held his arm against his body. One of Seth's eyes was so swollen he couldn't possibly see out of it, and he moved in stiff, measured steps. Dry blood caked a cut on Jesse's lower lip, and the shadow of a bruise colored his jaw. Yes, it was true every one of the men was injured in some way, but…

Mara turned back to Travis, cupped his painted face in her palms, and kissed him lightly on the mouth. When she drew away, she murmured for his ears only, "So are you."

His lips tightened, but he said nothing in response, only pulled out of her grasp and faced his men. "Are we all good with this new plan?"

"Yes, sir," they said in solemn unison and Mara was half surprised they didn't snap into salutes. Then again, maybe not. Although they had been well trained by Travis and Gabe and they were the most honorable men she'd ever known, at the end of the day, they were still a raggedy, headstrong bunch of mercenaries.

And in that moment, she both admired and hated every one of them.

"You're really going to let him go out there by himself?" She aimed the question directly at Jesse.

He stared at Travis for a long time, then nodded. "I don't like it, but we don't have any other choice."

"Don't give me that. You should go with him."

"He'll only slow me down," Travis said at the same time Jesse shook his head and said, "I'll only slow him down."

Mara crossed her arms and glared at each of them in turn. Finally, she gave up on Jesse, who appeared even less apologetic than Travis. Typical Jesse, stubborn as ever. She focused the full force of her glare on Travis, but he didn't look all that much more apologetic. She flung her hands upward in frustration and, honestly, fear so deep she felt the ache of it in her bones.

"Fine. Go play war and get yourself killed. See if I care." The statement lost some of its punch when she choked on the last few words.

"I know what I'm doing, sweetheart." Travis hesitated only a beat before pulling her into his arms again for a hard kiss. "I love you."

With that, he let go of her, took the rifle that someone held out to him, and ducked through the door.

Chest heaving with surpassed sobs, Mara stared after him. She couldn't explain it and was too terrified to analyze the sensation closely, but she experienced a sickening, sinking dread as the freezing night swallowed him up.

She should be happy. He'd said the words she'd wanted to hear from him since their very first night together.

But, God, why would he say those three amazing, heart-rending words to her *now* of all times?

Deep down, she knew exactly why, and as the realization bubbled up from her subconscious, she pressed her hand over her mouth to keep from getting sick.

He'd told her as a kind of deathbed confession.

• • •

The look of shock and horror on Mara's face…

Yeah, not exactly the expression he'd hoped for after dropping the L-bomb. Then again, he hadn't handled the situation well. Those three words had popped out of his mouth without his conscious consent, and it had scared the living hell out of him to hear himself saying them. So instead of manning up and facing the consequences, good or bad, he'd made like a ghost and vanished. Just like he always did when it came to Mara.

Fucking coward. Not honorable. Not even close to worthy of her, but fuck it. He was a selfish bastard, and he was done fighting his feelings for her. Didn't know how, but he'd make their relationship work. He'd give Mara the man she deserved and that baby a daddy to be proud of.

A chill shot down his spine and nailed him in the ass. Christ. Even now, the thought of being someone's dad freaked him out. He sure had his work cut out for him, but for the first time, he thought he might actually be able to do it. He might even be a good father if he looked at it like a mission.

Be advised, your objective is to raise a child from birth to adulthood so that she is a productive member of society. Minimum casualties.

Copy that, Quinn thought, then shook his head at himself and stopped moving, taking cover behind the Belyakovs' chicken coops. He sucked in a deep breath. His newfound determination in regards to fatherhood was all well and good, but he couldn't let it distract him now. If he did, he'd never even see the baby. He'd never be able to apologize and make it up to Mara for screwing up his confession of love so badly.

Focus on tonight's mission first. The rest he could deal with later.

Quinn sucked in a breath, let it out slowly through his nose, and slipped along the chicken coop until he faced the concrete wall surrounding the house.

If anything, this was the most dangerous part. He was completely vulnerable as he pulled himself up and over the wall—but nobody bothered him, and he landed on his feet on the other side without incident. Weapon in hand again, he low-walked through the short open space between the wall and the tree line of the forest. He found a tree trunk wide enough to offer cover and ducked behind it. Listened.

Nothing.

It was looking more and more like Liam didn't have as many men at his disposal as he'd wanted them to believe. Either that or he did have a platoon of men and they were all waiting at the front gate to storm the farm.

Nah. The first possibility was much more likely.

But that didn't mean these guys were any less dangerous. Whether he had ten men or a hundred at his command, Liam wouldn't tolerate anything less than brutal efficiency.

But still, shouldn't he be hearing...something? Up until now, between the taunts through the loudspeaker and the occasional potshots at the courtyard, Liam and his men had made no secret of their presence.

Why go stealth all of the sudden?

Unless they knew he was out here with them. And if that was the case, he might as well bend over now and kiss his ass good-bye. The element of surprise was about the only thing he had going for him.

Except his instincts told him he still had that element. Liam's biggest weakness was that he expected cowardice from his enemies—because for all of his specialized training and bluster, at his heart, he was a coward himself. He liked to blame Quinn for the murder of Rachael McDonald, the woman he claimed as his wife even though there was no marriage on record. But the truth of it was, he could have stopped her death from happening at any time before Quinn pulled the trigger. He could have warned Rachael that the cartel she did mercenary work for was about to crumble out from under her. He could have dropped the facade that he was an upstanding SAS operative and flipped sides to fight beside her. Hell, he was steps in front of Quinn when they went through that door—if he had loved her like he claimed, he could have even stepped in front of the bullet and taken it for her.

But Liam was a coward.

And he'd expect nothing less than that from Quinn.

So, no. Quinn was confident they didn't know he was outside the house. And, come to think of it, why hadn't they attacked yet? It had to be after Liam's midnight deadline by now.

Something else was going on here.

Quinn moved as fast as he could in the darkness and ankle-deep snow. His footfalls sounded like gunshots to him in the silence. A thin layer of ice crusted the top of the snow and cracked each time his foot broke through, but he couldn't take the time to stop and fashion himself a crude pair of snowshoes.

A shadow shot out of the trees at a dead run, no stealth whatsoever, and slammed into him before he could jump out of the way. They went down in a tangle of limbs, and Quinn let go of his gun in favor of his knife. He slid it into the guy's kidney and that was the end of it. Nice and quiet.

Quinn rolled him over and pulled off his mask. If he was a SEAL, Quinn didn't know him, but was that…?

Holy shit. He already had two other knife holes in his chest. No wonder he hadn't had much fight left in him.

Quinn pushed to his feet and grabbed the dead man's gun, scooped up his own, and continued picking his way toward the front of the property. But the closer he got, the more his skin crawled with unease.

Too. Fucking. Quiet.

The kind of quiet that only came with the dead. He stopped short, his nerves jangling, which was nothing new. If anyone said they weren't nervous going into a combat situation, they were either lying or sociopaths. But behind the usual nerves was a klaxon of alarm blaring that he needed to get gone. As in, right fucking now.

How had the guy ended up knifed?

Still, the panic could be his brain injury talking. Ever since the accident, he'd become much more reactive than he'd ever been before. He took another handful of steps…

Blood.

Huge swaths of it, dark against the snow.

And bodies. Seven of them littered the ground around

a still-running SUV, and among those was Bauer. He also recognized two more SEALs, a guy he'd worked with from Delta Force, and two of Liam's SAS friends whom nobody had ever expected of wrongdoing. The other man he didn't know. All were very, very deceased, unless a guy could live without his intestines inside his body.

Jesus Christ.

Quinn swallowed back bile. He'd seen a lot of nasty in his life, but this? It was Jack the Ripper–level brutality.

None of the bodies was Liam.

Quinn raised his weapon and circled to the driver's side of the SUV. He yanked open the door and found another man sitting up in the seat with his hands tied to the wheel. Someone had written "Captain Cold" across his forehead under a neat bullet hole.

For a half second, Quinn forgot how to breathe as he stared into a face very similar to Gabe's. Same dark hair, square jaw, hazel eyes.

Captain Michael Bristow.

Jesus Christ. *This* was the guy Gabe had recognized at the airfield. The man who had shot him and run away like a coward. His own fucking brother.

A megaphone sat on Michael's lap with something scrawled on the side of the bloodstained trumpet in marker…

Quinn's name.

He reached in to turn the thing over and realized a half second too late there was a trip wire attached. Something hit the floor with a dull *thunk*, and the vehicle's engine revved, its wheels spinning in the snow, looking for traction. He grabbed the megaphone and stumbled backward just as the SUV lurched forward, headed directly for the front gate of the Belyakovs' farm.

Chapter Thirty-One

Every minute after midnight that ticked by without an attack ramped up the tension in the room. The men were all getting twitchy, sweating, and the stink of their nerves had Mara's stomach rolling.

It was ten after midnight and all was silent.

"Somethin's wrong," Jesse finally said and a rumble of agreement went through the group.

"Maybe Travis stopped them," she offered, but Jesse didn't waste any time shooting down that frail hope.

"No. Somethin's wrong."

"Do you think he—"

Outside, the megaphone screeched again. "Get out of there! Out of the house! Now!"

Mara's blood froze in her veins. It wasn't Liam's voice on the megaphone, but Travis's.

The room around her burst into action. Jesse pulled open the trapdoor to the cellar. "Move! Go to the shed, out the back."

Jean-Luc scooped up Nadejda and carried her down the

ladder, while Rustam helped his wife.

Jesse motioned her down next. "Go."

"What's happening?"

He shook his head and gave her a gentle push toward the cellar door as a screech of metal on metal rent the night, followed by a crash that shook the whole house under her feet.

Heart thundering, she clambered down the ladder, and the team followed in quick succession until only Jesse was left topside. He tossed his rucksack down first then grabbed for the first rung—

A fireball exploded behind him.

• • •

The SUV crashed to a halt, wedged into the alcove outside the kitchen, and for a moment, nothing happened.

Quinn raced toward the twisted remnants of metal that used to be the Belyakovs' front gate—and the vehicle exploded with enough force to set off a chain reaction, blowing all of Ian's fertilizer bombs at the same time. The heat was incredible and seared Quinn's face even as the blast threw him off his feet. Fire soared into the sky, casting the world in an eerie orange-red light that danced across the glossy snow.

Dazed, he sat up and realized the burning sensation in his hand was the megaphone's plastic fusing with his glove. He yanked the glove off, threw it aside, and in the flickering light of the flames read the message left for him on the megaphone's trumpet.

Quinn,

This setup wasn't working for me. Until next time, here's a little something to remember me by.

Cheers,
—L

Oh, Christ. No.

Quinn shoved to his feet, but he couldn't get any closer to the house.

To Mara.

The team.

The flames were too hot. Even this close, his skin burned and his eyes watered.

Maybe he'd warned them in time. Maybe they'd gotten out or—

The cellar.

He ran around the outskirts of the property, slipping and sliding across the ice and snow, and found the shed still standing. Nearby, the chickens squawked in their coop and the Belyakovs' goat gave fearful bleating cries that burrowed into his brain with claws. His vision blurred, his skin prickled, and the light of the fire took on a colorful aura that warned of an impending migraine.

He had about twenty minutes until he was useless.

He yanked open the shed's wooden doors. Smoke poured from the back of the building, and he took the time to pull off his coat. He drew one last breath of the clean air, held the coat to his face and plunged inside. He couldn't see a fucking thing and moved by memory. The path from the shed sloped in a ramp down to the bottle storage area, then there would be another door and—

He bumped into someone. Rustam Belyakov.

"Where is everyone?" His voice was raw and completely unrecognizable to his own ears and the old man spared no heed to the questions as he ushered his family to safety.

Quinn noticed light streaming from the partly open door at the other side of the room. Not fire. It was soft, steady, and white—a flashlight. He ran toward it, shoved the door the rest of the way open, and came face-to-face with the muzzle of a weapon.

"Friendly," he choked out.

"Friendly," the man behind the weapon called to the rest of the team, but his voice was also shot and Quinn couldn't make out who it was at first. Then the guy cursed in French and the flashlight shifted to light Jean-Luc's soot-streaked face. "Holy shit, Quinn. What the fuck happened up there?"

"Later. Where's Mara?"

Jean-Luc's gaze skirted away. The Cajun stepped aside in damn near slow motion and shone the light farther up the tunnel and Quinn's heart almost stopped.

There she was. Alive.

Light-headedness set in, but the sharp breath he sucked in made him cough.

Mara was alive and whole and uninjured, leaning over something on the floor. Or, no, not leaning. She was giving someone mouth-to-mouth.

"Who?" Quinn demanded, striding forward.

Jean-Luc stayed right on his heels. "Jesse got caught in the blast. Not in the flames, but he was on the ladder, and the percussion threw him down here. He stopped breathing."

Mara sobbed every time she came up for air. "Jesse, c'mon. Please."

"Sweetheart, let me." Quinn touched her shoulder, and she stared up at him, dazed. Tears left trails on her dirty face, and her eyes were glazed with a wild kind of fear. She shoved him away, sucked in a breath, and bent over her cousin again.

Jesse wheezed, coughed, and his eyes flew open.

"Oh, God." Mara threw her arms around his neck, sobbed into his hair. "Thank you. Thank you. Thank you."

Lanie sat back on her knees beside Mara and released an explosive breath. "Goddammit, cowboy," she muttered and squeezed her eyes shut, pinching the bridge of her nose. "Just…goddammit."

Overhead, the ceiling gave an ominous groan.

"We need to move." As gently as Quinn could, he pried Mara away from her cousin and motioned Marcus and Jean-Luc—the least injured among the group—forward. They each wedged a shoulder under the semiconscious medic's arms and hauled him upright.

"Go!" Quinn said, scooping Mara into his arms, and Harvard and Ian took the lead through the thickening heat and smoke with Seth bringing up the rear.

Outside, the wind had picked up and felt like needles to the skin. Snow and smoke swirled around them, but a noise beyond the roar of the flames caught Quinn's attention.

Christ, he'd never been so glad to hear the *whap whap whap* of an incoming helo. He set Mara down but held her against his side and hoped to God these guys were friendlies.

Several ropes fell from the bird, and six white-clad men slid down. Once they were all on the ground, the helo swerved away, presumably to find a place to land, and the men made short work of securing the area, mainly because there wasn't a whole lot of area left to secure. Only the shed and chicken coops remained standing.

Finally, two of the men broke away from the rest and strode over.

"Looks like we missed one helluva fight," Tucker Quentin said. The billionaire owner of HORNET's parent company pulled off his hood and snow mask and gave his famous Hollywood smile. "Let me guess, we should see the other guys?"

Quinn sagged with relief, and the only thing that kept him from collapsing was the fact he still had Mara in his arms. "The other guys are dead, but it wasn't our doing. How the fuck did you get here?"

"Jace Garcia," Tuc said. "He picked us up in Romania."

Quinn's throat tightened. "And Gabe?"

"My medic's with him. Rex managed to stabilize him and they are on their way to the best trauma hospital in the U.K. as we speak." He smiled at Mara and held out a hand to her. "And you must be Mara Escareno."

She nodded and accepted his hand but couldn't seem to form words. She was going into shock, and Quinn hugged her close.

"I sincerely hope you have another medic with you. We have injured."

Tuc nodded. "My explosives tech is cross-trained as a medic." He whistled between his teeth. "Carreras!"

One of the men jogged over and smacked Tuc aside the head as he passed. "I'm not a dog, Hollywood." Stopping in front of Mara, he set his pack on the ground. He dug around inside, found a stethoscope and looped it over his shoulder, then smiled at her and softened his voice to something close to a caress. "Hi, there, sweet. I'm Sean. Let me take a look at you, okay?"

Quinn tightened his arm possessively around her. The way this Sean Carreras guy talked to her reminded him of Jean-Luc when the Cajun was in seduction mode, and he wasn't so sure he liked that.

"I'll take care of her." *So back the fuck off.* He bit the inside of his cheek to keep from saying that part out loud, but he was sure the message came across loud and clear on his face. After a moment, he added, "But some of my men are severely injured. One broken arm, some ribs. Our medic stopped breathing and we brought him back, but he's not stable."

"Got it." Sean offered Mara another quicksilver smile before picking up his pack again and jogging over to where Jesse lay in the snow.

And, yeah, Quinn really didn't like that smile, either.

"Don't worry about Carreras," Tuc said. "He's harmless."

Harmless, my ass. Carreras had the look of a panty-dropping predator, and he didn't want Mara anywhere near the guy. He steered her away from the fire and the men, and Tuc called after them, "We have transport arriving, ETA ten minutes."

He acknowledged the info with a thumbs-up and sat Mara down on a chunk of crumbled wall. He didn't like how pale she was or that she hadn't spoken a word since the tunnel. Maybe he should call Carreras back.

He cupped her cheeks in his hands and rubbed at the soot staining her face. "Mara?"

Her eyes tracked from the fire to him. "I want to go home."

"We're going, baby. As soon as our transport arrives, we're gone and I promise you—"

"No." She jerked away from his touch. "You're not allowed to make promises to me. I can't—" Her voice broke, and she stood, backed several feet away. "I love you, but I'm starting to realize you don't love yourself enough to stay healthy and safe. You'll just keep putting yourself in the line of fire like you did tonight. Again and again, until you get killed."

Quinn swallowed back the lump blocking his throat. "What are you saying?"

She trembled and wrapped her arms around herself. "I won't keep you from seeing the baby, but I can't live the kind of life you lead. I'm not strong enough, and I don't want to be the person they hand the flag to when they bury you. I—I can't."

Each word hit him like a blow, one after the other, but he sat there and took the beating. It was less than he deserved. And he'd known all along he couldn't be the man she needed, so really, why was he surprised by this?

"I hear you." It wasn't the right response. He knew it but couldn't come up with anything else. "I'll stay away from you if that's what you want."

"No, it's—" She bit down on her lower lip and stared at him as if willing him to say something more. But what was there to say? She was right, and the more he thought about it, the less he wanted to subject her to himself. Hell, half the time even he didn't want to be around himself, so why would he condemn the woman he loved to that?

The silence between them grew uncomfortable, and Mara muffled a sob behind her hand. She spun away, and it took everything he had in him not to chase after her.

She'd made her decision.

And, really, he couldn't blame her for it.

Chapter Thirty-Two

LONDON, ENGLAND

Another hospital.

Christ. Quinn was so fucking sick of hospitals. Hated the sounds, the smells, the creeping sense that death waited behind every door in the corridor. Unlike the other wards, where there was conversation and the constant murmur of televisions, the ICU was quiet. Unbearably so, and the silence ramped up his apprehension. He approached Gabe's room like he would a bomb, his palms sweating on the vase of flowers he'd bought at the gift shop downstairs because he hadn't been able to face Audrey empty-handed.

Gabe's wife was seated next to his bed, his limp hand pressed between both of hers.

He hesitated for a heartbeat. Every fiber in his body screamed to run in the opposite direction, and that was exactly why he finally tapped on the open door, ignoring the discomfort in his bruised knuckles. "Audrey?"

At the sound of her name, she gazed up with wet,

bloodshot eyes. "We're not going to lose him, are we? He's stronger than this, right? Please, Quinn, tell me he is. We can't lose him. *I* can't lose him."

The cheery bouquet seemed like such a stupid idea now. Flowers like this were for happy occasions. He set them down on a side table and wished he could tell her all the pretty, comforting lies boomeranging around in his skull, but none ever reached his lips. When he looked at the bed, with all the tubes and wires…

All he saw was a dying man.

His best friend.

Dying.

His vision blurred, and hot tears spilled down his cheeks. He dropped his gaze to the floor.

"Oh, God." She doubled over Gabe's hand, sobbing in sheer agony, and he couldn't stay still any longer. Gabe wouldn't want him to. Not when she was suffering and so obviously in need of human contact.

He strode around the bed and pulled Audrey up into his arms. She clung to his shirt as trembles racked her slender body. Maybe he didn't have the right words to say, but at least he could give her this little bit of comfort.

He rested his chin on top of her head and stared at Gabe. More tears rolled from his eyes. He kept hoping his best friend would sit up and start pulling out tubes while threatening bodily harm if he didn't take his hands off Audrey.

Gabe didn't move.

A sound worked up out of his tight throat, and it took Audrey's arms tightening around him before he realized he was sobbing right along with her.

Goddammit. He couldn't lose Gabe, either. Not now. Not like this.

Finally, Audrey released a shaky breath and backed away. Her cheeks were splotched red, her nose was running, her features still ravaged with grief.

He imagined he didn't look much better and rubbed his sleeve over his face. "Gabe would laugh his ass off if he could see me right now."

Audrey gave a watery smile and patted his chest. "If he did, I'd kick his ass. You're allowed to be upset. He's as much your family as he is mine. You're his brother in every way but blood."

Brother. He thought of Michael Bristow dead in that SUV and wondered if anyone in the Bristow family knew about it yet. His throat closed up again, and he struggled to clear it. "Yeah."

Audrey drew in another shaky breath and released it in a long exhale. "Can you stay with him for a few minutes? His family should be here any moment, and I've been commanded to meet them at the front door."

Quinn winced. "The Admiral?" That was a face-to-face he didn't want, not while knowing what he did about Michael and not having any answers as to why or how.

Her lips thinned at the mention of Gabe's father. "He doesn't approve of me."

"Don't feel bad. The Admiral doesn't discriminate in his disapproval. Probably wouldn't even approve of God if the big guy didn't fall into line like a good little sailor." He reached out to wipe a wayward tear off her cheek. "You don't have to listen to his commands."

"I know." She glanced over at her husband again, and her lips trembled. "And I don't want to leave Gabe for even a second, but it will make things…easier, I think, if I just do what The Admiral says. For now, at least."

"I'll go down and meet them."

"No. You stay here with Gabe. Please? I'll feel better knowing you're here."

If it meant that much to her… He nodded. "All right."

"Thank you." She leaned over the bed and pressed a kiss to Gabe's forehead, murmuring things to him that were too soft for Quinn to hear.

He felt like an intruder and turned away, only to spot a card on the wall signed by Mara. He opened it, read the heartfelt thank-you she'd written to Gabe, and his heart cracked in two.

I don't want to be the person they hand the flag to when they bury you.

Like Audrey would have nothing but a flag and her memories if Gabe died.

Oh, Christ. It was as if the world snapped into place in that instant. He got it, understood exactly why Mara had walked away. Every time he stepped into the line of fire, he was in danger of breaking her heart, forcing her to live through the pain and sorrow Audrey was experiencing right now. And it wouldn't be just Mara he'd hurt, but the baby as well.

When Audrey straightened away from her husband, tears glimmered in her eyes again, but she smiled. "The doctors say he can't hear us, but they're wrong. I know they're wrong, so talk to him, okay? I think he does better when someone talks to him. It gives him a reason to fight."

Quinn waited until she left, then lowered himself into the chair she had vacated. He stared at the bed for a long time.

Talk to him? What was he supposed to say?

"Hey." The word hung in the air, and he blinked hard to hold back another rush of emotion. He felt stupid—not because he thought Gabe couldn't hear him, but because he was still hoping beyond hope for some kind of reply when he knew one wouldn't come. He reached into his inner coat pocket and brought out the two envelopes Gabe had given him at the airfield.

"I have your letters for Audrey and Raffi right here." He smacked them against his palm a couple times. "But man,

I—I really fucking don't want to deliver them. Don't make me. I know you have the fight left in you because you've hung on this long against all the odds. So just—keep fighting, all right?"

Aw, fuck. He was leaking again. He lifted his arm to wipe his face on his sleeve and the envelopes slipped out of his hand. One landed face-up on the edge of the bed. The other slipped to the floor, but he barely registered it.

His name.

The one on the bed had his name on it in Gabe's handwriting, and the shock left him breathless. His gaze snapped to Gabe's face. "Why would you—?"

Voices in the hallway caught his attention, and he scrambled to pick up both envelopes and hide them away in his pocket again.

The Admiral stalked into the room, followed by his wife, Catherine. Raffi, the youngest Bristow brother, was still out in the hallway, comforting Audrey, who looked utterly defeated.

Quinn stood. "What did you say to her?"

"What are you doing here?" The Admiral demanded.

"Could ask the same of you. Since when have you given a flying fuck about Gabe?"

"He's my son."

"And my brother," Quinn snapped.

"Leave," The Admiral said, his features set in stone. So that's where Gabe got that implacable expression. And here Quinn had always thought Gabe hadn't inherited anything from his coldhearted parents.

Quinn squared off in front of the older man. "I'm not in the navy anymore, *Jasper*." He purposely leaned on the first name, knowing its use would rankle The Admiral. "Your commands hold no weight with me."

"Then we'll call the police," Catherine said. The woman

was dressed more like she was on her way to a fancy business luncheon rather than to sit vigil by her son's deathbed. And she hadn't even looked at Gabe once since entering the room.

Yeah, people handled grief in all kinds of ways, but the sheer indifference Quinn saw in her blue eyes made him sick. She reminded him of a more polished version of Cherice, his birth mother, and disgust roiled in his gut. Trash could come in all kinds of fancy bags, but inside, it was still trash.

He shoved between the pair, strode out into the hall, and ushered Audrey in to reclaim her seat at Gabe's side. She was white-faced, horrified, and visibly trembling.

Quinn knelt beside her. "What did they say?"

Her gaze moved from Jasper to Catherine before returning to Quinn. "They said they could make it so I can't see him."

"That's bullshit." He stood again and faced the Bristows. "Why would you do that to her?"

"This is family business," The Admiral said icily. "And despite your claims of brotherhood, you are not blood."

"He's more family to Gabe than you are," Raffi said, all calm and reason. "And, as I told Audrey, you have no rights in this situation. At all. She has power of attorney. And, so you know, I called security on you about three minutes ago, told them you were causing a scene in a coma patient's room. Might want to leave before they get here. Don't want to publicly tarnish those shiny halos of yours."

The glare he received from his father was so full of disgust and hatred, anyone else would have crumpled under the weight of it. But not Rafael Bristow. He gave as good as he got, but then again, he'd lived with that hatred every day of his adult life since coming out as gay. Quinn suddenly understood why Gabe had such a high opinion of his youngest brother, and his own respect for the man shot through the roof.

Raffi wiggled his fingers. "Buh-bye."

The door slammed behind the two of them, thanks to Catherine, in full snit mode, yanking it shut as she left.

"Well," Audrey breathed and slumped back in her seat. "That sucked. Now I hope Gabe *can't* hear us."

"Of course he can hear us," Raffi said and walked toward the bed. "But don't worry about it. He expected it, which is exactly why he drew up that will after you two married. Huh, bro? You knew they'd try to pull some kind of shit."

Quinn stood at the foot of the bed, watching as they talked softly to Gabe and each other. The envelopes in his pocket suddenly weighed a ton, and he cleared his throat.

"I need to go, but I'll come back later. Let me know if..." He couldn't say it. Wouldn't say it. "If anything changes."

Raffi nodded. "We will. Thanks for being here."

As if he would be anywhere else?

Outside in the hallway, Quinn leaned against the wall to catch his breath. His chest was too tight, and he wondered if he would ever breathe normally again.

He'd lost his adoptive parents. He'd lost Mara. And now he was losing Gabe.

The envelopes crinkled in his coat pocket, and he took them out. Why had Gabe written a letter to him? They had agreed long ago that the letters were only meant for family or significant others, not each other. He'd always thought they wouldn't need a useless piece of paper to know what the other felt. Like Audrey said, they were brothers. That forged-in-battle bond had always been an unspoken yet tangible part of their friendship.

But Gabe had left him a letter.

Part of him feared opening it would be like sealing Gabe's fate, but a bigger part had to know what he'd written and why he'd broken their rule.

Quinn pushed away from the wall and took the hallway

to a nearby waiting area he'd spotted on the way in. He was just about to round the corner into the room—

"Why the fuck is Quinn still alive?"

He froze. Was that Jasper Bristow's voice? He slid a soundless step backward and flattened himself against the wall to listen to the hushed one-sided phone conversation in the waiting room.

"He's like a cockroach," Jasper sneered. "Every time you stomp on him, he springs right back to life. Have you heard from Michael?"

A pause.

"Is he dead?" Jasper asked with a complete lack of feeling. "No, that doesn't sound like HORNET's doing. It was Liam, wasn't it? He's gone off the rails. I told you from the start, Bennett, he's unstable and his drug use—well, we should have rid ourselves of him the moment he was ejected from SAS."

Another, longer pause, and Quinn's blood started a slow boil. Jasper Bristow was involved in this ring of corruption up to his bushy eyebrows, and so was Augustine Bennett, Team Ten's former commander.

How high up did this thing go?

"No, if we make a move on Quinn now, we'll tip our hand. We need to lie low, let this all settle. We'll release a statement saying Michael and the other men died in a training accident, but spin it in a way that won't make Russia nervous about having our operatives on their doorstep. Last thing we need right now is to have Washington breathing down our necks for starting a war."

Long silence.

"You mean Gabe? Yes, I have no doubt he's put the pieces together, but he's not going to wake up," Jasper said in a tone that sent chills racing over Quinn's skin. "If by some miracle he does, I'll deal with it. He's my son, as wayward as he is. If anyone pulls the plug on him, it'll be me. And as for Quinn, he doesn't have the files anymore. If he did, he would have done something about them by now."

Files? What files?

Memories skittered along the outside edge of Quinn's damaged brain, hazy and just out of reach, but he got a vague impression of the feelings associated with those memories. Horror and rage and betrayal and—

And saving top-secret files to a flash drive the day of the car accident.

Holy. Fuck.

A headache sliced through his brain with the memory. He'd started getting suspicious of his commander and four other SEALs shortly after Liam Miller was ejected from SAS, but he hadn't had proof until after his team was sent in to rescue Seth Harlan from Afghanistan. There were discrepancies in Commander Bennett's reports of what had been found in that village with Seth. The numbers hadn't added up. Seized opium and weapons were never logged, so he'd started snooping and found more inconsistencies going back for years. He'd saved those reports to a drive mere hours before the crash that ended his and Gabe's careers. That's why he'd been in such a bad mood when he picked Gabe up that day.

And now—he searched through the fragmented memories of the weeks surrounding the accident but came up blank. He had no idea what he'd done with the drive, but none of the people involved could have known that, and it suddenly made a hell of a lot more sense why his place had been ransacked and his former teammates wanted him dead.

He had the power to blow their illegal operation wide-open.

Heavy footsteps thudded toward Quinn, and he backed away, ducking into the first room he came to. Luckily, it was empty, and he watched Jasper stride past the open door. He had the phone still clamped to his ear and was speaking in a brusque, businesslike tone. "Yes, this is Jasper Bristow. I need to speak to someone about contesting a power of attorney…"

The envelope in Quinn's pocket suddenly felt as heavy as a brick. He took it out, read his name scrawled in Gabe's messy script, and had a good idea of what he'd find inside. But, no, he couldn't read it here and tucked it away again. He needed the privacy of his hotel room before opening it.

Just because he knew what he'd find didn't mean it wasn't going to rip what was left of his heart out of his chest.

Chapter Thirty-Three

Quinn,

So it finally happened. We always knew this was a likely outcome, right? Every op, it was the risk we took. Though, I have to admit, I always thought you'd be the one in the casket and I'd be left behind to mourn your sorry ass. Bet you thought the same thing. Bet you're wishing right now that's how it all went down.

Yeah. I'm sorry, buddy. I know this sucks for you, probably more than it does for me.

I'm sure you're wondering why I broke our rule and wrote you a letter. Don't worry. Raffi and Audrey are still getting theirs. I put them both in the other envelope. But right now, you and the team are in the other room, preparing to go after Mara, and I decided I had things that need to be said, so I'm writing them down. Just in case.

When we were in Colombia, you called me a coward for walking away from Audrey, and you were right. I was terrified of losing her, of opening myself up to her and losing her, so I ran away instead of manning up and facing what I felt. But you know what? Not having her in my life was even worse than the fear. This is gonna sound sappy, but she made me whole, and I want you to find that with someone. I suspect you might have already, and if that's the case, if Mara is your Audrey, don't fuck it up.

And right now you're thinking, "Fuck you, Gabe. This is a different sitch than what happened with you and Audrey." No, it's not. It's exactly the same, and you damn well know it. Mara and the baby are the best things that have ever happened to you. They need you, and you need them. Don't make my mistake. Don't walk away from them.

And, Q, the whole fatherhood thing? Don't let that freak you out. You know more about being a good father than any of us. You got the blueprint. Just do the exact opposite of everything your old man did, and you'll be golden.

I'm sorry I won't be around to see your kid. Yeah, babies scare the daylights out of me, but still. I would have liked to meet Baby Quinn.

And now we come to the second reason I'm writing you. Fair warning, it's going to hurt.

I lied to you, buddy. When you asked me about the moments before the car accident and if you had said anything to me? Yeah, I lied. You did tell me something. In the days before the accident, you found files that proved widespread corruption, and you suspected it stretched all the way up the chain of command. I was so entrenched in the navy at that point, I didn't want to hear it, and we were arguing about it when the truck sideswiped us. I know you don't remember any of this, but you mentioned you put the files on a flash drive. You wouldn't give me any names of the people involved other than Liam, and I don't know what you did with the drive. You didn't have it with you because you were nervous they'd try something to make sure those files never saw the light of day. It's a good bet you were right to worry and that's what this clusterfuck is all about. I just didn't realize it until you spotted Liam here in Transnistria. Part of me hoped this all had something to do with Mara and not us. Should have known better, right? Given our track record.

Find those files, Quinn. ASAP.

You're probably swearing right about now. Pissed off at me, and I don't blame you for that. I should have told you sooner, but I was afraid for you, man. Afraid of the shitstorm it would have brewed up and what they'd do if you pushed them. So when you didn't remember any of this, I decided it was easier, safer for you, if I let it drop. It was wrong to let them get away with it for so long and I'm sorry for that. I just wanted to protect you.

I know I don't have much right to ask you for a favor at this point, but I'm going to anyway. Don't take your anger at me out on Audrey. If I'm gone, she's already hurting, and I wish more than anything I could take her pain away. Please look after her for me.

And look after yourself. Get healthy. Find some happiness. Have a good life. God knows you deserve it more than anyone.

I'd better not see you for at least fifty years, but when you do get to the afterlife, look me up. I'm gonna miss you, man.

Over and out,

Gabe

Quinn folded the paper and stared at the floor in his hotel room for…he didn't know how long. Too long, probably, but the note was too much to process, and his brain was scrambling to make sense of it.

Gabe had known about the corruption all along. And he'd ignored it, brushed it under the rug. To protect Quinn.

And…to protect Jasper and Michael Bristow?

No. Gabe had said he didn't know the names of the

people involved, and it made sense that Quinn would have kept that to himself…to protect Gabe.

Dammit, he couldn't be angry when he would have done the exact same thing in Gabe's shoes.

I'm gonna miss you, man.

He was going to miss Gabe, too, more than he could vocalize. Very carefully, he refolded the letter and replaced it in its envelope. He had to keep it safe because before this was over, he'd need to see his best friend's words of good-bye again. And maybe he'd need them every day until the hole Gabe's death created in his heart started to heal. But right now, he was cold down to the marrow of his bones and so raw that even the weight of the clothes on his back was painful. He tried to imagine his life without both Gabe and Mara in it and couldn't do it.

Didn't want to do it.

Didn't want to live it.

His cell phone rang, vibrating across the nightstand, and he grabbed it before it jittered over the edge. A cold pit opened up in his stomach when he spotted Audrey's number on the screen, and he silenced the call. He didn't have to answer. He already knew what she was going to say.

Gabe was gone.

Chapter Thirty-Four

The whole team was there, milling around in the hallway in front of Gabe's room. Quinn refused to meet their gazes, didn't want to see their grief when his own was sharp enough to slice him in two.

He drew a breath, fortifying himself before he went through the door, expecting to be overwhelmed by the sorrow of a widowed woman.

Instead, Audrey was laughing. She was leaning over the bed and laughing.

Quinn slammed to a halt, disoriented. Hope and adrenaline sang through his veins, and he moved forward on autopilot, his stomach fluttering.

Gabe's eyes were open, and they shifted from his wife to Quinn. He reached up with a shaking hand, and Quinn met him halfway, clasping their palms together.

"Hey, man. About time you stopped sleeping on the job. You know I hate being in charge."

Audrey gave a startled laugh. "Quinn!"

Gabe's hand slipped from his, and he made a scribbling

motion at Audrey.

"Oh. Okay. Hang on, honey." She turned to grab a whiteboard and a dry-erase marker. "His doctor is going to try weaning him off the ventilator later today. Since he can't talk until the breathing tube comes out, the nurse gave us this so he could communicate," she explained, handing him the marker. She positioned the board in front of him, and it took him a few tries, but he finally scrawled out, *F U, Q*. Then he emphasized it by sticking up his middle finger.

"Gabe!" Audrey said in the same half-horrified, half-amused tone she'd used moments ago with Quinn. Her husband gave her a reassuring thumbs-up before his hand dropped heavily back to the bed and his eyes fell shut.

Yeah, Gabe was back. He wasn't going anywhere yet.

Quinn leaned over the bed's railing and lowered his voice, "Gabe, do you remember what happened?"

Yes, he wrote. Then his gaze lifted, and despite the cloudiness brought on by pain meds, his eyes asked all sorts of worried questions.

Quinn nodded. "Yeah, I read it, but I'm not pissed off at you, okay? I get why you didn't say anything. I would have done the same to protect you."

He blinked slowly, a silent thank-you.

"But you know I can't drop it now, right?" Quinn hesitated. "And this is going to hit close to home for you."

Gabe nodded with his eyes more than his head and scrawled, *Michael shot me.*

"Yeah, I know. He's dead, but Jasper's in this, too, and he's more than willing to kill you to keep his secrets. He's already tried twice."

Gabe paused for a moment, his hand dropping with exhaustion. Then he wrote, *Twice? The car accident?*

"Wasn't an accident. And maybe Michael and Jasper weren't directly involved, but they knew someone was going to try for me, and they were okay with you ending up collateral damage to protect themselves." He tilted his head toward the ventilator that was currently breathing for Gabe. "And now Jasper wants to pull the plug on you."

"What?" Audrey demanded.

Let them. I can breathe on my own. I'll pull the plug myself.

Quinn chuckled. "That'll piss them off, huh?"

Gabe blinked twice, then added in big letters, *Not my family anymore. Fuck them over 4 me.*

"Hooyah," Quinn said. "I'll make things right."

Gabe swiped his palm over the board, erasing it. He had to pause for several long minutes to gather his strength, then he wrote, *Mara?*

Quinn huffed out a breath that was caught somewhere between a laugh and a sob. "Nag, nag, nag."

u already fucked it up?

"Probably." At Gabe's narrow-eyed glare, he threw up his hands in surrender. "All right, yeah. But I'll fix that, too."

Go 2 Mara 1st. He underlined the statement twice, then added, *rest can wait.*

"Yeah, yeah. When did you turn into such a romantic?"

Gabe dropped the marker and groped for his wife's hand. He raised it to his cheek, leaned into her palm.

Audrey laughed through her tears. "I think he's saying I'm rubbing off on him."

The conversation must have drained him because he drifted off just like that, his cheek pillowed on her hand. Audrey freed herself and lovingly stroked his hair. She leaned over to kiss his forehead.

Yup. Time to leave.

Quinn slipped out the door and closed it. The guys were still in the hall, and a hopeful optimism permeated the air.

"He's going to be okay now, isn't he?" Harvard asked.

Quinn looked at the closed door, and the fluttering in his stomach exploded into a sense of euphoria so heady it made him dizzy. He couldn't control the laugh that erupted from his chest. "Yeah. He's already issuing orders. He'll make it."

The bubble of tension surrounding the team popped. Shoulders relaxed, smiles appeared. Laughter rippled through the group. Someone cracked a joke. Someone else suggested a round of drinks to celebrate. They were in London, after all. You couldn't throw a stone without hitting a pub.

Quinn held up both of his hands. "Guys. Wait. This isn't over yet."

The noise settled, and everyone got serious again.

"Liam?" Jesse said. After his close brush with death, he'd let the doctors check him out but had refused to stay in the hospital.

"Yeah," Quinn answered. "Liam's a problem we still need to deal with, but after killing Michael and Bauer and the rest of them like he did, he's gone to ground. If he's smart, we won't be seeing him for a while."

"So then what's up?" Marcus asked.

"I need volunteers to guard Gabe's room."

"You should know you don't even have to ask," Seth said, and everyone else voiced their agreements. "But if not Liam, who are we keeping out?"

"His family. None of the Bristows except Raffi are allowed inside."

Jesse whistled. "Dayam. That's not gonna go over well."

Quinn nodded. "It could get ugly. I'm sure Gabe will also tell the hospital staff he doesn't want Jasper or Catherine around, but I'd still feel better knowing you guys were here to make sure they stay away."

"Why? What's goin' on?"

Quinn hesitated a beat, weighing his options. In the end, he decided the guys deserved to know. And, if something happened to him, they'd be able to take over where he left off. He explained everything as concisely as he could—the widespread corruption, the files, the car accident that wasn't an accident, the Bristow family's involvement. When he finished, there was a beat of silence.

Finally, Jesse said, "Okay."

Quinn managed to hide his surprise at the easy acceptance, but just barely. "Okay," he echoed. "I have to figure out what I did with those files. I know I wouldn't have kept them in my home. I would have stashed the drive someplace I knew nobody would ever look."

"Which would be where?" Harvard asked.

"Hell if I know."

"Would you have left clues for yourself?"

Quinn had to laugh. Sometimes he forgot how young Harvard truly was. "Nah. I didn't know I was going to end up with faulty wiring." He tapped his temple.

"We could fake the files easily enough," Harvard said. Everyone looked at him, and color stained his cheeks. "I mean, *I* could fake them. They'd be real enough to pull off a bait and switch. If we have something more concrete to turn over to the authorities—like a confession—we won't need the copies you made."

Jesse opened his mouth but apparently couldn't think of a protest, because he closed it again and shrugged. "It's actually not a bad plan, except for one thing. How we goin' to pass off the fakes as the real deal?"

"Well." Harvard pushed his glasses up his nose. "All we need is for one of us to convincingly switch sides."

Quinn glanced up as movement at the end of the hall caught his attention. "You mean like a traitor?"

Everyone followed his gaze to Jace Garcia, who hesitated a good ten feet away. "I know I'm not welcome, but I had to find out how Gabe's doing before I leave town."

Quinn sent Jesse a sidelong glance.

The medic glowered but then sighed and rubbed his temple. "You saved his life, Garcia. He wouldn't have made it without your help."

"So he'll recover?"

"The prognosis is good," Jesse said.

Garcia nodded. "Okay. Thanks for telling me."

Quinn let him walk several steps away before calling, "Hey, Garcia. We're big about second chances around here. Want to redeem yourself?"

• • •

"You sure we can trust him?"

Quinn lowered the binoculars and glanced over at Seth, who sat in the driver's seat of a rented SUV. "No. And that's why this will work. They think Garcia is one of theirs."

"Well, he's not one of ours," Jesse said from the backseat.

"No," Quinn agreed and lifted the binoculars again. "I don't think he's anybody's. He does what suits him."

Across the hospital parking lot, Garcia waited by the car Jasper Bristow had left twenty minutes ago. Any moment now, The Admiral would be returning to it, hopefully shaken by the fact Gabe was alive, awake, and strong enough to come off the ventilator today.

"Hey, there he is," Seth said and whistled. "Oh, man. He looks pissed."

"Not as pissed as he's gonna be when he realizes he's been had," Quinn said.

Jasper stopped short at the sight of Garcia leaning on his car. Words were exchanged. Garcia motioned to their SUV.

"Dayam," Jesse said. "What's he doin'? He's not supposed to expose us."

"Hang on. Give him a chance."

"Uh," Seth said. "They're coming this way. That was not part of the plan."

"No, it wasn't," Jesse said. "We've given him plenty of chances, and he keeps fuckin' them up."

Yeah, they were right. The pilot had just fubar'd all of their previous plans to use the fake drive to leverage a confession. Time to improvise. "Stay here and hidden until Jasper reaches for his weapon."

"You think he will?" Seth asked.

"I know he will." Quinn grabbed the handle and shoved open the door. He strode across the parking lot, meeting the pair halfway. "You're a liar, Garcia."

He shrugged. "It's what I do."

"You don't want redemption."

"Nah. Money's better. And speaking of…" He turned to the Admiral and handed over the fake flash drive. "This one's a fake, but I know what's on the real one. If you want my silence, you got it. For a price."

The Admiral took the drive and crushed it under his boot, then opened his wallet and pulled out several thousand in fresh five-hundred-dollar bills. "That should do."

Garcia's mouth kicked up in a smile as he pocketed the money. "For now. We'll be in touch." And with that, he jogged away.

Fucking Garcia.

"Once a traitor, always a traitor," Jasper said with a smirk. "So, Quinn. Here we are. I have to tell you, I only agreed to this meeting as courtesy to you. You were a good SEAL at one time."

"Funny." Quinn crossed his arms over his chest. "I was going to say the same thing about you. What happened, Jasper? Was it the money? Or did you just get bored walking the straight and narrow?"

"I don't know what you're talking about."

"Sure you do. It's why you're here, isn't it?" He pulled another flash drive from his pocket and held it up. "I suspected Garcia would betray us again, so yes, that drive he gave you is a fake. This one? Not so much. You know what's on here?"

Jasper's jaw tightened until a muscle in his temple jumped, but he kept silent.

"The top-secret documents I stole from the Department of the Navy. Actually, from you. I highly doubt the navy had any previous knowledge of these documents. And until recently I didn't have any knowledge of them, either." He tapped his temple. "Car accident scrambled my brain, and I didn't remember. But that accident wasn't an accident at all, was it? Was it hard to convince Michael that the only way to keep your pockets lined was to have his big brother—your *son*—killed? I'm betting not."

Jasper still said nothing, but he didn't have to confess in words. The guilt was written all over his eyes.

Quinn nodded. "Yeah. It was your way of trying to get rid of me—and Gabe, because you couldn't be sure I hadn't said something to him—without making it look like an obvious murder, which would raise too many questions. Kicker is, the whole thing might not have gone down as you planned, but it worked. If you hadn't sent Urban after Mara, I probably would have gone on not remembering. Hell, I still don't remember all of it. All I know is what I left for myself in a handful of notes when I downloaded the documents."

A red flush worked its way up Jasper's neck and into his face. "What do you want? I'm sure we can work something out and put this whole mess behind us."

"I want you to stop trying to kill me and those I love."

"I didn't have anything to do with that."

"Yeah, nobody believes that. You were just too damn afraid I'd spill your secrets to leave well enough alone."

Jasper ground his teeth together. "That car accident

should have been fatal. You were supposed to die."

"But I didn't." Quinn shrugged. "What can I say, I'm stubborn like that. Only thing I can't figure out is why you got Liam involved. You had to know he wouldn't play by your rules."

"He was supposed to be an easy scapegoat," Jasper said after a beat of silence. "All we had to do was dangle the possibility of revenge, and he was on board. If things went sour, the shit was going to fall on his head, not mine or Michael's."

"That worked out well. There's now a shitstorm bearing down on you."

"We didn't expect him to kill everyone. He was making money off us, too, and we assumed he wanted to keep our business arrangements intact."

"Yeah, that's the thing about criminals. Can't trust 'em. Which is why, Jasper, I didn't come here alone. So that gun you're reaching for to kill me? Wouldn't do that if I were you." Behind him, the SUV's door opened. He pointed downward, and Jasper gazed at the red laser dot centered over his heart. The hand that had been inching toward his side froze.

Quinn didn't bother concealing his smile. "You remember Seth Harlan, don't you?"

Jasper swallowed hard.

"Good. Then you know he doesn't miss."

Several police cars screamed into the lot, and Lanie and Marcus climbed out of the first one with Danny Giancarelli, HORNET's FBI contact.

"Hey, Quinn," Giancarelli said casually, as if they'd just run into each other at the store or something. "How's it going?"

"It will be going a helluva lot better if you tell me we got him."

"Oh, yeah," Marcus said.

Giancarelli nodded. “Heard the whole thing, loud and clear.” He unhooked a pair of handcuffs from his belt, grabbed Jasper’s wrists, and secured them behind his back. “Jasper Bristow, you’re under arrest for conspiracy to commit murder and…a whole shitload of other charges. You have the right to remain silent…”

Quinn walked toward Gabe’s father, stopping on his way to pick up the crushed flash drive on the pavement. “They were both fakes, but this one? Nothing inside but a microphone designed by Harvard. Indestructible, since we figured you’d try to destroy it.” He tucked the remnants into the pocket of Jasper’s coat, then turned as Jace Garcia approached. “Like you said, once a traitor, always a traitor.”

Garcia dropped the cash into an evidence bag one of the FBI agents handed him. “Helps to know which side the traitor is betraying before you trust them.”

Jasper stared down at his pocket in shock, then lifted his gaze.

Quinn leaned in, got in his face. “Keep it as a memento.”

As Giancarelli pulled Jasper away, Seth and Jesse lowered their weapons and came out from behind the open doors of the SUV.

“Could have warned us about Garcia,” Jesse said.

“Had to make it look real. Thanks for the backup,” Quinn said to Seth.

The sniper shrugged and shouldered his rifle. “Hey, my rescue was part of the reason they kept trying to kill you. It’s the least I could do. But,” he added with a crooked half smile, “if you don’t mind, I’d like to go home to Phoebe now.”

“Yeah,” Quinn said. “Home sounds like a damn good plan.” He turned to Marcus. “Did you and the FBI have any luck tracking down Liam?”

“No. We lost him in Istanbul. He’s gone to ground.”

“He’ll reappear. Eventually. He always does.”

Marcus clapped him on the back. "We know he's alive now. We'll be ready for him next time."

"Yeah. I hope so."

Marcus clapped him on the back one more time, then walked over to join the rest of the team by the SUV. Jesse started to follow, but Quinn grabbed his arm.

"Hey, Jesse? Can we talk?" He motioned away from the SUV with his chin, and the medic broke away from the group, following without protest.

Once they were out of earshot, Quinn turned to him. "I need your help."

"This about Mara?"

"Yeah. Listen, I want to be in her and the baby's lives, but…thing is, what the fuck do I know about being a good father, about having a family? I've never had one."

"Bullshit."

The vehemence in Jesse's voice brought Quinn's head around. "You got something to say, Warrick?"

"Bull. Shit," Jesse repeated. "I've told you before, and I'll say it again, you got more of it than a cow pasture. You see those men standin' over there? Why do you think they're here? Why do you think they all dropped what they were doin' to hop on a plane, fly halfway round the world, and dig you out of the black hole of Europe?"

Quinn opened his mouth. Closed it. Tried again. "Uh, I assumed it had more to do with Mara and the baby than—"

"You really did scramble that brain of yours, didn't you?" Jesse shook his head and pointed at the team. "Right there is your family. Yeah, it's fuckin' crazy and dysfunctional and infuriatin' as all hell—but speakin' as a guy with more relatives than *The Brady Bunch*, I can tell you that's how families are. And the one we've cobbled together here? It ain't half bad."

Quinn stared at the men, watched them interact. Seth

and Ian were leaning against the SUV, no doubt taking verbal jabs at each other as they liked to do. Harvard, Marcus, and Jean-Luc had gathered around Harvard's tablet and were watching something intently until Jean-Luc cracked a joke that made them all laugh.

Christ. He'd always looked at them as a team. Had practically brandished that word, "team," around like a shield to keep a modicum of distance between himself and the guys.

But they were more than just a team.

He faced Jesse again. "What do I need to do to win her back?"

Jesse grinned and looped an arm around his shoulders. "Grovel, pal. And grovel hard."

Chapter Thirty-Five

El Paso, Texas

"Hawkeye! How many times do I have to tell you, the box isn't for you?" Mara bent over and picked up her cat, who mewed his disapproval at being removed from the cardboard box yet again. She scratched him between the ears, then set him on the floor and took a moment to stretch her aching back before she finished packing up her dishes.

"Hey, Mar?" Lanie called from the living room. "What do you want me to do with this bag?"

"What bag?"

"This one." She came through the kitchen door and held up the canvas duffel. "Found it in the back of the closet. Doesn't look like anything of yours."

"Because it isn't." At first, Mara didn't recognize it and took it over to the table to unzip it. Inside, she found two changes of men's clothing, a small toiletry kit, a combat knife in a leather sheath, and a mystery novel. She picked up the book and ran her hand over the cover. Remembered how Travis had sat in her living room that first night of his assignment as her bodyguard, feigning interest in the book, pretending he wasn't the least bit attracted to her.

She opened the book. He'd marked his spot with a receipt—only ever made it to page fifty before lust got the better of them both.

Her vision blurred. She snapped the cover shut and replaced the book, then zipped up the bag. "I completely forgot I had this. It's Travis's. He left it here in July. You should take it to him."

Lanie shook her head and reached for a box of tissues, held it out. "Nah, girl. You should give it to him yourself."

She sniffled and rejected the offered tissues. "No. I'm done crying. And I'm done with Travis." She wiped away the tears with the backs of her hands. "God. What did I ever see in him?"

"Besides a hot bod?"

Mara snorted. "Besides that. And you shouldn't be looking at his bod." When Lanie didn't say anything more, she glanced over. "You're supposed to back me up here. Where's the Ben and Jerry's–filled man-bashing pep talk? That's like a post-breakup law in the BFF handbook. I'm starting to feel cheated."

Lanie bit her lower lip, indecision battling over her features, then she heaved out a sigh. She grasped Mara's hands in her own. "I am so proud of you…but you're wrong."

"Ben and Jerry's is never wrong."

"I can't agree more, but that's not what I meant and you know it. I'm talking about Quinn. You're wrong about him."

"If you think that, then why are you proud of me?" Mara tried to pull away, but Lanie held on tight.

"Girl, you've spent your entire life letting people walk all over you. I'm happy you finally stood up for yourself, but pushing Quinn away wasn't right. Do you have any idea what a disaster he was until we found you at Olesea's?"

"Disaster?" And there were the tears again, threatening to spill over.

"Total FEMA-level state of emergency," Lanie said. "Honestly, it would have been pathetic to see him like that if I didn't know how much that man cares about you. He's a good man. Sad, lonely, and God knows his head's fucked up six ways from Sunday. But a good man."

Mara shook her head. She didn't want to hear this. Especially not from Lanie. She wanted the Ben and Jerry's and righteously indignant man bashing. "I—I can't."

Lanie squeezed her hands. "You keep saying that, but what is it you're so sure you can't do?"

"I can't fix him," she blurted, and her cheeks heated when Lanie lifted a brow. "I mean, there's something broken in him, and it's not his head injury. I understand that. It's deeper than that. It's this self-loathing that makes him put himself in unnecessary danger, and no matter what I do or say, I can't make it better. I can't fix him."

"But if you fell in love with him as he is now, why do you want to fix him?"

Mara opened her mouth and realized too late she didn't have an answer.

The corner of Lanie's mouth kicked up in a smile. "Mara, you have a one-eyed cat, a three-legged dog, and every day you wear a watch that doesn't tick. You like broken. It's kinda your thing."

Across the kitchen, Hawkeye jumped into the box again and BJ was standing up on her one hind leg, peering over the edge like she was trying to decide if she could get in, too.

Mara called the dog's name softly. Her curled tail swished and she gave a goofy doggie grin before clumsily hopping up and over the edge of the box.

And, crap, Lanie hadn't only hit the nail on the head,

she'd driven it home with one strong blow of logic. Mara had never thought of her animals as broken, although many people would. Nor had she ever considered fixing her dad's watch, although anybody else would.

So why did she think she had to fix Travis?

"Oh..." She sank into a chair and dropped her head heavily to the table. "I'm an idiot."

"Yeah, I've heard love does that to people."

Mara turned her head to the side and scowled at her best friend. "You're having too much fun with this."

"Maybe a bit." She held her fingers an inch apart. "At least this much."

Mara pushed herself upright. "Don't get too smug there, Ranger Delcambre. You think I didn't notice the googly eyes you and my cousin were making at each other? Everyone noticed."

Lanie winced. "Everyone?"

"Yup. Everyone."

"Shit."

"I've heard love does that to people," Mara mocked in singsong.

"I'm not in love with Jesse." Lanie sighed and pulled out another chair at the table. "I'm...madly, deeply in lust. God, he is so hot, and I bet he's packing more than a fine ass in those Wranglers."

"Oh. Ew." Mara stuck out her tongue in disgust. "No, I don't want that picture in my head. Pass the brain bleach."

"You brought it up, girl."

"And you made sure I regretted it."

"Teaches you not to deflect a conversation."

"Lesson learned. Now I'm never going to be able to look at Jesse again without thinking about his...Wranglers. So much ew."

They sat in amused silence for a few minutes until Lanie

leaned forward and propped her chin in her hand. "So? What are you going to do about Quinn?"

"I don't know, but it's not something I have to decide right now, is it? He's still in London and—"

Her doorbell rang.

Lanie grinned. "You sure about that?"

Mara shoved away from the table so hard she frightened Hawkeye and BJ from the box. The both scampered toward the bedroom. "Travis is here? Right now? And you knew he was on his way?"

"Jesse called this morning and asked if I could hang out here until Quinn got in. Which, you know, I was here anyway helping you pack, so no big deal."

Nerves jangled around in her belly. "Oh, shit. No big deal?" She ran a hand over the messy topknot of her hair and cringed. "Lanie! You could have at least told me to shower and get dressed before he got here."

Lanie tilted her head to the side and pursed her lips. "Why? He's seen you braless with messy hair before. Obviously, or you wouldn't be knocked up right now."

"Ugh. You're so not a girl sometimes." She hurried toward the master bathroom and called over her shoulder, "Stall for me. I'll be out in five—no, ten minutes."

She shut the bathroom door, cutting off Lanie's groan of complaint, and stripped off her ratty shirt and cotton shorts. Her heart raced as she hurried through a shower. She'd had the same excited-anxious feeling during another shower months ago, when she'd made the decision to throw caution to the wind and sleep with Travis. It was only fitting and somewhat poetic that this new chapter of their lives also started with a shower.

She took the time to braid her hair and slather on her favorite berry-scented lotion before digging through her closet for something presentable but also comfortable. She spotted the blue maxidress she'd been wearing the day she met Travis. Its cut was loose enough and the fabric stretchy enough that it still fit her, so why not wear it again? Full circle.

She slid on a pair of sparkly flip-flops and crossed to the door—but stopped before reaching for the knob.

Why wasn't any noise coming from the living room? At very least, she should hear Lanie and Travis making small talk, but there was no sound of voices. Someone was definitely out there, because she could hear the scrape of footsteps—too heavy to be Lanie's—on her tile floors. But why weren't they talking? Had Lanie left? But she wouldn't do that without at least calling a good-bye into the bathroom.

Mara released the doorknob and stepped back. Every instinct she had screamed, *don't go out there!*

She kept backing away until her legs bumped her bed, and she sat down. Her room was all but empty, everything packed away for her impending move out of the duplex she could no longer afford. There was nothing available to use as a weapon, and those footfalls she'd heard were coming closer.

"Marisol, I know you're in there." The voice slithered over her skin as the door creaked open, and she got her first look at Liam Miller. He was thin and wild-eyed, and his smile chilled her to the bone. "Let's have a chat, shall we?"

• • •

Grovel.

Okay, he could do that. Right? He'd never groveled before in his life, but how hard could it be?

Quinn realized he was standing in front of Mara's duplex, bouncing back and forth on his feet like a yo-yo, and told himself to stop. He had to calm the fuck down, but he honestly couldn't remember the last time he was this nervous. What if she wouldn't listen to what he had to say? If she just flat-out turned him away, where would that leave him?

Out on the sidewalk wearing this ridiculous shirt, that's where.

All right. Enough stalling.

He sucked in a breath and strode to her front door, only to discover it was open about five inches. All of the nerves jangling inside him went silent.

He wasn't armed. Hadn't thought he'd need a weapon for groveling.

Fuck it. He'd have to improvise.

He pushed on the door with the flat of his hand and saw Lanie sprawled on the floor just inside the entryway. There was some blood under her head, but he couldn't tell if it was a fatal wound or not. He crouched beside her, checked for a pulse. She was breathing, and her heart beat strongly, if a little slow, under his fingers. The blood seemed to be mostly from an open wound over her eyebrow, as if someone had coldcocked her with something heavy.

And that someone had to be Liam Miller. This situation had the crazy bastard's stink all over it.

He'd made a huge fucking miscalculation in thinking that Liam would go to ground until things cooled off. He'd been thinking like Liam was still the man he'd known, the SAS operative who was smart and careful to a fault, and not the batshit-insane man who had managed to kill eight well-trained people before launching a car-sized bomb at an innocent family's farm.

Christ. That right there should have been his first clue Liam had gone completely wacko and couldn't be predicted.

"I know Quinn will be here any minute." Liam's voice floated out from the bedroom, and Quinn's stomach jolted, the nerves flooding back. Mara was alone with that nutcase. In the bedroom.

He left Lanie where she lay, moved farther into the house.

He detoured to the kitchen, hoping to find a butcher's block, but everything was packed away in cardboard boxes, stacked in a neat pile for the movers.

Fuck. There had to be something—

He recognized the canvas duffel sitting on the table. It was the same one he'd been missing for months, the one he'd thought he'd left in Colombia back in May. But he hadn't left it in Colombia. He'd left it here. And there was a combat knife inside.

"I've enjoyed watching you this past week," Liam continued in the bedroom. "Listening in on your conversations was…thrilling, but it's time to end this now."

"What are you going to do?" Mara's voice. She sounded terrified, but there was a core of steel underneath that had Quinn's chest swelling with pride. She had said she wasn't strong, but she wouldn't think that if she could hear herself now.

Hang on, baby. I'm here.

Liam chuckled. "I doubt you want to know."

"Why do you hate me so much?" she demanded. "You don't even know me!"

"I know you belong to Quinn, and that's enough."

Quinn moved on silent feet toward the bag and pulled on the tab of the zipper. Slowly, one clasp at a time, it came undone with a soft hiss, and he reached inside, searching for the knife.

"I don't belong to him," Mara said.

"Of course you do. You're carrying his child."

"That means we had sex," Mara said, and her voice took on a surprising edge. "You think I wanted this? I'm not even keeping it."

"Nice try, but I've been listening to you, remember? You love that kid and you love Quinn and I can't think of a better way to make him suffer than killing you both in front of him."

Mara cried out in pain.

Yeah, fuck the element of surprise.

As blood thundered in his ears, Quinn tucked the sheathed knife into the back of his jeans and kicked over one of the chairs at the table. "Liam!"

Liam appeared in the bedroom doorway, dragging Mara along by her braid. He pressed a gun to her temple. "Hello, Quinn. Nice shirt. Did you enjoy my parting gift at the Belyakov farm? Explosive, huh?"

"Stop with the games, Liam. You've wanted a shot at me for years." He spread his hands. "So here I am. Take it. I won't fight you. I'll let you do whatever you want with me—if you let Mara go. She's completely innocent in this."

Liam sneered. "And Rachael wasn't?"

"No, she wasn't. She knew the risks of a mercenary life like the rest of us." When Liam said nothing, he played a hunch and continued, "Why did you kill Michael Bristow and his men in Transnistria? You had us by the balls there, and we both knew it. You could have ended it at any time, and the only reason we escaped is because you let us."

Liam's grip loosened on Mara's hair. Quinn held her gaze, silently telling her not to panic. She had to stay still and not try to run. At least, not yet.

"It was too much," Liam said. "They wanted only to protect their paychecks. The corruption business is lucrative, and they saw it all slipping away. I assume you know by now who the mastermind is."

"Yeah, I know."

Liam snorted. "And I thought I came from a fucked-up family." He let go of Mara and shoved her to the floor but kept his gun aimed at her. "All I wanted was revenge, not money."

Quinn moved on automatic pilot, grabbing his knife and throwing himself in the line of fire just like Mara said he always did.

The gun exploded.

Pain blazed though his ribs at the same moment he let the blade fly and the knife sank into Liam's shoulder, close to his neck. Not a fatal wound, but he fumbled the gun and stumbled backward a step in surprise. He touched the protruding hilt of the blade, then met Quinn's eyes with wonder in his own. "You…took the bullet for her."

"Yeah." Quinn pressed a hand to his side. The bullet had cracked one of his ribs and he was starting to have trouble breathing, each inhale short and choppy. Pain speared throughout his chest and light-headedness swamped him.

"Travis!" Mara was suddenly beside him, keeping him up with an arm around his waist and a shoulder wedged under his armpit.

In the living room behind Liam, Lanie staggered to her feet and fumbled a small-caliber gun out of the holster at her ankle.

Quinn met her gaze for less then a heartbeat before turning his full attention back to Liam. "I'll take a hundred bullets for Mara," he said, hoping to buy Lanie the seconds she needed to get within kill range. "If you had loved Rachael, you'd have done the same. That's what you do when you love someone."

Liam's lips peeled back in a vicious snarl as he pulled the knife free from his shoulder and threw it aside. It skidded across the tile, leaving a trail of blood in its wake. He switched his gun to his other hand, raised it again. "Yeah? Let's see you do it a second time, mate."

Quinn shoved Mara out of the way and hoped like hell she knew he wasn't doing this out of self-hate. He loved her, loved the baby, and would do anything in his power to keep them safe.

Then pain burst through his skull and all he knew was

blackness.

• • •

The world slowed down to crawl.

Mara landed on her knees on the tile, but she didn't feel the impact as the gun's second explosion ripped through the enclosed space of her kitchen and left her ears ringing. She saw Travis's head snap back and his knees give out. He collapsed where he stood and didn't move again.

No.

No, no, no! He couldn't die like that when they had so much to talk about, so much to work through.

Her throat went dry, and her vision clouded. The knife lay right there by her hand, and she didn't fully register that she'd picked it up until she was on her feet. There were all kinds of noise around her—screaming and crying and more gunshots—but the pure rage roaring inside her head drowned it all out. Her vision tunneled on Liam, and all she knew at that moment was she had to keep him from hurting Travis again.

Liam dropped to his knees in front of her, his eyes wide with shock. He seemed to already be bleeding from holes in his chest, but she couldn't figure out why. Didn't care why. He'd murdered Travis, and it wasn't enough for him to just be bleeding. He needed to be dead.

She stabbed the knife into his chest with every ounce of strength she possessed. But it still wasn't enough. She didn't believe the wound would kill him, because how could it? He didn't have a heart like a normal person.

Sobbing, she tried to pull the blade free, so she could stab him again and again and again, but he toppled sideways and her fingers slipped off the hilt. She screamed and lunged for it—

Strong arms banded around her from behind, hauling her backward against a hard body. “Shh. Baby, stop. He’s dead. He’s dead.”

She stilled even as her heart threatened to leap out of her chest. That voice. It couldn’t be…

“Travis?” She ripped out of his arms and faced him. He was alive. A little unsteady on his feet with blood dripping down the side of his face, but alive and whole. She couldn’t believe it. “B-but h-he shot you in the head!”

“Lanie shot him first. It threw his aim off and the bullet only grazed me. See?” He turned his head to show her the gash along his scalp and winced when she gently touched it.

Her breath caught on a sob. “I thought he killed you.”

“Nah, I have a hard head.” He offered a weak smile. “And Lanie has a faster trigger finger.”

Mara gazed over at Liam’s body and shuddered. “I didn’t kill him then?”

“No, baby. He was already dying. You just put him out of his misery.”

She blinked hard. She wouldn’t cry tears for that man, and she most certainly wasn’t going to feel guilty. She turned away from him and resolved to never think of him again after today. “I wish I hadn’t. I wanted him to suffer. I wanted to kill him.”

Travis cupped her cheeks in his palms and thumbed away her tears. “I know, but I’m glad you didn’t. Killing’s not something people come away from unscathed.”

Across the room, Lanie finally lowered her gun and staggered, catching herself against the kitchen wall. She slid down it until her butt hit the floor and cradled her head in one hand.

Travis hugged Mara close, and she melted against him, still half afraid he wasn’t real. Her mind kept replaying the moment his head snapped back and he collapsed. Over and over again, like a horrible movie on repeat. Shaking, she wrapped her arms around his waist and held on tight. Underneath her ear, his heart beat strongly, if not a little too fast.

"I thought he killed you," she said again. "I was so sure."

He kissed the top of her head. "I'm here, Mara. I'm not going anywhere."

"Jesus," Lanie muttered and gazed up, exhaustion lining her face. "Is every mission like this for y'all?"

"Pretty much." He grinned at her. "Want a job? Mine's going to be opening up real soon."

"Jesus," Lanie said again.

Chapter Thirty-Six

Quinn knew where he was before he opened his eyes. Hospital. Part of that knowledge came from the training he'd endured to always know exactly where he was when he woke up. But he'd also spent so much of his recent life in hospitals that the sounds and smells—the rattle of a nurse's cart and the beep of machines, the acrid scent of antiseptic layered over sickness and death—seared his memory, making it impossible not to know.

For a moment, he couldn't remember how he'd gotten here, and claustrophobia threatened until he turned his head on the pillow and saw Mara sitting in the chair beside his bed, smoothing her hand over a piece of blue cloth on her lap.

His T-shirt from yesterday.

He relaxed as the memories trickled back. The ring of corruption was exposed, Liam was dead. Gabe was going to recover. And, most importantly, Mara and the baby were safe.

She noticed him watching her and smiled, showing him the folded T-shirt. "I asked the hospital to wash it. They just brought it back. They got the stains out, but it has a hole."

"Baby, I can get another one."

She unfolded it, shook it out, and ran her fingers over the lettering on the front. "I can't believe you bought yourself a World's Greatest Dad T-shirt."

He lifted a shoulder and winced at the pain it caused down the side of his body. "I wanted to prove to you that—hell, I don't know. That I'm not the world's greatest anything now, but I maybe could be. Except I fucked my apology all up. Proved you right—I did exactly what you accused me of always doing."

She hugged the shirt to her chest. "You saved my life."

"By jumping in the line of fire. Just like you said. I can't seem to stop myself from doing it."

"Yes, but..." Still holding the shirt, she lowered the railing on his bed and crawled in beside him. "I understand now. When I went after Liam with the knife, I didn't think about my own safety or even the baby's. I just had to protect you. That's not a character flaw for either of us, and I was so wrong to throw it in your face like it was."

Christ, he loved having her in his arms. He brushed a kiss across her temple. "You weren't entirely wrong. I didn't care enough about myself to stay healthy. That's why I stopped seeing all my doctors, was bad about taking my meds...but no more. I told the docs here what's been happening, and they ran some tests. They think the blackouts and fugue states are from scar tissue putting pressure on my brain. I'm going to have surgery in a few days to remove it, and the docs are working to find a med regimen to help me cope with the migraines. I figure if I want a shot at World's Greatest Dad status, I need to start taking care of myself."

Her lips curled into a smile against his neck. "I was going to name the baby Quinn."

He lifted his head to look at her. "You were?"

"If it's a boy, he was going to be Quinn Jackson Warrick, after you and my dad. For a girl, Quinn Rosa Warrick, after you and the women in Mom's family—they're all Rosas—and Dad. I plan to go back to using my dad's last name, too, but if you're serious about staying in our lives, I'd rather give the baby yours."

"I'm staying," he said and entwined their fingers together. He lifted her hand to his lips. "As long as you'll have me."

"So forever?"

The breath stalled out in his lungs. Nobody had ever wanted him for that long, and he wasn't sure how to react. He reached out, tucked a loose strand of hair behind her ear. "Yeah, baby. Forever."

"Good." Mara grinned like she'd won the lottery—though Christ knew why—and snuggled down beside him. She picked up his hand and placed it over her belly. Love swamped him, so hard and fast he was afraid he'd drown in it. He swallowed hard.

"Hi, little one," he whispered. "You don't know me yet. I'm—" The words seemed to catch in his throat. "I'm your dad, and I probably won't be very good at it." He lifted his head and met her gaze. "But I'm going to give it my best shot."

Tears gathered in her eyes and spilled over. "The baby will need a new name now."

His voice sounded like gravel and his cleared his throat. "I like Jackson Quinn for a boy, but you're right. Quinn Rosa Quinn for a girl doesn't sound right."

"No. It doesn't. So I was wondering if—if you—" She stopped short and worried her lip with her teeth.

"If I…?" he prompted.

"If you would be okay with naming her after your mother?"

His lip curled in disgust even as he tried to smooth his features. Why would she want to burden their child with his sordid past? Besides, Cherice wasn't the kind of name he wanted to saddle a newborn with. "I'd rather not."

"Oh."

The disappointment in her voice brought on a startling realization, and he sat up, wincing at the pain it caused. "Wait. Which mother?"

Her forehead wrinkled. "The only one who's ever meant anything to you. Bianca. I was thinking we could name a girl Bianca after your mother and Rose instead of Rosa."

"Bianca Rose." His mouth went dry. All of the moisture must have transported to his eyes, because suddenly everything blurred. He swiped at his eyes with the back of his hand. "I love it. And I love you. I haven't told you that again, have I?"

"No."

"I love you, Mara. I love you so much it feels like a grenade in my chest waiting to explode and kill me, and it scares the hell out of me. Christ, taking on the baddest bad guys the world has to offer by myself would scare me less than loving you."

She laughed and sat up beside him to wrap her arms around his neck. "My warrior. Always the romantic."

"I know. I'm sorry. I always say the wrong things, but I don't know of any other way to describe how I feel. I wish I could give you pretty, romantic words and flowers and—"

"And I don't want any of that. I love you, too, Travis. Exactly the way you are."

Quinn shut his eyes. "I—I don't think anyone has ever said that to me before."

She kissed him but then leaned back and wrinkled her nose. "Well, maybe not the way you are right at the moment. You could use a shower before they discharge you. You kind of stink."

Quinn laughed. It was exactly what he'd needed to hear,

because things were getting too heavy for him and he hadn't known how to handle it. "I don't have a change of clothes."

"Yes, you do." She scooted off the bed and opened the closet. "I had Lanie pick up your bag. The one you left over the summer? It has some clothes in it."

She set the duffel on the end of his bed and started pulling things out. A book landed on his leg, and he reached down, picked it up.

It was just a normal paperback book by one of his favorite thriller writers, but something about it had adrenaline singing through his veins. He couldn't put his finger on it, but there was something…

He flipped through the pages. Once, then again. Maybe he'd written something or…

Christ. Why couldn't he remember?

Mara had stopped unpacking the bag and watched him closely. "What's wrong?"

"This book. I feel like I should know something about it."

"But it's just a book."

"Yeah." He opened to the page marked with a receipt and read a paragraph. Nothing. He stuck the receipt back in, but stopped short and picked it up again…

And the missing puzzle piece clicked into place.

"Oh, fuck me," he breathed. "Someplace nobody would think to look."

She pulled the receipt out of his hand and read it. "What? It's just a receipt from a liquor store."

He took it back and stuffed it into the book, then folded his hands around hers. "Are you up for a trip to Baltimore when I get out of here?"

Her brow wrinkled, but she nodded. "Why?"

"Because…" He grinned. "There's someone I want you to meet."

Chapter Thirty-Seven

BALTIMORE, MARYLAND
Five months later

The late-spring wind was pleasantly warm, chasing away the last vestiges of a stubborn winter as Quinn led Mara through the cemetery. He'd needed the surgery to remove the scar tissue sooner than he'd thought, and this visit had been postponed longer than he'd have liked. But after spending far too many of the last few months in the hospital, he enjoyed the walk, the warmth of the sun on his face, and the comfort of Mara's hand in his.

Life was pretty damn good right now.

At the far end of the first row of graves, he stopped and let go of Mara's hand to brush some dry leaves off the familiar tombstone. "Remember the old man I told you about? The one who set me on the right track with his stories of the navy?"

She nodded. "Froggy. Is this him?"

"Yeah. William 'Bill' Thomas Beaty. I didn't know his

real name until after he died. He's always been Froggy to me." He rested his hand on the tombstone. "And he's been keeping secrets for me. Haven't you, Frogman?"

"What secrets?" Mara whispered.

"Hang on." He squatted in front of the tombstone, then used his Swiss Army knife to pry up a plaque engraved with the same cartoon frog he had tattooed on his arm. "Froggy didn't have any family left—or at least, none that cared to give him a proper burial, so I bought his tombstone. Had it custom-made with this cubby, wanted to make sure he always had his favorite drink. I used to come here once a year on the anniversary of my graduation from BUD/S to have a drink with him and thank him for steering me in the right direction, but I haven't been back since before the car accident."

Mara gasped. "The receipt in your book. It was for a bottle of Jack Daniel's."

"Yeah. And I'd been trying to read that damn book since before the accident even though reading gives me migraines now. Still, something told me I had to keep trying. I had to keep the book. And the receipt."

Smiling, she crouched beside him. "Your subconscious at work."

"Apparently." He reached into the cubby and pulled out an empty bottle of Jack Daniel's. Inside, swaddled in a waterproof bag, sat a small bundle the size of a flash drive. He grinned and held the bottle out for her to see. "Because I left something other than alcohol last time I was here."

The flash drive.

He dumped it out of the bottle and turned it over in his hands. "Hard to believe all this for something so small."

"And so big. Think of how many lives they've probably destroyed over the years. Not to mention the pain they've caused you and Gabe. And all for nothing more than money."

"The great evil."

"I suppose so." Mara propped her head on his shoulder. "Now what?"

"I'll have to get this into the proper hands, but at this point it's just extra ammunition for an already loaded gun. Hell, for all I know, the FBI has the original files in hand by now."

The two of them crouched there in the mud, staring at Froggy's grave for several long seconds. Finally Mara tried to stand, but she couldn't quite make it up.

Laughing, he pocketed the drive, then grasped her around the waist and lifted her to her feet. "C'mon, roly-poly."

Once she was steady, she punched his arm. "Jerk. You never call a pregnant woman roly-poly."

"Aw." He leaned down, kissed her nose. "You know I think you're adorable."

"I don't feel adorable," she groaned and rubbed her belly. "I feel fat. But I'm hungry. Again."

He bit back another laugh. He was a warrior, trained to know when to pick his battles, and this was one he'd definitely lose. "All right. Let's get some food." He linked their fingers together and led her toward the path that would take them to their car, but she pulled him to a stop.

"Wait." She let go of his hand and walked back to Froggy's grave. For a moment, she just stood there in front of it, not moving. Then she pushed up the sleeve of her shirt and undid the clasp of her father's watch. She laid it on the stone and rested her hand on top of it.

"Thank you," she whispered, "for pointing my warrior in the right direction. I wouldn't have found him otherwise."

With that, she left the watch and rejoined him on the path.

"Are you sure you want to leave it?" he asked, throat tight.

She nodded. "It's time for us both to let go of the past." Smiling, she took his hand. "Now didn't you say something about food?"

Epilogue

Christmas Day

If Mara didn't already love Travis Quinn, the scene before her in the kitchen would have sealed the deal. He cradled their daughter close as he fed her a bottle and softly sang the lullaby his adopted mother used to sing to him. "Too-ra-loo-ra-loo-ral, too-ra-loo-ra-li, that's an Irish lullaby."

Uninterested in the bottle, Bianca babbled, kicked her stockinged feet, and reached up with one chubby little hand to hook her fingers in his mouth. He laughed softly and set her down in her bouncy seat on the kitchen table. "All right, bumblebee I can take a hint. No more singing."

And he'd thought he wouldn't make a good father.

Mara couldn't stay silent any longer and, fighting back a smile, cleared her throat. "She likes it when you sing to her."

He looked up and color rushed into his cheeks. "Uh, hey. Did we wake you up?"

"No, BJ did, actually." The dog in question trotted after her as she crossed the kitchen to the pot of coffee he already had brewed. "How'd Bianca do with her cereal this morning?"

"Beautifully." Travis wiped the baby's hands and face with a cloth, then unbuckled her from the seat and picked her up again. "We were just getting ready for a bath."

The doorbell rang. BJ barked, startling the baby. She didn't cry but gazed up at Travis with wide eyes as if asking, *What was that?* He soothed a hand over her head even as his muscles tightened. Mara noticed his other hand twitched, as if he wanted to reach for a gun.

Poor guy.

Adjusting to civilian life hadn't been easy on him. In fact, the whole past year had been tough, and at times, Mara had truly feared they wouldn't make it. Although she never doubted for a moment that he loved her and their daughter with everything he had in him, she'd had to resign herself to the fact that living with Travis Quinn would never be easy. Her warrior would always triple-check the locks on the doors at night and sleep with a gun nearby, and he would always tense at the idea of unexpected visitors. But looking at him standing there with their daughter cradled in his arms like she was the most precious thing in the universe…

Well, who wanted easy, anyway? As he liked to say, the only easy day was yesterday. And after all these years, he deserved to be loved. He deserved the family they were building together.

Mara set down her coffee, took the baby from his arms, and gave him a lingering kiss as the doorbell rang again. "It's probably Lanie. She said she was coming by with some presents for Bee."

"Wait." He caught her hand and drew her back for another, longer kiss that made her legs go a little Jell-O. Yes, living with him wasn't easy. But loving him? That was the easiest thing she had ever done, and she wouldn't have him any other way.

Travis eased away from the kiss, smiled, and rested his forehead against hers.

"I love you." The words no longer sounded rusty on his lips. He'd made a point to say them every day, and every day it still made her heart flutter to hear it. She hoped she'd have the same reaction fifty years down the road.

"I love you, too."

The bell rang again—*buzz, buzz, buzz, buzzzzzz*—and BJ scampered toward the front of the house, barking. Mara laughed at the disgruntled look Travis shot toward the living room. "Go get the door before Lanie kicks it in. I'll dress and change Bee, then we'll be out."

• • •

Quinn watched Mara walk toward the bedroom. She sang his Irish lullaby to their little girl, making Bianca giggle, but even the beautiful sound of the baby's laughter did nothing to calm his racing heart. He shut his eyes. Breathed out in a huff. He couldn't remember the last time he'd been so nervous.

Oh. Yeah, he could. It was when he'd showed up at her duplex wearing the World's Greatest Dad T-shirt. That seemed like another lifetime now.

Cursing under his breath at the doorbell and whoever was now leaning incessantly on it, he dropped the silver-wrapped ring box back into the pocket of his sweatpants. So much for his plans. He'd wanted to have the baby fed and clean by the time Mara woke. He'd figured that was more romantic than something like breakfast in bed, which would have been an impossible task since he couldn't cook worth a damn and she had banned him from touching all kitchen appliances save for the coffeepot and dishwasher. But after a long night of making love to her, he'd awakened late, and prying himself out of bed had turned out to take more effort than he possessed. He had lain there for a good hour with Mara in his arms, enjoying the quiet, intimate moment. When he'd finally rolled over to coax her awake with another round of lovemaking, followed by the ring box and the question that had been burning a hole in his gut, Bianca's waking burbles over the monitor stopped him and he'd decided to stick to plan A.

Which was now fubar'd due to the unexpected visitor.

And he hadn't come up with a plan C. Dammit. How many backup plans did a guy need for a marriage proposal, anyway?

Okay, regroup and strategize. He had to do this right.

"Travis, are you going to get that?" Mara called.

He stalked through the living room, past the brightly lit Christmas tree—the first one he'd had since he was sixteen—and yanked open the door.

Lanie lifted her thumb off the doorbell. "About time. It's cold out here."

"It's Texas," he muttered. "It's never cold. Have you heard of a phone?"

Without answering, she dumped a towering handful of presents in his arms and breezed into the house, shrugging out of her coat as she greeted the now ecstatic BJ and her best buddy, Hawkeye.

"Christ. What is all this?" He juggled the gifts over to the tree. Setting the pile down, he checked the top tag. *To: Bianca. From: Aunt Lanie.* "You spoil her."

"Aw, what's up with all the bah-humbugging, Quinn? Did we interrupt something?"

"Yeah, you did." He straightened away from the presents and asked, "We?"

Lanie tilted her head toward the still-open front door, and he walked over to look out. Several cars and a van had filed into his driveway behind Lanie's vehicle. Audrey and Raffi climbed out of the first car, Seth and Phoebe from the second. Jesse, Jean-Luc, Marcus, Ian, and Harvard were working at unloading more gifts from the van while BJ and Tank sniffed circles around each other.

And there was Gabe, lifting himself out of the first car's backseat with Audrey's help. He looked good. Strong. Healthy.

Except for the wheelchair.

It still twisted Quinn's guts into ropes of guilt to see him in it. The bullet had damaged his spine, but his doctors had assured the paralysis was only supposed to be temporary. Nearly a year of therapy later, Gabe was slowly learning to walk again, and for a man who had despised using a cane, he was surprisingly carefree about the wheelchair. Quinn had never asked about it, but he suspected the way-too-fucking-close brush with death had given Gabe a new outlook on life.

Gabe wheeled himself up the sidewalk. Audrey rushed to help him navigate the one concrete step to the patio, but he waved her away, popped up the front end of his chair so that he was balancing on the back two wheels, and surmounted the step himself.

"Hey," he said when he reached the door.

Quinn told himself to breathe past the lump in his throat. "New wheels?" The chair, with a short leather seat and sleek fenders painted with green flames, brought to mind a motorcycle.

"Yup. Custom painted by the great Audrey Van Amee Bristow." He popped another wheelie and rolled forward and backward a couple times.

Audrey opened her mouth, the look on her face saying he was about to get a tongue-lashing. But before she got a word out, he caught sight of her and muttered a curse. He dropped all four wheels back to the ground and gave her his most innocent expression. "Happy now?"

She crossed her arms over her chest and shrugged. "See

if I help when you face-plant one of these times."

"You tell him like it is, Audrey," Lanie said. "These guys are so bullheaded, none of them know what's good for them." She scowled as Jesse approached with an armful of gifts and blocked his path. "Some more so than others."

"Aw, c'mon," he groaned. "Let it go already."

"He got us lost on the way here," she explained.

"No, I didn't. I knew where I was goin'."

Lanie harrumphed.

Huh, Quinn thought and glanced back and forth between the two of them. "I don't know if I should invite you two in. Those sparks get any hotter and you'll burn down the Christmas tree."

Lanie scowled. "What sparks? There are no sparks." She turned on her heel and marched back inside. "Now where is that beautiful niece of mine? I want to hold her."

Jesse chased after her. "Wait a minute, she's more my relation than yours. I get to hold her first."

For several beats after they disappeared, there was no sound on the patio.

"*So,*" Audrey finally said and grabbed the handles of Gabe's chair to wheel him inside. "Looks like somebody's met his match."

Gabe winced and tilted his head back to look up at his wife. "Was I that surly when we met?"

"Yes," Audrey and Quinn said at the same time.

"Well, fuck."

"Hey, watch the language, man," Quinn said and followed them in. "The baby doesn't need to hear that."

Mara joined them with the baby a few minutes later, and Bianca became the instant center of attention. She loved it, too, showing off to a captivated room by demonstrating her newest skill of rolling from her back to her belly.

Quinn would have laughed at his former teammates'

enthrallment if he wasn't just as taken with his daughter.

While Bianca entertained the room, he took the opportunity to slip away and put on something other than sweats. In the bedroom, he pulled on one of his newer pairs of jeans and a button-down shirt. But before he joined the party again, he dug the ring box out of the pocket of his sweatpants, unwrapped it, and slid the ring into his jeans pocket. Maybe an opportunity would present itself to ask his question, and he didn't want to be without the ring if that happened.

Quinn returned to the living room to a burst of laughter. Mara was sitting on the floor with Bianca, helping her tear open some of the gifts, but the baby was far more interested in Tank, who lay calmly at Ian's feet and endured the ear pulling with the dog equivalent of an amused expression on his face. He seemed just as fascinated by the baby as everyone else.

Presents were passed and opened, and Quinn watched it all with a weird sense of detachment. Between the baby's birth and his own medical issues, he hadn't seen the guys much over the past ten months, and he felt the rift of his leaving the team more strongly now than ever.

He didn't want to lose them.

And although he'd had the surgery to remove the buildup of scar tissue on his brain, he still wasn't fit for active duty and never would be again. He had the migraines—fewer of them, sure, now that he'd come clean with his doctors and was more consistent about taking the pills to help control them—but that meant he'd never again work as an operative behind enemy lines.

Admittedly, he was still trying to be okay with that.

After the last presents were unwrapped, the room got quiet. Quinn was sitting in his favorite recliner with Bianca on his lap and Mara on the floor in front of the chair. She glanced back at him. "What's going on?"

"Not sure." He studied the team, noticed Gabe and Jesse

exchanging a glance before Jesse left the room. "Gabe, what's up?"

"We have one more present for you from Tuc."

"Tucker Quentin?" Mara gasped.

"Yeah, he was sorry he couldn't make it today to give it to you himself."

"Oh, wow," Mara said. "Tucker Quentin was going to come here? That…kind of blows my mind."

Jesse returned with a large black leather document case and opened it on the coffee table. Quinn passed the baby to Mara and got up to study the documents. Or, actually, blueprints.

"You mentioned our need for training center once," Gabe said and nodded at the blueprints. "There it is. All we need is land and someone to whip the fuc—" He stopped, shot a look at the baby. "Er, I mean train the new guys. Tuc wants to expand our operations, and we'll need someone to provide a steady stream of well-trained, reliable men. There's no better man for the job than you, Q."

Stunned, Quinn set the blueprints down. "Where would we get the land?"

"Well," Jesse drawled, "that all depends on Mara."

"Me?" she asked. Then her eyes widened. "Oh. You mean Dad's land? Well, yeah, that would be the perfect spot. My dad left me and my brother some land in Wyoming when he died," she explained before Quinn could ask. "Matt doesn't really want it, and my uncle—Jesse's dad—is using some of it for the ranch, but it's mostly just sitting there, untouched."

Quinn met her gaze across the table, not daring to let himself hope. "Would you want to move to Wyoming?"

"I'd love to be closer to my family there. I don't see them nearly enough, and with Mom still under Ramon's thumb…" She shrugged. "There's no reason for us to stay in El Paso. If this is what you want—and I know you do—I say go for it."

"What about your job?"

"I can find work anywhere. There are plenty of veterinarians in Wyoming, that's for sure."

"All right," he said after a moment. He didn't even know why he was hesitating about it. Mara was right. He did want this, and if she had no objections...

"Let's do it." He reached over and gently clamped his hands over the baby's ears before adding, "Let's train ourselves some fucking new guys."

• • •

Later that night, Quinn spread his hands on the bathroom vanity and dropped his head forward, rolling his neck to work out the kinks. He was supposed to be brushing his teeth, but hadn't quite managed to work up the energy to get out the toothpaste yet, not to mention squirt some on the brush and do the whole scrub-spit-rinse routine.

He loved the guys. He did. But, damn, was he glad they had finally left. Thanks to them, he was going to be nursing a slight hangover by morning.

Mara came up behind him and slid her arms around his waist.

"Hey," he said. "The baby finally fall asleep?"

"Yup. I don't know why she fights it like that. She could barely hold her eyes open." She kissed his spine. "What about you? Tired?"

"Exhausted."

Her fingers skimmed down his stomach and inside the waistband of his pants. "That's too bad."

"On second thought..." He scooped her up and set her on the vanity, wedging himself between the open vee of her legs. He leaned in and kissed her, a long slow one that lit his nerve endings on fire and had her squirming under his exploring hands. He traced his palms up her outer thighs, under the hem of her nightshirt, and found her naked underneath.

And she was ready.

He broke the kiss with a groan as his fingers dipped inside her. "Oh, look at you, Mara. All wet for me already. Let's go to the bedroom and I'll make you come all night long."

She gave a sly, sexy smile. "No, we'll stay right here. And I'll make you come first."

"You think so?" He reached down and pressed his thumb against her clit.

She shuddered and freed his cock from his pants. "I know so."

"Are you challenging me?"

"Yes," she said in a breathless rush and closed her hand around his length. She had to know this was a dangerous game, like a mouse challenging a lion, and he could tell by the delicate shivers racking her body that she was already on the verge of losing. Except then she leaned down to swirl her tongue teasingly over his tip, and his thoughts fractured. His muscles went taut and his hand stilled between her thighs as she sucked him all the way into her mouth. Heat gathered along his spine.

Oh, hell. He was going to lose this little power struggle if he didn't pull away from her. Right. Now.

He didn't know where he found the willpower, but he managed to dislodge himself from the warm vacuum of her mouth.

"You," he said, chest heaving. He wrapped one hand around his erection and squeezed to hold back his climax. "Over here. If I'm going to lose, I want my cock inside you."

"Yes." She leaned back on the vanity and wound her legs around him. "No more foreplay. Hard and fast, Travis."

Oh, yeah. He could do that. He'd always been good at taking orders. He held her thighs open, positioned himself, and kissed her as he plunged in. Her body gave in to his invasion easily, accepting his entire length, and damn, she felt good. He held still as she writhed against him and continued to tease her clit until she shattered in his arms.

He chuckled. "I win."

She opened her eyes and scowled. "You didn't win."

"You can't tell me you faked that," he said smugly and moved his hips, thrusting deep. She caught her breath, and he grinned. "It was really fucking hot to watch. Bet I can make you do it again before I finish."

"Hmm. I'll take that bet. Something tells me you don't have as much control as you're pretending to." She tightened her inner muscles around him, and a fine sheen of sweat broke out across his forehead.

"Christ, Mara." Groaning, he gripped her hips tighter and pounded into her, hard and fast like she'd ordered.

Mara bucked her hips in time with his thrusts. The sound of their bodies slapping together echoed off the tile walls and mixed with her moans into an erotic soundtrack. Her breasts bounced under her nightshirt and she sat up, wrapped her legs tighter around him, and dug her nails into his shoulders. That bite of pain was the shove he needed over the edge of control, and he reached down between their bodies to tease her clit, then covered her mouth in a hard kiss to muffle her scream as she came undone with him.

He wrapped his arms around her and drew her in for a kiss. "I think," he breathed against her lips, "we both won that round."

She laughed and kissed him back. "I think you're right."

Once he caught his breath, he withdrew from her, tucked himself back into his pants, then smoothed her nightshirt down, taking time to enjoy the feel of her curves under his hands.

"Mmm," Mara said and leaned against the vanity's

mirror, her chest heaving, strands of hair sticking to the side of her face. He loved seeing that sated, well-loved look on her face. "Merry Christmas."

He leaned in, kissed her again. "If that was my Christmas present, I love it."

"Christmas present?" She laughed and nipped at his lower lip. "You get that every night."

"Yeah, I do. I'm a damn lucky guy."

"Uh-huh," she said dryly. "A lucky guy with super sperm."

He drew away. "What?"

"This is your Christmas present." She leaned over and pulled out the drawer in the vanity that usually contained the toothpaste. Inside, lying on his World's Greatest Dad shirt and topped with a silver bow was a pregnancy test. And the digital screen read "pregnant." He picked it up, stared at it, then at her, then at the test again.

"Are you fuck—" When she raised an eyebrow, he winced and finished, "Kidding me? You're on birth control."

"I was last time, too. And, yes, I take it like I'm supposed to. Told you, super sperm. It's the only explanation." She tugged on his ear to get his attention. "Hey. Talk to me. You're not silently freaking out, are you? I don't know if I can deal with all that again."

"Freaking out? No." A wild, incandescent joy burst through his chest. He grinned, scooped her into his arms, and carried her into the bedroom. "I love you," he said between kisses. "I love Bianca. And I already love our son and can't wait to meet him."

Mara laughed as he dropped her on the bed and she bounced. "You can't possibly know it's a boy," she said, pulling her nightshirt off over her head.

"It's a boy this time. You just wait and see." Turning his back to her, he found the ring in his pocket and stuck it between his teeth, then stripped off his jeans. If there was a better time to do this, he couldn't think of one.

"And if it's another girl?" she asked.

He crawled up the bed, pausing to kiss her cesarean scar and drop the ring there. "Then I'll love her all the same and we'll have to keep trying for a boy."

"Wait a minute. How many kids do you think we're going to have?" She reached down, picked up the ring. "What's this?"

"I want the family I never got, Mara. I want more holidays like today, big and loud and crazy. I want days we feel like we're going to pull out our hair in frustration. And the days we feel like pulling out each other's hair. I want more nights like tonight, with quickies in the bathroom. I even want more of the nights we fall into bed too exhausted to do anything more than sleep."

She laughed softly even as tears leaked from her eyes. "You say that now."

"And I mean it. I want all of it. The good, the bad. In sickness and in health. All of it, with you by my side."

Mara sniffled. "I want that, too."

"Then your answer to my next question should be easy." He took the ring from her and slid it onto her finger. "Marisol Rosa Warrick, will you marry me?"

"Yes." She gave a squeal that only female vocal cords were capable of making and threw her arms around his neck. "Finally!"

Quinn scowled and ducked out of her embrace. "Hang on. What do you mean, *finally*?"

"Well, you've had the ring for weeks. I didn't think you were ever going to ask."

"How did—wait, did Jesse tell you?" He never should have asked for the cowboy's input on rings.

Mara rolled her eyes. "No, of course not. Jesse wouldn't do that."

"Then how—?"

"Baby, you left the jeweler's receipt in your jeans pocket. I found it when I washed them."

"Foiled by a receipt again?" He released an exaggerated sigh. "I've lost my edge. Those trainees are going to chew me up and spit me out."

"No way." She patted his cheek reassuringly. "It's just that I'm a mother now, and all mothers have eyes in the back of their heads. You're not as stealthy as you think you are, Mr. Navy SEAL."

"You scare me sometimes, you know that? And, Christ, I love you for it." He nuzzled the soft skin of her stomach. It blew his mind that there was another tiny person in there, created by his love for this woman. "We're definitely pregnant again? It's not a false positive or anything like that?"

Mara stroked a hand over his head. "We'll have to go to the doctor to be sure, but I took more than one test and…I can't explain it. I just know."

So he'd have another small branch added to his budding family tree. For a guy who came from hatred and grew up broken, it was nothing short of a miracle to him.

His chest tightened, and he brushed his lips across her lower belly. "Hi, little one. You don't know me yet, but my name is Travis Benjamin Quinn. I've been a lot of things in my life. An orphan. A sailor. A SEAL. A mercenary. A lover—which I plan to be again very soon." He paused to kiss Mara's hip. She giggled, squirming as he swept light kisses across her flat stomach, along her ribs, the side of her breast, her neck, chin… And finally he tasted her mouth, long and slow and sweet.

When they broke apart, he stretched out beside her and laced their fingers together over her belly. "And soon I'll be a husband, and I look forward to that. But to you and your sister, little one, I'll just be Dad. And you know what?" He grinned at Mara. "It's the best thing I've ever been."

Acknowledgments

Funny story time.

In 2011, I started writing the first book in the HORNET series—SEAL of Honor. In it, I mentioned Travis Quinn's adopted mother by name, knowing when I got to his book, he'd have a daughter by the same name.

Fast forward to fall 2012. My sister was pregnant with my first niece and I had completed a (very) rough first draft of Broken Honor. Now my sister isn't a reader and has never read any of my books, not to mention any my ugly first drafts. So imagine my shock when she stopped by to tell me the baby was a girl and they had chosen to name her Bianca Rose—the same name I had chosen for Quinn and Mara's baby the year before.

Pretty sure my jaw hit the floor, cartoon-style. Really, what were the chances of that happening?

So this book is dedicated to my niece, Bianca. And I have to give a shout-out to my sister for laughing off the crazy coincidence. Thank you for not making me change my Bianca's name.

About the Author

Tonya Burrows wrote her first romance in eighth grade and hasn't put down her pen since. Originally from a small town in Western New York, she's currently soaking up the sun as a Florida girl. She suffers from a bad case of wanderlust and usually ends up moving someplace new every few years. Luckily, her two dogs and ginormous cat are excellent travel buddies.

When she's not writing about hunky military heroes, Tonya can usually be found at a bookstore or the dog park. She also enjoys painting, watching movies, and her daily barre workouts. A geek at heart, she pledges her TV fandom to Supernatural and Dr. Who.

If you would like to know more about Tonya, visit her website at www.tonyaburrows.com. She's also on Twitter and Facebook.

Don't miss the rest of the* HORNET *series…

SEAL of Honor

Honor Reclaimed

Code of Honor

Discover the Wilde Security series

Wilde Nights in Paradise

Wilde for Her

Wilde at Heart

Running Wilde

Too Wilde to Tame

Looking for more strong heroines and to-die-for heroes? Try these Entangled Amara novels...

Risking it All

a *Crossing the Line* novel by Tessa Bailey

Three years ago, Seraphina Newsom's brother was gunned down by a ruthless mob kingpin. In order to take down the killer, Sera has gone undercover unsanctioned. Alone. Her only protection lies with Bowen Driscol, the reluctant new head of South Brooklyn's crime family, who the NYPD blackmailed into pulling her out. But when the two meet and Bowen feels a deep, damning shiver of desire, he knows there's only one way to keep her safe...to claim her as his own.

Temptation and Treachery

a *Dangerous Desires* novel by Sahara Roberts

Andres "Rio" Rivera became his ICE profile years ago. Cold and calculating, he never promises anything beyond right now. But when he ends up with a cancelled flight and a shared hotel room with the secretive Celeste Patron, the fire behind Celeste's buttoned-up exterior melts every barrier. He may only have her for one night, but that's long enough to make her every fantasy come true.

Permanent Ink

a *Something to Celebrate* novel by Laura Simcox

Blair Whitaker has one goal: get the hell out of Celebration, NY. Her ticket out is helping the town take the grand prize in a parade contest. If not for Ben Lambert, that is. Blair will have to sideline the sexy, local tattoo artist's planned tattoo festival to get what she wants. But before she knows it, she starts to see Celebration–and Ben–as something more than a temporary distraction. Coming clean will turn Ben against her for good, and going forward means losing what she really wants and hurting the town she's grown to love.

Rules of Protection

a *Tangled in Texas* novel by Alison Bliss

Rule breaker Emily Foster just wanted some action on her birthday. Instead she witnessed a mob hit and is whisked into witness protection, with by-the-book Special Agent Jake Ward as her chaperone. They end up deep in the Texas backwoods. The city-girl might be safe from the Mafia, but now she has to contend with a psychotic rooster, a narcoleptic dog, crazy cowboys, and the danger of losing her heart to the one man she can't have. But while Jake's determined to keep her out of the wrong hands, she's determined to get into the right ones—his.